THE
SYNDROME

Also by Tony Moyle

'How to Survive the Afterlife' Series

Book 1 - THE LIMPET SYNDROME
Book 2 - SOUL CATCHERS

Sign up to the newsletter:
www.tonymoyle.com/contact/

THE LIMPET SYNDROME

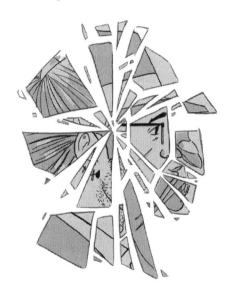

TONY MOYLE

PUBLISHING

First Published: March 2017.
Third Edition: October 2017.

ISBN 9781980524007

Limbo Publishing a brand of In-Sell Ltd
53 The Sands
Ashington, West Sussex RH20 3LQ

www.tonymoyle.com

Cover design by Lucas Media

*For Mr. Mark Summers,
my GCSE English teacher, Bassaleg
Comprehensive.*

*"Your constant criticism gave me
inspiration." T.M.*

limpet

'lɪmpɪt/

noun

noun: **limpet**; plural noun: **limpets**

   1: a marine mollusc which has a shallow conical shell and a broad muscular foot, found clinging tightly to rocks.

      ◦ used in comparisons to refer to people and things that cling tightly.

syndrome

'sɪndrəʊm/

noun

noun: **syndrome**; plural noun: **syndromes**

   1: a group of symptoms which consistently occur together, or a condition characterised by a set of associated symptoms.

      ◦ a characteristic combination of opinions, emotions, or behaviour.

CHAPTER ONE

DEATH?

One thing was for certain, John was dead. Everyone knew it. The ambulance crew, the fire brigade, several witnesses and, most importantly, the decrepit old man hurrying suspiciously from the scene. Only one person didn't know, and that was John. He couldn't be totally certain because he didn't feel dead. He assumed that death meant you didn't feel anything at all. But he was convinced there was certainly something *not dead* about him.

It wasn't a pleasant way to die, although there are very few good ways to go. If he'd been asked before the event for his perfect exit from the world, John Hewson would have opted to be smothered by two scantily clad, sex-crazed, nineteen-year-old models feeding him an unlimited supply of alcohol and more illegal drugs than you could shake a stick at. Unfortunately, not everyone is lucky enough to go with a smile on their face and he definitely wasn't wearing one. Anyone who had the misfortune of witnessing John's untimely demise would have described the look as horrified panic. It wasn't an altogether inappropriate facial expression, given that he was crumpled up in the driver's seat of his car, its bonnet fused to a red postbox with all the handiwork and finesse of a drunken welder.

Initially, John was nursing nothing worse than a cut to his head and a broken foot, both mere trivia compared to the realisation that he smelt the rich and pungent aroma of petrol. The smell wouldn't have bothered him had it not been for the fact he was totally unable to move from his position. It wasn't long until his worst fear came true, the fear of an uncontrollable spark. A spark that had soon turned the car into a fireball and John into something entirely indefinable.

How long ago the crash was, or what circumstances had led to it, was no longer in focus. He was struggling to identify what he was, let alone when he was. The one certainty was a dark and icy chill had infiltrated his body. Although he wasn't sure it was necessarily *feeling* that he was experiencing. *It* felt weird, whatever *it* was.

Very slowly strange entities formed in the darkness around him. There was a sense of electricity pulsating in the air that occasionally passed straight through him. This power source collected to form a dozen miniature electrical storms that drifted and bobbed elegantly at a height some two feet from the ground. They weren't the dark grey that you would associate with geological weather. These storms were electric-blue and discharged small sparks chaotically into the air. In the gloom they swirled, occasionally bumping into each other fighting for dominance and crackling with energy. They all shared one familiar behaviour. They were all floating along in the same direction towards, what John sensed to be, a doorway.

Attempting to get to his feet to follow them, he immediately answered one of the questions that was circling above him. He had no feet. He wasn't sure what he did have but feet were deficient to the tune of two. It didn't seem to matter because in the same manner as the other storm-like objects he, too, was drifting along and, if he wasn't mistaken, he appeared to be in a queue. In contrast to their lawless structures, one by one these little blue storms were patiently taking turns to go through a dimly lit doorway at the end of an otherwise vacuous space. As John got closer to the object floating next to him a sensation of curiosity washed over him, as if someone else's emotions were trying to supersede his own. The blue sparks were more than just electricity, they tingled with life.

Eventually it was John's turn to enter the door at the end of the room. Once inside there was no sign of the objects that he'd witnessed previously, as if the doorway itself had provided them with a permanent exit. All he sensed here was a shabby, woodworm-ridden desk lined with green leather, the sort you might expect to see in the office of a first-rate accountant. Behind the desk sat a woman who seemed as old as, if not older than, the desk itself.

Every disappointing and unpleasant experience that the world offered was etched over this woman's persona and yet her grimace suggested she was expecting more. Barely able to see above the table, her extreme age and gravity having conspired together to force her downwards, she sat scribbling on a pad unobservant of John's arrival. In an attempt to get her attention he tried to cough, the only result being a self-induced electric shock that vibrated through his mass. Finally she lifted her head. Her skin, shrink-wrapped to the bone structure fearing the consequences of letting go, dragged with it curly white hair, afflicted in places by lightly stained nicotine-yellow patches. As she spoke the air around her mouth ran for cover into the corners of the room.

"John Hewson, take a body please," came the stern voice, bouncing back at John from around the small and empty space.

In response, John's mass tingled with apprehension whilst a cascade of unanswered questions tried to force their way out simultaneously.

"Okay, enough," said the old woman. "Let me stop you there for a second. I can only answer one question at a time."

John couldn't remember asking any, at least not out loud.

"First things first. Yes, you are dead, boohoo, sob sob, poor you. Second question, where are you? You're in a place that we refer to as Limbo," said the woman, answering some of the questions that John had.

So that was it, then. At the tender age of thirty-three, John Hewson was no more, which was quite inconvenient really because there were so many things that he still wanted to do. All those plans that he'd considered making, ambitions that always seemed to be laid aside for something more important or urgent, would stay forever unfulfilled. Why had he spent so much time achieving nothing in his life? Why hadn't he just got on with it when he'd had the chance? 'Oh bugger,' thought John, 'I had a date on Friday night with Gemma from Purchasing. I suppose being dead is a good enough excuse for my absence.'

"Question three, why are you here? You're here because you're a neutral. Which means they need to judge you, decide what to do with you next. Now, for them to judge you, you need to be suitably dressed for the occasion. That's why I need you to go into that wardrobe on your right and pick a body," expired the woman in an uninspiring tone that indicated this was not the first time today she'd had to explain it.

On John's right he did indeed sense what resembled a wardrobe. He looked at it with surprise, as if it had appeared out of thin air. It was an ornate, old-fashioned piece of furniture constructed of oak, and adorned with intricate white gold handles and brackets. The doors were open but John didn't know how deep it went, as there was apparently no back wall. Nine feet wide and at least twelve high, on either side of a central space were two lines of outfits hanging from the ceiling like carcasses in a meat truck.

Still disconcerted by the comment, 'take a body,' he drifted towards the entrance to examine its contents. What he found was not outfits, but two rows of bodies, females on the left and males on the right. Hundreds stretched down the lines in every demographic you could wish for: fat, thin, black, white, bald, freckly, handsome, ugly, beards, big ears, small lips, even one with a huge wart right in the middle of its forehead. These bodies were best described as full body prosthetics, not fleshy forms but flaccid plastic skins of people previously sucked from their shells.

Each body was hung from the head by a piece of string, attached in turn to a hook on the wardrobe's ceiling. The bodysuits were all clothed, the male versions in smart but boring suits, the female versions in sensible and unattractive black dresses. John went to touch one and found that he had no hands to carry out such a task. He drifted back out of the wardrobe, where the elderly creature was tapping her fingers on the table in anticipation of the next tiresome question, eager to give the usual scripted answer and get on to the next.

"No, you don't have to find your own body. You can pick anyone you want, but I would suggest you don't take all day: they don't like it when people are late for their own trial. If you want to get inside, just float towards the mouth of the one you want. It will know what to do," she droned.

'*It* will know what to do' made it sound as if these bodies really were alive. John returned to the wardrobe. It was an interesting experience picking what you wanted to look like. Wasn't this every person's secret fantasy, to look like someone else? The chance to rid yourself of some hideous genetic disappointment that you'd always hated, all without the pain of expensive cosmetic surgery.

For the first time since a strong petrol smell filled his nostrils, John felt mild excitement. Crackling with energy, a now familiar blue spark emitted in front of him. He had a split second instinct to be a woman, but then realised he wasn't sure what was likely to happen to him. Although having breasts might be an interesting although slightly distracting novelty, he wasn't sure how impressed he'd be if he had them for the rest of eternity.

John floated past the column of male bodies examining each one and finding that he'd become incredibly picky. Too spotty, not tall enough, not sure about the moustache, big nose, freaky scar, funny hair and so on, as he went down the line. Eventually he came to a body he felt he might get away with. It was a Caucasian of about six feet, deep blue eyes, short, black hair, trim, and with interesting facial features. Most importantly there was nothing *abnormal* about it, although there could be some later shock when John got to look under the clothes.

John glided forward for a closer inspection. The body's mouth was open and at the back of its throat John sensed a valve made of white plastic. As he came closer to it he experienced a sudden sucking sensation pulling him forward with incredible strength. He tried to resist it, but the pressure was much too intense. After a short and pointless struggle, John gave in. What was the worst that could happen? After all, he was already dead.

Darkness took John once more. Not the icy darkness he had already experienced. This nothingness was not trying to create fear or doubt, it felt purposeful and organised. Every part of his energy and emotions was being stretched and distributed, as if he was expanding outwards into the many folds of a blow-up doll. After ten minutes the sensation stopped and for the first time, John felt as if some kind of normality had returned to death.

Before this moment none of his senses had been working properly, but in a strange way he had a *sense* of them all. Now he was able to feel with real touch rather than perception, see with real vision and hear true sounds. Opening his eyes he saw a line of female bodies hanging from the wardrobe opposite. He swung loosely above the floor, still hanging from the string that he'd seen attaching the body to the wardrobe's ceiling.

"Help!" John shouted.

To his astonishment he heard a voice shouting for help. It wasn't the voice that John had known for the best part of thirty years, but it had definitely come from him, whoever he was. The old woman lurched slowly down the corridor, holding an overproportioned pair of scissors.

"You've done it, then," she said to John, lifting the scissors in the general direction of his head.

She really didn't look strong enough to wield such a device, let alone use it. The scissors snipped wildly, accidentally shaving off part of his ear in the process, before eventually managing to cut the cord holding him in place. John fell to the wardrobe floor two feet below him.

"You've cut my ear, you silly hag!" he yelled, pulling a piece of plastic earlobe from the side of his head.

"Did it hurt?" replied the old woman inconsequentially.

John took a second to think about it, to double-check that feeling had returned as he'd first believed.

"Actually, no, I didn't feel a thing. Why not?"

"It's not your ear, is it?" she replied, in a style that John recognised as utter sarcasm.

"If it's not my ear, then..." John's attempt to respond came to a shuddering end.

"Look, I'm just the Tailor and I've got another fifty-three to do today. So if you wouldn't mind taking yourself, and your body, down to the waiting room, I can get on with my thoroughly fulfilling job."

John followed her out of the wardrobe and back to the desk, which now stood next to a set of iron doors. Above the door, in big, bold, old-fashioned font were the words, 'Waiting Room.'

"That wasn't there before, was it?" John asked the Tailor.

"Oh, just get on with it. Why do you all have to be so inquisitive? Even after death the human soul is still so bloody nosy! It doesn't matter, just go through it and let me explain the situation to the next poor sod that comes through my door, asking no doubt the same stupid and repetitive questions you asked me," she croaked, returning to the mountain of paperwork that occupied her desk.

John took the hint. As he wasn't quite sure who or what this woman was, or what powers she possessed, he decided to do what he was told. John moved towards the wrought-iron doors with his new hands outstretched in front of him. They behaved almost exactly like his old ones used to, although they felt stiff, not yet calibrated to his specification. Although they appeared heavy, the doors swung open with almost no strenuous effort. On the other side was a room furnished by three moulded plastic chairs, the type that John recalled he would often get his bottom stuck in back at primary school.

He took a mental note of the two doors in the room in case another should appear whilst he was off his guard. Opposite the one he'd come in through was an even bigger door, strangely mesmeric in appearance. He was sure it was made of metal, but of no type he'd seen before. The liquid moved chaotically in its frame, manipulated by whatever forces were being restrained on the other side. At the side of the door a skinny man with a short but crooked nose smiled, his hand outstretched in welcome.

"Hello, I'm hoping you're John, since I have no idea what you look like. Although, come to think of it, nobody knows which body you've chosen, so even your own mother wouldn't recognise you. How is the vessol, by the way?" said the man, chuckling at his own joke.

"Sorry, did you say vessol?" asked John.

"Yes, the thing you're wearing. A vessel that holds a soul, it's called a vessol. Is it comfortable, because sometimes we get all sorts of problems? Only last week we had one where the soul ended up inflated in just one leg." The man puffed his cheeks out and pointed to his leg in mock impression, as if John might have forgotten where it was. "Terrible mess, took ages to sort that one out. I bet you were tempted to have a female vessol, weren't you? You wouldn't be the first, you know. This bloke picked a female one a while back and I just couldn't get his attention, kept staring at his chest the whole time. The funny thing was..."

"Sorry to be rude, but who are you?"

"Oh, did I not mention that? I do get carried away. I'm the Clerk of the court for your trial, lovely to meet you," replied the man, still holding his hand out in the hope that John would finally shake it and complete the formality so he could put it down again.

John didn't and finally the Clerk gave up.

"I guess you have a few questions, then?" said the Clerk.

"A couple of things on my mind, yeah," John replied with a sarcastic inflection in his voice.

"Well, I hope you don't mind but I've got a little pamphlet for you. It saves me repeating it to everyone I ever meet, which is a lot, I can tell you. This will answer most of your questions."

The Clerk passed John a small and beautifully printed booklet which was entitled on the front in handwritten calligraphy, 'Welcome to Limbo – so you're neutral'.

"If this doesn't answer your questions, I'll be happy to help. Grab a seat and have a quick read," he added.

John noticed it was subtitled, 'All you wanted to know about being dead, but didn't like to ask'. After rereading the front about fifteen times, hoping that he might find it said something different but satisfied it wasn't going to, he turned the page.

So you're neutral – what does that mean? Most people believe that when you die, your soul is released from your body, and they're right. If you are not most people, sorry, but get used to it, there's much bigger surprises in store for you. Here's the science bit. What few people know is that the soul has both mass and charge. Every memory or emotion contained inside your human form was created by a physical reaction. Each of these emotions is constructed of conversely charged atomic particles. These are fixed inside a neural network in the brain to form a map of your character and personality. The combined mass of all of these emotions defines the quality and overall charge of your soul. Positive souls are a reflection of a surplus of positive emotions linked to the good deeds you did during life.

Right, here's the important bit. Positive souls are immediately attracted to Heaven when they leave the constraints of their physical body. Negative souls are, as you might expect, the reverse. Evil deeds (or sins as you may know them) create emotions and memories formed of negatively charged particles. Of course these souls are immediately attracted in the opposite direction, Hell.

Very occasionally, and it's a pain for us, I can tell you, a soul will have no charge at all and these are neutral souls, like you! They have no dominant negative or positive charge, an unlikely balance of both evil and good deeds, or quite possibly somebody that's spent their entire life in complete isolated boredom, never interacting with anyone or doing anything mildly exciting. Whichever it is, these souls have to be accounted for in some way. They can't be left to linger around or all sorts of nonsense will happen. So someone has to decide, on a balance of probability, whether they should be sent to Heaven or Hell. For more information refer to the document, 'My trial, what the hell's going on?'

John searched the sheet for further information. The only additional passage read: 'Please ask if you would like the agnostic version of this pamphlet, if you still need convincing'. John thought it highly unlikely.

"I'm confused. How can a soul be charged?" John said to himself, looking up from his pamphlet.

"That's an interesting question, and not the first question people normally ask if I'm honest," the Clerk replied, who John had completely forgotten was standing perfectly still in the background. "They usually start with, 'Why me?' or, 'I'm not ready,' and 'What about all my family?' That sort of thing. One person once asked if I'd take a bribe, which was really very silly…"

"Uh hum," coughed John. "Anyway, so the charged thing?"

"Oh yes…well, the soul is a complex thing. It's made up of tiny particles only visible under very specific conditions. They emit small electrical charges and travel around like a gust of air, or a little storm as some describe it. The combination of the charged particles can be positive, neutral or negative," explained the Clerk.

"So that's what I sensed earlier on. Those little blue storms were other people's souls," said John, thinking back to his first experiences of Limbo.

"Yes, just like you, except now you are inside one of our bodies," replied the Clerk.

"So if I'm just a ball of electricity. How did I experience those things before I got into this vessol?"

"I guess it's a kind of extrasensory perception. Your soul is built on emotions, characteristics and memories, which have feeling, sense and awareness. Alive but not quite living."

"But why is my soul neutral?" mused John.

"That's not for me to say. There may be any number of reasons, but that's what will be explored in the trial," answered the Clerk, checking his watch as if concerned by the schedule. "You'll be in soon, and you can find out. The reason can often be explained by how you died. Out of interest, how did you die?"

Although his last mortal moments were still very fresh in his mind, most of the details were clouded by a hazy veneer. It was as if his new anatomy was shrouding his vision and placing a veil over his closest memories. He remembered being in his car driving to the office when it had happened. He was a stickler for punctuality and routine, so it must have been about eight o'clock. Driving in a state of autopilot, he'd looked down momentarily to tamper with the radio. "This country will no longer be under the grip of fear…" John cut off the Prime Minister's announcement in mid-sentence. He hated politics these days and rotated the radio dial to more comfortable listening.

That's when she appeared. Right in front of him. Almost on top of his tired and battered Audi. In the middle of the road a young girl, no more than eleven, was standing calmly smiling at him, her bleached-white hair flowing around her like wisps of fog on a breezy day. The only other thing he remembered was his instinctive need to swerve away, his last conscious memory of her.

John visualised the moment he came around. A warm trickle of blood was running down his face and into his eyes as the smell of petrol fumes overpowered his nostrils. In the corner of his eye, through the rear-view mirror, he saw the shadowy figure of a man. The last fraction of memory was of a huge explosion, the sound of splintering metal being ripped apart around him and then darkness.

"I'm not sure why I died exactly, but I was definitely involved in some kind of car crash. It's all a bit vague," stuttered John, struggling to rewind the memories in an attempt to clarify them further.

"Some of your memories need time to adjust to their new setting. It's not unusual for you to remember more later on," said the Clerk, seeming almost sympathetic to John's situation as if he knew at first hand how he felt.

"Where is Limbo exactly?" asked John, not altogether happy to be recounting the manner of his own death.

"Well, the simple answer is it's on Earth. I'm not allowed to tell you where exactly. You're deep under the Swiss Alps and it's about time you saw it in its full splendour," said the Clerk, putting on a black robe that was nestled over one of the chairs and making his way to the liquid metal door.

"Wait! I'm not sure what to do?" pleaded John.

"Don't worry, I'll explain everything when we're inside. This door opens directly onto the court, the very heart of Limbo. It's made of a metal similar in characteristics to mercury, but unlike anything else on Earth. It's designed to stop souls escaping out of the chamber. Once you go in through this door you won't come back this way again." The Clerk held the key to eternity, but spoke with the simplicity of a tour guide.

He beckoned John to stand next to him. When there was no response he took him by the arm and led him towards a door that was deficient of lock, hinge or knob. Without knock or ritual he pulled a hesitant John straight into the liquid, which even for a soul protected inside a plastic body was an experience like swimming in a metallic hot tub. The metal solution flooded over him and began a frantic search for any gaps or openings in his vessol, welding them shut where they were found. It took several breathless minutes to reach the other side. As he finally broke through to the space in the next room he took a huge gasp of air, seconds away from drowning. No breath was forthcoming, an unnecessary, if not impossible, function for a dead person.

On the other side of the door was a sight of jaw-dropping beauty and wonder. A thousand metres in diameter, a huge, metallic sphere, made of the same substance as the door, opened up in front of them. One of the only non-metallic structures in the room was a white column. Like an oversized stalactite it stretched from the very middle of the ceiling almost to the floor. At about six feet from the bottom it stopped above a dock made of an intricate array of ivory benches. The room had no natural light, but was bathed by the glow from four huge pyres that jutted out of the sphere at equidistant points along its circumference. Below him, a less than obvious stairway flowed down to the centre.

"Welcome to Limbo," the Clerk added matter-of-factly.

CHAPTER TWO

THE TRIAL

The two of them made their long, careful journey to the bottom. The concave walls of the sphere shimmered from the light of the pyres as the liquid in the walls swam back and forward trying to escape to another part of the room. By the time they were halfway to the centre, John saw more of the court scene, which included three figures sitting along a large, raised platform behind a heavy, wooden counter.

"Who are they?" whispered John to the Clerk.

"They are the people who will defend, prosecute and judge you in the eyes of God. The judiciary, if you like. The man on the left in the tweed jacket represents God on Earth. The man on the right, the one that looks like he's just been pulled from a sewer, is the man representing Satan on Earth. They will decide your fate," explained the Clerk, pointing out the two people with his finger.

"What about the man in the middle?"

"You might find out later," replied the Clerk, "if it's appropriate."

When they had reached the centre the Clerk led John to the dock. The door to the four-foot-high, intricate structure was made of ivory, but they weren't animal bones. Exhumed human leg and arm bones were interwoven with jaws and skulls to create this macabre cubicle. Above him the white column had a hollow point at the end, like a giant was about to do some icing on a massively oversized wedding cake.

The Clerk made his way to a desk on the right-hand side, between John's dock and the three deadpan characters who sat quietly waiting for proceedings to start. The Clerk ruffled through crumpled pieces of paper, hastily making notes with a quill and ink. John glanced across nervously at the judiciary. The figure in the centre looked down at his hands uncomfortably, desperately trying to avoid eye contact. All three of them were male, but whilst the men representing the religious extremes were relatively young, the man in the middle was the oldest person that John had ever seen, and he'd seen the Tailor.

The weight of this man's personal trials had been captured in his forlorn eyes, only equalled by the signs of fatigue in his leathery and cracked skin. His filthy, old-fashioned pinstripe suit was slightly too big for him, bought at a time before his body had shrunk by several sizes. As his bent and withered body shuffled in its seat, a pair of thin spectacles balanced precariously on the tip of his flaky nose. They were helped to defy a seemingly inevitable fall by uncontrollably long and matted white hair like lambswool caught on a barbed wire fence.

"Case number 13,214,390,129, John Hewson versus damnation. Under the laws set out by the creators, all such neutral anomalies will be brought to Limbo to be judged as to their final resting place. In the documents set forward you will see that this case has been brought by Satan, who accuses John Hewson of breaking one of the Ten Commandments. If proven, he will be sent to Hell without reprieve until his soul is utterly spent. John, you have been accused as stated, how do you plead?" The Clerk stared in John's direction and for the first time seemed neither sympathetic nor friendly. There was a long and difficult pause.

"I'm sorry, I'm still getting over the fact that I'm dead. What do you mean, how do I plead?" replied John.

"Did you break one of the Ten Commandments?" reiterated the Clerk. "Innocent or guilty?"

John racked the area that until recently housed his brain, under pressure as to the implications of an incorrect response. The Ten Commandments: it was years since he'd been to church or studied the Bible. Could he remember them all, let alone remember whether he'd broken any? He tried to recall the easy ones. Murder, theft, adultery, he was certain he was clear on the first two, and since he wasn't married there was no chance of the third. What came after those? He seemed to remember something about honouring his parents, one about graven images, and another on bearing false witness. He was convinced that he hadn't knowingly gone against any of these, although he recognised the twisted irony of the last one if he gave the wrong answer.

"I do need an answer. We have other cases, you know."

"Innocent!" John blurted out, on the basis of hope more than good judgement. He prayed the chap resembling a bearded hippy, the eyes of God, might remember more about his life than he did.

"Then the case will proceed with the evidence for the defence." The Clerk sat down, the pre-agreed signal for the hippy to creep unstably from his chair and approach John's dock.

"Hey, man, I'm Angelo. I'm here to help you."

As Angelo smiled his eyes tried unsuccessfully to cross sides, unable to get past the bridge of his nose. It was most disconcerting to concentrate on his counsel, the man between him and who knew what horrors, when he kept looking at John's knees. On top of this the smell from Angelo's life of record-breaking shower-less sit-ins was making him nauseous.

"I'm sure you understand the importance of your honesty and can guess that there is little need for you to say the oath on the Bible," stated Angelo, whose smile instantly evaporated from vaguely odd yet mildly reassuring, to a mad, 'I don't live in the real world' expression. If this man wasn't away with the fairies he was most certainly waiting patiently in the departure lounge clutching his boarding pass. "John, how would you describe the way you lived your life on Earth?"

"Well, I think I live…sorry lived, a very fair life. I never willingly or consciously harmed anyone. I wasn't very active in my visits to church, but I prayed occasionally. I gave money to charity, looked after my friends and…and…never stood on spiders," John rambled, trying to unlock positive memories in a puzzled mind swirling around a prosthetic body.

"Excellent, John. No more questions," affirmed Angelo, addressing his colleagues on the judiciary.

"Is that it?" John declared, pulling Angelo back by his tank top.

"Is that what?" replied Angelo, more bamboozled than if he'd been asked to complete an IQ test after a rather potent spliff.

"My defence, is that it? A brief character reference from the very person on trial," replied John in exasperation, certain that he'd not been given the best resources to help him. In fact he'd decided this guy had probably never been in a court before, let alone worked in one.

"That's about it, yeah. It's an open-and-shut case. I've seen their evidence, the prosecution haven't got a leg to stand on," replied Angelo. As John was soon to find out, the prosecution did have a leg to stand on, they also had several spares, all of which were about to be used to kick him to pieces.

"Our evidence suggests that this man has led an honest and fair, if not totally devoted existence on Earth and has not broken any of the Commandments. This is a classic case of low-level religious belief coupled with some foolish misdemeanours, which explains why his soul is neutral. We've seen it a thousand times before. If Greco can find any evidence of major religious wrongdoing, then let him bring his evidence forward."

The man furthest right stood forward. His crazed grin exposed his rotten teeth and blackened tongue, whilst his greasy, dank hair drew attention away from his pox-ridden skin and bloodied nose. As he scuttled towards the dock the slime and dirt followed in his wake. If there was anyone in this room more suitable to be sitting where John was, it was this man. Surely he must have a criminal record longer than his arms, and they showed the needled evidence for at least some of his misdemeanours. Oddly, Greco was the only person in the room enjoying themselves. He approached with a strange device in his vein-ridged hands.

"It is our belief," croaked Greco, "that John Hewson has broken two of the Ten Commandments, evidence which I will put forward to this court."

Greco's voice, deep and sore from years of self-inflicted abuse, echoed several times around the sphere. "The first breach relates to the Ninth Commandment, thou shalt not covet thy neighbour's ass."

"I object," chirped Angelo dreamily. "I thought you might bring this one up, Greco."

"Let's hear it, Counsel," said the Clerk.

"Staring at his neighbour's *arse* doesn't count as breaking the Ninth Commandment," replied Angelo, directing his comments to the elderly man sitting on the bench, apparently half-asleep.

The decrepit figure briefly looked up and uttered, "Sustained."

John reflected on the young brunette student who used to live next door to him. She was in her early twenties and did have a fantastic bottom, which he had to admit analysing on a number of occasions when she left the house for her daily walk to university. But to be damned for eternity on a technicality would have been extremely harsh.

"Okay, well, if you can't accept that I have overwhelming proof that he has broken the Third Commandment." Greco held aloft his device in triumph.

"Thou shalt not make wrongful use of the name of God," clarified Angelo quickly. "What have you got on that, then?"

"What I have is John himself breaking this commandment at the very point of his death. In fact it is my belief that, as this commandment was broken as the wave of life broke on the shores of death, it demonstrates the direction in which he was heading," said Greco, seemingly with information that Angelo had not been briefed on based on his sudden look of unhelpful anxiety. "If the court will allow, I would like to play for you the last moments of John's life."

"This is most irregular, Greco. But if it is real evidence, then it must be heard. I am concerned, however, as to how you came across this most unorthodox of instruments," replied the Clerk.

"I am not at liberty to divulge the source, Clerk, but safe to say this is genuine, as I am sure the defendant will verify." Greco leaned forward, passing the silver-coloured box to the Clerk.

The Clerk, completely confuddled by its technology, searched around for a way to make it work. Eventually he found a pad on the side, which caused it to amplify its hidden recording at maximum volume around the court. The first noise was a screeching car forcibly applying its brakes. The next sound was the impact, as broken metal, glass and plastic combined. A radio station was doing its best to play through the commotion. Greco indicated to the Clerk to stop the tape.

"What was playing on the radio at the moment of your car crash, John?"

John could remember changing the radio channels moments before the crash from Radio 4 to Radio 2, and strangely he *did* remember what music was playing. "Ironically, it was 'Stairway to Heaven' by Led Zeppelin."

Greco motioned again for the Clerk to restart the tape. In the background they could hear the same track with the added backing vocals of a clearly injured driver.

"Uh no...no don't do it – oh shit...Jesus Christ, you'll kill me...I don't want to die...Jesus."

The last noise heard was a muffled gunshot.

"John, can you confirm that was your voice?" asked Greco, poised for the killer blow of his cross-examination.

"It sounds like me, yes, although I have no recollection of saying it, or of a gunshot. It sounded like a gunshot, didn't it?" replied John, worried and confused in equal measure.

"Having no recollection is no form of defence, I'm afraid. 'Oh, Your Honour, I know I have two kilos of cocaine in my colon, but I have no idea how it got there': do you think that's going to work?" Greco mocked. "Quite clearly this man has broken one of the Ten Commandments and therefore the prosecution rests."

John was torn between the events in front of him and the contents of the tape. It sounded as if there had been some other force at work that had resulted in his death. But there was no context to his comments on the tape. Who had he been shouting at? Why would there be a gunshot if he died in a car crash?

The Clerk stood up.

"This case is unusual but we have been given very strong evidence. Angelo, does your client change his plea based on the evidence?"

"He does not. This evidence is, in my view, inadmissible in this court unless we know who provided it. If the court is determined to go ahead, I must strongly urge a third-party view."

"Laslow," said the Clerk, addressing the elderly man, "it seems we need your impartial view as the

Arbiter in this case. You have heard the evidence before you, what is your decision?"

Laslow Kreicher rose with a new vigour and more power than his initial withered look had suggested. Without making eye contact with John, he opened his mouth and uttered, "Guilty," immediately turning to walk from the court. Before he could get more than three feet from the bench, Angelo interjected.

"I call for the Decree of Redemption!" shouted Angelo, the final roll of the dice that was left to him.

Laslow stood motionless as he faced away from the court.

"Under what grounds?" spat Greco.

"Under the terms of this court, evidence from an unknown source has been used without my prior assessment. Unless you are willing to reveal where you got it from, this man must be given a chance to make amends," responded Angelo.

Before Greco could answer the attack on his sources, a final word from Laslow echoed in the sphere.

"Agreed." Laslow swiftly retreated up the stairway.

The Clerk approached John's dock, where he stood drained and utterly flummoxed.

"What does that mean?"

"It means you will be sent directly to Hell with the rare opportunity to redeem yourself. If you are successful in whatever task Satan sees fit to deal you, then you will get a second chance," said the Clerk.

"No. I'm not going to Hell on any deal. I've done nothing wrong, this is a set-up, I demand a retrial. I'm not going there. Over my dead body," screamed John.

"Not over yours, John, someone else's," the Clerk pointed out quite accurately.

John didn't want to meet the Devil, let alone do a job for him. Scared and angry, he unwisely attempted to jump the ivory dock. Anticipating the move, the Clerk grabbed the escapee in a headlock and pulled him upwards so that he was directly below the white pillar. The pillar moved towards John's face until the tip connected with the valve in his throat, which he'd used hours earlier to occupy this temporary body.

"Good luck, John," said the Clerk, throwing a switch on the side of the pillar. In a flash he was gone and in the Clerk's arms lay a limp plastic body ready for its next occupant.

CHAPTER THREE

THE DEAL

John ran his hands over his body to confirm that everything was where he'd left it. His fingers found the cold flagstone floor where he was currently lying face-up. Reassured by what his hands discovered, he opened his eyes. Six feet or so above his head he could see a white column, conical in shape with a hollow point at the end. Had he gone anywhere at all? Yes, he was convinced he was somewhere else, given the uncomfortable circumstances of the last two or three minutes.

The first thing he remembered from the moments after the verdict was a feeling of incredible pressure as his soul was drawn out of its body with the precision of blood being drawn from a vein. Like an elastic band, his soul had been stretched to the point of breaking as it was sent with unfathomable velocity up through the inside of the white column. As it crashed through the air outside, landmarks flashed instantly in front of him before being immediately replaced by something new. First the mountains, then sky, the Earth, the Sun and the Solar System all roared past in a blur. Then there was nothing but space as he passed out of sight of human endeavour towards a patch of utter darkness.

As he approached the nothingness, he felt all of his memories and emotions being compressed and crushed into an incredible density. As he hit the darkness, almost instantly he was on the other side. Here his soul seemed to lose its sense of direction for a while before another force connected with it and again he was off, pulled towards an unknown destination. A few seconds later it was if he'd hit an invisible wall, the point on his journey that John remembered feeling the most uncomfortable.

All around him he heard voices whispering in the darkness, encouraging his own deepest feelings to reappear around him. Most of the voices were unfamiliar and gave no impression that they were talking to him. The voices overlapped, making it difficult to understand what any of them were saying. To his horror, though, some of the voices *were* recognisable.

Here in space, getting clearer and fighting for an audience, he heard his father. Although he'd died in combat during the Falklands War when John was only a young child, his voice was now shouting loudly and clearly all around his soul. Even though the recollections of his dad were sketchy, he knew the circumstances of his death. Now those details were being broadcast to him thirty years on, his father's voice screaming with the pain of his injuries and shouting out for help. John wanted to reach out to comfort him, but had no control over his movements or senses. Finally the voice was cut off, as if the macabre play that was being acted out amongst the stars was suddenly cancelled.

The other voices closest to him were faint but crystal-clear. As he listened he realised that they were his own memories replaying events that had had an impact on his life. There were hundreds of his voices all fighting desperately for John's attention, trying hard to remind him of moments of weakness or regret. The last voice he heard was so close he swore it came from within him. It spoke in a dull and lifeless tone and was the only message that John did not recognise.

"I know why you are here. I know what they have done to you. Find the way, John."

The final sensation was now a familiar one. One of being injected into a white plastic nozzle and filling a lifeless plastic body, his third different physical appearance today.

The whole experience had been somewhat unsettling but John assumed the worst was still to come. Regaining his composure he pulled himself to his feet and looked around at his surroundings to calculate what sort of place it was. Foul-smelling air swirled around, seeping out from the numerous passageways in the sides of the cavern's walls where John now stood. One side of the cavern was completely open to the outside world. A short distance into space stood a translucent wall. On the other side of this, a thousand stars were distorted by the effects of the barrier, reducing their sharpness as if viewed through water. John stood for a while transfixed by the sight as if surveying a newly discovered world and needing to take a mental picture to mark the achievement.

"Impressive, isn't it?"

John jumped. He wasn't the only person looking out at the view. Some ten feet behind, gradually thumping closer to him, the voice spoke again.

"It kind of takes your breath away, doesn't it?"

John didn't know where he was, but he was sure what it was: Hell. A place certain to take your breath away, one way or another. He glanced over his left shoulder to see who it was that had spoken. At first he saw nothing, until he lowered his gaze down to the floor. Below him, standing no more than three feet from top to bottom was the figure of a man, but like no man that John had ever seen.

The first noticeable thing about him was that he was smoking. Not the conventional human way. The smoke was coming out of his skin, a composition of solid and molten rock that burnt with the intensity of the sun. The man's smile showed off his chiselled, pumice rock teeth, and as a result a small crack opened across his stone face, releasing a small line of lava. Even though he was made entirely of rock, most of the normal human characteristics were present. He wheezed as if struggling for breath, coughing a putrid, sulphurous plume of gas in John's direction.

"Welcome to the second gateway to Hell, reserved for souls like yours and other anomalies. We call it the back gate," he coughed again, "and they call me Mr. Brimstone. Although what my real name was has long been forgotten and is of little consequence."

"So this is Hell, then. I thought it might be a lot....hotter," quipped John. It's hard to make small talk when you're confronted with a man seemingly made entirely from the contents of an active volcano.

"One of many misconceptions spun by ill-informed religious imbeciles to scare witless and God-fearing humans. The reality is somewhat worse, I might add, at least for those that listened." Brimstone shot John a wry smile, further opening the gash on his face and allowing the molten lava to drip onto the floor, burning a small hole in the flagstones.

"It looks quite small when you're standing here, doesn't it?" said Brimstone, clomping past John towards the view.

"What looks small?" asked John.

"Your Universe," replied Brimstone in a tone that suggested he was slightly disappointed with John's response. "We are on the very edge of your Universe. The barrier that you can see out there in space is the end of a wormhole, the point between our Universe and yours. On this side, time, at least as you knew it, hardly exists. On the other side it continues along, oblivious to our existence. Slowly it changes, ageing, as we watch over it like shepherds watch a flock."

John took a fresh perspective of the view, feeling more invisible than he did when he was just a soul back in Limbo. To think that no one could possibly know where Hell existed, unless they had the means and the motivation to pass through the wormhole, and then they'd never return to tell anyone about it anyway. It was the perfect illusion.

"Are you telling me I've been through a wormhole to get here?"

"Two, actually. The first took you from your Solar System to the other side of your Universe, and this one took you over the bounds of your Universe into this domain. That's where you were held before we could bring you in." He pointed to an area on the other side where a blue gas swirled erratically.

"It's really not what I expected, though. I expected it to be louder, more harrowing, full of screams, the sound of punishment being meted out, hands placed in manacles, that sort of thing?"

"Well, for the majority of souls that's the case. Even those that normally come in through here would be transferred immediately to one of the ten Circles of Hell that lead from this chamber," replied Brimstone, pointing to the passageways in the walls of the cavern.

"Now that's familiar to my vision of Hell. Wasn't that how Dante described it in *The Divine Comedy*?" stated John, who had been a keen student of classical studies at school.

"Quite similar, yes, although Dante's writing was mere guesswork, as we now know. We could stop off and ask him how he feels about it, if you like?" suggested Brimstone, grinning further.

Was Brimstone toying with him or did he just have a slightly perverse, warped sense of humour? John didn't dislike this creature, even though he was unsure what it had in store for him.

"So, why this treatment for me?"

"Well, you're special. You've been given the right to a reprieve, which is in itself a very rare occurrence. I can't tell you how long it's been since we've had one. What it means is we need you, because we have a job for you, and we don't want to damage you before you've done it," replied Brimstone.

THE DEAL

He rummaged around his only piece of clothing, a thick, solid silver belt that had pouches hanging along it like a very expensive builder's tool belt. Having seemingly found what he was searching for, he pulled an envelope from one of the pouches.

"Before I tell you what that job is, I think it might be time for a quick look around on our way over to the front gate."

Brimstone motioned for John to follow him.

They headed towards the nearest archway in the walled side of the cavern and, once inside, quickly climbed at a steep gradient. Even with his short, heavy body this didn't seem to hamper Brimstone's progress, as he marched impressively upwards. After they had walked for several minutes, John heard noises in the distance much more comparable to those that he expected when he'd first arrived. The sounds were not screams but whimpering voices begging forgiveness. These pitiful pleas were undoubtedly aware that the compassion they sought would not be forthcoming.

The tunnel opened up into a much lighter, larger area. When they eventually stopped climbing, John and Brimstone stopped to establish their bearings, neither able to facilitate the need to catch their breath after their hike. This was the very belly of Hell. Stretching to John's left and right ran towering cliff faces each dotted with a million cell-like caves that went on infinitely. Like the steps of an Inca temple, several more identical cliff faces, each one set further back than the last, were above and below him over the edge of a hollow space. The ends of these cliffs were unsighted, but he guessed they met somewhere to produce huge, oval-shaped levels that returned a hundred feet across the abyss, which dropped below their feet and into the ground.

Just over his left shoulder, in the nearest cell, a harrowing sight attracted his attention. A female inmate was clasping her head with both hands. Tremors shook her body in an exaggerated epileptic fit, as blood-curdling moans emanated through gritted teeth. Eyes red with fear or panic, her mumbled, crazed words were horribly disturbing. The pain deep within her soul was tangible and she reached out from the bars that held her in her public misery, her voice aimed in John's direction.

"What have they done with my girls? I need to find them...get off me. I never touched them...something made me do it...in my head...shouting at me. No, I can't take it...get that creature away from me..."

"What's happening to her?" John asked.

"She's being cleansed or punished, depending on your point of view. The punishment is always chosen to suit their soul and the evils within it. Sometimes we garnish it with things that we know scare them to pieces, just for fun. I assume that's what the creature reference is all about. Her mutterings reflect her life's crimes, now replayed in her head and around her for the rest of eternity," explained Brimstone rather clinically.

"When does it stop?"

"That very much depends. Most people eventually succumb to the relentless, haunting psychological and physical punishment and their soul diminishes, thoroughly defeated and empty. These become totally harmless and are effectively lifeless. Our job is done and they are released back into your Universe to make up future matter, part of the circle of creation."

"Why do you do that?"

"There is nothing left to do, their soul has been cleansed and we need the space. Hell's big but it's not infinite, you know."

John couldn't fathom the likelihood of Hell having a space problem as he once again took in its vastness.

"Anyway, welcome to the Third Circle of Hell. There are two further rings below us and seven more above." Brimstone pointed over the edge of the hollow and then into the opening above as if John might have missed an important part of the tour. "Hell works a bit differently to the version that no doubt you had imagined. The levels reflect how evil you've been in your physical form back on Earth. The more evil you are, the higher up the circles you are placed. The higher the number of the level, the easier the afterlife."

Brimstone continued with the tour by walking along the cliff edge to the left from where they had entered.

"I'm sorry, the *more* evil you are? That's not right surely?" replied John, hurrying after him, convinced that he must have misheard Brimstone's croaky description.

"Yes, the more evil you are the better your treatment. Some of the souls on level ten are like royalty."

"But why?"

"Think of it as the reverse of Heaven," replied Brimstone. "There, the better you are the closer to God you will be. Same theory here. Satan is pure evil and relishes anything that has a similar level of malevolence to him. Therefore those souls are kept as close to him as possible. The souls that have marginal negativity get the most frequent and harshest punishment. They deserve it, too, for their naivety and foolishness. The nastier you are, the better it'll be. Level ten is where you get all the warmongers, madmen and murderous dictators. Satan loves them."

As the two of them walked along, the line of cells continued to sprawl out in front of them, each containing a new and shocking example of self-hatred. Each was slightly different to the next, but all were extremely difficult to witness. The poor souls on the bottom circles might have been there simply because they did not, or could not, believe in God. They'd done nothing particularly wrong or right in their lives, yet they had to endure the most unbearable punishment. Then others, who had destroyed lives and in some cases whole countries, were treated as if they were saints, or more appropriately anti-saints. It was no surprise that this news had never managed to reach

Earth: imagine the consequences to society if people found out.

In the distance, John made out a bridge spanning their side of the third circle across the abyss to the other side. In effect, the bridge was the result of the cavern having been carved out around it, reminiscent of a piece of work that the builders had not completed due to budget constraints. When they were about halfway across, John could truly gauge the full size and extent of the Hell that surrounded him. All ten levels were visible, each cowering in the shadow of the next, the lowest sitting astride a dark, stagnant lake, lifeless and still.

Which level would he have found himself on if he hadn't decided to go to work on that sunny morning the day he'd died? How much longer would he have lived, and would his life have taken him further towards Heaven or Hell? He suspected the latter. John had been an active Christian up until his mid-twenties but had forsaken the Church when those around him, who had professed to be so devoted, used the Church to gain personal profit and influence. This wasn't the sort of profit that John was searching for, and eventually he became disillusioned.

He stopped attending church, developed a new circle of friends, and forgot most of the teachings that had been his default behaviour for so long. His soul must have been positively charged until he went off the rails. At that time he'd been determined to catch up on the fun he'd missed out on. Inevitably, this landed John in trouble on more than one occasion, perhaps erasing some of the positive charge, slowly creating a balance that had led him to Limbo.

As they reached the other side of the bridge they were met with the same moans of misery from the countless inmates within earshot. Directly in front of them another tunnel, much wider and more impressive than the last one, burrowed into the rock face. Unlike the ones leading up from the back gate, with their foul and unpleasant smells, this one felt fresh and welcoming. A great relief filled him when Brimstone gestured for them to enter. It was an extremely unpleasant experience for a person, even a deceased one, to see former humans in so much pain and anguish. It was a relief that none of those that he'd seen were people he knew personally: what would his reaction have been then? It had all seemed to wash over Brimstone as if he was totally desensitised to it all.

"How can you live with this, doesn't it affect you?" asked John.

"No. It has never had an impact on us."

"What exactly are you? If you don't mind me asking," asked John, hesitant with his question as he wasn't entirely sure that he wanted to hear the answer.

"I'm a demon. I was created at the very dawn of the Universe when Satan first played with creation. Satan created us in the same way that *he* created man in *his* image, only Satan's creations were more sinister and disgusting. The elements were his ingredients: water, fire, minerals, air, space and time. Satan wanted to better *his* creations, to challenge *him*. At first we looked almost completely human, although there were no souls or any capacity for them. Slowly over time we degraded into the elements that formed us. We are bound to Satan's will, the guardians and the workers of his domain." Brimstone showed no emotion in his explanation; he felt no pity for his situation or any ability to do so.

"There are others like you?"

"There are others, yes, but none of us look the same. Each was created from a different elemental starting point. I was moulded from the dust that erupted from the initial creation, what you refer to as the 'Big Bang'. You may meet some others if you are unfortunate."

As they discussed the birth of life, it dawned on John how close the competing views of religion and science were to each other. In past debates he'd had on the subjects, their compatibility with each other seemed paradoxical and had fuelled many an argument. There was never even a close compromise between people with sacred views, the two subjects having divided generations of scholars and beer drinkers alike.

Now he could see how both had some validity in their polarised positions. At the very least he could no longer argue and reject the existence of a greater being. Neither could he pour scorn on astrophysical calculations that he had read in scientific journals about the probable outcomes of passing through a wormhole. He had personally witnessed both of these events in the last few hours. What a unique position that put him in. No doubt a Nobel Prize would be winging its way from Sweden, if only he had any proof of what he'd seen, or an audience close enough to hear it.

"Okay, we are here," stated Brimstone as they passed through the end of the tunnel.

As John scanned the scenery he noticed one main difference in a room similar to the one at the back gate. Instead of the white column that had brought John's soul in through that entrance, there sat a very different piece of machinery. It resembled a massive cannon with a huge, clear, bulbous base where you might expect to find the trigger. The barrel extended out into space through the void in the cave, right up and partially through the wormhole. At the base of the gun, conveyor belts carried plastic bodies that stretched all the way to the back of the cavern and up through one of the tunnels.

A figure was carefully loading empty vessels to the bulbous end of the gun, where they were attached to a white, plastic nozzle. These bodies were manacled at both the arms and legs and blindfolded around the face. A second figure, seated to the nearest side of the equipment, was pressing a complicated array of buttons and levers on the side of the barrel.

At regular intervals the plastic bodies would expand and come to life, before being immediately led away on the conveyor. As each new empty vessol was loaded, and at each pull of the lever, a huge pulse of blue electrical energy was fired through the transparent barrel into space. After a fraction of a second, a similar but weaker blue spark came bouncing erratically back into the bulb, eventually forced into the body that was waiting for it. The whole mechanics of it were an extremely impressive sight, managed with the utmost efficiency and organisation.

John had been so immersed in it that he was unaware that Brimstone had made his way down to one of the figures and was now in discussion with a solid gold version of himself, which John guessed to be one of Brimstone's demon colleagues. The golden creature, who had been the one operating the controls, stepped down from his seat and beckoned to his colleagues to help him.

All four of them grabbed hold of a massive red lever and with all of their force pulled it down to the floor. The machine still appeared to be working, or at least it was still pulsing with blue energy into space, but this time no bodies were being filled. The machine's demon crew walked away towards a further tunnel and Brimstone beckoned for John to join him. John walked cautiously across the floor.

"Let me introduce you to the Soul Catcher," Brimstone pointed quite unnecessarily to the machine that had been the focus of John's attention.

"You're now standing at the main entrance to Hell, otherwise known as the front gate. This is where we process the majority of those that are unfortunate enough to be attracted here," said Brimstone. "It's usually a job that never stops, although we've managed to put a freeze on it for a while so we can talk in peace. This is where I work, and the Soul

Catcher is my responsibility. Which brings me to my reason for bringing you here."

Brimstone again took from his pouch the envelope that he had shown John at the back gate. It was clear that the niceties of his arrival were over. They were going to get down to the real business. What task was he about to be dealt?

"Hewson, we have a problem," said Brimstone, looking serious, even worried. It appeared that it wasn't just John who was concerned about the contents of the envelope.

"To get to the point, we have had a minor incident with the Soul Catcher. We have lost a soul that should have been attracted here but has not yet arrived. We need you to recover that soul and bring it back to us. In return for successfully completing this task, your debt will have been repaid and Satan will honour your reprieve. Your soul will be positively charged and you will be allowed to travel, if you wish, to Heaven. That is the deal if you choose to accept it?"

"I don't suppose that I have much choice in the matter?"

"There is an alternative," offered Brimstone. "You can be taken immediately to the fourth level and be housed in a cell right next to your father's."

"My father isn't in Hell. He was a war hero and highly decorated for it. He saved lives…you're lying to me," shouted John.

"I'm afraid not. I suppose you were too young to know the truth. Your mother told you what you wanted to hear. Tell me, John, did you not hear his voice in the ether before you came in through the back gate? Where did you think he was?" taunted Brimstone. "You can see for yourself if you like. It's only a short walk, but I'm not sure you want to take it."

John idolised his father, or at least the image of him that he'd pieced together. When he was seven years old news reached the UK that his father, a Navy officer, had died when his ship had been bombed and sunk with the loss of all but a handful of the crew. The story he'd heard portrayed how his father's heroics had saved the small number of survivors; he'd even met one of them and got the story first-hand. This new twist was devastating. How could he face the prospect of seeing one of the people he loved in the same predicament as those he had already witnessed?

"Whose soul do you want me to find?" John answered meekly.

Brimstone opened the envelope as if he were about to announce the winner of an award.

"The man's name is Sandy Logan."

"Sandy Logan, the Minister of Homeland Security for the government?"

"Yes, well, the former," replied Brimstone. "What of it?"

"I know him," responded John.

"Yes, we thought you might," replied Brimstone, his smile expanding across his face, leaking more lava than ever.

CHAPTER FOUR

THE MINISTER FOR HOMELAND SECURITY

Finding your way around the corridors in the Palace of Westminster was a challenge for all but the longest-serving employee. But for a brand new civil servant they were a complete nightmare. The building was a myriad of passageways, cabinet offices and debating chambers. There were literally thousands of doors, each concealing an important person busily influencing the direction of our lives in their nominated discipline. Some of the departments along these hallowed corridors were more important than others. Some, such as the 'Department for the Protection of British Culture', were small and invisible in the public consciousness. Very few people knew what they were; even fewer knew where they were. One of the newest departments in this beacon of democracy was extremely well known: the 'Department for Homeland Security'.

Recent events meant you couldn't go a day without reading or hearing about it across the media. Formed by the last prime minister in the early part of the 21st century in a direct response to the devastation of the attacks in America, it was created to develop a clear and strategic approach to national security. Part of the Home Office, its job was to bring together the security services, GCHQ, MI6 and MI5, to co-operate as a seamless intelligence body. Cynically most people believed that the British Government was obediently following the US's lead, adding further fuel to the fire that our prime ministers were just lapdogs, ready to bound to the president's side at a moment's notice. The government were insistent that the department's main purpose was to demonstrate that they *were* taking it seriously. So much so that they appointed someone who could act as a mouthpiece to the country, communicating progress and allaying the public's fears. The man responsible was the Minister for Homeland Security.

Whether the department was seen as important or not didn't make it any easier to find. The panic-stricken civil servant, currently sweating from head to foot, would have to agree. He lurched from corridor to corridor, stopping sporadically to appeal for directions, his grey suit a mere excuse for the one he remembered putting on that morning. It flopped around loosely as he quickened his pace, glancing frequently at his wristwatch. It had now passed three o'clock and his message had still not reached its destination. The sweat accelerated, dripping under his glasses and down his face. Just as he was about to give up, retrace his steps and start again, he found a door that read, 'The Rt Hon. Sandy Logan. Minister for Homeland Security.'

The man stopped for a few seconds to regain his composure before tapping firmly on the door. There was no response. He put his ear against the door and heard the sound of paper being hurriedly hidden away, followed by heavy footsteps pacing quickly towards the door. It swung open and the civil servant tumbled through, just stopping himself hitting the floor on the other side. The tall, heavy-set man holding the door open scanned the empty space up and down the corridor, before quickly closing the door behind both of them.

Sandy Logan returned to his chair, sitting his large frame awkwardly behind a desk that was much too small for its occupant. Rubbing his beard in quiet contemplation he continued working, ignoring the new arrival. Relieved that he'd finally found the right office, the disjointed civil servant stood vacantly, having completely forgotten why he was there in the first place.

"Well, what is it?" snapped Sandy impatiently, still looking downwards to something more important.

"The Prime Minister has requested your presence, a matter of urgency as I understand it," replied the man.

Sandy took in his dishevelled appearance.

"You pronounce it to be a matter of some urgency, yet you have clearly been trying to find me for some time. You might advise the Prime Minister to make better use of his email in future. I'm a little busy at present to repeat the same pointless journey that you have just been on," said Sandy, in no mood to be summoned as a master calls a servant.

"He did say that you might not be keen to meet," replied the civil servant, his wits returning to him. "He said that if you were not in his office by three-thirty, then you would not be in yours past four."

Sandy's humourless, unpleasant laugh filled the office, brimming with contempt for the preposterous nature of the threat. Sandy picked up his phone and pressed a few numbers. Sitting motionlessly he waited for the tone on the other end to be answered, all the while staring at the fragile man in front of him. Finally, after what seemed to the civil servant as several minutes, the line was answered.

"I need to meet our illustrious leader, I'll be a little late...no, I see no problems...carry on as planned. I'll get there when I can." The call was short and sweet and the moment the phone had been replaced in its charger, Sandy got up and reached for his jacket. "Let's see what all the fuss is about then, shall we? I'll show you the way back: after all, it is *urgent.*"

Sandy led the man towards the door and out into the corridor. The mid-afternoon sun was streaming in through the floor-to-ceiling stained-glass windows that were positioned at regular intervals along the passageway. When they had walked the length of it in silence they descended a vast staircase for several floors. The civil servant tried to keep pace with Sandy's quickening steps, whose urgency to get to the Prime Minister's office now appeared greater than the original request. Several more winding corridors, each resembling a clone of the last, flashed by before they reached an area of the Houses of Parliament more decorative and well kept. It was also more occupied; doors were now guarded by security personnel, two of whom stood either side of the door that they were approaching.

Sandy flashed his official security badge in the direction of one of them, and without knocking opened the door and entered. On the other side a vast office, with little resemblance to Sandy's own, bustled with fervent activity. In the distance three people stood in deep discussion, whilst here and there several more were engrossed in vast mountains of paperwork, or deep and meaningful telephone conversations. There was a heightened sense of anxiety felt in both the actions of these people and the urgency with which they were being carried out. Sandy had been here before: this wasn't normal, something was happening.

The three figures at the far end stopped their discussion as Sandy burst into the room in a manner of overimportance. The Prime Minister, Byron T. Casey, a greying, bushy-haired, slightly overweight man with the ubiquitous cigarette dangling from the corner of his mouth, stood in the centre wearing the expression of someone who had just been told his house was on fire and that all the exits were blocked. The man to the Prime Minister's right was also someone that Sandy knew well, the Home Secretary, his immediate boss.

Smartly dressed in a sharp, black suit, Sandy had not seen the third man before. Handsome and muscular, the light glistened off his dark, greased-back, blond hair, and the obvious bulge in his jacket indicated that he was an agent from one of the security forces. Sandy's present role had brought him into contact with these people, so he knew how to spot them without seeing the unnatural bulge. The only surprise was that he didn't know who this one was.

As he moved towards them, Byron beckoned for the other two to leave. The agent left by another exit, but not before he assessed Sandy for some unknown threat.

"Okay, I need some time with Minister Logan, so I want everyone else out," the Prime Minister announced loudly to the congregation of employees who, accepting his decision, unanimously filtered away.

"What is it this time, Byron?!" bellowed Sandy before he'd reached the Prime Minister and the collective had finished leaving the room.

The Prime Minister waited until the throng had left before acknowledging Sandy. His demeanour suggested the weight of an uncomfortable few hours was about to explode out onto a few others, and he was not at all in the mood to suffer Sandy's insolence.

"An ideal question. One that I feel is more relevant for me to ask of you," growled the Prime Minister. "If I had any belief that you had done your job correctly, then perhaps I might be illuminated by the response. However, as I suspect this is not the case, at least I can witness your discomfort. A position that I have occupied for most of the day."

"I take it, then, that there has been an incident?"

"How dare you be so blasé?" Byron barked in reply. "Do you call the death of three government scientists an incident? Would you tell their families quite so calmly? I'd say it's a bloody catastrophe. An 'are you considering your position'-sized incident, given the recent past, wouldn't you say?"

The Prime Minister thrust a memo into Sandy's chest. Sandy opened the now crumpled document and read the headline that leapt out from the page:

Saturday March 25th (9.06am)
Zytech Facility Bombing – Three scientists killed in latest terror attack.

Sandy took several minutes to read the rest of the briefing, partly absorbing the information and partly considering the best way to respond. Clearly this *was* a big deal for his department, and only hearing of it several hours after it had happened, instead of several weeks before, was sure to cause him embarrassment.

"Who did it?" enquired Sandy, his response typically reserved.

"I thought that you might shed some light on that yourself," shouted Byron in dismay. "Is it not your department's responsibility to identify these types of groups and prevent such an attack. I think I'm right in saying that in the past six months this is the twelfth such attack on similar facilities. How many of these have you foiled?"

Sandy showed no reaction.

"None. Not one. Not even a warning."

"Can I remind the Prime Minister that one of the most notorious perpetrators in this particular war has been run underground on the information and actions of my department? He will also remember that I informed him, no fewer than three times, that the budget he has given me is wholly inadequate to win this fight. If we are to make an impact, I need twice what he has given me. What has he done with this request? Nothing. Instead he pumps millions of pounds into the government research laboratories that these people endeavour to attack," retorted Sandy sternly, both men standing nose-to-nose, trading verbal punches with the other.

"Do you remember why I gave you this job, Sandy?" asked the Prime Minister, his tone softening as if suddenly talking to a compatriot rather than an adversary.

"Yes, I know exactly why you gave it to me. It's because I have a unique insight into this world."

"I gave you this job because, prior to your miraculous victory in the Blackpool by-election, as a one-issue candidate, you were within the inner circle of these groups. You vowed to work with me to destroy the renegade elements of these organisations. What did I say that I would do in return, Sandy?"

"You agreed to abolish all animal testing in Britain, sir," replied Sandy, realising how poorly his part of the bargain had been delivered and the weakness of his position.

"I did, and I will. But I need to see progress first. This country is in the grip of the worst bombing campaign since the early 1980s, and now for the first time we have fatalities. The press and the public are baying for my head. I need to give them something. I have just been battered in a press conference in which you were noticeably absent, and, although numerous attempts have been made to get this news to you, it is clear that you had other priorities. How do you think that makes both of us look? Now I can tell you something for certain, they *will* get someone's head, but it won't be mine. Would you like it to be yours or someone else's?"

"What do you want me to do?" asked Sandy.

"I need you to give me Violet Stokes."

Sandy stood quietly for a moment. He'd been backed into a corner. Both of them knew that Violet was one of the most infamous activists in the country and that Sandy had previously been in cahoots with her. Whether Violet was behind this spate of attacks was unimportant. The press would see it as success and allow the government time to identify the real culprits.

"You know that she is underground?"

"So I hear," responded the Prime Minister, "but she's not invisible. I suspect you know under which rock she has crawled."

"She's more of a symbol in their world now. It won't stop others from copying what she stands for."

"It doesn't matter. She was previously involved, and no doubt will be in the future. It's her head or yours," demanded the Prime Minister, laying the ultimatum clearly and squarely at Sandy's door.

"If I bring you Violet, then you must agree to the immediate abolition of vivisection?"

"My foremost thought is to stop any further loss of human life. I care little if a couple of mice die in the process. You must decide whether you have more chance of achieving your objectives in your present role, or out of it. I have more important things to worry about. You have a week."

Before Sandy reached the door the Prime Minister added one final comment.

"Don't forget where your allegiances lie, Sandy. We put you where you are: don't do anything that might force us to put you back. Without us, you'd be an outcast. A politician in name only. Devoid of any influence or power. You must decide what it is that you hold most sacred."

Sandy left the office. Rather than return to his own office, he made his way to the nearest exit to pick up his ministerial car.

The Prime Minister sat down on his throne-like leather chair, and leant back in quiet contemplation. He reached into a side drawer and removed a bottle of fifteen-year single malt whiskey and poured a large measure of the brown, viscous liquid into one of the fine crystal tumblers arranged neatly on his desk. He swirled it around the glass for a few moments to decide if his clarity of thought would be improved from its consumption. Placing the glass to his lips, he emptied it in one gulp, before resting the tumbler back on the table. As the warmth of the whiskey flooded through his body, he knew what he had to do.

He picked up his telephone handset and placed it on top of the secure scrambling device that was used to ensure none of his conversations could be infiltrated by undesirable ears. The familiar numbers punched into the keypad, he picked up the handset and after several rings an encrypted male voice, which sounded more like a computer than a human, answered.

"Byron," said the distorted voice, "has he gone?"

"Yes, he knows his choices. Let us see what decision he makes."

"Do you want us to follow him?"

"No, whichever choice he makes does not immediately concern me. You have to understand that Sandy would kill his own mother if he thought he might lose his power or any chance of more." Byron didn't show much trust in Sandy, which was probably a well-placed judgement of character. "I think he will make the right choice, but I can't risk his failure if he doesn't. My mind turns to more important matters."

"Emorfed," replied the voice, knowing instantly what he meant.

"Yes. It must be protected at all costs. I cannot risk it being damaged in one of these attacks. If Emorfed is discovered it will stop us creating the type of country that I want. The type of country that the people deserve. I need you to double the security at the Tavistock Institute. I am making you personally responsible for its safety. Is that understood, Agent 15?" demanded Byron.

"It's understood."

The voice was replaced with the monotonous sound of a disconnected line.

CHAPTER FIVE

THE SOUL CATCHER

During the spring of nineteen ninety-seven, in a town hall near Blackpool, a fresh-faced, idealistic and worldly naive John Hewson met a man who would shape his young adult life. Drawn symbiotically to each other by the same cause, the fight against animal cruelty. Both had their own unique reasons for their involvement and both had chosen the campaign group, 'The Movement Against Animal Cruelty', as their vehicle. John had always been passionate about animal welfare and needed little persuasion to join the group when confronted by campaigners in his local High Street. The graphic and shocking pictures that they presented of vivisection and animal experimentation horrified him and he vowed to do what he could to raise awareness.

His first campaign meeting was a rally outside the gates of a local pharmaceutical company that had been known to test products on mice and rabbits. The march was a totally peaceful event, although with the mass of demonstrators no one from the company would be foolish enough to stand in their way. John couldn't deny, though, that the mere chance of conflict, the opportunity to take the law into his own hands, gave him an unexpected sense of rebellion. For the first time in his adult life he felt he belonged. He no longer needed the teachings of the Church to tell him what he could or should do. He'd discovered his own drive.

The man in charge of the campaign group was Sandy Logan, and everything that Sandy did was impressive. An eloquent speaker for a relatively young man no more than thirty years old, he could captivate an audience like a hypnotist. Moulding their views and opinions to his, he handed out his passion and conviction to anyone willing to listen. It was infectious and John was unable to stop himself being compelled to act as directed. Sandy also had everything that John sought in himself. Everything that he currently wasn't: handsome, funny, the centre of attention and a hit with the female members.

Sandy soon recognised that John's unwavering commitment could be fashioned to his every command. Although this aided Sandy greatly, he secretly mocked the weakness of John's mind. Soon the two were at the very heart of the group's activities, working closely together to design campaign leaflets, organise rallies and demos at local businesses seen to be supporting animal cruelty. The campaigns continued peacefully, but always on the edge of legality.

Sandy's desire for attention, and his irritation with the limited progress of the group, made him envious of other organisations that took a more shocking and dangerous approach. It wasn't just because this furthered their cause, it also brought their leaders increased levels of publicity and exposure. Sandy sought publicity more than anything, his real motivation behind his actions.

He became convinced that the only way forward was to join forces with another more national campaign group called 'Justice for Animals, Whatever Species', known more commonly as J.A.W.S. This outfit made headlines by publicly naming and then terrorising the senior management of government research laboratories and multinational companies. Their success had driven their founder, Violet Stokes, into the spotlight. The press latched onto her, creating an image of a dangerous freedom fighter who continued to evade capture.

THE SOUL CATCHER

Eventually John found that he was unable to back such a violent philosophy, arguing that their approach affected humans also. In John's mind humans were included in 'whatever species', too, contradictory to the group's very name. Sandy's unstoppable quest for power and notoriety drove him to a position at the right hand of Violet. He no longer needed John's 'high horse' morality and ignored any views that he held. Eventually the two men drifted out of contact. John left the movement and rejoined the normality of employment. Sandy used his powers of persuasion to canvass for local and central government elections, joining the mainstream parties as his only realistic chance of gaining the power he so craved.

All of this information flew through John's mind as he sat on the floor at the front gate to Hell, his head buried in his hands. He never really comprehended what task he was going to be set. But he certainly hadn't considered that he might be used because of *who* he was, rather than what he was. Emotions in a heightened sense of suspicion, his first question was why it wasn't feasible for an entity like the Devil himself to go and find Sandy's soul.

"Sandy Logan. That's someone I haven't thought of for a very long time. I didn't even know he was dead. How did he die?" said John, buzzing with questions once again.

"We don't know exactly, but suffice to say we know he is dead. What we also know for sure is that he isn't here, and believe me, he definitely should be. So when you put two and two together we know that he is, or at least his soul is, somewhere else. We know he died about the time you did. But as to where or how, that's unclear," replied Brimstone. "Friend of yours, was he?"

"He was, but I couldn't say whether he still is. He compromised our friendship because of his insatiable ambition. The last time I even thought about him was when he became a Member of Parliament. He had a

59

way of using people to get where he wanted to go, rather than fight for the ideals that he so passionately spoke of. Why do you need me to do this? Surely you have the means to do it yourselves?"

"You'd think so, wouldn't you?" answered Brimstone. "Unfortunately we are all tied to this place and the boundaries of our own Universe. Our time travels much faster than yours: a few minutes on Earth would take several years here, so crossing the time-space continuum through the wormhole would be impossible. We would suddenly age at an incredible rate, disintegrating before we got anywhere near our destination. We could travel there if we had a soul, but that isn't the case for all but one of us at least. Anyway, these events are so incredibly rare there's little call for it."

"How did it happen? Surely you have processes in place to stop this stuff happening?"

"Well, for me to answer that question I'd need to explain the principles of the Universe and how the Soul Catcher works, which might take a while."

"I seem to have the rest of eternity and an almost timeless location. What say you we give it a go?" replied John, getting tired with Brimstone's demeaning approach to what he clearly thought was a lack of mental capacity.

"OK, you don't have to get like that. If I told every soul that came through here the intricacies of how everything worked, I'd never get anything done," he snapped in response.

Brimstone stood up and strolled towards the Soul Catcher, a look of pride on his craggy face, as if a father was about to talk about a highly successful offspring.

"This magnificent device is responsible for detecting negative souls and attracting them through space and time to the edge just outside of the wormhole." Brimstone pointed out into the darkness where the end of the Soul Catcher poked out, almost lifeless except for regular pulses of energy that jetted into space.

"What's the blue stuff?" John asked, less than intellectually.

"The energy that you see being emitted from the barrel are forces that suck those souls into the base. At any point there might be thousands of souls colliding with each other inside the bulb, which I am told is a rather unpleasant experience. All the evil charged emotions rub off on the other souls around them. It's like a personal hell all of its own."

"It's like a big magnet," mused John out loud.

"Yes and no. It draws things to it like a magnet, but it's not magnetism. It uses the fifth force, but it'll be several more centuries before the human race has fully understood it."

"Why doesn't it attract other electrically charged objects as well as souls?" asked John, fascinated by the unexpected science lesson. John's pre-death career had been as a climate scientist and this was right up his street.

"It does on occasion. We had a particular problem at one point, got all of these aeroplanes and ships from the Atlantic Ocean. They called it the Bermuda Triangle, which made us laugh, I can tell you."

John recalled a story that he'd once read about a B-52 bomber that had been found on the moon. Just goes to show you should never completely write something off, however farcical it seems.

"The fifth force should only attract atomic particles that have been released from an organic entity. Before the soul is released from the organic object where it resides it is subjected to the bigger forces, like gravity."

Brimstone walked around the side of the Soul Catcher towards the control panel. The centre point of all the knobs, buttons and leavers was a screen, split in half down the middle.

"This screen splits the souls into two lists. On the left is a list of souls already trapped inside the machine, and on the right-hand side a list of the souls that are due to be captured in the next ten minutes. Now, we can look at this list backwards and forwards to see who has been here and who is due here. When a soul is not accounted for the screen flashes like crazy and all hell breaks loose, if you pardon the pun. Now because it so rarely happens, we tend to be unprepared for such an instance. On the day Sandy's soul was due here his name never crossed from the waiting list to the in-soul list on the left." He indicated the movement with a craggy finger, sending a miniature pyroclastic flow over the screen. "The rest of course you've seen. When the vessol is ready at the end of the Soul Catcher, the souls are injected and sent off for processing to the relevant level."

Brimstone had obviously worked on the machine forever, but sounded almost scared when mentioning what had gone wrong, as if the responsibility was laid squarely at his door.

"So, why did it go wrong for Sandy?"

"We're not sure, to be honest. Every few hundred years something like this will happen. Some demons think it's a problem with the machine, some say it's a user error. My personal belief is that, once in a while, the soul itself is to blame. I think that somewhere in its composition is a force unknown to us that rejects the attraction of the Soul Catcher. It may be that they have the strength to remain on Earth, some higher level of need for one last deed left unfulfilled. I've heard it referred to as the Limpet Syndrome. The soul stays firmly stuck to the Earth, irrespective of how much force is applied by an external source. Even with the power of the Soul Catcher, it remains where it is."

"Where has his soul gone?"

"Ah well, that's less of a mystery. A soul can't survive in its purest form on Earth; there are just too many electrical sources to mutate it, and the pull of the fifth force will catch up with it eventually. It has to go somewhere. This is where the human soul exhibits its ultimate instinct – survival. It seeks out and finds another vessel to occupy until it can be laid to rest, or complete its last purpose. In all other such examples that we've seen the other vessel is a body, just as the souls here are placed into a vessol. In the case of a soul on Earth, it could be anything that has yet to contain a soul. You know it commonly as reincarnation. The only other possibility is possession. But that's much less likely. With possession the soul enters into another human, which already contains a soul, so it's a lot harder. It either results in the human going crazy and killing themselves, or they are eventually exorcised. In both cases the soul returns to us."

John reflected on the possibility that Sandy could be wandering around the Earth in a million different guises. How was he going to find him? It appeared an impossible task. If John's original view on reincarnation was still valid he could be any living thing on the planet. John had never believed in reincarnation as a possibility. His view on the afterlife had been a conventional Christian one, until about ten minutes ago at least.

"Do you know what he has been turned into?" prompted John, unconvinced he was going to like the answer and having visions of him trying to coax a cloud of blue sparks out of an uncooperative elephant.

"That's what you need to find out. We have no idea what he's become. Come to think of it, we have no idea how the Limpet Syndrome works either. It's not of our design, you see, more a quirk of nature, a mutation, an anomaly if you will. There are people who may be able to help you, though," replied Brimstone quite unhelpfully.

"If Sandy's soul is in some random animal, why can't you just leave it there until it dies and eventually passes up here anyway?"

"As I said before, it's not our design, so we don't know what the possible consequences are. We think the most likely outcome will be the complete destruction of your Universe," Brimstone answered without the required level of concern.

"The end of the Universe. What makes you think that?"

"Obviously we don't know for sure. Clearly it hasn't happened before or we wouldn't be having this chat. Neither are we prepared to sit back and see if it does. We're only going to get one chance to find out, aren't we?"

John weighed up his predicament. He had to find the soul of someone he didn't really like that much, which was inside some kind of animal, somewhere on Earth. What's more, no one here had the foggiest idea or helpful suggestions as to where. If he didn't do it, the whole Universe was probably going to collapse around his ears. If he didn't take the deal, or failed, he was personally going to spend an afterlife somewhere on the lower levels of Hell, being emotionally and physically bothered for the rest of eternity.

That was before he even considered how he was going to get back to Earth to try. He was dead: that must be a major restriction. It wasn't an everyday choice which he was used to. In the past the hardest decisions he had to make were which restaurant to eat in on Friday night, or what direction he was going to take to go to work. This took more consideration and thought.

"Not that I'm suggesting this, you understand, but what happens if I say no?" John asked in a manner designed to suggest the question was hypothetical.

"This is your only chance to get back to Heaven: there is no choice. We need you because you have first-hand experience of the persons in question, and that has always been vital in the past. The alternative is that I break out the sharp, whizzy, pokey devices that make life particularly uncomfortable and go get your room key." Brimstone had the expression of someone holding a royal flush, whilst John had at best a pair of two's and a very poor poker-face.

"I'm sorry, I might have misheard you then. Did you say 'persons'? That's plural," replied John, who had been paying close attention to the response, which he hadn't liked at all.

"Yes, there are two of them. Did I not mention that earlier? How remiss of me. That's what makes this case so absolutely fascinating," explained Brimstone, seeming to think it was humorous.

"Who's the other one?" asked John, his vision now expanded to dealing with a herd of elephants.

"His name is Ian Noble and he was due to come at precisely the same time as the other one. We think that both incidents might be related."

"Oh, they're related all right," replied a now exasperated John, "Ian Noble is Sandy's right-hand man; he hangs around him like a lost dog. He was always the one that carried out Sandy's more difficult or risky jobs. Unfortunately he wasn't very good at them, very accident-prone, that's why he was nicknamed Cher, as in Cher-nobyl."

"I knew you were the right person for the job, John, you already know more than I do. What is your choice?"

"It doesn't appear that I have one."

"That's the spirit: worse things can happen, you know. Think of all those poor sods circulating around in there." Brimstone pointed at the base of the Soul Catcher.

John did consider the possibility of this for a second and, although he would not have volunteered for this mission, it perhaps could have been a lot worse. After all, it would seem that he would get a chance to return to Earth, one last time. It might give him a chance to do what no other dead person had ever been able to do: right a few wrongs.

"Ok, there really isn't much time to lose," said Brimstone. A ridiculous phrase in a place where only nanoseconds had been lost since John's arrival.

"You need to get those souls back before the summer solstice. Now to my reckoning you got to us in early April and they died at the end of March. That only gives you a couple of months to get it all done," said Brimstone, talking to himself rather than to John.

"What's significant about the solstice?"

"We believe that this is the point at which any lost souls would be noticed. Do you know what the solstice stands for?"

"No," replied John, shaking his head. He guessed that it was some Greek or Latin derivative, but all he knew was it represented the longest or shortest days of the year.

"'Sol' means sun, and 'stice' comes from the Latin 'sistere', which means 'to stand still'. Of course, 'sol' also has links to the word 'soul'. At the point when the Sun is in its most northerly position it appears to stand still. It is believed that at this point any souls that are unaccounted for will themselves appear to stand still, ready to be counted. Any imbalance in matter, matter that should not exist, means the Universe is not in balance. This in turn could set off an unstoppable chain reaction. The reverse of the Big Bang," explained Brimstone.

"I need to get on with it, then? But how do I get down there?"

"I'll explain that later, that's the easy bit," said Brimstone, stretching to his full height and flapping aimlessly at the hot steam 'sweating' from his brow. "Before you go, I think I might be able to take you somewhere that might help. Somewhere that very few people, including many of us, have ever been. Are you ready to have your eyes opened, John?"

CHAPTER SIX

THE TAVISTOCK
INSTITUTE

"Rough day?" asked Sandy's driver, as his ministerial car made its way across Westminster Bridge and on to the South Bank.

"No more than usual, Frank," replied Sandy plainly.

The car weaved its way through the congestion, zigzagging to avoid the suicidal cyclists that bobbed and ducked amongst the rest of the rush hour traffic. Sandy always referred to cyclists as moving organ donors for this very reason.

"Where to, sir?" asked Frank nosily.

"S.I.S., I need to speak with Ian," responded Sandy distantly, as if he was answering his own question rather than his driver's.

The car turned right onto Lambeth Palace Road, and took off as quickly as it could towards Vauxhall. In the distance in front of them, nestling on the very edge of the Thames, was the unmistakable outline of the SIS Building, that housed the British Secret Intelligence Services. The building itself stood to attention, keeping guard over London as a reassurance and a warning. The sun shimmered off its huge, layered, step-like construction, the light occasionally blocked out by the shadow of the step above. It was ironic how one of the most secretive places on the planet was also one of the most distinctive in the capital.

When the car arrived it passed through the normal array of security checks without delay. Sandy effectively ran this building and his security clearance was of the highest level. This was the building that never slept. The threats didn't just come between the hours of nine to five of the working day, so it was occupied twenty-four-seven. On this late Friday afternoon it was occupied by someone that Sandy had specifically placed within the confines of its walls. He stepped out of the car and gestured for Frank to wind down his window.

"I won't need a lift back, Frank. I've made other arrangements. See you at the normal time on Monday."

"Okay, sir, have a good weekend." Frank put the Jag into a right-hand lock and sped off towards the security gate at the front of the complex.

Sandy walked through the entrance and up to reception. As a regular visitor he barely stopped at the front desk before he was being waved through, passing underneath the metal detectors and x-ray machines that scanned all personnel and visitors that entered or exited the building.

Sandy had been the Minister for Homeland Security for over four years, ever since the present government had been first elected to power following a decade or more in opposition. Originally he'd been elected to parliament as an independent, but soon defected to the government when it became clear that power was nothing unless it had some influence. It was hard to use your power if the only influence you had was on the constituents of Blackpool, and for Sandy that was nowhere near enough. He was the second person who had served in this role and it was a well-held public opinion that neither of them had been particularly good at it.

This building was as familiar to him as his own house. Over the years every department had felt his presence in one way or another. He kept a keen interest in everything that was being carried out there. Many commented that he spent more time here than he did in his own office. Some of the staff found the ever-present attention of a minister reassuring, some found it suspicious. This was hardly surprising given the nature and character of some of the people that worked within its walls. The people who avoided him most were the field agent handlers. It was a matter of both national and personal security that very few people ever came into contact with the people they protected. Not that Sandy hadn't tried, mind. He wanted the ultimate control of everyone that worked under him.

Sandy wandered through the building, taking in the activities that he saw through the glass partitions, occasionally making eye contact with some of those involved. When he reached 'Conference Room C' the door was ajar and a man sat typing violently into a laptop computer. Frustrated with the instrument, he tapped the keys in an overdramatic fashion as if they might respond better to force.

"It's an electronic device, Ian, not a mechanical one. Using extra force won't help you." Sandy's voice had been the first indication to Ian that he had company. Sandy entered the small conference room and shut the door behind him.

"Stupid bloody thing," replied Ian. "How am I supposed to save the planet if I can't even get into this piece of shit?"

"It might help if you plug it in," replied Sandy, who could see that, although the power cable was plugged into the back of the computer, that's as far as the connection went to any actual power source.

"How are you going to help me understand the inner sanctuary of the Secret Service if you repeatedly insist on demonstrating how much of a tit you are?" Sandy added frustratingly, "You're meant to be inconspicuous."

"Look, I'm trying, but it isn't easy, you know. I can't get anyone to help me, I think they suspect something."

"I suspect they also think you're a tit. Do you know how difficult it is to get employment here, Ian."

"I don't know really. Quite difficult, I guess," answered Ian, his head dropping at the question.

"Quite difficult," replied Sandy, mimicking Ian's reply in a less than complimentary fashion. "Let me tell you. You have to have the highest level of qualifications, a clean police record, a sound family history, agree to the Secrecy Act, be constantly scrutinised, and have an IQ the size of a moderate cricket score. How many of these things are true of you?"

"Well, I don't know. I suppose I have always had a good understanding of…"

"None." Sandy cut him off halfway through his incoherent babbling. "Absolutely none. Not only is it none, but also in the six months that you have worked here there isn't a single person that doesn't know you exist. Now is that because you have set the world alight with your talents?"

Ian's mouth opened but the words took too long to form.

"Not quite," offered Sandy. "In those six months, what *have* you managed to do? You've set fire to your own office because you were using a magnifying glass on a hot day to make the font size on your laptop look bigger. You've worn a badge into work that said, 'Is that a gun in your pocket or are you pleased to see me?' and you've destroyed a state-of-the-art prototype bugging device when you accidentally dropped it in your Diet Coke, costing the department tens of thousands of pounds, I might add."

"Hold on, Sandy, I can explain some of that…" Ian tried unsuccessfully to defend himself, knowing full well that he couldn't.

"All that pales into insignificance of course with your pièce de résistance. The great Ms. Diaz fiasco."

"Anyway, Sandy, to what do I owe this…" Changing the subject also had no effect.

"You must remember the head of the Spanish security services, Maria Diaz. The woman you rugby-tackled in reception because, in your words, she was the least convincing-looking woman you'd ever seen and therefore must have been an imposter."

"She looked suspicious. How was I to know she was a *she*?" pleaded Ian.

"The normal female characteristics weren't a clue, then?" scoffed Sandy. "Yes, you're right, Ian; I really can't understand why there isn't a queue of people outside your office who want to help you. If there was, they'd be medical experts."

"Look, you don't have to be like that, you've known me for twenty years, you know that I'm a bit... clumsy."

"Ian, it was me that gave you your nickname Cher." Sandy had thought up the name after the Russian nuclear tragedy, something that resembled Ian Noble on an almost daily basis. "I suppose I shouldn't blame anyone but myself: after all, I put you in here in the first place. Unfortunately you are the only person that I had, the only person that I can trust."

It was a stark truth that Sandy had very few allies left in the world, many of them having been trampled on in order for him to climb the greasy pole of power. Ian had been different, though, Sandy never saw him as a threat. In fact he pitied Ian for his inferior intelligence and unusual appearance. Ian, the palest man the world had ever seen; even when he had been in the sun the only result was he tanned to white, was a scrawny individual with the unfortunate image of looking greasy and unwashed.

What drew most people's attention, though, was his eyes. His left eye was blue and relatively normal, whilst his right eye was brown and always looked in a different direction to the other, a condition he'd had from birth. You couldn't be sure if he was looking at you or at something more interesting twelve feet behind your left shoulder. The few people that engaged in conversation with Ian were constantly turning around to see what was happening behind them.

"The Prime Minister has given me a choice: either I hand in Violet Stokes or I fall on my own sword," said Sandy, much more calmly than he had done hours earlier in Byron's office, time having softened his anger and focused his mind.

"You're joking: why her?"

"Because he knows he can. He wants to test my resolve and loyalty. There's something else as well that I can't put my finger on. He could have got me to do this years ago, and I don't know why now."

"What are you going to do?" Ian whispered, remembering where they were.

"For the moment, nothing. I need to talk to her. Do you know if the next target is Tavistock?"

"It certainly is. It's the only one left that hasn't been affected, and it's the jewel in their crown. On top of that, for the first time it is clear who's running it."

"What have you learnt?"

"It's undoubtedly a government facility, but it's impossible to uncover what they're doing there. Even your security clearance couldn't find out."

"Do you know when they might strike?"

"The early hours of Sunday morning."

"OK, then we need to get personally involved in this one. Is the van here?"

"Yes, everything is ready. It's fully equipped as you instructed."

"We need to be extremely careful that we don't bring any undue attention to ourselves. I want you to get the security details for Tavistock and anything needed to get close. I want names of personnel, entry codes, blueprints, whatever you can find. If I'm found anywhere near the place then I can say goodbye to my knighthood. I'll see what I can find out that might help us. Take the van tonight. I'll walk. Make sure that the plates are untraceable, even within this building, and make no attempt to contact me in the meantime. Pick me up on the corner of Dunraven and Green Street: there aren't any cameras there. Two o'clock on Sunday morning. Any questions?" asked Sandy.

Ian, wanting to demonstrate his intelligence and mend his already damaged ego, thought about this for a moment.

"Do you want me to bring breakfast?" he asked.

Sandy stood up and moved to the door, shaking his head as he left. On the other side of the door he put his hands across his eyes. What was he about to get himself into?

*****

A black Transit van pulled up alongside the kerb and an unhealthily pale, skinny man wound down the electric windows. The van itself was normal enough, with the exception of two notable features. The windows had been blacked out and there was a longer than usual aerial flapping in the early morning breeze. A man dressed in black trousers, jumper, shoes and gloves opened the passenger door, jumped in and fastened himself into the seat. The van moved away at a pace that suggested a certain haste, but without drawing undue attention.

"Where have you been, Sandy? I've been circling the block for about an hour. I would have rung but you told me not to contact you," said Ian.

"Then you must be early," replied Sandy, looking at his watch. "I hope you've brought a balaclava with you, Ian? You look like a magician has just pulled an exceedingly ugly white rabbit out of an oversized top hat."

"Yes, I have, but I didn't think it was the best thing to wear while driving around London at this time in the morning," Ian responded with unfamiliar good sense.

"I see you brought the sat nav. I had fears that you'd take me to the West Country rather than the Tavistock Institute." Sandy glanced across at the colour display on the dashboard as the arrow indicated their movement north along Park Lane.

"Did you manage to speak to Violet?" asked Ian, breaking a long period of silence.

"No, not yet. It appears she may have gone further underground than I had first imagined. Let's just see if she turns up when we get there."

"So are you going to hand her over, then?"

Sandy ignored the question.

They travelled north out of London, passing many of the illuminated sights of interest at that end of the city. The still brightly lit arch of Wembley Stadium loomed to their left as they joined the motorway, travelling in silence, each contemplating what they would find when they arrived. The M25 was deserted and for the first time in its creation a car was able to drive to its designated speed limit. At junction eighteen they joined the main road into the heart of Buckinghamshire.

"What did you manage to find out?" asked Sandy, keen to see what information Ian had gained about their destination as they drew closer to it.

"There's absolutely nowhere to get breakfast in London at two in the morning."

"Tavistock, Ian, Tavistock."

"Oh. It's definitely animal testing, that's for sure. But there's no information as to the purpose. The secrecy around this place is immense."

"What's your hunch, what do you think they're doing there?"

"It's anyone's guess, but it's definitely government-financed and it's definitely new. There are absolutely no records of this place more than four years old. It's almost as if it was purpose-built."

"How do you know there is animal testing?" asked Sandy trying to punch holes in Ian's theories.

"Same as normal, our friends the activists. They have witnessed birdcages being unloaded, but they can't say what was in them for certain."

This was a smart piece of intelligence. Whenever the government was up to its knees in something they had the perfect circumstances for hiding information, even from their own secret services. The people that they couldn't hide things from, though, were the general public. The government would happily play down any insights as misinformation or outlandish conspiracy theories, a sure-fire indication that it was really true.

"We're almost there," said Ian, as he pulled over into a quiet country lane lay-by, pointing to the sat nav that indicated that they had two more miles to go. He turned off the engine and both men walked calmly to the rear of the vehicle.

Inside the van were an array of instruments lined up on solid metal shelves. This was a secret service vehicle, brimming with the most up to date surveillance equipment the government could buy or steal. Amongst the computer screens, thermal imaging equipment, data recorders and a vast array of weaponry were the most incongruous of items. A row of empty cages were positioned at regular intervals amongst the 21st-century paraphernalia.

"Let's have a look at the blueprints for this place." Sandy motioned for Ian to load them up on-screen and after several moments of uncomfortable computer flapping he succeeded.

"Here we go. As you can see, for somewhere this secretive, it's strangely unprotected. It only has a few security guards or guardhouses. It's as if they want as few people to know of this place as possible. There are two main entrances. The main gate and a service entrance at the rear of the grounds. The place is covered extensively by CCTV, but that won't be a problem, we can interfere with the signal. We have the entrance codes for the gate and I have managed to get two security passes for the main building. No one should suspect us getting in. The guards patrol the building on a regular pattern: if we use the passes it will appear that we are them," explained Ian, pointing to various parts of the plans as he gave his summary.

"What about the guards that are onsite now...won't they see something?"

"I had some special cakes sent to them that should knock them out for a fair few hours," Ian replied proudly.

"I'm impressed, for once you seem to have everything in order." Sandy could be extremely cynical towards Ian, but he had to give him his dues this time.

"Thanks," replied Ian cautiously.

"Here's the plan. We'll drive up to the service gate and pass through the delivery hatches. Once there, we can get in with the passes. It's a big site: where is the best place to wait?"

"There is a main lab on the first floor, not far from where we get in. That will be the natural place to start," replied Ian.

Sandy consulted a few of the screens and turned on some of the instruments. "OK. Let's get it over and done with."

Both men pulled their balaclavas over their faces, clambered back out of the vehicle and into the front seats. Ian pulled away slowly, following the winding road down to the institute. It was the sort of road that you wouldn't choose to drive down, narrow and littered with potholes. There was certainly no indication in the road itself, or the occasional signposts, that one of the UK's leading laboratories was waiting at the end of it.

The service entrance was located on the farthest side of this massive site and from what Ian had uncovered it was normally unoccupied at night. The main entrance, just off the main road, was far more conspicuous, being the normal entrance for the staff that worked there. That side had a security post where the two full-time guards watched any activity on their CCTV screens. The service entrance on the other hand was secured by a large, eight-foot-high, automatic metal gate. As the black Transit van pulled up alongside it, Ian leant out of his window and typed in the eight-digit security code that he'd written on a scrap of paper.

The gates parted slowly, but rather too noisily for Sandy's liking, allowing them to drive through to the delivery hatches at the back of the building. The delivery hatches resembled those that you would find at a logistics warehouse, where lorries would reverse in to load and unload their cargo. Sandy suspected that these had been constructed for the purpose of secrecy, rather than ease of use. At the side of one of these hatches an entrance led into the facility.

"You'd better put one of these on," said Ian, throwing a pair of night vision goggles in Sandy's direction.

"Is that really necessary?" Sandy glared at them unconvinced.

"Well, unless you want us to put all the lights on, then it might be useful. We could stand there with a big sign that said 'Intruders' instead, save the aggro."

It had been many years since Sandy had taken any active role in this kind of exercise and he was very much out of practice. They placed the devices over their eyes and immediately the distinct green effect coloured the objects in front of them.

"Let's keep totally silent once we're in. If I think we need to go back to the van, I'll point to the exit," added Sandy with one final word before they left the van to move towards the door.

When they reached it, both swiped their security cards through the electronic lock situated on the wall. After a moment the red light turned green and the door lock buzzed opened, allowing them entrance. There were no signs of any recent activity: if they didn't know better they'd have thought they were inside an empty warehouse. Using the plans that they had seen in the van, they made their way a short distance towards the main lab. Entering the unlocked room they were knocked back by the smell that hit them. Both of them spontaneously covered their noses. It stank. It was the unmistakable smell of faeces, and the source of the smell was quite obvious.

Past the rows of benches, fridges, and cluttered apparatus, were row upon row of cages. There were hundreds positioned throughout the room. Neither of them had to go very far to realise what they contained. On top of the smell they were met by a barrage of cooing, the noise that only a pigeon can make. In fact it was the sound of a hundred pigeons, all cooing along in an irregular pattern, like a loud, looped version of the chorus line to, 'I Am the Walrus.' Coo, coo, cajew.

If they needed any proof that these were the subject of scientific experiments, they found it in the appalling physical condition of the animals. They had been hand-plucked ready for the pot. Others had horrific scars, the result of sharp objects forcibly inserted or removed. Since stepping back from the hands-on approach to focus on his ability to make changes through political pressure, Sandy had forgotten the harsh realities of vivisection. He felt physically sick as his body shook with anger and the blood start to boil in his veins. Although he hadn't planned for it, he was compelled to act.

Sandy whispered, "I don't want you to answer, just do it. Take all of these poor creatures back to the van. All of them: put more than one to a cage if you have to."

Ian's mouth dropped down to his chin as he mimed furiously at the difficulty and the scale of the task. It was too late to get Sandy's attention, who had already made his way to the first set of cages and was placing as many birds to a cage that he realistically and humanely could. Once the first cage was packed, he moved on to the next. Ian finally picked up Sandy's instructions and followed suit. Once they had four or five cages ready, Sandy pointed to the door as their agreed signal for returning to the van, carefully picking up as many cages as they could. In the back of the van, Sandy transferred some of the birds into the empty cages that were already arranged on the shelves.

"We'll never get them all in, Sandy, and if I'm honest, I'm not sure this is what we came for," pleaded Ian, hoping that Sandy might see some sense.

"Maybe not, but we have to try. It's what we believe in. You finish off the rest. I want to check out that office just off from that main lab, see what I can find out about this place."

Ian had seen this thrill-seeking side of Sandy before, and above all else it was usually him that suffered most off the back of it.

"And get the bomb ready," Sandy whispered as he leapt out of the van and scurried back to the building.

Ian couldn't remember how many trips he had made in total. But after about twenty minutes all the birds were packed and transferred to the van. Trying to estimate how many of them they'd rescued, he made a final guess of one hundred and twenty. The noise which had been loud in the lab was now deafening, making Ian edgy about the unwanted attention it might draw.

He shut the back door to insulate the noise levels and reached onto the shelves, pulling down a rectangular metal box. On the front glowed an LCD screen and two metal nuts, one attached with a crocodile clip and one wire hanging loose at the side. Ian peered down at his wristwatch which was now showing 4.55 a.m. Using the buttons below the screen, he set the bomb to 6.00 a.m, which was now flashing in red from the tinted blue screen. He was just attaching the last wire to the other metal nut when

Sandy emerged from the gloomy distance, his face almost as white as Ian's.

"What's happened?" asked Ian when Sandy reached the van.

"I know what they're doing in there. I can't believe they could have gone this far, it's worse than I could ever imagine. They've got to be stopped. This isn't just about animal rights anymore, this threatens every person in the country," replied Sandy, shaking uncontrollably with both rage and shock. "Is the bomb ready?"

Ian nodded in confirmation.

"Then let's rid the world of it," announced Sandy.

"Okay, the bomb's in the front cab ready to go. I've set it for 6.00 a.m. I've got all the birds out, too," replied Ian, all in all feeling it had been a good night's work for him.

"Ian, I think for the first time in your life you've avoided doing something stupid," said Sandy, following Ian into the front to collect the device.

"How does it feel?"

"Overdue," replied Ian.

"What's that ticking noise?" asked Sandy.

"That'll be my new watch, it's on the dashboard there. I took it off to set the time on the bomb."

Ian pointed to the passenger seat sill next to where Sandy was now sitting. He picked up Ian's watch and held it to his ear before giving it a gentle shake, finally peering down to his own golden wristwatch for comparison.

"Ian, why does your watch say almost 5.00 a.m when mine says it's almost 6.00 a.m.?"

"That's the time, Sandy," replied Ian. "Five o'clock in the morning. I double-checked."

Sandy looked again at the two watches in either hand.

"Oh no...I can't believe that you would be so stupid...even you aren't capable of this. Tell me you put your watch forward by an hour tonight?"

"No, was I meant to?"

*****

Agent 15 peered through the window of his blacked-out Land Rover, spinning the barrel of his old-fashioned Smith & Wesson pistol, removing and replacing the six bullets in a way that only a true obsessive-compulsive can know how. He was bored. He absolutely hated stake-outs. He joined the services for excitement, and this wasn't it. There was no value in a man of his notable reputation sitting on his backside. The only saving grace was that he had one less hour than usual to sit there, thanks to the change to British summertime. The building that was the focus of his lack of interest was the Tavistock Institute.

It stood in front of him, grey under the darkness of this early Sunday morning. Most of the expansive complex of buildings was nestled in the valley. But he could see the main entrance on the other side of the iron security gates from where he sat in his car. Except for one solitary security guard, probably half-asleep in the gatehouse, the place was unoccupied. Having sat there for several hours, he felt the whole task lacked a degree of purpose, even though he knew the importance of this place. The Prime Minister had given no indication of what might happen, apart from a general fear for the safety of the thing that lay within the perimeter.

Agent 15 knew that the Tavistock Institute was a government laboratory founded by the eminent scientist Paul Tavistock, now more commonly known as Lord Tavistock. Other than that it sat on the edge of a sleepy town in Buckinghamshire, he knew very little else about it. What he did know was what it now contained, and given the current climate he recognised the Prime Minister's nervousness. The Institute was one of the few government-run facilities that hadn't been the subject of an attack over recent months. It was only a matter of time before they would try.

He peered up at the car's clock, just above the rear-view mirror, and watched it flick to 5.59am. Deciding that this was as good a time as any to stretch his legs, he got out of the car to contemplate how long he would remain waiting for nothing to happen. As he stepped outside, the dimly lit morning was suddenly brightened by a spectacular explosion. A huge column of fire and smoke stretched into the sky from somewhere at the rear of the institute building. Agent 15's eyes twinkled: finally his night was about to get interesting.

CHAPTER SEVEN

PRIME MINISTER'S QUESTION TIME

"Ladies and gentlemen, thank you for gathering here so early on a Sunday morning," announced Byron T. Casey, whose hands gripped firmly on the rostrum as he stared out into the crowd of waiting journalists. "In the current climate it is important that we share with you any updates on the battle against the terrorist scourge that has plagued this country as soon as the news breaks. It is with great heart that as of now, that war is won."

He waited for the rapturous applause to wash over him. After several disappointing seconds none was forthcoming.

"The people of this country need no longer tolerate the grip of fear from radicalised groups determined to destroy our way of life. At six o'clock this morning a bomb exploded at the Tavistock Institute in Buckinghamshire."

Shock and confusion gathered on the faces in the crowd. Byron, realising that his dramatic pause had come too early, hurriedly continued to remove their concern.

"Instead of destroying its intended target, it killed the bombers that tried to carry it out. One of our agents, who had been dispatched to the scene on my command, witnessed the explosion and was the first person on the scene. It seems from early indications that the bomb malfunctioned and went off in the terrorist's vehicle."

Byron paused again, believing that now the congregation was fully informed, applause would follow. A couple of journalists coughed. What did he have to do to get these people onside? They'd always had it in for him, whatever he did. If he'd had Britain's ten most wanted criminals manacled to the desk they'd still have attacked him.

"Today I want to send a message to those willing to follow in these dead men's shoes. If you attack us we will retaliate, if you scare us we will hold firm, if you try to destroy us *your* world will be dismantled, either by our hands or your own. I will not rest until every person can be secure in the knowledge that our values of peace and freedom are a reality, not just an aspiration. We will not rest until we have hunted you down."

This was Byron at his most impressive, communicating to the masses, acting presidential. It was well known that Byron had little warmth or skill when it came to dealing with people one-on-one. People were drawn to Byron because of his ideals, aided by the fact that the opposition were acting like a fart in a trance. When the public had voted Byron and his party into power they were the best of a bad lot. My God, had he paid for it over the last four years. One of his responses to their attacks was to fuel the fire by being as belligerent and cantankerous as possible.

Byron may have felt that the press were against him, but for them this felt like a new prime minister compared to the one that had fronted so many recent press conferences. This prime minister was on the attack. A far cry from the one that they had been writing about, ineffective, powerless and isolated. This time he had the answers, not just the usual rhetoric. The secret to Byron's performance wasn't delight at what had unfolded but pure relief. He knew that his one chance to deliver on his manifesto, to deliver the people from themselves, had come close to being destroyed. Emorfed was safe, and so was Byron's future.

"I will take a few questions," he announced, confirming the end of his announcement. The watching journalists jostled for position, arms in the air like primary school children eager to answer the teacher's question.

"Julian Mundy, BBC News. How can you be sure that this war is at an end?" asked the first to receive Byron's outstretched finger.

"Our intelligence tells us that these attacks were being conducted by a small band of extremists. Some of them may be left, but this will have dented their confidence and capabilities. We also hope to use the evidence collected at the scene to track down the rest of the group," he replied.

As the Prime Minister batted the questions comfortably away with both wit and skill, his thoughts lingered on what to do about Emorfed. Tavistock had until recently been a secret, even within the government. Now its home was being broadcast across every television network from Scotland to the Scilly Isles. Tavistock was no longer a safe place for it to be kept. Maybe it could be used before the tests had been successfully completed? Was that too great a risk? There would be one chance, and the timing had to be right.

"Gillian Trees, ITV. No doubt this is a huge achievement for the government, but yet again your Minister for Homeland Security is missing from another press conference. Where is Sandy Logan?"

"Mr. Logan is fully aware of our recent success but is unavailable for comment. He is currently following up on an extremely important piece of information linked to these attacks, but I can assure you, Gillian, I will be very keen to see Mr. Logan at our scheduled meeting this afternoon." The Prime Minister's response had been delivered with the well-rehearsed certainty that someone would ask it.

In reality, Sandy had not been seen since their showdown in his office three days ago. What had his decision been? Was he due to hand in the cherry on top of the terrorist cake, or open the trapdoor to his own political oblivion? Byron didn't know what his choice would be, and nor did he care. He could no longer trust someone whose erratic behaviour was liable to make him self-destruct at any moment, possibly taking Byron down with him. It was time to flush him out. Whatever the outcome, Byron would win. Either Sandy brought Violet in and showed his own past links to her world, or he got relegated to the backbenches. It might make Byron's life uncomfortable at moments like this, but his plan was faultless.

"Fiona Foster from The World Today. How would you respond to accusations that the government has been producing illegal biological therapies, designed as weapons of war, at Tavistock for the last four years?"

The auditorium fell silent as they focused on the source of the question.

"I'm sorry, who did you say you were?" asked the Prime Minister, squinting towards the middle-aged blonde sitting at the very back of the room.

"Fiona Foster, The World Today," repeated the journalist.

"I don't remember your name being on the list invited to this function, but in response I would say that you have been reading too many science fiction novels. Clearly your publication, which I am unaware of, is designed for readers only interested in conspiracy theories."

The room erupted in laughter at the particularly cutting response, Byron revelling in the audience's sudden shift to his side.

"I'll repeat my question, sir. How do you respond to my sources who have been inside the Tavistock Institute and have witnessed secret testing on animals, said to be with therapies designed for use on humans as a type of biological conditioning?" demanded Fiona, now standing and pointing fiercely up at the rostrum.

"I'd say that your source was on the same medication as you. I would be happy to accept your claim, if you can accept that this room is made of fudge, The Queen is actually from a small planet on the outskirts of Saturn called Jinbut 3, and that German cooking is undoubtedly the best in the world." More laughter burst out from the journalists and camera crews, charmed by the Prime Minister's newly discovered humour. "I am unsure how you have come by these absurd suggestions, but I will not tolerate them anymore."

Byron nodded towards two burly men stood at the back entrance of the auditorium and within seconds they had moved over to where Fiona had been sitting. After a brief and pointless attempt at resistance she was physically removed from her chair.

"Now, unless anyone has any questions that are substantiated or relevant to my announcement today, I have important issues to attend to," bellowed Byron, ignoring the fact that almost everyone had their hands in the air.

"Please remove your hands from me. I am perfectly capable of leaving this room in the same manner that I entered!" shouted Fiona, aiming one final comment at the delegation as she was dragged away. "Just remember the word Emorfed. Ask him about that, see if he will deny any knowledge of that."

"Paul Eaves, *Sky News*. What is Emorfed?"

"There will be no further questions; I refuse to answer questions that have no basis in reality."

Byron picked up his papers and left to a barrage of further questions and a shower of crackling flashbulbs.

Any empathy that he had created in the last five minutes had just evaporated. Byron disappeared behind the curtains.

"Get Agent 15 in here at once!" shouted Byron at the closest aide that he could see. "And I want to see Sandy Logan when you have dug him out of whichever vast hole he is hiding in."

Byron's rage was palpable. What had started out as a great victory had somehow developed into an open season. How was it possible that an obscure reporter from a two-bit rag had been so well informed? Only a handful of people even knew the name Emorfed, let alone knew what it was capable of.

"Agent 15 is waiting in your office, sir," said the aide, having just come off his mobile phone. "He's managed to identify the bombers. He says he's got all the data with him."

"Good, let's see who these bastards are," replied Byron as he headed for his nearest exit.

*****

Agent 15 was sprawled on the red leather sofa in Byron T. Casey's private office, arms outstretched along its back, dressed as he always was in his dark suit, dark tie and shoes polished to within an inch of their lives: the classic spy clichéd dress sense. He always argued that this was the best appearance for meeting dignitaries as he'd fit in with all the other civil servants, security guards and hangers-on. In his left hand was a large brown envelope, sealed and marked 'top secret'. Byron came through the doors of his office so forcibly that they almost came off their hinges.

"So what have you got?"

His anger had not yet abated and it was clear he was in no mood to be messed around. Byron removed the tie he always hated wearing, sat down behind his desk and waited for Agent 15's report. Agent 15 stood up and approached the Prime Minister's desk.

"We now have a positive ID. There were elements of two human bodies in what was left in the debris. The explosion was so powerful they are still finding fragments in nearby fields." Agent 15's style lacked emotion. Sights and scenes that would have turned most people into blubbering wrecks were delivered in a factual, almost heartless manner. "There were, in fact, no bodies to speak of, sir, just a lot of splatter. The job was made more difficult for the scientists, given the presence of non-human DNA in the remains."

"I'm sorry, Agent 15, what do you mean, 'non-human' DNA? What are you saying?"

"There was a large quantity of bird DNA present, almost certainly pigeon. These birds were seemingly removed to the vehicle from the laboratory, which gave us the impression at first that the perpetrators were animal rights protestors. They would no doubt have released them at a later date, but accidentally killed them instead. Ironic, isn't it?"

"I feel quite sorry for the poor things: at least they would have survived if they were kept where they were. So who were they?"

"Our first clue comes from analysing the wreckage of the vehicle. Interestingly, the van that they used is untraceable."

"Explain?"

"Firstly, the bomb exploded inside it, so there is very little of it intact, and secondly the serial numbers that we've recovered are not recorded at DVLA or any other official body."

"What does that mean?" barked Byron, getting impatient with this clinical and seemingly round the houses description of the incident.

"Quite simply it means that it was either a government vehicle, or a vehicle from abroad. If you will let me continue I can demonstrate it is not the latter." Agent 15 continued his summary on Byron's nod of the head. "We know that it *was* a government vehicle because we know that one of the deceased was on the payroll of MI5."

Agent 15 opened the envelope and passed him a dossier of information. It included a black and white photograph of a pale and gaunt individual.

"His name is Ian Noble," added Agent 15, "and there's very little detail on him. At least not that we can find. He's been on MI5's payroll for three and a half years but his personnel file has been encrypted and only one person can get access to it. Now there are very few people within the intelligence community that have the ability to do that. Would you like to hazard a guess as to whom?"

"Sandy Logan?" Byron answered with an air of self-expectancy and a tone reserved for those difficult moments in life when mistakes are about to come home to roost.

"I'm afraid so, Prime Minister."

Byron's reflexes launched towards his mobile phone.

"If you are about to call him, let me save you the job," added Agent 15, guessing whose number was about to be dialled.

"I'll kill him. Not a quick end, no. I will reserve the most unpleasant demise you can imagine. I'm going to string him up by his soft nether regions from the very hands of Big Ben. I'm going to suck his heart out with a straw."

If Byron's blood pressure had been high after the press conference, it had now surpassed all medical records.

"Again, let me save you a job."

Agent 15 passed across a second dossier from within the brown envelope. The Prime Minister's jaw dropped and for several minutes he stared unbelieving into the face of the second photograph. There the unmistakable features of the ex-Minister for

Homeland Security, the late Sandy Logan, smiled back at him.

"Oh shit," gasped Byron, dropping the dossier onto his desk and placing his hands through his greying hair. "Who else knows about this?"

"You and I. Even the scientist that ran the test doesn't know who he is," replied Agent 15.

"If this gets out into the open we are finished. Can you imagine the Minister appointed to destroy the terrorist network was actually running the bloody thing? Oh this is bad."

"His treachery runs deeper than that." Agent 15 removed his smartphone from his inside jacket pocket. "This call was made at ten to six this morning from Sandy's mobile phone."

Agent 15 held up the device and pressed play. The recording was muffled but most of the conversation was comprehensible. The first voice was unmistakably Sandy Logan's, panic-stricken and angry.

"Violet, if you pick this up you need to act quickly. I've got into Tavistock. We thought you might beat us to it. I've just broken into a safe in one of the offices... I can't believe what they're doing here...it's some kind of biological weapon called Emorfed. They're testing it on animals, but that's just the beginning."

"The recording gets a bit muffled at this point. It seems he may have been distracted by something," added Agent 15, as the recording became distorted and fractured.

"Go to the press, get this out in the open. If it is what I think, then we'll all be in big trouble. It threatens our very way of life," came Sandy's voice, tailing off.

"So that's how that bitch found out," added Byron through gritted teeth. "Have you traced where the message was sent?"

"Yes, but the property was unoccupied. They must have picked the message up earlier today and scarpered, knowing what had befallen Sandy and knowing that we would come after them. Clearly they didn't waste any time spilling the beans to the reporter from The World Today. What do you want me to do, sir?"

Byron composed himself. If nothing else, Byron T. Casey was a fighter. He'd won the ugliest general election campaign the country had ever seen. He'd fought dirty to get into this position and if necessary he could do the same to stay there. He had previous.

"Our only good lead is the reporter. We know that she must have got her information from Violet Stokes, or one of her people, and one thing's for sure: if she's still around we still have a problem. I want you to find this Fiona Foster. I want you to stick to her like glue. I want to know where she goes, who she meets, where she lives, who her friends are, and even what brand of shampoo she uses. Is that understood, Agent 15?"

"It will be done."

"Oh, and if you have to silence her, then use all your powers, legal or otherwise, but keep it out of sight. This stays between the two of us." Byron stood up and walked to the window. Rain lashed down on the rooftops of a blustery London.

Agent 15 departed through the nearest door, or at least that's what Byron had thought he'd done. The moment after the door had closed, it opened again, then shut, opened, shut again, and for a third time opened and closed. A confused Byron walked to the door where Agent 15 was already halfway down the corridor.

"What was that?"

"What was what, sir?" replied Agent 15.

"All that mad door-shutting," he asked, flapping his arms forward and back in mock reconstruction.

"Oh that. Obsessive-compulsive disorder," replied Agent 15 as he returned. "I have to shut every door I open at least three times or unspeakable things will happen to me."

"O.C.D., really? But you're an agent. How did you manage to get the job in the first place?"

"Only started after I joined the service. Something to do with deflecting anxiety."

Byron returned to his office. "That's all I need. The only person that I can trust is a bloody freak."

CHAPTER EIGHT

LEVEL ZERO

The very first resident of level zero was a rat called Li Xeng. The day she arrived in Hell had been a most memorable one. Li Xeng was the very first person to demonstrate the effects of the Limpet Syndrome and no one had seen anything like it. Her soul had finally been returned to the Soul Catcher by the efforts of a fellow Chinese man by the name of Zhang Heng, averting the certain doom that awaited the Universe. On his return from the afterlife, Zhang went on to be the Chief Astronomer for the Chinese Emperor, having inexplicably catalogued some two thousand unnamed stars. On top of this he had an uncanny ability to create inventions using mechanics and gears never previously seen on Earth.

When Li Xeng's soul had finally been released from its rat-like form it was a complete bugger to catch. Like all souls, she had made her long and meandering journey through space and time to the very edge of the Universe. The soul had been altered in such a way that when it entered the Soul Catcher it would not accept the prosthetic human version of Li Xeng that had been laid on for it. For days the soul lay siege inside the machine refusing to budge, the effects almost destroying it. Every time a normal soul was incarcerated with it, the unusual union produced the weirdest and most wonderful pulses of energy emitted in every colour and direction out into space.

There was great concern amongst the demons that the Soul Catcher would be permanently damaged, and after much deliberation an alternative vessol was created to keep Li Xeng safe. A vessol shaped in the form of a rat which Li's soul finally accepted as its last resting place. The idea had come from the quick thinking of a demon called Mr. Primordial, who, in turn, was given the responsibility for storing and dealing with Li Xeng and all other such cases in the future. A post he still held several millennia later when, unbeknown to him, a recently deceased man from Surrey was about to see how he was getting on.

John and Brimstone stood at the lowest visible level of Hell on the bank of the stagnant lake that John had seen from the bridge on his earlier walk around.

"I've never been where we are about to go, John, but I'm hoping that we will find out something that will help you in your task," Brimstone announced, searching around the edge of the lake. "Now somewhere around here should be a switch...ah here it is."

Brimstone placed his hot, stony fingers around a piece of rock protruding from the wall. As he pressed on it the once still and stagnant water of the lake started to froth and ripple, swirling violently around the edges, as if someone had removed the plug from the bottom. Within a minute the water was suspended against the side of the lake, held invisibly by centrifugal forces. The bed of the lake was laid bare. But from the flicker of the lanterns adorning the walls, John could make out some stepping stones winding down to a trapdoor. Brimstone was already stomping down the stairs like only a creature made of granite can, his pounding footsteps echoing through the cavernous city of cells.

"Are you coming down or not?" Brimstone asked as he disappeared through the previously concealed entrance.

The scene that greeted John, when he'd finally made the decision to follow his demon guide, was a very different one than he'd been used to in his brief experience of the levels above. The entrance led into a vast underground forest, dimly lit but magnificently real. Trees stretched upwards towards the heavens and a carpet of fragrant-smelling flowers, that sheltered under their canopies, were joined by an assortment of coloured fauna that circled all around him. The deep solitude and anxiety that had weighed so heavily on him for the majority of his death evaporated like a cheap perfume. He could not adequately describe how he felt, but he knew that here, underneath the horror, there was a degree of peace.

"Welcome to level zero," said Brimstone, breaking John's calm.

"What is this place?" asked John quietly.

"It's where we keep the…well…anomalies that we receive," replied Brimstone cautiously. "The victims of the Limpet Syndrome are brought here. We like to call it the zoo. Now all we need to do is find him."

"Who do we need to find?"

"Primordial."

"Who's he?" asked John nervously.

"He's responsible for managing level zero. I haven't seen him since he first created this place."

As they strolled gradually through the undergrowth they weren't sure if it was the enchantment of the place or their own intuition that created a sense within them that they were not alone. John had convinced himself that a bush had just rustled to his left, but as he peered closer any movement was non-existent. They ambled through the grass, occasionally stopping to examine some exquisite new find, adventurous, carefree children on a voyage of discovery. A golden eagle swooped down from an unseen eyrie, landing on a withered beech tree, thick and ancient, grown from a seed planted at the dawn of this place. Several metres above them, the eagle bobbed its head up and down, scowling at the two new figures that had just trespassed into its world.

"Is that one of them?" John tapped Brimstone gently on the shoulder, whispering out of the corner of his mouth and pointing up at the bird of prey. Brimstone's attention had been focused elsewhere.

"Am I one of what?"

"What did you say?" John asked Brimstone.

"Nothing," replied Brimstone.

"I said, what do you mean, *one of them*?" repeated the voice indignantly.

Very slowly John looked around, hoping to find the source of the voice *elsewhere*. It was clear that it had come from the eagle and no one else.

"Hello," John said hesitantly, raising a hand in the air to wave in greeting. "Was that you who spoke?"

"Of course it was. My name's Malcolm Truman and if by *one of them* you mean a reincarnate, then yes, I am one," said the Eagle, gripping the branch with his long, dangerous talons.

"Did you know that they could talk?" John whispered again from the corner of his mouth, as if not to draw the eagle's attention or in some way offend it.

"No. Fascinating, isn't it?" replied Brimstone, depicting an interested botanist that had suddenly discovered an exciting new species.

"Why are you two here?" asked Malcolm the eagle.

"We are looking for Primordial," replied Brimstone.

As Brimstone spoke, a giraffe's head poked out of the dense thicket of trees just to the right of where John and Brimstone had been conversing with a bird.

"What's going on, Malcolm?" asked the giraffe, his voice muffled slightly by the clump of leaves on which it was currently munching.

"They're looking for Primordial, Alan."

"I haven't seen Primordial for a while. Didn't he go on holiday?" offered Alan.

"I don't think demons go on holiday," Malcolm replied, raising his eyes to John as if to indicate that Alan was not quite all there. "By the way, how's your friend, Penelope: she managed to remove her trunk yet?"

"I don't like to interrupt," said John, raising his hand in an attempt to get in on the conversation.

"No, she had to have it chopped off. I told her not to go sniffing around in the crocodile pond, but she wouldn't listen…"

"STOP!" shouted John. "I can't deal with this. I'm watching a conversation between a giraffe and an eagle. This day is just too weird. What's next? I suppose that muddy puddle over there is about to get up and do a tap-dance?"

John's eyes hadn't just been opened, as Brimstone had warned, they'd been removed from their sockets and violently stamped on. Unfortunately John's sanity wasn't improved by what happened next. The patch of mud on the path in front of them *was* moving. It wasn't just moving, it was getting up.

"What are the odds on that?" John commented. "Usually I'm rubbish at predictions."

A muddy, disjointed arm emerged from the ground, grappling forward onto the path to secure its grip. The arm pulled itself along the ground, quickly followed by a head, and then finally a body lurched out in front of them. Before long, the full figure was standing upright, dripping and oozing on the ground a few feet in front of them. It was a humanoid shape but with no obvious features, a mass of filth and dirt from head to foot.

"I understand you want me, Brimstone," said the creature, gliding forward with a path of detritus in its wake. "It's been a long time since we have had a visit from those above. Do I guess that we are due a new specimen?"

As he spoke, more creatures started to mingle around the clearing, excited that for the first time in a long while something new was happening on level zero.

"You are correct, Primordial. We have another case that will need your attention, a couple of new animals for your zoo," replied Brimstone. "This is the man who has been chosen for the task. Say hello, John."

"H..e..l..l..o," John stuttered, mouth agog at the thing that was Primordial.

"Who the hell picked this one? He doesn't even seem capable of speaking properly. You've chosen an idiot for a job that requires someone truly brilliant," replied Primordial, his voice gurgling out of some unknown orifice.

John suddenly came to his senses. As much as he was finding it hard to accept his surroundings, he couldn't but be annoyed that he was being mocked by a pile of mud.

"I'm sure that I am as capable as anyone," John said defensively.

"Then you are misinformed," replied Primordial. "You can't possibly understand what you are about to be subjected to. Are you prepared to have your soul, your very existence, forced backwards through the heart of the Universe? Ready to be manipulated so that you see all of your past mistakes replayed in front of you? To be subjected to a degree of pain that you could never imagine was possible?"

This certainly wasn't the way that Brimstone had painted it. But it was a bit late to complain or ask for a refund.

"Look, Primordial, let's not jump the gun here, don't forget the safety of their Universe is on the line," replied Brimstone.

"Exactly, then you understand my concern."

Primordial had moved closer to John so that they were face to filth. Primordial was a zoo all of his own. John could see an army of tiny organisms growing and living symbiotically in the muddy, sticky flesh of his form. Primordial had no recognisable eyes, but even so, John could feel their glare burning into him.

"The job you have received has previously been conducted by some of the wisest and cleverest members of the human race. What is it that *you* did on Earth to merit such company?"

"I was a meteorologist," replied John, feeling inadequate.

"Well, it's not the usual benchmark for those that have preceded him." Primordial stared at Brimstone. "I'm used to luminaries. This is a nobody. I wonder whether he can do it."

"He is the one, as it is written," replied Brimstone.

"Really? We will soon see, won't we?" replied Primordial. "So, what is it that you want from me?"

"We need to know how to recognise the target, what they have become," replied Brimstone.

"Another sign of his unsuitability. Most people can work it out for themselves. I think a test is in order, come with me," signalled Primordial, his body instantly collapsing to the floor to create a small, muddy river that meandered into the distance.

Brimstone and John followed a few feet behind as Primordial slithered through the undergrowth and around tree stumps that blocked his route. When they reached a clearing in the trees he stopped and reverted to his humanoid form. A number of animals had collected around a small stone cairn, excitedly waiting for the curtain to rise and the show to start.

"This cairn was the first habitat I made on this level. Built to shelter the very first of its inhabitants, Li Xeng. Level zero spread from this central point, evolving into all the different habitats needed for those that were brought to me. Lakes to the north of here for the aquatic species, arid lands to the east, Arctic conditions to the west, and the forests to the south that you have already seen. Everything here was created by my hand," explained Primordial, clearly proud of what he had built. A Hell for animals that was both his creation and his domain.

The ability to create so many habitats that were as fake as they were impressively realistic was no mean feat. This place had a beauty about it. A place that had been fashioned with care and attention to detail. The rest of Hell was devoid of anything other than desperation. Was that why very few demons came here? Perhaps this area was as alien to them as the levels above were to him? Or maybe because Primordial was as much the lord of this realm as Satan was the governor of those above it?

Primordial lifted a rock from the top of the cairn. It almost disappeared into his body as the life forms under his skin crawled out and over it like a swarm of bees. He threw the rock into the air, where it landed in the middle of the clearing with a thud. What was Primordial trying to accomplish? Eventually he could hear and feel the ground under his feet shift and move. A mound of earth pushed upwards onto the surface of the ground until a mole's head popped out from the centre. Primordial leaned down to the mole's level.

"Greetings, Bert."

"How can I serve you, master?" replied the mole.

"If you want to know how to recognise a reincarnated soul, let's see if you can prove your worthiness, John. What do you notice that is different with Bert, compared to a normal mole?"

John, further annoyed with Primordial's constant references to his inability, was more determined than ever to take on Brimstone's task and prove them wrong. Was this what Primordial was aiming to do? John assessed the mole trying to identify the differences. One was obvious.

"Well, most moles on Earth don't have red spots all over their faces."

"Correct, but not hugely insightful. A four-year-old could have told me that. Take a note, Brimstone, for reference when you are next choosing candidates. What else?"

John tried again. What else was different? As a whole he was very much like...well, a mole. John looked at the other animals that had collected around the clearing. Of the creatures that had congregated, a white rabbit was hopping around trying to get it on with any other animal that it came into contact with. A monkey was swinging through the branches from tree to tree, and an ant was scurrying around on the top of the cairn. That's when it struck him. The cairn was about fifteen feet away but he could clearly see the ant. Surely he shouldn't be able to.

"The animals are bigger than they should be?" John said out loud, although not intending to do so.

"I'm mildly impressed," replied Primordial. "You're right of course. The animals are all about a third bigger than the average for their species."

"Why is that?" asked Brimstone, protecting John from asking the very same question.

"When the human soul enters an animal it tends to enter at or before the creature's birth. The presence of the human soul, the mass of energy fighting for free space, seems to accelerate the growth of the animal. The smaller the animal, the bigger the growth. We have a great white shark down here called Xavier, who's hardly any bigger than normal. But for most they would appear much bigger than normal."

"That's great, now I know how to recognise Sandy and Ian. There is one teeny-weeny thing that might still be a problem," replied John calmly.

"What's that?" asked Primordial.

"I don't know what animal they've been reincarnated into," John shouted angrily, as if Primordial had been wasting his time. Difficult to do in a place where your time doesn't exist, mind you!

"I can't help you with that, there's only one person who can," said Primordial.

"I'm sorry, are you telling me that after all of your bullshit, all your taunting, you don't know where they've gone either? You actually don't know any more than I do."

Primordial sank into the ground completely disappearing from view and for several minutes nothing happened. John and Brimstone wondered if Primordial was gone for good. Just as they were about to give up and return to level one, Primordial soared out through the Earth, right under John's feet, totally engulfing him. In complete darkness, John could feel Primordial all over his false body, the organisms that lived inside crawling over him, through his hair and on his skin. Creatures oozed into his mouth, attempting to infiltrate his body and suck out his life force. The sensation was one of the most unpleasant feelings that John had ever experienced, even more unpleasant than death itself.

"Remember who you are talking to, John?"

Primordial's voice enveloped him in the darkness, harsh and dangerous. Struggling for air, each gulp followed by a heavy dose of filth down the white funnel of his vessol.

"Don't you know what I am? I was created from the first pool of life that gave birth to the organisms in the Universe. I'm the creator and taker of life. The bringer of death, the decomposer of flesh. Dead or not, I could consume you. If you succeed or fail you had better wish you never have the misfortune to meet me again, John. You have no idea how painful that might be. I do not know what your target has become because it is not of my doing. Let's hope you have the wits enough to find out yourself. I spoke of one who knows. His name is Laslow Kreicher."

Primordial slid away from his body, disappearing into the ground for the final time, allowing John to gasp at the fresh air. John hit the soft mud, struggling to find some type of normality. Brimstone loomed above him, something he was unaccustomed to doing.

"I think you might have pissed him off, John."

CHAPTER NINE

ONE IN A BILLION

"That went rather well," commented Brimstone as they emerged back through the trapdoor of the dried-out lake.

"What!?" replied a flabbergasted John. "I almost drowned in the filth of a demon."

"Yes, but you didn't, which was a much better result than I was expecting." Brimstone pressed the button, which allowed the water to collapse from around its banks and submerge the route that they had just taken.

"I'm sorry, you thought we wouldn't be coming out again?"

"No, not quite. I thought *you* wouldn't be coming out again! Primordial doesn't care if you're human or animal, but he wouldn't harm a demon. In the past all the demons who have dared to take someone else down there have come out on their own. He's a nasty piece of work, but I could handle him," replied Brimstone, a degree of arrogance in his voice.

"There was me thinking you were on my side," said John, shooting Brimstone a disconsolate frown.

"I'm not on your side, John. I just don't want your Universe to crumble around my ears and suck everything into an infinitely dense void. As long as that doesn't happen, your final destiny doesn't concern me."

"But surely we are outside of my Universe: this place would remain untouched, wouldn't it?"

"That's true, but without your Universe there are no humans. Without humans there are no souls. Without souls we have no reason for being, nothing to fuel us, nothing to feed on," replied Brimstone, in a distressingly cannibalistic manner, as if he would have quenched his insatiable thirst on John's soul right now if he hadn't been sanctioned not to. As he clumped awkwardly towards a block of stone that rose up through the middle of level one, for the first time John felt a sense of unease towards this once seemingly harmless character.

"Now I understand. You don't care about my Universe or anything in it. You just want to save yourselves. As long as you get your fix, is that it? Everyone else can rot," replied John, realising there was no real help in this vast, desolate place and ultimately the only one who cared enough to save humanity was him.

"That's about right. What would you have me do, John? Repent? Fall on my knees and beg forgiveness? I can physically or spiritually do neither, even if I wanted to," countered Brimstone, his patience in dealing with a mortal stretching thinner by the second. "So, you know the question, what's your answer?"

John hadn't really decided for sure what the best choice was. Primordial certainly hadn't painted a very pleasant picture of what would happen if he said yes, and the alternative of doing nothing didn't sound like a blast either. On the bright side, if he was successful he had the chance of getting out of this place forever.

"I'll do it," said John begrudgingly, glancing around a final time at the alternative.

"Good," replied Brimstone. "Okay, let's go to the library and decide where we are going to put you."

John was almost able to ignore the deafening cries of terror and pain that accompanied their stroll along the lowest level of Hell. How in the world was he going to be *put,* as Brimstone described it, back on Earth? They entered a steel-based lift, now visible in the face of the stone column towards which Brimstone had been leading them. A list of numbers that ascended from one to twelve on a crudely chiselled keypad crept down the furthest wall. A steaming hand reached up and pressed number eleven.

"You said there were ten levels of Hell?" said John.

"There are, for inmates at least. But as you have seen, there are some supplementary areas. The eleventh level is where we keep all of our records from the past, present and future."

With the sound of a motor desperately overdue a service, the decrepit lift cranked slowly up through the levels. As they reached each level a bony hand indicated their position on an old-fashioned dial at the top of the lift door. It reminded John of the old-fashioned Victorian hotels in London he used to visit as a young child with his father. Treasured moments, that were all too few, of happier times when they'd take weekend trips to the capital's attractions. Some of the few real memories of his father's existence that he still had.

As they reached the eleventh floor the steel gates creaked open. When he stuck his head nervously out of the door the sight of a gigantic library running left to right in the same oval shape as all the other levels he'd seen, but with one significant difference. The abyss, that featured so prominently through the centre of the tiered caves, was replaced by an even floor constructed of smooth and polished graphite that enabled easy access from one side of the cavern to the other. In certain areas of the black carbon hue, John could make out faint but indecipherable writing, eroded by continually passing feet.

Across from John, elongated bookshelves teetered precariously under the weight of their contents, which were books of every shape and size stuffed unwillingly into position. On the far shelves were thick volumes with weathered spines, thumbed through by generations of readers like a favourite reference book in constant use. Behind him the books newer and thinner, flaunting their unread or unwanted shiny laminated covers, a Christmas gift that the recipient had never got round to reading. At the end of the room towards the thicker books a vast bonfire burnt with intense white light, and leaping flames competed to be the first to lick the ceiling. Even though it was at least a hundred feet away the heat from it was almost unbearable.

At the other end, near to the thinner titles, stretching out as far as the walls would let them, were a pair of ancient oak trees whose branches stitched themselves together symbiotically. There was no librarian bustling about, moving books from place to place, or organising them back into their correct order. Here the books *themselves* were moving. Big, tatty volumes shot off their racks from every section of the shelves as they competed for airtime with inferior slimmer cousins. As they left the shelves the books on either side shuffled along to make space for new entries at the other end.

It was now abundantly clear to John why the bonfire was burning so fiercely. It was the books that were fuelling it. Each time a new volume flew into the flames the bonfire momentarily exploded, embers dancing chaotically into the air. As rapidly as the books were being burnt, even brisker was the activity of the two trees. A constant stream of individual parchments were being shed from the trunks with no external influence, each page floating one at a time into the spaces that had been vacated by those books that headed further down the line. John walked up to one of the trees to take a closer look.

Before the pages were invisibly cut from the trunks, John saw that they had writing etched on each page, and unlike the writing on the floor, this was clearly legible. It was tricky to read each individual document as the trees were producing them at the rate of an industrial-sized printer.

'Cassie Sahota, Female, Orlando, 9lb 2oz, D.O.B. – 7th April'

'Franco Solita, Male, Venice, 5lb 6oz, D.O.B. – 7th April'

'Umba To'onga, Male, Fiji, 6lb 6oz, D.O.B. – 7th April'

The last entry never made it to the shelves. It stopped in mid-air, hovered for a second, as if awaiting orders as to where to place itself in the maze of shelves. Finally it made up its mind and floated like a plastic bag caught in an updraft along the hall towards the fire.

"These are a list of human births, aren't they?" said John solemnly.

Brimstone, who had been studying John's movements with a great deal of intrigue, replied, "Yes, they are."

"And that one, the one I've just read, the Umba boy. Why isn't he going onto the shelves with the others?" John asked, as he watched the single piece of paper being consumed by the fire in a blink.

"He didn't make it."

"How can you be so cold about it? A newborn child has just died before our very eyes, probably because he was born in the wrong country, at the wrong time, and all you can say is, 'He didn't make it.' Have you got no sensitivity?" replied John, his voice rising to a shout to lecture Brimstone, whether he meant to or not.

"To be frank, John, no. I have no emotions. It intrigues me that you care so much. If the consequence of emotion is weakness, then you can keep it. You're getting angry because you've witnessed the death of a child that you have no knowledge of," said Brimstone, as his short frame appeared to grow and his voice became deep and direct.

"It's still a life. You could have done something."

"Ask yourself, John, who is responsible for his death? Is it us? Did I cause his mother to give birth in a country without adequate medical resources? Was it us that squeezed the world's money into a tiny minority of the world's population? Was it the Devil that failed to train the local witch doctor in the safest method of childbirth? Or was it humanity that caused this boy's death? We are not the cause of death, merely the receiver of it. Before you deal out your moral judgement on me, perhaps you should ask yourself what you did to save this child."

Even though Brimstone had made a valid argument, it did not make John feel any better. He'd heard this type of argument before and, even though he accepted there was corruptness and inequality in his kind he could not act as if the death of an innocent child was just some inconvenient statistic.

"Emotion is not what makes us weak, Brimstone. It's what makes us human. The ability to care, even if people often do not."

"Mankind doesn't care," replied Brimstone scornfully. "If it did, then his death would have been avoided."

John stood with his back to Brimstone, tears welling in his borrowed eyes, unwilling to show this so-called weakness. As he watched one of the trees, another leaf of paper had just stopped in mid-air, just as he had seen moments before. Instinctively, and without knowing the consequences, John grabbed it with both hands. The force on John was intense as the paper wrestled him towards the fire. He felt the friction in his hands burning towards his soul as he was hauled along closer to the flames. Eventually, with a power of its own the sheet sliced through John's fingers leaving a large paper cut across the palms of his hands.

In response, John's plastic body hissed like a punctured tyre from the sound of his soul escaping from the wound. The cuts in his hands glowed bright blue and he felt himself being drawn out through his vessol towards the cut. John's emotions panicked. Nervousness, worry, fear and cowardice jostled each other to be the first to the exit door, these escaping emotions asphyxiating his life force like he was being strangled for air. Brimstone, who had moved casually towards him, lifted a stony finger to his brow, removed a clump of molten lava from one of the cracks in his face, and wiped it across John's gaping wound. The plastic in John's hands sealed over to the sound of his excruciating screams.

"John, you're a dead human in a plastic body: what makes you think you can play God? The only person you can affect is you," explained Brimstone, grabbing John by the arm and lifting him from the floor where he had slumped in pain.

"I did what was right. What my instincts told me to do."

"You can't change destiny, John. It changes you. It's not for you to choose what is right."

"I'll keep that in mind."

"Shall we get back to our main reason for being here?" offered Brimstone.

"Ok, let's do that."

"What you have probably guessed by now is that this place holds the records of every living person on Earth. As they are born their records are collected, and as they die they are recycled into the fire. At which point most arrive with us at the Soul Catcher. Every action and emotion that is worth noting is documented into these books, and all of that information is managed by this," explained Brimstone, pointing at the glass screen on the table in front of them. "What we need to work out is who would be the most appropriate person for you to inhabit down on Earth."

"So when you said earlier, 'where to put me,' what did you mean exactly?" asked John, having regained his composure and concentration.

"There are only two options available to us if we are going to get you back on Earth. The first is we put your soul into an unborn child. This is by far the safest route because pre-born infants have no soul. The soul only develops in the early days of the child's life as the emotions develop. Of course this also has its downsides in our present situation."

"Downsides?"

"Yes, I thought a clever man like you would have guessed. The downside is that your Universe will have disintegrated before the new infant John is out of nappies. You'd only develop about a third faster than a normal child. So at best when you were twelve you'd look and act like an eighteen-year-old. But that would still be too late. I'm guessing you are going to get about twelve weeks to find Ian and Sandy?"

"Why only twelve weeks? I thought our time didn't exist in Hell. Can't you send me back earlier and find Sandy *before* he becomes reincarnated?"

"Unfortunately not. We can't go back further than your own death otherwise there would be two of your souls swirling around down there. That would be worse than having Sandy's soul on the loose. We know the date when Sandy and Ian *died* was the twenty-sixth of March and you have until the summer solstice on June twenty-first to recover them."

John considered the time frame to be fairly short given his complete lack of knowledge about what they had turned into.

"The only realistic approach is the second option, possession. We place you inside another person who already has a soul. There are a couple of issues with that, too, though."

"Go on," replied John, an air of doom to his voice.

"First, you will have to learn to control the other soul so that you can properly use their body. Secondly, getting you inside the selected person is not an exact science," explained Brimstone, turning to the glass table and carefully placing his finger onto the top right-hand corner, a testing thing to do when you're made of stone and the device is so fragile. The glass lit up and several strange labels appeared in an alien language.

"What is it?"

"It's our computer database."

"Computers were a human invention?"

"Typical human, such a high opinion of yourselves. John, our kind created everything in the Universe. Don't you think that it's just possible that we might have invented the same things as you, given *we* invented *you?*" huffed Brimstone.

John nodded in agreement. Although it made sense, the human condition of self-importance was still part of his make-up.

"Let's think about what sort of person you should be. We know Sandy and Ian died in the UK and it's likely, given the movement of souls, that they went into something close."

"Why's that?" replied John, trying to keep his questions as sensible as possible after his last rebuff.

"A soul's natural place is inside a body, so it will quickly search for the sanctuary of an empty vessel before the fifth force takes hold," replied Brimstone. "Let's bring up all the adults between twenty and fifty in the UK as a starting point."

Brimstone tapped the screen several times and with the cacophonous sound of a million books lifting from their shelves, they hovered in the air suspended in front of them. The collective noise of all of these volumes moving was seismic and made John hold his ears, a pointless reflex given the useless bits of plastic on the sides of his head. Brimstone showed no such effects. A number flashed on the screen indicating the search results.

"That's clearly far too many. Any preferences, John?"

What was important to him? He had to take control of someone's soul and by all accounts that wasn't likely to be easy.

"No women please. I've had enough problems trying to communicate and understand them when I was next to them, I'm not sure I would have any more luck if I was possessing one. Plus I'm fairly sure that

Sandy and Ian would have been in the London area, so let's go for that, too."

Brimstone added a few more taps to the screen and about three-quarters of the books rushed back into the gaps that they had vacated.

"1,760,345 returns, according to the computer. What else should we look for?"

"Let's lower the age range to about the mid-thirties. I think I'd feel more comfortable with someone of my own age. Also someone inconspicuous: give me someone with a normal job. I can just imagine suddenly finding myself inside an airline pilot in the middle of a transatlantic crossing."

"That's good thinking. Let's say office job and thirty-five," replied Brimstone, for a third time entering the search criteria to the screen as more volumes returned to their places.

"112,401, still too many for us to consider."

"Brimstone, what dangers will this person be in?"

"I expected this from you, John, and I don't see what difference it makes."

"Humour me."

"Basically, they might go just a little bit mad during or after the event. They will, after all, have someone else inside their heads. If they survive the ordeal that you put them through, they may never suffer again, but I doubt it."

"Okay, no one who's married or has kids. Perhaps an orphan or, failing that, a traffic warden, I've never liked those guys."

"7,245," Brimstone announced, as the now familiar sight of books flying back into shelves had finished. "One more search I think should do it."

"What do you think would help?" asked John.

"The only thing that I know is that one of the biggest issues is mentally controlling the person you are in. I'd suggest that the lower the mental strength, the more chance you have."

"Okay, let's go for low IQ levels, but not too low. I don't want to be inside a complete dunce who can't even read or tie their own shoelaces."

"Fair point. Let's go with an IQ of between seventy and eighty," said Brimstone, tapping the screen for the final time. "72 returns, that should do it. Let's see who we've got."

Brimstone pressed one final button and a list of names appeared on the screen in front of them. It was a strange feeling for John to look at a list of people that he was potentially about to possess. It felt like picking a rescue dog out at the local pound. He was about to change someone's life forever and he felt the need to take the decision seriously. Just as he had done in Limbo, he went through the list rejecting the smallest and most unimportant of characteristics. One was too short, another was into fly fishing, and one was rejected on no other foundation than that he had a silly name. This was the second time that he had had the chance to choose his appearance, and this time he had more time to think. Was he really John Hewson at all anymore?

"I like the look of Edward Reece," said John. "He's a civil servant, and given that Sandy works in government, Edward might move in similar circles. He might also have access to some of the places that I need to go. On top of that it appears he has no strong social standing."

"Okay, Edward it is," replied Brimstone, sending the unchosen books back to their positions.

"How do I get inside his head?"

"Effectively it's the opposite way that you got here, John, and for that we need to go back down to the Soul Catcher," replied Brimstone, noting down the co-ordinates given for Edward's whereabouts for March the twenty-sixth.

They took the lift back down to level one and followed one of the descending tunnels that they had taken earlier in their travels. As they reached the Soul

Catcher, the machine was back running in full flow, a procession of bodies were being filled and led away by the workers on this endless process.

While they walked, John's mind wandered back to the subject of the task at hand. If he did find Sandy and Ian, in whatever they had become, which John doubted in itself, how was he going to remove their souls and send them through the Universe to the waiting Soul Catcher?

"How do I get the souls out of Ian and Sandy if, I mean when, I find them?"

"That's the easy bit, John. All you need to do is kill them and then utter the chant, 'erior wit solsta trak' repeated three times when the soul is out of its body."

Brimstone stomped over to the workers busy in their duties and talked to them in a language quite unfamiliar. They turned off the Soul Catcher and scuttled away to nearby tunnels. The machine sat quietly, receiving the pulses of light from outside of the wormhole and storing them inside its vast interior.

"It's time to go. As I said before, it's not an exact science getting a soul inside someone else. We have the co-ordinates for Edward but you have to do your bit when you get near him. You'll only get a few seconds before your soul does its own thing," suggested Brimstone.

Brimstone walked over to the terminal and pressed a large red button that protruded out of the console. The contraption jolted as if the mechanism had been suddenly halted, which wasn't far from the truth.

"I've placed the Soul Catcher in reverse. This isn't going to be very pleasant, I'm afraid, but at least you've been shot across the Universe at the speed of light before. The difference this time is that your soul is going against the flow, it will want to come in this direction rather than in the way you're heading," informed Brimstone, who stood John beneath the long, white funnel that normally received souls to place them in their foreign plastic bodies. Brimstone inserted the funnel into the valve in John's throat and returned to the console.

"Good luck, John. You're on your own now." Brimstone pulled a lever and the whole cavern was engulfed in a flash of blue light.

*****

Edward Reece was at the front of a large, noisy and sweaty crowd that swarmed around the confined space of the Assembly Rooms, a concert venue in the heart of London. About two thousand people were pushing him forward into the barrier, erected to keep the crowd away from the stage but not, unfortunately in Edward's view, the crowd from him. It was an understatement to say that he was uncomfortable and was enjoying himself much less than the dancing, bouncing population of people around him.

Did his ears still work? They throbbed and quivered with the blast from the speakers stacked to the ceiling, belting out hundreds of decibels of rock music, which to him might as well just be a recording of an orchestra of jackhammers. He really didn't want to be here. He'd been pressured into coming by some of his work colleagues who he normally didn't socialise with. His real reason for attending was his huge, but hidden, crush on Nancy from the legal department who was currently ricocheting around him, reminiscent of someone who had just lit a firework in their pants.

'The Wind-up Merchants' had just finished the second hour of their concert and Edward hadn't recognised even one of their songs. Radio 4 never played much music. He couldn't wait for it to finish so he could go to the doctors and have his ears syringed, after they were sown back on, that is. Maybe his prayers had been answered? The band had finished their last song and were leaving the stage to a rapturous chorus of "encore" that drowned out one faint voice of "no more". Clearly God had decided not to listen to Edward's request and the band returned to the stage to a symphony of excitement. The crowd waited for the lead singer to announce one of their favourites and continue their enjoyment, and Edward's nightmare.

"Thanks, London, you're amazing. I'd like to introduce you to the band that has rocked the foundations tonight. On drums, Ian McMillan."

Edward ducked as a drumstick catapulted just over his side parting.

"On bass guitar, Brian Fox."

The resulting bass solo sent the P-wave from an earthquake directly at him from the nearest speaker.

"On lead guitar, Stan 'mad man' Jenkins."

'Please, please, for pity's sake, STOP.' Nancy thought she saw Edward mouthing to the stage, but it was washed away by the sound of an epic guitar solo.

"And on lead vocals, me, Nash Stevens."

On each announcement of the band members, a roar of shouts and screams echoed around the room. That wasn't the loudest noise of the evening, though. Directly after the introduction of the lead singer a huge thunderclap ripped through the air, followed by the most brilliant flash of blue light. The crowd went wild, assuming that this was some amazing special effect planned as a great finale by the band. A beach ball-sized cloud of blue gas was floating above the stage, moving erratically, unsure which direction it wanted to go in. Finally it gave up hope and shot forward into Nash Stevens, who crumpled to the floor on impact.

There was a spontaneous gasp of breath from two thousand fans. Even Edward joined in, this being the first piece of audience participation that he had entered into. Nash pulled himself to his feet using the microphone stand as a prop and shouted to the crowd, "There's someone in my head!"

The audience went wild with excitement, presuming that this announcement was a new song that the band was going to play for the first time.

Through Nash's eyes, John witnessed two thousand faces waiting expectantly. There was a guitar in his hands that he was unable to control, and he produced one single simple word.

"SHIT."

Edward Reece remained squashed, still bored, still hopeful of an earlier-than-expected finish and absolutely oblivious as to how close he came.

CHAPTER TEN

OUT OF THE DARKNESS

The darkness that surrounded Sandy was absolute. Not a single chink of light could penetrate it and even time itself was struggling for relevance. Minutes, days, years, or very possibly an eternity had passed since the point when normality had last put in an appearance. Perceptions and memories in equal measure had been blended, shaken and whipped into a muddled soufflé, anxious about their chances of rising to the top to see the light. As time had elapsed it signalled for the space around him to reduce. The smooth, concave floor that lay beneath him slowly shrank and heightened his sense of claustrophobia. Now there was almost no free space, an abundance of darkness, more time than he cared to wish for and a hard enamel surface pushing up against him, making it increasing difficult to breathe.

Forced to sit immovably by his surroundings, he attempted to catalogue his memories back into an acceptable order. The explosion in the van felt like an experience that was not altogether his own. Somewhere deep within his psyche a scar ached from the forces of two lives being ripped apart and separated in a fraction of a second. That vague pain was the start and the end of his thoughts, everything else having been substituted by a vacuum that tried to cast doubt on his very existence. For a long period he believed his isolation in this nothingness was just the experience of death.

As time crept immeasurably onward, the possibility of him not being dead looked more promising. The lack of space around him had brought the realisation that he had a physical presence in this void. As he regained the ability to move and touch, it seemed to trigger his ability to think and feel more clearly. Perhaps it was the space enclosing around him that triggered the emotion of fear that finally affirmed that he wasn't dead, panic not being something dead people think much about. Whatever this existence was, it was definitely not the one he was used to.

The fact that he had a sense of his past meant that this state was a hybrid of the then and now. Some of the emotions that washed over him were undoubtedly familiar. He had a concept of who he was, where he had come from and what he had been, yet there was another part of his instinct which was alien and highly disturbing. This perverse alter ego generated a weird sensation of vulnerability in him, and as the cocoon had shrunk it was this part of his psyche that had felt the need to escape.

Driven inextricably by these acquired instincts, he pushed outwards in the search for a weakness or escape route from the smooth walls that encased him. He reached out to find the handle of a door that would suddenly become visible, but he was unable to locate any. There was no door and, more worryingly, there were no hands to open one with. Something else occupied the space where his hands had once been, but they certainly weren't hands. On discovering this he panicked and threw his head towards the wall. A crack echoed around him and the whole place rocked back and forth. Undeterred, the new odd portion of his instinct told him to do it again. The second head-butt was even more forceful than the first and sent the cocoon rolling over the top of itself like a human bowling ball.

Sandy tried to wriggle himself back to what he hoped was an upright position, if that was possible when your feet seemed to be constantly somewhere around your head. A thin stream of light seeped in from a crack in the wall, allowing Sandy more certainty of his position. Encouraged, he made several more successful attempts to widen it, creating a large hole that flooded him with light and fresh air. A sea of green shook and shimmered in the sky above, an alien world waiting to welcome him.

Sliding his body so that his head was near enough to the hole for him to see, he pushed it through to get a better understanding of where he was. As his face met the fresh air for the first time in months, his relief was instantly replaced by panic. There in front of him, blinking merrily, was a round, feathery head the size of a beach ball with a beak like an ostrich. The head belonged to a massive pigeon that cooed maternally, eager to introduce herself after enduring a long wait and a sore arse.

"MY GOD!" shouted Sandy, ducking back inside.

What had once been his prison now became a welcome sanctuary. Over the last few weeks he would have given anything to escape his smooth, dark cell. But now he felt a lick of paint and it could be a cosy place to stay, forever. It would be better than going out there again. He wasn't the only one in shock. The pigeon, who had expected Sandy's first response to have been something along the lines of, 'Coo,' had just heard a human voice and before long, it started again.

"Sod off," came an echo from within the egg.

The pigeon took a step backwards.

"Where the bloody hell am I?" he whispered to himself.

Sandy peered again through the gap to get a better look and make sure he wasn't hallucinating. As well as a pigeon the size of a horse, who had now backed away even further, he could see that there were about four or five eggs nearby. These were also massive, at least based on what Sandy remembered the size of eggs to be, relative to him.

"What do you want with me?" Sandy shouted out to the pigeon.

Neither of the current inhabitants of the nest seemed to be pleased by their predicament. Both were feeling confused and stressed. Both had expected quite different outcomes, and one at least was finding the situation altogether too much to deal with. The pigeon flapped its wings and flew off into the vicinity of another tree a few yards away.

Sandy took the opportunity of the pigeon's retreat to get out and explore. Struggling out onto the loosely constructed nest he stretched his body to its full height, loosening limbs and muscles that had spent too long fused together. As he did so he noticed why he had no hands. Where his arms and hands would normally have been were long-feathered, blue-grey wings. Convinced that his eyes were malfunctioning, he glanced to the other arm and found the same outcome. As the wind breezed through the feathers, he felt them tug gently on his skin. There was no escaping the fact that these strange appendages belonged to him.

"What am I?"

He moved his wings experimentally to see how they worked and what they would do. They seemed to work very much like arms apart from the obvious visual differences. It wasn't just his arms that weren't as he remembered them, there had been other changes. The last time he'd seen his feet they were covered with a pair of sturdy, black Dr. Marten's boots, but now they weren't even covered with hair. Instead, an excess of leathery grey skin clung loosely to the bones as if they were intended for someone with slightly bigger feet. Finally he raised a wing to his face to explore his features, immediately discovering the most noticeable difference from the past: a stiff, pointy beak.

"I'm a pigeon? No, don't be stupid, get a grip on yourself. Oh please, please tell me I'm in a coma?"

There was a sudden 'CRACK' from one of the other eggs and Sandy looked around for the source of the noise. After another 'CRACK,' Sandy located the egg where crazy paving fractures now ran chaotically down the side. With one final 'CRACK' the bright white head of a young pigeon forced its way through the top of the shell.

"OH SHIT. A monster pigeon," came a voice that retracted its head gopher-like back from where it had come.

Unfortunately, Sandy knew immediately who it was. He cursed his luck that, wherever he was, coma, dream or reality, it seemed impossible to shake off his incompetent companion.

"It's just my luck that I'm landed with you again, you cretin," said Sandy.

However badly Sandy's memory had been affected by recent ordeals his soul would take a long time to erase the stupidity of Ian 'Cher' Noble. Ian re-emerged cautiously from his shell, head bobbing up and down, casing the creature that stood in front of him.

"It's me, Ian, or as far as I can make out at least, it's some of me."

Sandy watched as Ian went through the same roller coaster of emotions that he had gone through minutes earlier, although it was going to take Ian more time for it to sink in. All Ian knew at the moment was there was a pigeon the size of a cow telling him, "It's me."

"Who are you...strange, talking bird?" murmured Ian, his head half in and half out of the broken egg.

"Sandy. I'm Sandy. That poor sod whose life you have seen fit to ruin, and seemingly will continue to ruin in the afterlife or whatever twisted reality we have found ourselves in."

The cogs in Ian's feathery head went into overdrive for a moment. This couldn't be a coincidence? It sounded remarkably like Sandy, even if it came from something that didn't look remarkably like him. Ian took in this strange incarnation of his friend. After more than a pause, unsure what to say next, he broke his silence.

"I hate to be the one to tell you this, mate, but you appear to be a…a…pigeon."

"Ian, it's not just me. So are you."

"Look, I know you must be upset about this Sandy, but don't be daft. I'm not a pigeon: that's impossible, ludicrous."

"Ian, do me a favour, can you give me a hand? I seem to have a small piece of shell in my wing. Could you pick it out for me?"

"Of course, mate."

Ian struggled to crawl out of his egg, eventually landing in a heap on the nest. He picked himself up and hopped over to Sandy and after much flapping, found the piece of eggshell to which Sandy was referring. After several bungled attempts to remove it, Ian sat down on the twigs.

"I can't seem to remove it. I think my arms must have got cramp from being inside there all this time," he announced, pointing at the broken shell without the slightest mental connection.

"It's not cramp, Ian. I think you'll find they're called wings."

Ian raised his arms in front of his face to see that his *arms* were covered in white feathers. As he did so, Sandy walked up to him and pecked him directly in the middle of the forehead, sending Ian tumbling backwards and almost off the edge of the nest.

"That's for killing me," said Sandy, helping Ian to his feet as best as he could. "We're both pigeons, so let's get over it and think about what we need to do."

"How did we get like this?" asked Ian.

"That's the big question, isn't it? That's if this is real in the first place, which, if that peck hurt you, I believe it probably is," said Sandy.

"Hurt like hell."

"What do you remember after the bomb blast?"

"Not much really. I remember feeling pain and then I remember seeing bits of my body all over the place. After that I remember travelling incredibly fast before a long period of darkness," replied Ian, who was able to recollect far more of the incident than Sandy had.

"Do you believe in reincarnation, Ian?"

"Not really."

"Then I think you might need to think again. I believe that somehow we have been reincarnated. Did you feel that you had a choice when you were looking down at your bodyparts?"

"Yes, I think so. I remember thinking how mad you were going to be that I'd screwed everything up. I knew I needed to make it right. What about you?"

"Similar, I remember thinking that I needed to stick around to stop what I saw happening on that night, although I can't remember what it was now. After that came the darkness."

Both of them sat down on the floor silently contemplating what might have happened and trying to force out further memories of that early morning in March.

"So, what do we do now?" asked Ian.

"Coo."

"What did you say, Sandy?"

"I didn't say anything," replied Sandy.

"Yes you did, you said, 'coo' or something?"

"No, I really didn't," replied Sandy forcibly.

"Coo."

Both of them glanced around in simultaneous slow motion to find that they were no longer alone in the treetops. Sitting behind them was a newly hatched pigeon. It smiled warmly, or at least that's how Sandy would have described it, not understanding pigeon expressions that well yet.

"Is that one of us?" asked Ian.

"I guess it might be a half-brother or half-sister," replied Sandy surreally. "The half being the pigeon half, that is. This is starting to freak me out. We need to get out of here before something tries to eat us, or sit on us, or worse."

"I guess that there is one thing that might help," said Ian. "Pigeons can fly."

"Yes, but are we *real* pigeons?"

"We have wings, don't we? Should be feasible, shouldn't it?"

"Coo," affirmed the new arrival.

"Only one way to find out, Ian, give it a go," said Sandy mischievously.

Ian walked to the edge of the nest and peered over the side at a drop of probably no more than twenty feet by human standards. Although they seemed to be somewhat bigger than the other pigeon that had just joined them, it was still a long way down in their present form. Ian flapped his wings in a rather amateurish fashion. However much he flapped his feet were still very much on the floor. Jumping up and down didn't help much either.

"Maybe you have to jump off to get the velocity right," prompted Sandy, either helpfully or wickedly.

Ian stood on the edge of the nest looking downwards at the distant muddy ground. He took two paces backwards and did a run and jump, flapping furiously all the time. For a split second Ian hovered momentarily in mid-air before the realisation that gravity was always going to win this contest. Ian plummeted towards the ground, accelerating as he fell in a symphony of ruffling feathers and wind-effected screams

Sandy and the other pigeon rushed to the edge, both seemingly interested for entirely different reasons. Ian wasn't there. Seconds later the ostrich-sized pigeon, that Sandy had seen previously, landed behind them with Ian held firmly but gently in its claws. Even with these peculiar offspring the maternal instinct would not allow her to ignore his fall, much to Ian's relief. When Ian had come to rest safely on the nest floor, he shuffled over to Sandy.

"It appears that we can't," stated Ian.

CHAPTER ELEVEN

BROUGHT DOWN TO EARTH

Nash Stevens woke with the mother of all hangovers. When he'd finally convinced himself it was safe to do so, he opened his eyes and tried to focus on the ceiling of his posh hotel bedroom. The blurred wallpaper did nothing to help him piece together the prior evening's events that had led to his present state. He stretched out his hand, fumbling to find the pint of mineral water that he placed religiously next to his bed for lunchtimes like these. After all, it was part of the lifestyle to be ignorant of mornings. Only some of the glass's contents made their way into his mouth, whilst the rest was used to unintentionally wash his chest and some of the pillowcase. As one hand attempted unsuccessfully to unify glass with table, the other went to massage his throbbing head.

John Hewson woke up and didn't know whether he had a hangover or not. Above him was an unfamiliar, pale blue ceiling and, unsure of his whereabouts, he, too, tried to retrace the evening's events. Or at least he would have done if his attention hadn't been drawn to his arms moving without his permission. 'I hate mineral water, why would I drink mineral water? Not just drink it, but also throw it on myself. Why am I rubbing my head? My head feels fine.'

Nash stumbled out of bed but, rather than falling in a heap on the floor as gravity had a right to expect, some strange instinct stopped him before face met carpet. In the gloom he felt his way to the bathroom, crouched over the toilet, and threw up twice as a combination of being suddenly vertical and the previous night's vodka and cannabis overdose caught up with him. Feeling the need to wash his mouth out, he stood at the sink and caught the reflection of his bloodshot eyes and unshaven face in the mirror.

John felt himself being pulled out of bed. He was quite comfy and not altogether convinced that his body would make it. He felt himself fall, but quickly made his legs fight the sensation. 'Why don't I turn the lights on? It's dark in here. I better feel my way along the wall.' As he reached the toilet he unexpectedly sank to his knees. 'Hey, look at all of those colours coming out of my mouth. Oh God, that's grim, I need to wash that away. How do I look this morning?' A smack of realism rose like a cold sweat as the mirror reminded him where and who he was.

"Hey, mate, I really need your help," came a voice out of Nash's mouth that wasn't his own.

Nash couldn't believe that his lips had moved entirely of their own accord and that it was the same voice he'd heard last night. Quickly, he put his hands over his mouth hoping to stop any encore. 'I thought it was just the drugs. What's happening to me?' A muffled sound tried to escape through Nash's fingers. It was happening again. Gingerly, and with a strange sense of intrigue, he moved one hand away.

"Look, you're not imagining this. I know you are going to find this hard to believe but I have possessed you. My name's John Hewson."

Nash replaced the hand slowly but this time there were even louder muffles and his teeth were trying to bite his hands.

"Look, I need to use your body for a while to find some friends of mine."

"Stop talking," replied Nash under his breath.

"I know you're not going to accept this but I might as well tell you now. It's only marginally weirder than finding out someone has possessed you."

"I'm not listening to you. I don't care what you say, I'm just not listening," he answered, audibly humming a song out loud.

"Look, there's no time for this. My friends have been reincarnated as some sorts of animals and if I don't find them, the whole Universe will collapse!" shouted John, interrupting Nash's innate melody.

Nash picked up the two empty bottles of pills that were on their sides in the bathroom cabinet and scanned the labels for possible side effects.

"It's not the drugs, although I'm sure they're not helping. It's real, look."

John concentrated all his efforts on Nash's left arm, picked it up and slapped Nash across the face with it.

"Owww!" shouted Nash, his face stinging from the blow.

John couldn't feel a thing.

"This is the weirdest trip I've ever had," whispered Nash, rubbing his face. "I need to find Herb." He left the bathroom and searched for the door to the corridor. Without meaning to, he turned the lights on as he went.

'Who's Herb, and for God's sake, turn those bloody lights on?'

Nash hurried down the corridor, glancing at each door in search of room number three hundred and five. Hammering on it with both fists he waited several minutes and numerous heavy knocks before a short, fat, balding, elderly man opened the door.

"What's wrong with you? It's twelve o'clock, far too early to be getting up," he yawned in a deep Scottish accent whilst rubbing his eyes in a vain attempt to focus them. "Why are you standing in the corridor in just your pants?"

'Who's he?' asked John, this time without the necessity of opening Nash's mouth.

"Look, it's Herb, my manager. Now shut up."

"Who are you talking to?" replied Herb quizzically.

"It's the voice in my head again, I can't shift it."

"Look, you'd better come in before the paparazzi get a photo of you in just your grits," replied Herb, beckoning him inside.

Herb was one of those old-fashioned rockers, famous for his rock and roll lifestyle more than his actual musical ability. He had the air of a man who had taken too many drugs and too much alcohol but was absolutely convinced he was just getting started. Teetering on the edge of his mid-sixties it was unclear how much of his appearance was from the natural ageing process and how much was due to the visual effects of an extremely enjoyable life. Contrary to his arthritically ravaged body, there was still a faint twinkle in the man's eyes that sent the message, 'I could be rebellious at any moment, if only I wasn't so knackered.' Inside his room the TV had been pushed over to the open window and lay on its side, dented but fully functional. Herb had attempted to throw it out in a spontaneous moment of drunken rock and roll, but by the look of his stooped walk he may have put his back out in the process.

Herb swaggered around in a pair of overly small jeans which openly presented several layers of stomach fat that each competed to be the first over the edge of his belt. Faded tattoos covered the entirety of his naked, hairy chest other than a spot where a two-inch scar ran across his left breast. It wasn't incorrect to say 'breasts' for Herb. A good bra technician would have done wonders for eliminating his back pain. Herb collapsed out of breath onto a settee, reached for a packet of cigarettes, and sparked one up with an old-fashioned Zippo.

"So, what's going on, then, Nash? Is it the drugs?"

"No, it's not the drugs. I didn't have anything major last night."

"That's what I mean. You didn't have *enough* drugs, that's the problem."

"Sad, wasted, fat loser."

"Look there it goes again. I'm telling you this is real, Herb."

"What's it saying now?" asked Herb.

"Ah, he said…nice tattoo," replied Nash, not wanting to hurt anyone's feelings.

"Tell him you're going to take a few weeks off."

"No, I'm not taking some time off," replied Nash to himself.

Herb found it quite off-putting to have a conversation with someone who was arguing with themselves.

John would have to work out how to control Nash a lot faster than he was currently managing, if he was going to have any chance of getting on with what he was supposed to be doing. Brimstone had told him that possession wasn't easy. He didn't know the half of it. What he'd worked out so far was if he concentrated his entire soul on one part of Nash's body he could take control of just that function. The issue for John, as with all men on the planet, was multitasking. It was no good just controlling a foot if the rest of the body was doing something completely different. It was time to concentrate for the moment on Nash's mouth and work the rest out later.

"Herb, I need to take a couple of weeks off," said John.

"No, I don't. I'm fine, I just need something to relax me," slurred Nash, fighting to regain control.

"Well, which one is it, Nash? Make your bloody mind up," replied Herb.

"Time off," said John before Nash had a chance to respond.

Nash's hands leapt to his mouth to stop himself talking against his will.

"So you do want some time off, then?" clarified Herb.

"Yes," replied a muffled John.

Nash's head shook vigorously in denial.

"Hold on, now you're saying yes and suggesting no," replied Herb, completely baffled.

"No," shouted Nash before he could be contradicted.

"Look, you're obviously quite confused. We haven't got another gig for three nights so I suggest you go back to your room and take something to relax you. I've got a couple of tranquillisers somewhere you can take," said Herb, getting up gingerly with his hand on his back and going over to rummage in his suitcase.

"Look, I don't know why you're inside me, but I want you out. Right now," whispered Nash to himself.

"It's not exactly a holiday for me, you know. The only way I can leave you is if you help me. I need to get to Switzerland. Like it or not, believe it or not, you're stuck with me and all of our fates are now interlinked. If I fail then we all fail."

"No way. If you don't get out of me right now, I'm going to, I'm going to…"

"You're going to do what exactly? It's not like you've got much choice, my friend," said John, concentrating his effort on Nash's tongue which he used to blow a raspberry.

"Oh very pleasant. I'm just trying to help," said Herb as he passed Nash two huge green pills that would tranquillise a hippo. "Take these, lie down and I'll come and check on you later."

John wasn't entirely sure what effect these pills were likely to have on either of them, and he certainly wasn't going to hang around to find out. As Nash left Herb's room a struggle broke out in the corridor. Nash's left leg and the rest of his body seemed to be heading for his bedroom, whilst his right leg had decided to head full pelt for the lift at the other end of the corridor. Nash collapsed to the floor under the impending pain of the splits. In response to this surprise tactic, one of his arms pulled itself along the carpet towards his bedroom as the other hand tried to impede its progress. Two cleaners, who had been standing chatting over a cleaning trolley, stopped and watched the one-man commotion with interest.

"Look, this is getting us nowhere!" Nash shouted out.

"You're right, until we can agree on this, no one's going to win. Okay, I promise I won't try to stop you anymore."

Nash sprinted towards his room and got halfway there before John double-crossed him. With the precision of a professional boxer, a clenched fist punched him squarely in the jaw, sending him crashing to the ground again. Taking advantage of Nash's disorientation, John swivelled him around and hopped one-legged towards the lift. Blood gushing from Nash's nostrils, he regained his senses and grabbed hold of the lamp that was fixed to the corridor wall.

The more youthful of the two cleaners gazed vacantly at the sight of a man trying to hop in one direction whilst gripping the wall light for dear life with the other. The other cleaner was staring at John. Not at Nash. At *him*. Her eyes shone with a faint, pale blue sheen and were transfixed at the point where John had taken up residence in Nash's heel.

"Nie niepokoi, John. Pozwalany on bierze ego lek," said the cleaner in a deep, ugly voice that he hoped wasn't her own.

John understood. Even though he didn't speak Polish, he understood every word.

"I DON'T KNOW WHAT YOU'RE SAYING, BUT HELP ME, YOU STUPID BITCHES!" Nash shouted at both of them.

The teenage cleaner, breaking out of her own trance, attempted to pick up her walkie-talkie to signal for help, but was quickly stopped and led away by her colleague. They exchanged dialogue in Polish and both quietly moved away from the scene.

"Okay, Nash, let's have it your way. Let's go to your room, I won't stop you this time, I promise," said John, pleased that his friends and family hadn't overheard that sentence as he'd not have lived it down.

"You promise? You won't hit me in the face again, which hurt like hell, by the way."

"Believe me, you've no idea how much hurt there is in Hell. Anyway, it hurt me as well," John lied. "I promise I'll not stop you."

Nash tentatively made his way back to his bedroom. When he got through the door, which he had left unlocked and open, he went straight for an unopened bottle of mineral water. Placing both pills in his mouth at the same time, he washed them down with the remaining water and lay back on the bed to await the results.

John was no longer concerned about the effects that the pills might have. The cleaner had clearly indicated that no harm would come to him, however strange that seemed to John. He had no reason to trust her, but deep down some compulsion insisted on it. What concerned him most was how he was going to manage to find Sandy and Ian if he couldn't even influence his body to go down to reception. Not for the last time he questioned whether he'd made the right decision to take on Brimstone's task. Maybe this was what was meant by 'damned if you do and damned if you don't'.

Whilst Nash lay on his bed, John decided to explore. It was very hard to explain how John occupied Nash's body. Through vein, organ, nerve and sinew he slithered, each time at the speed of a heartbeat, moving like a virus that was condemned to only one part of Nash's body at a time. Although these journeys were smooth and unnoticed by the host, they still didn't allow any sort of control. If he was going to gain any, he would need to occupy every part of Nash at once.

The answer seemed to present itself whilst John was exploring Nash's left knee. John had spent all his strength focusing his soul on the one thing that he wanted to move. So if he wanted to punch Nash, as he had in the corridor, he'd move all of his efforts to a hand, leaving all other parts of Nash to him.

"You idiot," thought John.

"What are you doing now?" inquired Nash, already feeling exceedingly groggy from the effects of the pills.

"The brain. That controls everything, it's the nervous system."

"Stop right now!" exclaimed Nash.

Although unaware of it, John's timing had been impeccable. Whilst Nash was tranquillised, his thoughts and senses had been weakened and for the first time it allowed John to move his soul into Nash's brain, who was powerless to stop him. In time the thin fog of his soul crept across Nash's body with the same effect that a warm drink has on a cold day. Now he had the helm of a boat and not just the crow's-nest.

John sat bolt upright like an uncoiling spring. No resistance was forthcoming. He swung his legs out of bed and onto the floor. Again nothing stopped him. He got up and got dressed in the most practical clothes that he could find, which wasn't easy given the rock-style fashion that Nash appeared to favour. Settling for some stonewashed jeans, cowboy boots, Iron Maiden T-shirt, a leather jacket, and all topped off with a pair of dark sunglasses, he was ready to reveal yet another new persona.

"Where are we going?" thought Nash, newly relegated to cabin boy on a vessel he was recently in full control of. Well, almost in full control of anyway.

"Now don't panic, old boy. We're just popping out to save the world," replied John. "I promise I will do my very best to leave you in one piece at the end of it."

John had no idea whether this was feasible or not. But he did feel genuine responsibility for Nash: after all, it was John who was borrowing him. Keeping Nash unharmed wasn't going to be easy, and from what Brimstone had told him it wasn't solely down to him. The strength of Nash's soul was also going to be tested.

John made his way to the lift and pressed the zero button, crossing his fingers that this would be a more pleasant experience than his last visit to a level zero. The mirrors on three sides of the lift reflected the fourth incarnation of himself in a matter of days and he had to say he liked this one best of all. This is what he imagined cool felt like, experienced for the first time in his life. Little did he know how much he was going to live to regret not finding his way into Edward Reece, a geeky, plain and uninteresting civil servant.

In the lobby of the hotel a scrum of photographers were lying in wait for the lead singer of 'The Wind-up Merchants', which today just happened to be John Hewson. A hundred flashbulbs went off as he came out of the lift into a throng of journalists forcing questions and microphones at him.

'Nash, how famous are 'The Wind-up Merchants'?'

'We've just had a number one single, number one album and a sell-out tour,' replied Nash sleepily.

"Nash, how's the Prime Minister's daughter?!" shouted one of the hacks. "Any reaction to the PM's comments that he's going to have you arrested?"

"What was she like?" shouted the most seedy of the contingent.

"What are they talking about, Nash?"

'Oh yes...and I slept with the Prime Minister's seventeen-year-old daughter. The pictures ended up in all the newspapers and now her father wants me dead,' replied Nash, prouder of this achievement than any of those by his band.

"Brilliant, just brilliant. I'm on a secret mission to locate something impossibly difficult to find and I'm in

137

the body of a man being tracked by every paparazzo in the country and probably the police as well. Congratulations, John, that's the way to be inconspicuous," he whispered, forcing his way through the mass of bodies, out of the hotel and into one of the waiting taxis. "Heathrow Airport, and go quick."

CHAPTER TWELVE

FLIGHT 237

Just after three o'clock in the afternoon, Herb got to Nash's room to find it empty. There was no sign of Nash and his stuff was still strewn around the bedroom where it had been thrown. Herb casually picked up the hotel phone on the bedside table and called reception.

"Yes, sir, how can I help you?" answered the receptionist in a bright, foreign accent.

"Has Mr. Stevens checked out?"

"No, sir, but he did leave in a taxicab about three hours ago. There were quite a lot of photographers down here, as you can imagine," replied the receptionist.

"Thank you, Miss," Herb replied, replacing the receiver but quickly picking it up again to dial a number he knew by heart. The phone was eventually answered by a deep, male Irish voice that danced out of the speaker like an enchantment.

"Dr King? It's Herb."

"Hello, Herb. It's been a long time. What can I do for you, my dear friend, after all these…all these…you know?" croaked Dr. King, gasping for the end of his sentence.

"Years," prompted Herb. "Yes, it has been a while, but you always said to call if I ever needed you. One of the band has got some issues that I think you might be able to help with. How quickly can you get to London?"

*****

When the taxi finally pulled up outside Heathrow Airport, John jumped out and made quickly to Departures. He was going to buy a ticket to a place he knew little about or why he felt so compelled to go there. The nearest sales representative, whose impossibly stretched smile was neither welcoming nor dismissive, wore a pristine outfit daubed in the brash corporate colours that she represented. The name on her lapel read, 'Sandra Wheale' in fancy bold black print.

"How can I help you, sir?" she asked, before John had even reached the counter. Painfully, her perfectly manufactured toothy grin competed with those of her colleagues to see who could be the first to break their own jaw yet still hold an effective conversation.

"Yes, I'd like to check some flight times," responded John vacantly. It was obvious to anyone that he was distracted and fascinated as to how this woman's face managed to stay vertical under the weight and layers of the make-up that she wore, single-handedly propping up the sales performance of the cosmetics industry.

"So, where would you like to go?"

Where was he going exactly? He knew very little to be sure of his destination. All he knew was he had to find Laslow and the last time he'd seen him he was in a huge, metallic sphere somewhere in the heart of the Swiss Alps, a mountain range that ran for more than a thousand miles from west to east. How on Earth was he going to find the right spot in only three months was anyone's guess. Anywhere would be a start.

"Geneva," he eventually replied, thinking that he might as well start from one end.

"The next flight to Geneva leaves in three hours, sir," replied Sandra.

"That's fine, thanks. Can I get two tickets please?"

"Absolutely, who else are you travelling with? I need to take both your details down."

"I'm sorry, did I say two tickets? I meant one. I'm a little confused today, been working far too hard," replied John, finding it difficult to separate himself from the other passenger on this journey.

"I know," Sandra replied. "I saw your concert last night. Amazing effects at the end, although I think everyone was a little concerned when you collapsed like that."

"Yes, that part didn't quite go to plan," replied John, thinking about Edward for the first time since he'd left Hell.

"It's a shame I've met you here. If I was anywhere else I'd get you to sign my breasts," she whispered, giving him a sly, suggestive wink.

John stared back at her, paralysed by this character's chameleon-like ability to appear so prim and proper at first but then degenerate into a slutty groupie. John felt the temptation to misuse his current position in order to have sex with hundreds of ordinary but beautiful women, an opportunity that might have been possible if John had been dealt a different set of priorities. It was going to be a constant battle against flirtation without any chance of getting more than a raised eyebrow. John shook himself back into life.

"How much will one ticket be, please, Sandra?"

"£249, if you take the supersaver. That means you have to return on a Monday between four-thirty and six in the morning."

John placed his hand inside Nash's leather jacket and pulled out his wallet. Inside was an array of credit cards and a gold frequent flyer card. After prevaricating over the choice of cards, he placed the gold card and an American Express onto the counter.

"Okay, Mr. Stevens, you'll be able to access our first-class lounge and all I need from you is your PIN number in here please."

PIN number? A signature he could have forged but a PIN number gave him no chance. Well, actually it gave him three chances, which was as good as none given the millions of possible four-digit combinations. Motionless he stood for a moment as he scanned through Nash's brain desperately seeking answers. Although he had possession of Nash's emotions, he could not tap into his knowledge. He concentrated harder to reveal the information but nothing happened.

"Is there a problem, Mr. Stevens?"

"No, not really. I have so many cards. I've gone blank as to which PIN goes with which card. Just give me a couple of minutes and I'll remember it," he lied, turning his back from the desk and walking away a few paces. Sandra watched intently as he muttered incoherently to himself.

"Nash, I need your PIN number for your Amex card," thought John to himself. Nash had been altogether silent for the last few hours as the tranquillisers had numbed his senses and John had developed his ability to control him.

"I'm not giving you my PIN until you give me back my body."

"Look, the quicker we get this done, the quicker I'll be gone."

"Then give me back some control or we're going nowhere."

"OK, but no messing about," demanded John, temporarily loosening his mental grip on Nash's brain and drifting to the bottom of his head. Walking back to the bewildered Sandra, Nash pulled a piece of paper from his back pocket and slid it across the desk.

"This *isn't* your PIN number, Mr. Stevens."

"I know, but if you're still interested in getting your breasts done you can use that number. You'll get much more than a plane ticket, you'll get a trip of a lifetime, I can promise you," replied Nash with a wink.

"Oh for God's sake, I avoided that temptation, you tosser. Can't you focus on anything else other than

your libido?" added John. *As he circulated around Nash's body he found a region that clearly showed he couldn't. John moved on rapidly.*

"That sounds like fun," replied Sandra, blushing and leaning forward across the desk. When the two of them were within a few inches of each other, Nash whispered into her ear.

"You have to help me. I'm being held against my will."

"But," she replied, "you're on your own."

"For God's sake, Nash, just buy the ticket or I will poke you in the eye with your own finger," thought John.

Nash picked up the machine and reluctantly entered his PIN.

"You are joking, aren't you? You have a PIN number 2666. To 666, to the number of the beast!" John proclaimed.

"What's significant about that?" replied Nash out loud.

"Can you stop answering me verbally? It's starting to scare people. Just think it and I will hear you."

This was indeed the case. Sandra now looked at Nash with a sense of worry rather than lust. She passed him his ticket and pointed the way to the gold members' lounge. A gaggle of cameramen and photographers charged noisily across the vast departure hall in their direction. They jostled each other for position like some insane horse race where jockeys whipped each other rather than their horses. As flashbulbs shattered the serenity and their shouts drew closer, the general public were being drawn to the commotion.

"I think we should run," thought Nash.

"That's the first time we've agreed on anything."

Together they put all of their focus and energy into Nash's tightly clad, skinny legs and forced them to bolt as fast as they could in the direction of the members' lounge.

"Call me!" Sandra shouted out, quite against company policy, as they sped off into the distance.

In the sanctuary of the quiet lounge, Nash slumped into the nearest sofa, unconsciously picked up a newspaper and read the front-page headline. 'The truth about Tavistock, by Fiona Foster.' As Nash read the article, John tried to figure out what his next move should be. The words that Nash read floated aimlessly in the background of John's mind, until a name stopped it in its tracks.

"Nash, read that again," thought John.

"Read what again?" replied Nash to the whole of the first-class congregation.

"To yourself, Nash, like when you're reading," replied John, noticing that several people sitting close by were wondering if they'd been asked the question.

"Read what again?" thought Nash.

"Now you're getting it. The article, there was a name I heard, read it again."

"The World Today has uncovered the shocking truth about the Tavistock bombing. The hundreds of pigeons that were killed in the explosion were being used to test a secret biological weapon being developed by the government. Even more mysteriously we can exclusively reveal that the bombing was carried out by a faction within the government itself. CCTV footage recovered from the site has identified a vehicle with plates that are not listed at DVLA, and it is our belief that it was being used by the security services. With the strange disappearance of the Minister of Homeland Security, Sandy Logan, still unexplained, The World Today is unable to verify the vehicle with the authorities…" read Nash.

"There you are, Nash, now you know. That's the person I need to find," thought John.

"What, Fiona Foster?"

"No…Sandy Logan," corrected John. "I know why they haven't been able to find him. He's dead, or at least his body is."

Nash pulled an unusual expression, as if a lemon had just exploded in his nostrils, completely befuddled by the concept.

'That explains it. Sandy was killed in the bombing. He's back to his old tricks again. The timing's right, it's in context with his character and undoubtedly he would have had Ian with him as well,' John thought to himself.

"What old tricks?" replied Nash unexpectedly.

"Sorry...I didn't say that to you," thought John. "I was just thinking to myself."

"I know, but I've been concentrating on you over the last hour and I've discovered that I can infiltrate your thoughts, just as you can mine."

This worried John. With his brief successes since the hotel, he thought foolishly that he was now able to control Nash without consequence. It was clear that they were both becoming entwined with each other. John suspected that possession might actually damage both of them in the long run.

"If your thoughts are true, John, then I do need to help you, otherwise who knows what will happen."

"Passengers for flight 237 to Geneva, please proceed to border control," announced the loudspeaker across the lounge.

"There is one thing that I can't figure out," thought Nash.

"I know what you're going to say. How are we going to find two souls that could be in any kind of animal, anywhere on the planet, and then how on God's Earth are we going to encourage them out?"

"No. I was thinking how are we going to get on the flight without my passport?"

John panicked. All he constantly thought about was what was happening at that immediate point. After all, there was a hell of a lot to think about. How were they going to get past border control without a passport?

"I've got an idea, leave it with me," thought Nash.

Nash walked nonchalantly up to the immigration desk with an air of utter confidence about him. When he reached the desk, John felt Nash's self-belief evaporate. Behind the desk stood a burly, grumpy jobsworth, whose only purpose in life was to annoy other human beings. The type of person who revels in the disappointment and pain of others.

"What's the matter?" thought John as Nash stopped in his tracks.

"I was very much placing my hopes on it being a sexy bird that I could charm."

"Passport?" grunted the man from across the desk.

John needed a miracle. Standing against the lounge doors, keeping watch over the rich and famous that were lucky enough to afford the luxuries that first-class offered, was spotty young security. There was a tinge of blue in his eyes.

"Passport?" repeated the man even more gruffly.

"Only if you say the magic word," replied Nash, stalling for time.

"Passport. Now," came the response.

With a nod to John, the young lad flung open the main doors of the lounge to unleash a torrent of bustling and determined journalists. Mayhem broke out. Security guards jumped to their feet from all positions, forced into unaccustomed productivity quite in contrast to the usual state of standing motionless and looking threatening. Noticeably irritated by the unauthorised disruption to his kingdom, the burly passport controller stood up and shouted at everyone and no one at the same time.

"Get them out of here at once, or I'll start breaking legs."

"What do you think?" thought Nash.

"Run!" thought John.

"Agreed."

In the midst of the melee, quietly but quickly, Nash jogged down the corridor towards the gate. Before anyone had noticed, he had made it down the gangway, up the stairs and onto the plane. As the gold lounge passengers were always last to board they wouldn't have long to wait to see if they'd made it.

Waiting at the entrance of the plane was an unnaturally constructed stewardess. It wasn't unfair to say she was Barbie-esque as it was clear that, out of the two of them, she contained more plastic than Barbie.

"Oh, Mr. Stevens, it's such a pleasure to have you on-board with us today. If there is anything, and I do mean anything, I can do for you, please don't hesitate to send for me."

"Do you get this everywhere?"

"Pretty much. It does get a bit boring after a while," replied Nash.

"Oh yes, I can see why an endless array of beautiful women offering you their bodies without so much as a chat-up line must be absolutely awful for you," replied John, impressed that he could think sarcasm.

Nervously they sat in their seat hoping that the flight would take off without anyone noticing their breach of security. At 6.15 p.m., as scheduled, the flight taxied onto the runway and took off into the darkening sky. It was an hour into their two-hour flight when their luck turned.

John had been calculating what to do when he got to Geneva, when 'Barbie' approached them. John assumed that this would just be another sickly attempt for her to proposition Nash. It wasn't.

"Mr. Stevens. We've just been contacted by security at London Heathrow. It would appear that you did not present your passport before departure. I'm sure this was just an oversight because of the security breach down in the airport. If you can just show me your passport now, I can put the matter to rest."

"Well, um…do you know…you have the most beautiful eyes that I've ever seen, they dazzle like diamonds?" replied Nash, turning the charm-o-meter up to maximum.

"Oh God, can a soul be sick?"

"I'm sure they are, but I still need to see your passport," she replied, unmoved by Nash's advances.

It was obvious that Nash was taken aback by his failure. There was an audible little bang as his balloon-sized ego popped.

"I don't have it with me," replied Nash sheepishly.

"Then I'm afraid you will have to be detained at Geneva Airport security when we arrive. They will have to validate your identity," she replied before pulling out a pair of handcuffs.

"That's more like it, baby, now we're talking," replied Nash, grinning as she fixed the cuffs in place around both of his wrists.

"Nash, it's absolutely not what you are thinking."

CHAPTER THIRTEEN

THE ARBITER

For a change the Prime Minister was sitting down for dinner with his own family. It was a change because most evenings were consumed by an endless schedule of dinner dates with dignitaries. There was always a national president, religious leader or foreign ambassador making requests for his time, and food always seemed to play its part. Why did people always want to 'do lunch'? When you had to contend with a multitude of contrasting opinions and incompatible beliefs, perhaps eating was the one subject that people agreed on. The need for it at least, even if they often couldn't agree on the variety of cuisine. Although at times an intensely tedious and tiring exercise, in some respects he had to admit favouring these obscure V.I.P. luncheons over meals with his own flesh and blood.

It's a peculiar life being Prime Minister. Many of his predecessors had warned that the nature of the job meant it would become all-consuming. Byron in his naive arrogance initially brushed off this advice, declaring that he would always have time for his family. How wrong he was. In reality it became impossible not to spend every waking moment thinking about work, or to receive a phone call from someone else who was thinking about it.

When he did have a so-called normal family meal there was no subject of conversation that he didn't have some degree of knowledge or opinion on. Any subject outside of his self-proclaimed expertise wasn't worth commenting on. It wasn't just his understanding of topical subjects that had changed over the last four years, his attitude to others had been equally affected. In parliamentary circles his almost unlimited power to force through his will had suppressed his sensitivity to how other people might feel about it. Anyway, they rarely complained, at least not more than once. Of course this approach didn't go down quite so well when sitting around Number 10's dining room table with his wife Michelle on one side and his only child, Faith, on the other.

Apart from the Leader of the Opposition, the person he found it most difficult to connect with was his daughter. Faith had spent the majority of her teenage years living in Downing Street, a ludicrously alien environment to grow up in. Arguably if there was a time in life when a daughter most needs, but least wants, paternal guidance, then it's the teen years. A responsibility that Byron was both unable and unwilling to find a gap in his schedule for. Faith was marooned in an overprotective environment and left to work things out for herself by absorbing wisdom from a vacuum. To make matters worse, her every move, rebellious or otherwise, was being monitored, exposed and reported on.

On the rare moments when she did step out of line, which inevitably every seventeen-year-old does, the personal consequences were much more magnified. This was also true of the punishment for her misgivings. As an example to others she visibly carried the can for all her teenage counterparts around the country. Byron felt it was his duty to demonstrate to parents the right way to raise the children of Britain. This hard-edged, arm's-length, lead-by-example parenting made his relationship with his daughter more than a little fraught. As the pair of them sat silently waiting for dinner to arrive, one stared anywhere but at the other, whilst the other desperately attempted to find an uncontroversial topic to connect them.

"Dad, the bloke that won Rock Star on TV is doing a gig at the Millennium Stadium on Friday," commented Faith.

"What star?" huffed Byron, his thoughts still seemingly elsewhere.

"Rock Star, it's a talent contest. You should watch, it might give you a connection to younger voters."

"No, it wouldn't. I'd look like a sad old man trying to act cool," he responded, quite correctly.

"I just thought you might like to watch it with me," replied Faith dejectedly, proving to herself that there really were no subjects that were safe ground.

"Don't you have more important things to do with your time?"

Faith rolled her eyes, correctly predicting the forthcoming lecture.

"Do you know what I did today?" said Byron, using one of his favourite catchphrases, aimed at inflating his overimportance to the person he was addressing. It was almost impossible to better the story or event that he was about to reel off.

"No," said Faith reluctantly.

"Today I spent the day at an inner-city school. Almost all the children there are living under the poverty line. They are in that position, more than likely, because their scumbag parents use the government's money, my money, on booze, fags and drugs, rather than spending it on their family's welfare. I don't expect those kids get time to waste on watching Rock Man."

"Give her a break, Byron," encouraged Michelle, as she brought dinner in from the kitchen, placing a large, orange casserole dish in the middle of the table.

"It's Rock Star, not Rock Man," huffed Faith. But recognising that her mother's protection was close at hand she picked up the courage that she'd been waiting for. "Dad, I wanted to know if I could go to that concert on Friday night with a few of the girls from my college?"

"Absolutely not, you know you're grounded," replied Byron, as he scooped a large portion of lamb hotpot onto his plate. He'd missed lunch due to a poorly organised day of ministerial meetings and select committee hearings. Lamb hotpot was by no means his favourite but he was so hungry he could have eaten chipboard.

"How long are you going to act like this? It's so completely unfair, Dad. just because I'm the Prime Minister's daughter I get treated differently."

"You get treated differently because other parents do not lift up their Sunday newspapers to find their semi-naked teenage daughter in an uncompromising position with a minor celebrity in a posh London nightclub. A nightclub that you were in illegally," replied Byron sternly.

"Everyone in my school does these things. I'm just a normal teenager. I wish you were a normal father."

Byron had decided to ignore this comment, believing food to be more important than a fight. This was one of those moments when he wished he could turn to the Italian Prime Minister and discuss the merits of further sanctions against Zimbabwe. He lifted the first forkful of casserole to his mouth but, interrupted by his mobile phone, it never made contact. If he answered, it would keep him from his dinner but also deflect him away from his awkward dining companion. On balance he decided to answer it.

"Some good news, Prime Minister," came the distorted voice of Agent 15.

"I think you should let me be the judge of that," replied Byron as he got up from the table and walked to a quieter corner of the room. "What is it?"

"We've got Foster's apartment and office bugged up to the hilt. On top of that I've got surveillance on her twenty-four hours a day."

"That just sounds like news, nothing particularly good about it," replied Byron, aggrieved that this rather unexceptional information had interrupted his hunger. "What have you actually learnt so far?"

"She buys Pantene shampoo, sir," replied Agent 15 sarcastically, "and she hasn't made any contact with Violet Stokes as yet."

"I was being metaphorical when I said I wanted to know what shampoo she bought. Look, let me know when you get a proper breakthrough. Now if you'll excuse me, I'd like to at least start eating dinner with my family, even if I don't get to finish it," replied Byron, sitting back down to his casserole and about to close the call.

"There is one more piece of news you might be interested in," added Agent 15.

Yet again, Byron lowered his fork. "I seriously hope so."

"Nash Stevens has been arrested on a flight from Heathrow to Geneva. Apparently he didn't have his passport on him and was acting extremely strangely. They have him held in the airport prison. He's asking to see the British Embassy. Would you like to intervene?"

"Now *that* is good news," said Byron looking at his sullen daughter as she averted her eyes from her father. "Tell them to let him rot."

*****

According to the Red Cross the worst prison in the world is the Tadmor Military Prison in Syria. Conditions are bleak. As an inmate in Tadmor you have a one-in-three chance that you will die or be killed before the first anniversary of your incarceration. Cells are approximately sixty four feet square and regularly occupied by more than six prisoners. Cockroaches crawl through the bedsheets and temperatures fluctuate between minus six degrees during winter nights, and over forty-five degrees in the summer months. The Army-enlisted prison guards randomly choose inmates for ritual torture, some of whom are brutally maimed or killed in the process. Cholera and dysentery are common side effects from the defecation left in rain-soaked, muddy trenches that line the courtyards. There is no reprieve, no parole and no appeal.

The prison at Geneva Airport is not the worst prison in the world. In fact it wouldn't make the top hundred. In most people's opinion it was quite pleasant, as prisons go. Nash Stevens was not *most* people. As far as Nash was concerned this was the worst prison in the world. Life's all about perspective. When you are treated to the luxury lifestyle that celebrities of Nash's standing are, anything lower feels substandard. If a normal member of the public stayed in a two-star hotel they'd probably have quite an enjoyable stay. To Nash it would be like staying in a YMCA and eating in a lay-by greasy spoon. Let's just say when you're pampered more than you deserve, it's not easy adjusting to a lower standard of living. This for Nash was lower than a standard of living got.

John and Nash were in a single-occupancy cell with relative opulence. It had a TV, toilet, air conditioning and plenty of natural light. It wasn't smelly or cramped. The food was adequate and the guards pleasant. This sort of environment would be bearable for most people if they had to stay for a few days. An inconvenience put down to experience and laughed at jovially later in life, so long as the reason for the visit was resolved quickly.

Having been cooped up in this cell for the last four weeks, John and Nash were getting just a little bit pissed off. John had wasted a month of the three that were available to him to save the Universe. Nash had missed countless parties and a few concerts, and thought his testicles might explode from the lack of sex. On the positive side, that certainly wouldn't have been the case if he had been in the Tadmor facility. There he'd probably be getting it twice a night.

Neither of them could forecast when they were likely to be released, as the British Embassy staff had been and gone on several occasions. Inexplicably they could not verify Nash's claims that he was a British citizen. According to them, there was absolutely no record of Nash on the passport register and therefore they could not agree to his release. In these days of global hostilities it was just not safe to release someone if it was impossible to confirm their identity.

"Nash, there's something that I can't quite work out. Why can't they find your name on the register?"

"I've absolutely no idea," Nash replied sheepishly.

"There must be a reason why they're holding you for so long. Have you ever had another name, an alias?"

"Well, yes," replied Nash as if it was of no significance.

"Have you lost your bloody mind? Why didn't you tell them?"

"It's a bit embarrassing. I have a reputation to keep, you know. If the press got hold of my real name it would be the end of me."

"Oh that's all right, then. A bit embarrassing is far worse than being stuck in prison for a month with someone possessing your soul. I forgot you love it here! Are you telling me that your embarrassment has meant I've lost a month? What sort of imbecile are you?" John clenched Nash's fist.

Nash ducked it successfully, something he'd learnt to do really well in the last few weeks.

"So, what is it, then?"

"Well, Nash is my rockstar name. I changed it from my real name in my teens. I would never have made it in my profession with my real name...Barbara Stevens?" Nash replied timidly.

"Barbara!"

John's soul exploded with what he guessed to be laughter. Laughter is not a physical thing in a soul like it is in a human. In a soul it comes through as emotion, and an emotion in a soul is an electrical impulse. Nash's body lifted off the ground and did a fabulous star jump, his long hair leapt out towards the ceiling, and a small puff of grey smoke came out of his nostrils. John was not immune to the reaction as he went pinballing the length, breadth and width of Nash's body.

"What the dear Lord was that?" Nash said out loud.

"I think I laughed. Let's not do that again," John replied, trying to right himself.

"Please don't," agreed Nash, trying unsuccessfully to encourage his hair to come back towards his scalp.

"We need to get the Embassy people back here right now."

As Nash went to beckon the guard, the door opened in on them. In the entrance stood one of the neatest dressed and most unlikely-looking prison guards imaginable. The guards here were so polite, John and Nash might as well have been staying in a two-star hotel. They weren't used to dealing with celebrities, or people who were in residence for more than a couple of days. They'd become quite attached to Nash.

"How are you today, Mr. Stevens?" asked the guard in perfect English, but affecting a Gallic accent.

"Tingly," replied Nash.

"What is tin-ga-lee?" asked the guard.

"It doesn't matter. We need to see the Ambassador, quickly."

"Well, you have a visitor here to see you, maybe that's someone from the Embassy?" replied the guard. "I need to take you to the visitors' room."

Both John and Nash could find the visitors' room blindfolded. They'd been there once a week, every Monday, for the last four weeks. Not to see friends or family, as other inmates would, but on every occasion they had met Sir Noel Cavendish, the British Ambassador to Switzerland, an intensely boring and humourless man. The visitors' room was separated by a clear perspex wall which divided the tables between the visitor and the inmate. On either side of the glass were telephones which allowed those on either side to speak to each other. When they entered the room it was clear that this was not another visit from the stuffy-nosed, upper-class, Eton-educated Sir Noel.

On the visitor's side of the table sat a shadowy figure in a dark cloak, his face almost totally hidden from view by his hood. Two bony hands lay flat on the table top, twitching uncomfortably. As Nash sat down opposite, their intriguing visitor beckoned the prison guard over. Whispering something into his ear, the guard, without question or comment, walked from the room, closing and locking the door behind him. John knew this was quite against prison procedure, as a guard was always present at any meeting in this room. One of the bony hands picked up the receiver on his side of the wall. Nash sat motionless, transfixed by the figure sitting opposite. After a moment the man's other hand pointed at Nash with an outstretched and ominous finger, indicating for him to pick up the other receiver. Nash complied.

"Hello, John," came a gruff, ancient voice which seemed familiar to John, even though he couldn't immediately place it.

"John? You've got the wrong person. My name's Barb...Nash, I don't know who you are."

"Well, Barb-nash, if you want me to help you get out of here, I strongly recommend that you let your friend speak. Let me speak with John," replied the dark figure in a soft, sympathetic tone.

"Nash, you need to let me take over. Somehow he knows that I'm here. Let your mind go."

Nash was in no mood to argue, and if it resulted in freedom, he was happy to go with it. He let go of his mind and allowed John to take over his senses.

"Who are you and how did you know it was me?" asked John sharply.

The stranger pulled back his hood to reveal a face underneath that was old and weathered. The skin on his face hugged his skull so tightly that it was like viewing a living skeleton. His dark and dangerous eyes devoured the available light like the centre of a hungry black hole. Was he smiling? It was hard to tell, as none of his skin appeared to move. It was either a smile, or he was just baring his gap-filled teeth. It was clear that this person would find it hard to distinguish between empathy and psychopathy.

"I see you don't remember me, John," said the dark voice echoing through the room, piercing Nash's skin and targeting John's resting place.

"I feel something. It's not recollection, though, it feels more emotive," replied John, confused by the sensation that resonated around him.

"What emotion are you feeling?" croaked the visitor.

"Wrath."

"That's not surprising. You have no recollection of me, John, because the last time we met you were dead and you looked at me through plastic eyes. A soul cannot visualise like a human can. It has no power for visual memory. That's a function of the brain, and as you had no brain at the time we last met, that would be impossible. What a soul can do is record memories as emotions. My name is Laslow Kreicher, and I am the Arbiter."

John's emotions bubbled with tension as this new information brought a fresh perspective. This was the man responsible for sending him to Hell rather than Heaven. This was the man responsible for his current predicament and according to Primordial this was also the only person who could help him. In the chaos of the last five weeks he hadn't contemplated what his reaction would be when he met Laslow again, even though it had always been his intention to find him. On the one hand, he wanted his anger to leap forward and attack in a fit of revenge. On the other, he knew that wouldn't help in the long run. He had no choice but to rely on him, however hard an instinct it was.

John sucked in his emotion: there might be another time for it.

"Why shouldn't I kill you?" replied John, anger still fighting with the rational part of his internal argument.

"I don't think that would be particularly easy for you to execute in your current position, but part of me would thank you for it," replied Laslow. "After all, it is inevitable anyway. If you fail, we all die."

"I see that there are upsides to the end of the world," spat John through gritted teeth. "How did you know I was inside Nash?"

"I have certain abilities that most humans do not."

"What the hell are you?"

"You really should choose your words more carefully," he replied, glancing upwards. "As I told you, I am the Arbiter and have been since 1769. I make the final decision as to who goes East and who goes West, but you know that bit anyway."

"You're over 250 years old, but you said that you're human. How is that possible?" said John, struggling with the maths.

"It's possible because I am sitting in front of you in the flesh, although I have barely any left. It doesn't matter why or how it is possible, you just have to accept that it is. I'm sure over the last few months you have accepted many things that previously you didn't believe."

"True, but it doesn't stop me trying to understand them."

"Rationalising of your belief system will have to wait. I believe there is some haste needed. You've already lost a month and are no closer in your task. I am here to help you as much as I am allowed to, or am willing to. What do you need from me?"

John had a million questions that he wanted to ask but got the feeling he might not get to ask that many.

"What is the Limpet Syndrome?" he blurted out.

"A wise and intuitive question, start at the beginning. The truth is no one is absolutely sure. It is not of any creator's design. It's a mutation. If humans worked as they were designed to it would not, it could not happen. Over the centuries the human mind has evolved a stronger connection to the inner self and has taken more interest in its own soul. In the past, humans relied on faith in religion for comfort and the pursuit of answers. It's not the first time in history we've seen it. It occurred in some of the ancient civilisations."

"Like the Egyptians?"

"No, not quite, I'm talking about civilisations that are much older than that, but I'm not here to give you a history lesson. It's believed that when a human is strong enough, or motivated enough, it can momentarily halt the natural process of death. It can't stop its body dying, not yet at least, but it can stop its soul dying. It will cling to any form of life that it can find. Its purpose may be varied but every example has a shared need to remain in some form in this world. Lingering to put right something that it deems to be wrong. When a soul does that it is almost impossible to remove, like a limpet stuck to a rock after the tide has gone far out to sea."

"How do you remove the soul if it's stuck to a rock?"

"Well, just like the limpet, when the tide comes back in it can be loosened and picked off quite easily. You just need to know which rock it's stuck to and when the tide is high."

"So which rocks are Sandy and Ian clinging to?" asked John, fascinated by the Arbiter's explanation. It gave him hope that his own soul could show some powerful attributes.

"Well, you probably know already that the soul has to move rapidly into another carbon-based life form. Normally that has to be done in seconds. In almost every case the soul is drawn towards the last carbon-based form that it has seen in life, it sticks like a flashback. Now if you're very lucky that's a tree. It's much easier to find a tree. If you're really unlucky it's a type of insect, a really small one," explained Laslow, seemingly disinterested with his own explanation. His hands searched around in his cape for something to preoccupy them.

"Pigeon," replied John, speaking as much to himself. "They've been pigeoncarnated!"

Laslow's hands found what they were looking for. A thin ivory smoking pipe about seven inches long and beautifully crafted. The tobacco end had been carved with microscopic detail to reveal the outlines of a collection of mini-planets clumped together in some unknown solar system. The pipe was made of a liquid silver material that captured the light that gleamed in from the high windows, prompting the planets to move around in their own gravitational fields like a tiny physics lesson. When Laslow drew a long lungful of air through it, the resulting sweet-smelling camomile smoke instantly transformed the atmosphere from unease to calm.

"How can you be certain?" Laslow said between puffs.

"I have a copy of a newspaper article. Both of them were involved in an explosion in which they were rescuing pigeons from a government lab. It's the only paper that I've had for the last month and I've read it over and over again."

"That sounds plausible to me," replied Laslow. "What were they making in this lab?"

John stopped momentarily before responding. Why did Laslow care what they were making? It would seem to have no relevance. Even if it did, what would Laslow do with this information to help him? The old man felt John's hesitation and the one thing that he disliked above all else was...well, pretty much everything, actually. Laslow pierced Nash's eyes with his pitch-black stare, seeking for the information that, hesitation or not, he would eventually uncover. After a period of resistance, John's mind gave way.

"It's a drug of sorts. It seems to have some mind-altering quality. It's not really clear from the article."

Laslow's pupils, the only part of his face which showed any sign of emotion, expanded slightly. "That's interesting. Thank you for indulging me."

"I didn't really know I had," responded John.

"Is there anything else that you need from me, John?"

"There is one thing," asked John, unable to resist asking the one question that was most important to him. "Why did you choose Hell?"

"What if I told you, John? Would it matter, would it change anything?"

"I deserve to know, you changed my future," said John, standing up spontaneously and stabbing his finger against the glass.

"Deserve to know? No, you do not deserve to know. You were dead at the time and now all you are is a spirit, John. As far as I'm aware there is no Geneva Convention covering the rights of souls. You're a dot, an insignificant speck in many histories," replied Laslow, unflinching to John's suddenly more animated nature.

"I could still have received a different outcome if it weren't for you?"

"If I told you why, I would be disclosing information that you would have absolutely no way of understanding and even less chance of accepting. Stick to your task. There are forces at play here beyond your wildest comprehension. Precarious is your route on the tightrope of fate. Fall on one side and you will witness the destruction of the world that you hold so dear. Fall on the other side and we will witness the destruction of my world and I won't allow that. Unless you place every sinew, every ounce of effort, every atom, and every recalled emotion into that thin line, not only will you fail, but also you will see me again. If you do see me again…I will burn you."

Laslow replaced his hood, lifted himself away from the table and walked towards the door. The conversation was over. Raising a bony finger for the last time, he pointed at John who suddenly felt an intense heat, as if an invisible flame was bearing down on him. The glass, which he still had his finger on, started to bubble and melt. Large lumps of molten glass were running down the centre, coagulating in heaps on the table. Finally with a crack the wooden table split in two under the intense power of the heat. All that stood in front of John now was a three-foot-wide gap in the screen, a pool of melted glass and shards of wood. By the time John had made it through to the visitor's side of the room, Laslow was gone.

Had Laslow done that to free him or frighten him, or both? Torn between making a run for it and returning to his cell, he moved carefully and quietly towards the exit. When he reached the doorway, what he saw told him that he was going to need to run. The first clue to this was that the hallway outside the visitors' room now featured the corpses of two guards, one at either end. They were fully clothed, but what was left of their bodies had been turned from flesh to scorched bone. The unbearable smell of putrid, burnt flesh wafted through the passage. John lifted his jacket sleeve to stop himself gagging on the smell and the wispy, dark smoke that still hung in the air. It was a truly gruesome sight, even though he was viewing it through someone else's eyes.

These people had no chance of escaping the power that had so easily melted glass and burnt wood that John correctly guessed to be the cause of their deaths. What scared John more than the power that Laslow carried was the disregard for life and the ease in which he dispatched it. Out in the main reception more bodies were scattered around, killed at the spot where they worked. It was unclear why they had to be victims. If John had touched a nerve it wasn't the fault of these innocent bystanders.

John and Nash knew they had to get out, and fast. If they were found here in this devastation they wouldn't just be facing false passport charges, they'd be up for mass murder. They both ran for it, both for once in the same direction.

"That was a bit intense," thought Nash.

"Did you get most of that?" replied John puffing out of the main doors and down the street away from the airport compound.

"Yes, and at least I believe you a bit more now. There's stuff there that I never wanted to hear and certainly never want to see again."

"You're not alone. I think I've seen enough of Switzerland for a while: what say you we get back to London?"

"Agreed, but I don't think we're going be able to go commercially again."

"You're right, we didn't get here that well using domestic airlines, but how else are we going to get back?" said John between puffed-out strides.

"I could call my friend, Syd? He's got his own charter plane. We've used him a lot when we've done gigs in Europe, if we can find a phone I'll call him and he can organise a pick-up."

"That seems like a good move, although something tells me we could have saved a lot of stress if we'd thought of that on the way out," replied John.

CHAPTER FOURTEEN

FLIGHT 44

It was a beautiful May morning in Buckinghamshire. The warm sunlight shone down upon the wooded valley bathing it in a shower of golden glitter that played hide-and-seek with bush and thicket. The spring plumage that covered twig and branch was a kaleidoscope of pastel shades. Flowers of red, yellow, white and blue quivered in the brisk wind and danced in time to a secret melody. It was a small part of the world at peace. Fauna and flora entwined in harmony, working together in a perfect balance of symmetry, just the way nature intended it. Perfect symmetry? Maybe that was a little over-the-top. It was *almost* perfect. The animals, insects and plants that lived there in the wood were demonstrating some rather strange behaviours. They all felt that there was something unnatural amongst them and it made their instincts twitch.

Peculiar behaviours in animals isn't that unusual of course. It's said that a cow can sense a change in the weather, even when there are no obvious signs of one. It is these same evolutionary instincts that cats use to perceive danger well before the event. What was strange in this valley was that all of the animals were acting oddly, as if the valley species had gained a combined sixth sense. As a consequence of this new power, none of them would go anywhere near the large oak tree next to a group of silver birches at the foot of the valley. Almost all life forms had moved away from it over the last five or six weeks and their anxiety was not totally inappropriate.

The pigeons were the only species that went anywhere near that strange oak and it wasn't just the group that normally lived in it. Their population had expanded rapidly over the last week in anticipation of some great unscheduled pigeon convention. None of the other creatures knew the reason for this migration and they wanted nothing to do with it. Well, almost nothing. Although no animal ventured to the tree itself, that didn't stop it from being the only topic of conversation amongst the twitters, hoots, growls and croaks.

Throughout the generations humans have learnt from the strange, intuitive behaviours of animals, and the opposite is also true. Most pet owners will swear that their animals demonstrate human behaviours copied from their masters. Maybe they're right, or quite possibly their brains have been addled by the overexposure to pet faeces? What all animals, including humans, share is a natural sense of inquisitiveness. In most neighbourhoods people tend to be a little bit nosy. A curtain in a second-floor window ruffles to reveal a little old lady spying on an unannounced guest arriving at a neighbour's house. Some minutes later the rumours spread around town of an affair between Mrs. Hitchins and the man from the gas company.

Just occasionally the pigeons noticed the nose of a fox poking out of an old tree trunk just within earshot. When a feathery head had turned in that direction a rustle of leaves was followed by the rapid retreat of an embarrassed wren. The animals were on watch. Perhaps out of fear, perhaps out of natural nosiness, or perhaps because two pigeons as big as pheasants now lived in that tree. On this particular May morning, these abnormally sized pigeons were sitting in the nest of that old oak tree fighting over a worm.

"I really don't want it," said Sandy. "Is it too much to ask to have something different once in a while? I mean, a snail wouldn't go amiss?"

"Yeah a good, juicy snail would be great. It would feel like normal food," said Ian.

"Look, one of us is going to have to eat it or she'll force it down our throats again. I still haven't stopped coughing from the last time," added Sandy despondently, virtually retching at the very thought.

Over on the other side of the nest two infant pigeons sat watching them intently but with a touch of fear. Sitting as far as possible from Ian and Sandy without falling out of the tree, they watched their oversized siblings curiously, waiting to see what strange habits they were likely to reveal next. Over the past month Ian had given them names to pass the time, uncertain if this was a sign of insanity or normality. The one on the left with the blue head was called Fred, and to his left was Emma, his sister. Ian didn't know biologically whether she was a *she*, but had decided the white and brown colour made her look more feminine.

"Do you think Em or Fred want it?" Ian said to Sandy. "They look like they need some feeding up, they're nowhere near as big as we are."

"What did you say?"

Occasionally Sandy experienced a flashback to his past life. A connection that he could not fully control would seep out of his left brain activity. It was like déjà vu, although not something that he'd seen before, something he had been before.

"I said that they aren't as big as us."

"Not that bit," said Sandy shaking his head. "It may not have crossed your pea-sized brain but we are bigger than every pigeon that we've seen. Given that we eat less than any of them there must be some other reason for that, don't you think?"

Ian shrugged, clueless to Sandy's thought-process.

"What was the other bit you said?"

"I said Em or Fred might want it. The worm," Ian added in case he'd omitted even the smallest piece of the message.

"Em or Fred," muttered Sandy slowly, several times over and over again.

"Those two, remember I called them EM and FRED," replied Ian, even more slowly as if talking to an idiot.

"I've got this word Em-or-fed circling around me. It's something important but I can't work it out. Does it mean anything to you, Ian?"

Ian sat for a moment trying intensely to show that his face was concentrating. In truth, Ian's brain had always been a bleak place, desolate from any true intellectual capacity. Even when he did try to *really* think, all that popped into his head was something completely random. His eyes stared upwards and his tongue hung from his beak as he vainly attempted to demonstrate thought.

"Is Emorfed a...type of cheese?" replied Ian randomly. This was a bluff. What he'd actually been thinking about was what colour of offspring you'd get if you bred Emma and Fred together.

"No, it's not a cheese, you spastic," Sandy glared, rubbing his head with his wing in an attempt to massage the answer out. "God, I wish I could think straight, my brain's completely jumbled."

Ian hopped over to Fred and Emma to offer the worm that was still wriggling around fighting for life. Both pigeons shuffled away as Ian laid the worm in front of them like a holy sacrifice.

"Would you say that Fred's head is blue, or more a violet colour?" Ian asked, still contemplating baby colours.

"Violet."

"So that would make their chicks a sky-blue colour, I'd guess."

"Violet," Sandy repeated.

"I know, you said that."

"Not the colour," Sandy replied calmly. "Violet Stokes, I'm starting to remember."

"Violet, who?" said Ian.

"I phoned her just before we died in the bomb," said Sandy, now ignoring any noises that came from Ian in case he lost his train of thought. "I phoned my friend, Violet Stokes. I phoned her to warn her about something. What was it? Yes, I know, I phoned to warn her about Emorfed, that's it."

"What's a phone?"

The pictures were becoming clearer. Connections were flashing around in Sandy's head. The pieces in this mental jigsaw only fell into place if he blurted them out loud in case he lost the ability to recall them.

"Now I remember Violet, she was my second-year primary schoolteacher," Ian chirped.

"Shut up," replied Sandy curtly. "She was the leader of J.A.W.S., the animal welfare group."

"Oh, that Violet," Ian replied, not altogether convinced. "Why did you want to warn her about cheese? Is she lactose intolerant?"

"Remind me to smack you when I get my hands back. Emorfed is not a cheese, you idiot. It's the drug that they were developing at Tavistock. It's what they were testing on the pigeons in preparation for using it on the whole of the British public. What's more, I am absolutely sure it's the reason that I wouldn't let go of life. Why part of me remained when the rest of me died. It must be stopped and we, scrub that, I, am the only one who can do it."

Ian continued to look blankly at him.

"I'm not really sure why I'm explaining this to you, I'd be better of telling those two over there."

Both Emma and Fred nodded in agreement.

Ian tried to compute what Sandy had said. Whether Ian would have understood it even if he was still in his human form was questionable, so the chance of a Eureka moment now was low. Ian decided wisely not to comment and just nodded, not wanting to demonstrate less intelligence than two *real* pigeons.

"I think it's time for us to leave," said Sandy.

"How are we going to do that? We haven't worked out the flying thing yet."

Sandy couldn't argue with this. Between them, they had now recorded exactly forty-two unsuccessful attempts. Flight forty-one had almost come off until Sandy had engaged too much force on lift-off. He'd gone upwards alright, but after hitting one of the boughs above him, had descended just as quickly. Flight forty-two had also shown signs of promise. That time, Ian had definitely flown. Unfortunately, he'd flapped too hard with one wing which sent him into a fast and painful circular crash. What had disappointed them most was that both Fred and Emma had earned their wings weeks ago. Sandy had put it down to them having only pigeon instincts and no human baggage. Secretly, though, he felt quite inferior and as jealous as any sibling would.

"Ian, ask Fred to give us another demo."

Sandy had never engaged directly with his so-called brother and sister. It was penance enough to have to deal with Ian every waking moment of the day, without the indignity of stooping even lower. Ian shuffled over to the others. Neither Sandy nor Ian had learnt to communicate in pigeon. Whenever they spoke, they spoke in English. They discussed why this was but neither had come up with any provable reason. Sandy had surmised that their human souls had retained certain memories that projected outwards, controlling their speech. Ian guessed that they were just quicker learners than the average pigeon and eventually Fred and Emma would catch up, especially if Ian spoke loudly and slowly to them.

Sandy watched Ian communicate his message using a bizarre form of mime to act out what he wanted. He flapped his arms and pretended to leap off the edge of the nest. Occasionally he would point a wing at one of them and shout very slowly, 'YOU FLY!' It was like watching the warm-up routine of those idiotic bird-men that jump off piers on summer days wearing only a cardboard plane and a pair of flippers. Surprisingly, though, Fred did seem to understand the request. He stood up and bobbed over to Ian.

"I told you they were just slow learners. He understands me now," Ian said, beckoning Sandy over to see the expert at work.

Fred walked to the edge of the nest, spread his wings, bent his spindly knees just slightly and flew effortlessly out of the nest. He hovered a few feet from the tree, waiting in hope for Ian to follow him. Sandy watched intently as Ian attempted to repeat Fred's processes. More reminiscent of a long jump than flight, Ian leapt expectantly from the tree, flapping furiously. He floated for a few moments before the inevitable loss of control. This time he did at least fly forward, albeit whilst lurching uncontrollably from side to side and finally careering into one of the silver birches that encircled the oak tree.

As he flopped onto the floor in a heap, a startled grey squirrel landed next to him, dislodged from its hiding place from the impact of Ian's collision. The nervous squirrel bolted off into the undergrowth, constantly peering backwards to see if the monster pigeon was about to follow.

Not for the first time Fred chirped to Emma to assist Ian back into the tree. The two of them flew down to where Ian lay, clutched him softly in their claws and lifted him back up to where Sandy was watching. Dejected, Ian waited naively for some moral support. None came.

"Rudder," said Sandy.

"You don't have to be like that Sandy, it's not easy, you know. I am trying my best," replied Ian apologetically, shaking his feathers to remove the dirt that had accumulated on landing.

"Rudder, you idiot. That's the reason we haven't got it right. If you watch Fred, he's using his tail as a rudder to balance the direction he's going in. All you're doing is using your wings."

"But…I don't have a tail."

Sandy promptly kicked him in the rear.

"Owww!" Ian squawked as he hit the twig surface of the nest.

"You may not have had a tail when you were a human but I think, as I have just proved, you do have one now. We just have to work out how to use it. It must be a bit like trying to wiggle your ears. Not everyone can do it, but that doesn't mean that it can't be done. Right, we need to concentrate on trying to move it."

The many other creatures in their secret, shady hideouts witnessed an extraordinary sight. Two pigeons were apparently gurning at each other as they put all of their willpower into moving a part of their bodies that until recently wasn't there. The outcome was varied. Beaks twitched, feathers shook, heads wobbled and a foot did a little dance. Every bodypart moved, except the tail. Ian concentrated on his butt so much he managed to defecate all over his feet, which didn't help Sandy's concentration one bit.

"I think we're approaching this the wrong way," said Sandy after much loss of energy. "Ian, put your foot on my tail and move it up and down, maybe then I'll get to feel which muscles I need to use."

Ian placed his foot on the end of Sandy's tail and, like a man trying to pump up a lilo, moved it up and down. Sandy felt the muscles at the bottom of his spine moving. For the first time his brain connected to it, two parts of his body making their acquaintance for the first time.

"Okay, stop. I think I've got it."

Sandy's tail moved unaided. He raised his wings in the air, bent his knees and put his full force into a bounce from the floor. Using his newfound tail for balance, he flapped his wings and rose majestically from the nest, hovering a foot in the air.

"I've done it!" he shouted. "I'm flying!"

The experience was exhilarating. Sandy had hated the fact that he was caged in this new body. He hated eating bugs. He hated being stuck with Ian. He hated not having hands. For the first time in six weeks none of that mattered. He was doing what probably no human had ever done in history before. He was flying and he loved it. This power made Sandy feel like Sandy again. He landed smoothly back onto the nest. Once Sandy had demonstrated the use of his own tail feathers, he attempted to help Ian to control his own bodyparts. After a much longer time than it had taken Sandy, Ian waggled his tail. They sat down to contemplate their next move.

"We need to get back to London. The only person we can trust now is Violet. We need to seek her out and help her to stop Emorfed," said Sandy, uncertain as to how this was even possible. "The only problem is, we don't know where we are, and we don't know in which direction London is."

"Don't pigeons home?" mumbled Ian.

"Do you know that might have been the most interesting and helpful thing you've said in your entire life, pigeon or human."

Ian wasn't quite sure why he merited praise, or maybe just didn't recognise it as praise. It'd never happened before.

"You are right, of course, pigeons do home. But are we homing pigeons? Is there enough pigeon in us for that and do our brains know where home is?"

This peaceful little valley, which had been their home for the last few weeks, now felt like a tiny wilderness in a much more complex world. Which way were his instincts pointing him? He felt strongly that a point to his right under the midday sun was the direction they should follow. Maybe it was instinct or maybe a blind gamble.

"I think it's that way," said Ian, pointing a wing over the brow of the hill in exactly the same direction that Sandy had indicated to himself.

"That's where I was thinking, too," said Sandy. "Only one way to find out, I guess. You ready to go?"

"Not quite," replied Ian. He stood up and hopped over to Fred and Emma. Using his unique communication style of mime and piercing stares, he shouted, "THANK YOU!" in the loudest and slowest English that he could muster.

Sandy and Ian went through their newly learnt pre-flight routine, which still needed a high level of conscious thought. They lifted off from the nest for what they hoped would be the last time, passed out of the forest and up above the treetops. Brilliantly bright yellow rapeseed fields spread out for miles, keeping villages and thickets at bay on their perimeters. An astounding view that they could have stopped and watched for hours if they had more certainty of the dangers that might face them on their journey. As they got into their rhythm and were flying at what they thought was top speed, Sandy was aware that they were now food in the eyes of a great many creatures.

Behind was a sight he didn't expect. Flying about fifty feet away was a swarm of pigeons. He couldn't count how many there were, but they were flying in formation and they were most definitely following them.

CHAPTER FIFTEEN

THE SCOOP

As the Cessna light airplane touched down at Fairoaks Airfield just outside Chobham in Surrey, John contemplated his next move. What he knew so far was that Sandy and Ian were pigeons, probably bloody big ones with certain characteristics that resembled their human forms. That meant that somewhere in the world there was a pigeon with a beard. From all accounts their souls wouldn't have survived a long journey on their own, so they were likely to be somewhere in the South-East of England, quite near to the Tavistock Institute. That's if they had stayed where they were, and there was no guarantee of that. What would he do next? It was already the start of May and the solstice would be in six or seven weeks. Time was running out.

"There we go, Nash, we're here," came the voice of the pilot from the cockpit, having just taxied them to one of the private hangars at an airport so small even some of the neighbourhood weren't aware of it. "I still can't understand what you were doing in Geneva without transport, though?"

"You really don't want to know, Syd," replied Nash. "Did you phone Herb to pick me up?"

"Yes, he should be here already. He was very pleased that I called, seemed very eager to see you," answered Syd.

"I bet he was."

As he disembarked he shook Syd's hand in a manly fashion in order to demonstrate, without verbalising, his debt of gratitude. God knows how he would have got out of Switzerland in such secrecy without him. In the hangar, leaning against a 1985 Porsche 911 that had seen better days, was an extremely grumpy Herb.

"What the fuck have you been up to?" grumbled Herb, as Nash reached the red sports car. "Do you know the grief that you have put me through in the last four weeks? I said, have a *couple* of days off and relax. I didn't say go to Geneva to be imprisoned for a month, before getting embroiled in a mass murder. You're a wanted man and your career, well, that's going to disintegrate quicker than an O. J. Simpson getaway."

"Look, Herb, I know you don't understand but I really have got someone inside my head telling me what to do."

"That's just what Charles Manson said," replied Herb in a tone teetering between genuine concern and utter bewilderment. "Get in the car."

Herb squeezed his nineteen-stone frame into the driver's seat of the most inappropriate car he could have picked for himself. The car had been a present newly bought for himself in the 1980s when the excesses of that period made it compulsory to own a vehicle like this. Unfortunately twenty years later and about the same number of additional waist inches, it made him look quite ridiculous. Herb was convinced he was still the zenith of cool, partly due to the fact that no one had the courage to tell Herb how utterly ludicrous he looked. They sped out of Fairfax on the small lanes that wound haphazardly across the countryside.

"What should I do?" said Nash, after an awkward period of silence.

"There's no choice. You have to give yourself up. Clear your name!" shouted Herb over the roar of the engine.

"Oh yeah, great idea! Let's sit in prison again trying to argue that a man more than three hundred years old, who's possibly in cahoots with the Devil,

killed a load of people using an invisible heat-ray that came out of his index finger! That'll be the shortest trial in history, although it won't, because whilst we're there the Universe will implode around our ears. Good idea, Herb, you idiot," thought John.

"Yeah, I agree with John," said Nash. "If we try to explain that, they'd lock the door and throw away the key."

"Who's John?"

Nash pointed to his head.

Herb shook his.

"Look, if you're not going to hand yourself in at least let me help you with your head. I have a friend, Donovan King, he's a priest who helped me straighten myself out in the late-1960s when everyone was tripping their tits off."

The wind whipped Herb's preposterous comb-over into his eyes as they sped along with the car roof down to enjoy one of the rare moments in the British calendar when it wasn't raining. John didn't know what would happen if this mysterious vicar was let loose on Nash's head, or more importantly his soul. It was up to him to get them out of this situation and he'd have to use his one and only good lead to do it. But to do that he'd have to convince Herb that this was in Nash's best interests.

"Look, Nash, we both want to get rid of each other and you want to clear your name. The only person that connects Sandy and Ian to what we know is that reporter from The World Today, Fiona Foster. Why don't you give her an exclusive interview and set the record straight about what happened in Geneva, whilst I find out what she knows about Tavistock?" suggested John cleverly.

"I like that idea better than having some priest mess about with my brain. Herb, I need you to get hold of Fiona Foster at The World Today. Tell her I want to do an exclusive interview, and it must be today," demanded Nash.

"Look, it's your life, Nash, but if you will insist on doing this you need to give me time to set it up. I can't just get hold of her immediately like that. Come back to the flat. I'll make some calls and you, and your imaginary friend, can sleep on it," replied Herb.

"Is this imaginary, fatty?" thought John, as he lifted Nash's middle finger up in Herb's direction.

*****

Not since the hotel in Camden over a month ago had Nash woken up in a comfortable bed. It was even longer since his mind had been this clear and his body so relaxed. In fact it was, as he recalled, the first time in some years that he'd woken up in a nice bed without a hangover, a full memory of where he was and what he'd done the day before.

There was no doubt that Nash had used and been abused by alcohol. Performing onstage had always felt as alien to him as a cat trying to roller skate. Thousands of adoring fans waited expectantly every night for the person they thought he was to perform on cue. It was a persona that Nash knew he could never live up to, as much as he tried. Writing the music was what drove him on, not playing it to thousands. It was the messages in the music he wanted to get across to the public, not just a catchy, three-minute tune that they could dance to.

When the band had been propelled into the spotlight it meant he was forced to play in front of bigger audiences, and only alcohol gave him the confidence to perform. It was this enigmatic, yet inebriated, version of Nash that the fans really loved and he hated them for it. All this doppelgänger did was reinforce the illusion of success, whilst the real Nash grieved the failure of each song and project to achieve a greater purpose. The consequence of which was he drank more in a vain attempt to achieve it.

In latter years he no longer used alcohol to build his confidence: alcohol was using him to satisfy its own addiction. When days merged with nights, friends transposed with strangers and normality was easily substituted for celebrity, it was the gang of four that were really in control. Alcohol, cocaine, acid and sex had executed a slow hostile takeover, self-appointing themselves as his management team. Was it them that freed his mind to write brilliant music, or was there a more fundamental innate ability somewhere in the back office struggling for recognition? He didn't know, but the fear of not knowing had always driven him to 'back the management'. Surely they knew what they were doing?

Today he was free of them. Without John with him, the last month would have been the same old story. An endless night of binge drinking, staggering from one party to the next, oblivious of his own actions. Perhaps John had become his new drug? Who was really in control, him or John? When, or if, John ever left, what would remain of him?

"John, what do you do when I'm asleep?" asked Nash as he sat up against the headrest.

"To coin a phrase, Nash, I wander lonely as a cloud," thought John, who knew all too well what he did and it certainly wasn't sleep. John didn't like the question because he hated the real answer.

"What do you think about?" asked Nash, probing John's altogether ambiguous response.

"I think about everything, Nash," replied John, sensing an unusual air of pity towards him.

"Like what?"

"Mostly I think about things that I have no influence over," replied John.

"Tell me," asked Nash softly.

"I think about my mother and how devastating my death must have been and I hope she has found some way to overcome the grief. I think about my friends and sister. I think about what I could have achieved in

my life, if it had not been cut short. I think about the children I never had the chance to raise and the wife I never fell in love with. I think about why these things were robbed from me. I think about the millions and millions of souls that I have felt suffer, and I pray for them. I think about my father, and ask how he could have ended up in that place, when I know in my heart that he was a good man. Mostly I think about how I want nobody else that I love to suffer that fate, the fate that I have seen at the end of life. Finally, I remember that the key to most of this is finding Sandy and Ian."

Nash wished he hadn't asked. He wasn't good at dealing with emotion, and certainly wasn't good at offering advice. He'd usually say something stupid like, 'Never mind, it'll be all right in the end,' or, 'Look on the bright side.' Nash's advice was the equivalent of asking a mental health patient to 'pull yourself together'.

"What do I do when I'm asleep and you're thinking?"

"Dream mainly."

"What sort of dreams?"

"Some are downright pornographic and I get as far away as possible. Most are quite fascinating. It's clear your mind is packed with ingenuity. I see songs and lyrics building, like a painter experimenting with colours. A musical melody forged by memories, thought and unthought. I know it's only a matter of time before they emerge from your subconscious into something amazing. It's all in here, Nash, it's all you need."

Herb opened the door to Nash's bedroom. He was already dressed, if you can call denim shorts, flip-flops and an unbuttoned shirt 'dressed'. "Breakfast's up. Full Irish."

Nash knew all too well that 'full Irish' meant two pints of Guinness, an Irish coffee and anything that Herb found in his fridge that wasn't growing a bacterial culture on it and could be microwaved. Michel Roux, Herb was not.

Given Herb's cooking, John had expected his house to be on a scale between NATO air strike and communal squat: unclean, unloved and unfurnished. He had visualised it having an unnecessarily large collection of musical memorabilia that adorned every wall and hall, each with a personalised story that Herb would give without prompting, each one ending with, 'We were totally wasted.'

In reality Herb's house would have been quite at home in the pages of *Country Living* magazine. Every room was immaculately decorated with antique furniture that enticed you to explore further. The paintings were intelligent and well placed, and each small detail was lavish and thoughtful. Nash and Herb sat around the grand kitchen table like marble chess pieces waiting for battle. Around them the perfectly designed kitchen clashed incongruously with Herb's bespoke cooking style.

"How did you sleep?" asked Herb between gulps of Guinness.

"OK, I felt a bit strange when I woke up, though."

"Well, that's because you had an early night," Herb reminded him, "I did try to get a session going but you sent yourself to bed."

"That's why I felt strange. Good strange. My face didn't feel like I'd had it in a bowl of sewage all night. Did you manage to set up the interview with Foster?" said Nash, chewing on a spoonful of out-of-date dry cornflakes.

"Sort of."

It hadn't been easy for Herb to organise the interview. After all, he was now aiding and abetting a known suspect. Through various contacts he'd managed to source Fiona's number without raising too much suspicion. It was fair to say that Fiona had not initially been enthusiastic about doing it: from her reaction she had her own problems.

"She wants to meet you in Trafalgar Square at noon. She was very insistent about meeting somewhere crowded. According to my contacts she's hardly been in touch with anyone since the article you mentioned came out in the press," added Herb.

"We were trying to be inconspicuous. Why don't we get a banner made up just in case we're not spotted and a full-page spread in The Times *for good measure?"* thought John to Nash.

Herb downed the remaining half of his Guinness and collected up the dry bowls and inedible breakfast sacrifices.

"We need to talk about how to play this," John thought to Nash. "Whatever happens, don't mention me at any point, it might scare her off. What we need to do is find out who her source is. She's going to find it strange that we want to talk about Tavistock. There's absolutely no connection between you and it. So we need to invent one. Tell her you know Sandy and Ian. Tell her you want to find out more about how they died. Only give her a sniff of your story: we might not have too much time if you're identified in the crowd."

*****

"Sir, she's on the move. Over," came the message on Agent 15's radio from the operative stationed outside Fiona Foster's flat in Brick Lane.

"Where's she going? Over," came Agent 15's underwhelmed response.

"We picked up a mobile phone conversation this morning with an unknown caller who set up a meeting with a Nash Stevens at noon in Trafalgar Square. Over."

There was a long silence.

"Come again. Over," replied Agent 15.

"She's meeting a Nash Stevens in Trafalgar Square at noon. Over."

Agent 15 had been an undercover agent for a very long time and prided himself on his uncanny intuition to second-guess what people were going to do, often before they knew it themselves. This reliability had given him a reputation that meant failure just wasn't on the menu. As the most revered and trusted of MI5's agents, and the closest to the Prime Minister, he worked tirelessly for it to stay that way. In Agent 15's occupation it was unacceptable to receive news that made no sense like this.

How on earth did Nash Stevens connect to Fiona Foster? He'd done the homework. He knew every possible turn that she might make based on meticulous research of her friends, her political views and everywhere she went. He even knew what bands she liked, and 'The Wind-up Merchants' weren't one of them. There must be something he'd missed, and he wasn't going to miss it again.

"Okay, this is a level one surveillance operation. I want Trafalgar Square surrounded by agents. I want microphones in every nook and teams on every exit. I want it all and I want it yesterday. Do you understand me? OVER!" shouted Agent 15 across all frequencies.

"Understood. Over," came several replies all at once.

Agent 15 jumped out of his seat, eager to be there to ensure that nothing was left to chance. Speed was of the essence. By the time he'd started the engine on his blacked-out Land Rover Discovery, he'd opened and closed eight doors, three times each, at world record pace.

*****

"I'll drop you off here and keep circling," said Herb. "Here's your mobile phone. I found it at the hotel before you left for your jaunt in Geneva. If you need to get out quickly, call me."

Nash jumped nimbly out of the Porsche before it pulled away.

Trafalgar Square was teeming. As one of the most popular London landmarks, it was crowded almost twenty-four hours a day. In the daytime it was the art galleries and statues that drew the crowds and by the evening its rowdy bars and nightclubs made up the entertainment. It was the heart of a vibrant and exciting city, and Saturday afternoon was when visitor numbers were at their peak. Whatever reasons Fiona had for choosing it, solitude was not one of them.

Nash walked through the crowd, hoping that his dark glasses and hood would avert the gaze of any devoted fans. In London, people would barely notice another human being if they were painted fluorescent orange, naked and running through the fountains of the Square pretending to be a horse. But they were able to pick out a minor celebrity at five hundred yards in the dead of night.

Nash took up position on a bench next to one of the stone lions that stood in each corner of the Square around Nelson's Column. Trying to balance being unremarkable and inquisitive at the same time, he tried to pinpoint his interviewer. John noticed an old man selling bird food to the public at the other end of the Square. All around him a throng of pigeons were jockeying for position, each eyeing up the potential for a free meal or possibly, for some, an unfortunately discarded cigarette butt. This must be the centre of the Universe for pigeons and he considered the possibility that in their search for Sandy, he just might be sitting on top of this stone lion, watching them. John moved Nash's head around in search of any unusually big specimens.

"Can you stop moving my head around like that, it makes me look like the girl from *The Exorcist*," barked Nash nervously, glancing around to see if anyone had noticed him.

"Sorry, just wondered if any of these are Sandy or Ian. Too much to hope, I guess."

Neither of them noticed that a middle-aged blonde woman had taken the seat next to them and was sitting closer than any two strangers would naturally sit. The mild spring wind that was circling around them blew her long wavy hair into Nash's face.

"Do you mind? There's loads of space around here, love," whispered Nash over his left shoulder.

"Do you want the interview or not?" the woman replied without making eye contact with her subject.

The woman was holding a dictaphone that she planted quickly into the pocket of her neat leather jacket. Tired and dishevelled, an uncharacteristic appearance for someone in Fiona Foster's profession, she was also a lot older than Nash had imagined, the wrinkle lines on her face bringing undue attention to her years, something that a generous helping of foundation would no doubt have fixed.

"Yes," said Nash apologetically in response to her question. "I'm sorry I didn't know it was you. I didn't know what you looked like."

"No, nor do I anymore," replied Fiona, who was peering around as much as Nash had been. "I don't have long, it's not safe here for either of us."

"Either of us?"

"I'm being watched," said Fiona, as her attention was drawn to a couple sitting on a bench nearby. The girl was wearing a puffer jacket, which seemed excessive given the relatively warm yet breezy day. On the top of the National Gallery her eyes were drawn to a shard of sunlight that momentarily reflected off a piece of glass.

"You're being watched. I'm sorry I thought it was me that was in trouble. Are you telling me I've just walked out of the rain and into a storm?"

"It's possible. Look, let's get this done. Why did you choose me? I know you could have gone to a journalist with a much higher profile and a greater readership than my paper. This isn't about you, is it?" asked Fiona, her journalistic instincts highly tuned to the possibility that all was not as it seemed.

This response didn't come as a surprise to John. It was far too easy for an idiot like Herb to set up this liaison quite so quickly. Fiona clearly had put her life on the line to be here and she wouldn't have done that for a scoop.

"Turn the microphone up, I can't hear them clearly enough," demanded Agent 15 from his hidden location somewhere around the Square, via radio to the woman in the puffer jacket.

"I need to know about Tavistock," said Nash.

"Then buy my newspaper. I'm not here to enlighten you, Mr. Stevens, quite the opposite," replied Fiona angrily, although her tone of voice remained level and low to avoid drawing any attention.

"What do I do?" Nash thought to John.

"Get to the point."

"Sandy Logan and Ian Noble aren't dead," announced Nash, expecting her to make the universal sign language for madman before making a swift exit.

"Impossible," said Fiona and Agent 15, both in unison from their positions hundreds of yards away from each other.

"Extremely unlikely yes, impossible no," refuted Nash.

"They are dead, I've seen the DNA reports," said Fiona.

"Me, too," reiterated Agent 15.

"Whatever you do, don't mention reincarnation," thought John.

"You're wasting my time. How could you possibly think they are still alive?"

"I didn't say they were still alive. I said they weren't dead. It's a subtle difference. I don't know about the DNA reports, but they didn't recover their bodies, did they?"

"That's because there was nothing left of them, you imbecile," Agent 15 muttered to himself.

"That doesn't mean they're not dead, though, does it. What proof have you got?" said Fiona.

"A mutual friend, John Hewson, has seen them both, and I believe him implicitly," replied Nash.

"Nice one, Nash. Which part of 'don't mention my name' didn't you understand?"

"I want everything we have on a John Hewson," Agent 15 told the colleague sitting next to him. "Whilst you're at it I want every possible test known to man done on the samples of Ian and Sandy's DNA. Get the lab on it immediately."

Fiona Foster sat in quiet contemplation. Her instincts told her that not only was this a lie, it was also a trap. A way of discrediting her or even exposing her to further dangers.

"Clearly you are a total madman. Thank you for putting me in even more danger than I think I'm currently in," said Fiona, standing up to leave.

"What do I do now?" thought Nash.

"Stall her."

In a panic, Nash grabbed Fiona by the hand spun her around and planted a lingering kiss on her lips.

"You can't stop yourself, can you? Surely you must know other ways than that?"

"I panicked," thought Nash in reply.

Considering the anger demonstrated by Fiona's face and her clenched fist, John could see things were not improved. Fearing that this might be the end of their only lead, he took things into his own hands.

"I know what they were making in Tavistock. Sandy told me, I mean John told me. What they are developing there must be stopped," said John taking control of the conversation through a quick and unauthorised mission to Nash's vocal cords.

The sudden change to Nash's accent and tone gave her further reason to flee. But she couldn't help thinking that if this information was true it could only have come from someone entrenched in the government itself, or someone who'd been inside Tavistock.

"You could have got that from my article? What is it called, the thing you say they are making?"

John didn't know, he'd bluffed and lost. There was no way of stalling her any longer. As she left, a London bus caught his eye as it passed the South African Embassy. The advert along its side, that until recently had been advertising a fast-food restaurant, now read EMORFED in bold, luminous two-foot-high letters. As quick as it had been there it was gone again.

"It's called Emorfed," John called out to Fiona through the crowd.

"You couldn't know that," she said with her back to him.

"I need to know where your information is coming from," asked John.

Fiona returned to the wooden bench and sat still for a moment. Should she tell him? He knew as much as her contact did, and that person had given more information on Tavistock than anyone. More than anything she wanted to uncover the secrets, to find out if the government was up to their necks in it as she suspected. The strange calls, suspicious noises and people following her was enough evidence to tell her that she was getting closer to the answer. Could she trust him? She took out her pad and pen from her handbag and quickly wrote something, folded the paper in two and passed it to John.

"If I give you this, I never want you to contact me again, understood?"

"That depends on what it says," replied John as he opened it.

"I want to know what it says. Where's the camera, why can't I see this on-screen?" screamed Agent 15. The dense crowd was obscuring the dozen cameras and CCTV.

"Thank you. You have my word," replied John.

"I want her picked up now. I need to know what was written on that piece of paper. Leave Nash, but have him followed," shouted Agent 15, now more animated than his calm character would normally allow.

Nash and John watched as Fiona hurried away from the Square. As she reached the subway to the Tube station two men, who had been reading papers at the news-stand near the entrance, scooped her up by both arms and bundled her into a parked car. In a matter of seconds she and it were gone.

"Shit," Nash whispered, having re-established control over his voice. "What should we do?"

"There's nothing we can do for her at the moment. Call Herb, Let's get out of here before it's us as well."

Nash dialled the number. "Herb, let's go."

"Did you see that, two blokes just bundled a woman into an unmarked Volvo?" replied Herb down the phone, as his Porsche came around the Square without delay. Herb hadn't come to a stop before Nash was in the passenger seat.

"Get a shift on, Herb!" shouted Nash.

"Are we being followed?" thought John as he spun Nash's head around once more.

"I can't see anyone," said Nash. "What did it say on the paper?"

"It suggested we've got one final visit to make," replied John.

The black surveillance helicopter far above their heads locked onto their position and proceeded to follow the car through the city.

CHAPTER SIXTEEN

EMORFED

"Do you know how many meetings I still have today, Agent 15?" the Prime Minister said, leaning across the table towards the secret agent.

Agent 15 shrugged.

"Twenty-seven," Byron stated. "It's 9.24 in the morning and I have already had four meetings. So that's thirty-one in total. As you can no doubt appreciate, that means time and speed are critical factors when you're the Prime Minister."

Agent 15's gormless expression continued to lack understanding.

"What I'm saying to you is, I'm a very busy man, and for the last twelve minutes you have sat in my office staring vacantly at me, occasionally opening your mouth producing no audible sound."

Agent 15 opened his mouth and his eyeballs scurried into the top left of his eye sockets in a vain attempt to make sense of his retained memories. His mouth shut in disgust, frustrated that his friend, the brain, was making him look stupid again.

"WHAT DO YOU WANT?" Byron shouted, slamming his fists onto the table and dislodging a number of official documents to the floor.

The sudden impact shook Agent 15's brain into life. His mouth smiled in victory.

"I think you need to cancel some of your meetings, sir," said Agent 15, connecting his mouth and brain successfully for the first time since he'd entered the room.

"If this advice is based on your inability to talk at more than four words a minute, then I'm afraid that'll be a no. Unless you have something important to tell me?"

Over the last twenty-four hours Agent 15 had struggled to reconcile the pieces of the jigsaw that he'd uncovered. Explaining it to someone else would be the equivalent of trying to successfully explaining the offside rule to a two-year-old child. It was always more difficult to explain something when in your heart you didn't truly understand it yourself. It was important he got it right: after all, he had a reputation to uphold. Blurting out an incoherent list of information was likely to get him demoted or, with this particular news, possibly sectioned. All night he'd spent trying to formulate how to do it, to communicate it so that he came out on the other side untarnished. Ready for the plunge, he drew a deep breath and crossed his fingers.

"Sandy Logan, Ian Noble not dead...um...Nash Stevens went to see Fiona Foster...er...mysterious man helping them...we think he's meant to be dead, too...Emorfed...piece of paper, don't know what's on it...secret lab...um...DNA not right."

It hadn't gone the way he'd planned it.

Byron's pupils expanded on every part of Agent 15's garbled briefing. Still perplexed, he casually picked up his phone. Agent 15's heart stopped, expecting the Prime Minister to have him carted off. He wouldn't really blame him if he did.

"Alice, cancel all my morning meetings," he said calmly before replacing the receiver. Agent 15 finally exhaled the deep breath that he'd taken moments earlier.

"Let's start at the beginning. How on earth can Sandy and Ian be alive?" demanded Byron in a whisper, in case anyone else might hear such an absurd phrase and believe he, too, had gone barking mad.

"Not alive, sir. I said not dead, it's a subtle but important difference apparently."

"Sorry for being picky, but if someone isn't dead how can they *not be alive?*" Byron replied sarcastically.

"Well, if part of them survived they could be neither dead nor alive, so I'm told."

"Let's backtrack," appealed Byron. "How do you know this?"

"This is where it gets truly strange. Our friend, Nash Stevens, met with Fiona Foster…"

"Stop. This would be the Nash Stevens that is the main suspect in an international murder hunt. The same Nash Stevens that slept with my daughter and the Nash Stevens who would appear to have absolutely nothing in common with Tavistock?" interrupted Byron, losing his patience.

"It would appear to be the very same, although I think there must be some connection. He told Fiona Foster that a John Hewson had told him that he'd been in contact with Sandy and Ian."

"And you believed him?"

"No, not at first, but then I asked the Scientific Intelligence Agency to investigate and…"

"I'm sorry, but who the sodding hell are the Scientific Intelligence Agency?"

"Right," hesitated Agent 15, "this is a bit sensitive. It's a secret laboratory that explores some of the stranger cases that the government uncovers."

"Oh I see. This'll be the one that NO ONE has told me about," thundered Byron.

"With respect, sir, it's above your security clearance…"

"I'm the bloody Prime Minister, how can something be above my security clearance? Can I remind you at this point that not only is your job on the line here, but also quite possibly your life," warned Byron. He knew it was an idle threat, but when you back a vicious creature into a corner don't be surprised if you return missing significant and valued bodyparts.

It was a paradox that, although he worked for the Prime Minister, Agent 15 knew far more about the way government worked than Byron did, and he wasn't alone. There were hundreds of people that really controlled the country, silently manoeuvring it into position like the path of a giant container ship. Quite often the captain at the helm knew little about what was going on in the engine room, unless it was impossible for him not to know. This was one of those occasions. All concerned would have preferred if their activities remained concealed from the other in case the situation was made permanent. The Prime Minister knew now, and he did have the power to change it permanently. Unbeknown to him, they also had the power to remove him if they so wished. In a battle of hundreds against one, the power of one will generally lose. It was the first time in Byron's premiership that he realised that the well-run ship was not being powered by him, just steered.

"As I was saying, the SIA…"

"SIA?" Byron asked in a much less aggravated fashion.

"Scientific Intelligence Agency," Agent 15 repeated slowly.

Byron nodded to confirm his acceptance of this new department.

"Anyway, they ran every known test on the DNA samples of Sandy and Ian. What they found was most definitely their DNA, but the samples were found to be mutated."

Byron and Agent 15's facial expressions had traded places in the last ten minutes.

"Now, we already know that they found a large quantity of bird DNA, probably pigeon, amongst the remains of the bombing. What we didn't know until now is that these aren't separate samples. It's one sample. The two strands in the double helix come from each creature, one human and one pigeon. We also didn't know that there were missing links in the DNA structure," stated Agent 15 regaining his composure, sure that Byron was still reeling from not knowing about the SIA.

"So, what conclusions have they come to?"

"There's absolutely no way of categorically proving this as there's only ever been one suspected example in the past. But the portion of DNA that's missing is the part they associate with the creation of emotions. You could say it's the part that determines the make-up of the soul."

Calmly Byron sat contemplating what all this meant, being careful not to ask any stupid questions yet still interrogate the truths that Agent 15 was presenting to him. The revelation of the SIA had already damaged the level of trust he felt towards his ally.

"How can DNA govern the soul? I thought that was all about how you were moulded by society, by community?"

"Apparently, although I'm no expert, it's both. You can't escape your genetics completely. If you have been built with fundamental weakness, there's not much you can do about it."

"I should have guessed that, given what I know about Emorfed. So what has happened to them?"

"SIA believe that Sandy and Ian have been reincarnated," announced 15. "In all likelihood they would have been reincarnated as pigeons, if the last case is anything to go on."

It was the conclusion that Byron had already made in his own head. Although this outcome was unlikely, so was the idea that there were government agencies that he knew nothing about. His concern was not for the why or the how, but the what. If the only people outside of the government that knew about Emorfed were still alive, what repercussions would it have on the plans he'd already set in motion?

"You don't look as shocked as I thought you might."

"My only concern is for Emorfed. If there is even the remotest chance that you are right, then we need to find them. They must be destroyed," replied Byron.

"If I'm to do that, sir, then I need to know more about Emorfed. What is it exactly?"

Byron paused. Like the captain of the container ship, he was uncomfortable giving someone from the engine room unnecessary information, although he accepted that without the engine room the ship would hit the rocks and Byron could not afford for that to happen. Whether he trusted him or not, he had no choice but to secure his help.

"Imagine a world with no crime, no murder and no war. Imagine a world of harmony and peace. A world in which you would feel safe every time you left your home. A world in which every race, religion and creed lived without prejudice. A world in which human beings had no dependence on anything other than themselves. There would be no reliance on cigarettes, alcohol, drugs, sex, power or control. This government could really govern. It could set the human race on the right and proper path. In a world like that we would save billions of pounds of pointless expenditure previously destined to fail. That is the world that Emorfed will bring. A new utopia," Byron said calmly.

"It's the ultimate nanny state," replied Agent 15, with more than a touch of anxiety in his voice.

"Who wouldn't want to live in a world like that?"

"But could people really live in a world like that? Isn't it those conditions that make us human?"

"NO. Those conditions, as you call them, have limited the human race's potential. It's the wrong side of human nature that has destroyed millions of lives and could quite possibly destroy this planet if we carry on without action." Byron's eyes burnt with a fire of conviction so fierce you could have toasted marshmallows off it.

"Why do you want to do it?" asked Agent 15, shocked by the words coming out of the Prime Minister's mouth, as if some invisible hypnotist was orchestrating him from afar.

"Without addiction and human frailty the world will be free. Imagine the society we would live in if it was devoid of jealousy or desire. The savings for the Home and Health departments alone would be enormous. On top of that the people will reward me for this freedom by keeping this party in power, and you will be rewarded for your support, Agent 15. You will not be forgotten."

Agent 15 held his own counsel. The whole idea scared and intrigued him in equal measure. Maybe this therapy would rid him of his OCD affliction, but at what cost to who he was?

"How was this substance discovered?"

"It wasn't discovered. It was given to me."

"Who gave it to you?" questioned Agent 15, whose natural curiosity for the truth was searching between the lines. The inference was that this was a natural, rather than a man-made substance.

"That will remain mine to guard, it is of no consequence to you. Will you support me or not?"

"I will support you, but I expect to be rewarded well for my efforts."

"You will be. Now tell me how Nash Stevens came to know that Sandy and Ian were alive."

"Not dead."

"Whatever."

"That part is the biggest mystery. Nash said a John Hewson had told him. There appears to be no connection between the two of them. However, there is a connection between John Hewson and Sandy Logan."

"Go on…" prompted Byron.

"In the mid-nineties they were both involved in the animal rights movement along with another friend of ours."

"Violet Stokes," answered Byron correctly.

"Our missing link," said Agent 15. "I have Foster in my care but she refuses to give me anything that would lead me to her, or anyone around her."

"Well, let's bring in John Hewson, let's see what he knows."

"That's not possible, sir, he's not alive either."

"Hold on, does that mean he's dead? I'm getting confused," asked Byron.

"Maybe," answered Agent 15 cautiously. "It was a very unusual case. He appears to have died in an accident that, according to eyewitnesses, involved an elderly gentleman who was never formally found or interviewed. The suspect disappeared without trace. John's autopsy states that he died from a gunshot wound, which suggests it wasn't an accident. We had his grave exhumed and I passed the results on to the SIA for tests to be done. Want to know the results?"

"There was a piece of DNA missing. I'm guessing it's the same piece that was missing from Logan and Noble?" replied a perceptive Byron.

"Dead on. So it's possible he is not altogether dead either."

"Reincarnated as well? Jesus, I'm worried about walking the dog tonight in case he asks me if I want to go for a pint."

"Not this one, sir. There was no other alien material in his DNA. We just don't know what has happened to him."

The clock on the Prime Minister's wall had just clicked past 10.45 a.m. He'd missed four meetings. What worried him more was that his paradigm on life had been flipped on its head in just over an hour. The one thing that hadn't changed was his desire to deliver Emorfed and make the world a better place.

"You mentioned a piece of paper," said Byron.

"Fiona Foster passed a piece of paper to Nash Stevens. We couldn't see what it said from our surveillance positions and she won't tell us what was on it. We know from her conversation with Nash that it's linked to Fiona's contact, and it might lead to Sandy and Ian. We had Nash followed so we know where he is. Do you want me to bring him in?"

"Not yet. If we want to know what's on that paper we need to find another way. If we bring them in, they won't be able to lead us to Violet."

It was often said of Byron that he would have sold his own grandmother if it worked in his favour. It wasn't just a figure of speech, he really would have. Byron knew that there was no obvious connection between Nash and Sandy, but there was a connection between Nash and him. She was called Faith.

"Where is Nash now?" Byron asked.

"Kensington. Flat B, 106 Gloucester Road."

Byron reached inside his jacket pocket to remove a mobile phone at least ten years old and the size of a house brick. It was nothing like the type of mobile phone that was widely available. Byron was a technophobe who hated even having a mobile, even if it was a useful device from time to time. He'd refused to upgrade it to something more advanced with fancy applications and time-consuming features. Why did he need to know where he'd parked his car? He could just *remember* where he'd parked it. Why did he need to know what was on TV tonight? He never got time to watch it. Why did he need to know what the weather was like? He just looked out of the window. All he wanted to use his phone for was...calling people. That was the point with a phone, wasn't it? It didn't matter to Byron that it was the weight of a gold bar.

Faith's phone was a little different: in her view it could do anything. It could find out who won the 1978 FA Cup final, get traffic reports for the M25, and tell her the time in Taiwan. All of which were utterly pointless to a seventeen-year-old who had no interest in football, couldn't drive and didn't have the remotest idea where Taiwan was. It also had as many ringtones as money could buy. At the moment it was humming

'Papa Don't Preach' by Madonna, the ringtone she had purposely chosen for her father. She considered not answering. Her father didn't often ring but when he did it was important, usually more important to him than to her.

"Hi, Dad, I'm just about to go into a class," she lied. "Can I call you back?"

"I'm sure you can be a little late, how often do we get the chance to talk these days?" replied Byron in an uncharacteristically friendly tone. They both knew that he would never willingly suggest that she was late for anything. Lateness was something Byron hated almost above all other things. "How's college?"

"It's fine, I've got a sociology lecture next."

"Ah very important, learning about the world and how society should work," he replied, hoping that there would be no need for such lectures in the future if Emorfed worked as planned.

"Dad, I'm not being funny, but you never ask me about college, are you okay?"

"Yes, I'm fine. Just because I don't normally doesn't mean that I can't, does it? How's your friend, Nash, have you heard from him recently?"

"That would be quite difficult. He's on the run from the police and I think you said you would have him shot by the SAS if he came within a mile of me," she replied sarcastically.

"I know I did, I think I might have overreacted a wee bit there. I know from what your mother told me you're really very fond of him?"

"I am, Dad, but I can't believe Mum told you that."

"I also understand that he is in the clear now. The police in Geneva have arrested a suspect." Byron thought nothing of lying to his own daughter: he lied to the whole country on a daily basis and after all she was one of them. "Why don't you go and see him?"

"I don't know where he is."

"Well, I do. I thought as an apology I would tell you, as long as you did something for me?"

The bait was on the hook.

"What do you want me to do?" Faith asked hesitantly.

"He has a flatmate called John Hewson, who has, by accident, received some very important government information. It's written down on a scrap of paper, which was planted on him by one of our agents, by mistake. It's very important and it mustn't fall into the wrong hands. I need you to get it for me," asked Byron, his ability for thinking on his feet on overdrive.

"Why don't you just go and get it yourself?"

"I think, given what Mr. Stevens has gone through in the last few weeks, it would be a little insensitive of us if we sent a crack squad of agents in to recover a scrap of paper. On top of that I thought you might like to see him. But if you don't we'll go with the crack squad idea."

Faith couldn't escape the fact that she was being used, or the fact that she was desperate to see Nash. After all, how else was she going to get the chance to see him. She didn't have to find the piece of paper, she just had to look for it. If she failed, she failed.

"Okay, Daddy, I'll do it for you, but I might have to stay with him overnight so that I can get the information whilst he's sleeping. It'll be easier that way," she replied, knowing if she was going to lose the battle she might win the war. Faith had inherited more than a bit of her father's ability for game-playing.

"So be it, call me in the morning when you have what I need, and Faith, if he takes advantage of you in any way, I'll still have him shot," replied Byron as he turned off the phone. "I'll do more than that if I get my hands on him. Agent 15, set up a surveillance team outside the house. Once you have what you need, make sure you keep her somewhere safe."

"Consider it done, sir. I'll lead it myself."

Of all the missions that he'd been given over his career, none had been so interesting, yet so surreal.

Torn between his loyalty to the Prime Minister and his concerns as to the whole Emorfed strategy and whether it was really in the interest of the British people. He reminded himself his job was to do, not to grow a moral compass.

As he reached the door a flash of blue light hit the twelve-foot-high windows with a dull thud, basking the room around him. Before investigating the curious light, a voice, rather than a door, stopped him from leaving the room.

"One more thing before you go. My hand has been forced and I need to move my plans forward. Go to the Party Chairman and ask him to announce an election for June the 19th. It's time to get re-elected, and by the time the election comes around the people will do exactly what I tell them," announced Byron.

CHAPTER SEVENTEEN

THE POP-STAR AND THE POLITICIAN'S DAUGHTER

"We're probably homing pigeons," Sandy tutted to himself in mock impersonation of Ian, as he caught his breath perching precariously on the top of a statue.

For two straight days they had flown, each route influenced by Ian's intuition that this time they were definitely heading in the right direction. So far, Ian, Sandy and their uninvited flock had reached no fewer than four incorrect destinations. Twice Ian had led them back to the large oak tree in the valley from where they had started. Once, he'd taken them to the blackened remains of the Tavistock Institute, whilst the highlight of his ineptitude was their two hundred-mile journey to Bristol Temple Meads train station. Sandy understood the first three errors of judgement: after all, they had been *home* for Ian at some point in his lives. Ian's only explanation for the Bristol disaster was that he'd been delayed on a train there for eight hours in nineteen ninety-three.

It was after this explanation that Sandy took charge of navigation in order to reduce the potential of Ian leading them to another part of the world where his twisted mind recalled a randomly insignificant event. Whether it was by design, utter fluke, or a little of both, they had finally reached their destination, London. In the end they'd simply followed the M4 motorway, hoping that they'd eventually find the capital of England and not Swansea.

THE POP-STAR AND THE POLITICIAN'S DAUGHTER

The shadow of Nelson's Column painted on the ground beneath them proved that they had indeed reached their desired destination. Ian and Sandy watched as their adopted pigeon family explored the tourist attractions, as equally bewildered as they were intrigued to see how their city cousins lived. Their journey here had not been without incident. Twice they had been ambushed by buzzards on the lookout for a tasty lunch, only escaping thanks to the amazing efforts of their followers. It had surprised Sandy that they fought off these predators as if he was one of their own. But in the flock's mind that is exactly what they were. It doesn't matter how strange you look or act, family is family and you always defend what you hold most sacred. That's what the pigeons had done. It wasn't a conscious decision, just instinct.

"I'm starving," grumbled Ian. "Let's get one of those hot dogs over there?"

"Remember what you are, Ian," replied Sandy. "Maybe we'd best stay as low-key as possible."

This was easier said than done when you were thirty percent bigger than the thousands of pigeons that called Trafalgar Square their home. Sandy had already seen a small child pulling on its mother's jumper saying, 'Mummy, look at that pigeon, he's massive.' It was to Sandy's relief that the mother was too preoccupied to take any notice of the young lad.

"I think we'd best eat from the conventional sources like the rest of the *family,*" said Sandy, pointing a wing to where the pigeons from the oak tree were scurrying around, dubiously analysing the seeds being scattered by the excitable tourists.

If a pigeon can look dumbfounded, then this was their expression. The concept of being fed just didn't make sense to them. Normally they searched high and low for their food and this just seemed far too easy. They assessed the collection of discarded seeds with the same suspicion as a housewife confronted with a door-to-door salesman promising to save her money on the gas bill. Were the seeds poisoned? Would something come down and attack them the moment they picked one up, some deadly trap? Once one of them had weighed up the risk of certain death against a free meal and nothing untoward had happened, the rest willingly followed suit. Having gained hundreds of flying hours, Ian and Sandy elegantly glided down to join them.

A horde of confident urban pigeons hopped around a weathered-looking man, cooing in greeting of an old friend. They stalked the gaggle of people surrounding him, as he handed out small, one-pound bags of seeds. Some of the birds landed on his shoulder in order to carry favour as if it was normal behaviour. The encircling Japanese tourists, eyes glued behind almost invisibly small, futuristic cameras, pointed at the wonder that was a bird eating a seed. Over the crescendo of finger-clicking and wing-flapping, a group of Americans were about to burst with excitement.

"Hey, look at that, a man selling bird seed, how quaint. Come and look at this Bobby, ain't it sweet?" announced a seismically loud American pensioner from under the darkest sunglasses ever made, despite the sun having not been sighted in London since late-April.

Sandy stopped in his tracks overcome by the strength of her perfume, a sickly aroma so potent that it must have been hosed onto her using a water-cannon. Bobby, a man so large he took up both sides of his family tree, barged in past the Japanese contingent who had been photographing every possible combination of their group standing next to every possible combination of pigeon. With the Japanese knocked down like skittles, Big Bobby continued to shove his way through the crowd until he had grabbed the seed seller's attention, whether the man liked it or not.

"Hey, buddy, how much money to feed the birdies?" he bellowed in a volume that suggested everyone he talked to was profoundly deaf.

"Five pounds a bag, governor," he replied, moving to block out Bobby's view of the one-pound sign on the railings. Having rebounded from the floor like Subbuteo players, the Japanese group giggled at his stupidity like a bunch of schoolkids.

"Wow, that's amazing! I'll have ten bags. What a bargain. I've got them, Betty!" he hollered, as both of them made a beeline to the pavement where Sandy and Ian had just landed quietly to avoid attention.

"Hey, Bob, look at that. Get the camera, honey, those are the biggest doves I've ever seen," yelled Betty.

While Bobby tried to excavate the world's biggest camera from amongst the other rigmarole that was contained within his massive bumbag, Betty weakly threw seeds at the two birds.

"Did she just call us doves?" Sandy said to Ian.

"Ya, I fink so," he mumbled through a mouthful of sunflower seeds, a handful of which landed on Sandy after an unusually strong throw for someone as frail and thin as Betty.

"Hey, careful, watch where you're throwing that," Sandy said spontaneously in Betty's direction.

Betty froze to the spot. It wasn't the first time that she'd heard voices, but usually they came from inside her head. After eighty-one years of devout Christianity you assumed, even expected, that sort of stuff to happen eventually. Even if you had to convince yourself that you'd heard it.

"Bobby, did you hear that?" croaked Betty.

"I didn't hear anything!" he shouted, probably because the only thing anyone heard when Bob was around, was Bob.

THE POP-STAR AND THE POLITICIAN'S DAUGHTER

"Jesus Christ," coughed Sandy, spitting his mouthful of sunflower seeds onto the ground. "I thought slugs and snails were bad, but this shit tastes like bloody cardboard. Look, darling, I'm not on a diet."

Bob and Betty gawped in Sandy's direction, the first waking silence to surround the pair in months. Bobby was the sort of person that believed in anything, however strange or unlikely it might seem. Nothing was in the realm of the impossible. If you told Bobby that a giant lump of Angel Delight had just been fired at London by the Russians, he'd have looked up and shouted, 'Where?!' Not only was he willing to believe in anything, he was also totally unfazed by it.

"A talking pigeon, that's awesome. It must be some kind of robot," stated Bobby, leaning forward to pick Sandy up to get a better look at the way that it worked.

If Bobby had been totally at ease at the sight of an oversized, talking pigeon it was nothing to the shock that Sandy had that a human understood what he was saying. He had always thought that when Ian and Sandy talked to each other in English it was only them that understood each other. He'd guessed that they had been chirping all the time, but deciphered those sounds as English words, inaudible to pigeon or person. This proved not to be the case at all. They were speaking English and people heard them. Sandy jumped to one side to avoid Bobby's advancing chubby fingers.

"Get your filthy, fat hands off me."

"Hey, how did he know that? This isn't a robot, it's real. Quick, pass me the camcorder, honey, we've gotta get this on film. We'll be famous, Betty, just like I've always hoped."

"Ian, we need to get out of here. If they catch us on film, I think you can safely say we won't be low-key anymore."

"But Sandy, I'm still hungry. Let me just finish this lot off first," replied Ian, hoovering up as much of the free food as possible.

Bobby was already fumbling excitedly with the buttons of the camcorder and it wouldn't be long before he got what he needed.

"Ian, NOW! He's going to get us on film," shouted Sandy, pushing Ian away from his feast before launching himself into the air.

"It's always me, me, me, with you, Sandy."

Click went the sound of technology jumping into action. Bobby was waving his tree trunk-sized arms in the air in a sign of victory. Ian needed no more hints to get out of there.

"Did he get you on film?" Sandy asked, when Ian landed back on top of the stone lion next to him.

"I think he might have done," Ian replied meekly.

"Fantastic. You never fail, do you? Scrub that, you always fail, that's the problem. Now that obnoxious tourist will tell the world and every person in London will be on our tails."

"I'm sorry, Sandy. Let me make it up to you," pleaded Ian, head stooped like a scorned infant.

Limited by his options, and quite against Sandy's better judgement, he was going to allow him to do just that. At least he could try. Sandy couldn't afford to get caught, but he was quite happy if Ian did.

"After a lifetime of disappointing me, Ian, you are bound to get it right one day. I just hope for your sake that day is today. The only positive thing to come out of this is that we can ask someone for help because people will understand what we are saying. I want you to go and find Violet. Tell her where I am and that I need her help quickly."

"I promise I won't let you down this time. I think I'm only here because I need to repay you in some way. Where will I find Violet? I thought you said she was in hiding."

"She will be, but I know where. Go to Number 12, Blackhorse Way, you'll find her there. Once you've found her, bring her back to me."

*****

"Is it still out there, Herb?" asked Nash, whilst his manager peeked out of his net curtains into the evening sky.

"Yeah, it comes and goes but they're definitely still watching us, I can hear the hum of the blades going around," replied Herb, his bloated stomach impeding him from getting closer to the window and a better view of the sky. "What's the plan now?"

"I think only John can answer that question?"

Herb rolled his eyes, still unconvinced that Nash had been possessed and wasn't in fact just having the world's worst and longest bad trip. There was certainly no way that Herb was going to ask John the question himself: far too weird.

"Ask him, then," said Herb.

"John, what's our next move?"

"What's the date today?"

"It's the twenty-first of May," replied Nash.

"What day of the week is it?"

"Monday."

"Okay, Nash, the plan is tomorrow you get rid of me. Although I wouldn't raise your hopes up, things rarely go to plan. We can only go where we need to on a Tuesday, so I suggest we all chill out and hope that no one comes knocking at our door between now and then," replied John, so that both Nash and Herb heard the response.

"OK, very funny, Herb. Stop knocking the table," said Nash, as a light knocking noise came from the front door.

"I didn't, I swear."

John contemplated whether he had been given some additional powers that he'd not been told about when he was sent back to Earth. It was evident that when he was in the most difficult of spots the answer came to him as if by magic. There was the Polish cleaner in the hotel, the security guard at the airport, and the advertising sign on the bus in Trafalgar Square. If it wasn't him, then some other force, out of his control, was interfering. He really hoped it was him. Every time he was desperate for help it had come to him. The only difference this time was that he *didn't* want the knock at the door. Perhaps he did want it to happen but didn't know why?

"It was the front door alright," whispered Herb who, having made his way there, was now squinting through the spyhole.

"Don't open it, Nash. I don't care if it's The Queen," thought John.

"Who is it?" asked Nash, walking to the front door to have a look for himself as a second set of firmer knocks echoed through the hallway.

"I think…it's a girl," said Herb, whose eyesight was poor at the best of times. Nash's pace suddenly quickened.

"It's Faith," said Nash slightly too loudly, having bundled Herb out of the way.

"Hello, are you in there, Nash?" came the voice from the other side of the door.

"Who the hell is Faith?" John replied as he moved all of his soul up to Nash's eye sockets to get his own unique perspective.

"She's a friend. She's harmless, John: let me open the door. It would be good to have some company other than you two for a while. Please, John, before she leaves."

John peered again, first through his own spyhole of Nash's eyes, and then through the one in the door, to check out the young woman on the opposite side. At the door was a young, fashionably dressed twenty-something, although her real age had been concealed by the way she was tarted up for a night out. John was transfixed by her deep, beautiful blue eyes, like a Caribbean swimming pool enticing him to dive in. So vibrant and alive was this girl it crystallised his own loneliness for the first time. He, too, had only had a fat, bald roadie and a hairy-arsed popstar to look at and talk to for the last six weeks. Without answering Nash's plea, John placed his hand onto the door handle and opened it, just before Faith was about to give up and leave. She smiled at John, ran forward and gave him a long firm and lingering hug.

"I've missed you so much," she expired.

It was the first time that John remembered feeling happy and unburdened since he left his own body. Faith's very presence lifted his soul by simply walking in and smiling.

"If she's going to stay, for God's sake, shut the door," Herb wheezed as he stumbled towards the kitchen to top up his empty beer mug.

"Well, you're a sight for sore eyes. What are you doing here?" asked Nash.

"I've come to see you, of course. I was really worried about you. I've tried calling but only got your voicemail," replied Faith, still clinging to Nash like an infant monkey.

John was consumed by a new emotion that he couldn't find a name for. So far he'd only felt his past emotions, those attached to the physical form that he'd left behind. Just blurred memories and feelings from another life. Significant moments that he experienced triggered his emotions. Loneliness, love, guilt, fear, anger and hope had all been very real to John, even if the memories that they related to were not always clear.

Take the accident that caused his death. He only remembered cloudy visions of what happened. The figure of a man leaning over the bonnet of his car. The young girl with the lightning-white hair that he'd swerved to avoid. All echoes of his mind that lacked visibility, whilst the emotions linked to those events were as real as the pretty girl that stood before him.

What was new about Faith's entrance was that this emotion wasn't linked to a real-life event. This emotion was linked to Nash's real-life event. The name that he had been struggling for was longing. It might even be called jealously. Jealous that Nash was the one she was in love with and not him. It meant that his soul was evolving, reacting to real-life external stimulus and not confined to the ones from the past. His soul had some kind of future and the potential to change. John might have recognised the importance of this moment if he hadn't been distracted by Faith's bosom.

"How did you find me?" said Nash.

"Daddy told me where you would be."

"That was nice of him," said Nash, clearly in the same trance that John had fallen into.

John was not really following what Faith said: it was enough that her lips moved and captivating sounds came out. Then, as if his attention was catching him up, he took a double take, the specific words finally correcting themselves into the right order.

"Sorry, who's her father?"

"Byron T. Casey," Nash thought in reply.

"Who's he?"

"Prime Minister."

"Oh, Prime Minister, I see," replied John flippantly.

Cautiously, Herb returned to the lounge with an exceptionally large glass of red wine and a two-inch-wide cigar, already filling the room with a thick, grey smoke. Aware that Faith's arrival would mean another drinking session for one, he slumped onto the furthest sofa from the canoodling popstar and his latest groupie.

THE POP-STAR AND THE POLITICIAN'S DAUGHTER

"Daddy said that he's had Nash exonerated for the Geneva thing and that he wanted to send me over as a kind of apology. He's really sorry that they've been chasing you, Nash," said Faith, smiling innocently.

"Sorry to interrupt but who's she talking about, Nash?" asked Herb, from beneath his tatty copy of a 1970s *NME* magazine.

"Her father is Byron T. Casey."

"Have you gone bloody mad?" scorned Herb, jumping out of his chair with the force of a thousand volts attached to his buttocks. "She's the daughter of the very person who would like to see you banged up in the Tower of London while he watches the ravens take turns to peck your eyes out."

John was suddenly shocked out of his own dream. In the time that John had occupied Herb's world, he'd put him down as a whacked-out hippy who was incapable or unwilling to react with any level of concern. It wasn't as if Herb was in any significant trouble if Nash was caught. Therefore this unusual reaction was guided by a spontaneous and unconscious desire to protect. Maybe there was more to Nash and Herb's relationship than John had understood. Now that he was thinking clearly again, John knew Herb was right.

"It's all right, Herb, she hates her father," replied Nash.

"It's true, I do."

"Look, what I know about politicians is that they are vicious arseholes who will do anything to get what they want. At the moment Byron wants Nash, for more than one reason. One of those reasons is sitting in my living room. He's got a helicopter circling our house and it's not to keep an eye on her, it's to keep an eye on you. She has to leave," Herb shouted at Nash, attempting to frogmarch Faith to the door.

"He's right, Nash. I think it's a trick."

"Look, it's not a trick, she loves me. She's staying and that's that," snapped Nash, engaged in a bizarre tug-of-war with Herb over Faith's skintight clothes which were already bursting at their seams.

"You're a fool," raged Herb. "If she stays, then I go, and good luck to you and your friend, John. I'm done with both of you."

Releasing Faith from his grasp, he staggered out of the room more than a little inebriated from the night's alcoholic intake. Clumsily he slung his coat on back to front and pin-balled down the hallway before slamming the front door and tripping head first down the steps of the house. John heard a muffled, limping Scotsman lurching away from the house, clattering into empty dustbins as he went.

"Who's John, Nash? Is that your flatmate, John Hewson?" asked Faith now that the commotion had died down. Remembering her part of the deal with her father if she could get that out of the way she could spend the rest of the evening without guilt.

In John's mind the acknowledgement of his existence created an even stronger bond between them. No longer was this someone who Nash knew: he was now captivated by someone who knew he existed. It never entered his mind *how* she knew about him? What it meant of course was that the government knew about him. If they knew enough they could make the link to Sandy and find out every detail about him. How he died, and who he knew. The consequence of this was massive. It potentially put everyone that John knew in danger. Like a bee to honey, his only focus was on Faith and how to find more ways to connect to her.

"He's not so much my room-mate, more my... soulmate," replied Nash, unaware of the irony.

"Look can I stay here with you tonight?" asked Faith.

"Definitely," replied Nash and John in unison.

THE POP-STAR AND THE POLITICIAN'S DAUGHTER

*****

It was Tuesday morning and Nash was snoring loudly, crashed out in the middle of the king-sized bed in the opulent spare bedroom of Herb's house. As always, John was awake. But he wasn't the only one. Faith was out of bed, fumbling around in the dimness of Nash's room. Incapacitated by Nash, whose eyes were firmly shut in deep sleep, John was unable to see what she was doing. What was she doing? Focusing all his concentration on Nash's left eyelid, he managed to peel it open. There was Faith, semi-dressed in a skimpy, ivory silk nightie, rummaging around in the pockets of Nash's clothes.

'What was she looking for?' thought John.

Faith opened Nash's wallet and riffled through the receipts, cash and assorted oddities that he kept within it. She stared at some of the numerous photos of naked women stashed underneath his credit cards, a visual diary of previous conquests. Most women would have been enraged by finding such trinkets, but Faith went past them as if they were library cards. Finally she stopped rummaging as she unfolded a piece of notepaper. John knew instantly what it was. Fiona Foster had given it to him not more than twenty-four hours ago. To the unknowing eye the information would be meaningless, so her interest in it was intriguing at best. Faith assessed it for some time, before placing it back into its place. She shot a cautionary glance back at Nash.

"Hey, baby, you're awake."

John knew that Nash wasn't awake, even though one of his eyes appeared to be winking up at her. What should he do? Should he acknowledge her? He desperately wanted to speak to her as John, but he didn't have the courage to reveal himself. She'd freak out, wouldn't she?

THE POP-STAR AND THE POLITICIAN'S DAUGHTER

"Nash, wake up. WAKE UP!" John shouted internally.

Nash sat bolt upright searching around for the source that had so abruptly removed him from his slumbers. All he saw was Faith moving towards him like a beautiful dream. She approached the bed, leant over and kissed him on the lips.

"How was last night for you?" she whispered in his ear.

"Fantastic," replied Nash.

"Like watching your parents have sex. But worse," added John silently. "In fact much worse. Like directing your parents in a pornographic movie. The result of which is that you would be more than happy for someone to shoot you in the head at any point."

It wasn't pleasant having to live through the whole sordid evening of Nash and Faith, incapable of escape. On the positive side he had learnt some new moves. Although he didn't think he'd get to use them in his present situation. What made it worse was that it was with Faith. What he would have given to be in Nash's place instead of being in the weirdest and most surreal ménage à trois imaginable. Faith jumped out of bed and got dressed.

"I need to go, Nash. I said I'd be home by morning. If I don't, my dad will probably never let me out of the house again."

"Don't go, then. Stay here. Just for a little while at least?"

"There's nothing I'd rather do, but you don't know what he can be like. He's just too powerful for me."

"When will I see you again?"

"I don't know, but if everything goes well today I hope he'll never stop me seeing you again," she replied, leaning forward for one final kiss before she left the bedroom and made her way out of the house.

*****

THE POP-STAR AND THE POLITICIAN'S DAUGHTER

Hurrying down the front steps, Faith glanced anxiously at her watch to see if she was going to be late. A large, black Land Rover, clumsily parked on the kerb in front of the house, caught her attention. The passenger door swung open, blocking her route down the pavement.

"Hello, Faith. Had a good night, did you?" said a voice from the car.

"I thought my father's cronies wouldn't be too far away from here," she replied, her body frozen to the spot, eyes still focused with tunnel vision towards the horizon.

"I'm not one of his cronies, Faith. I'm far more than that. You might get to see much, much more of me in the coming years."

"I hope not," she murmured.

"What was on that piece of paper?"

At no point did Agent 15 look at his prey, always glaring forward, always coiled to pounce at a moment's notice and unaffected by the Medusa effect that had so befallen Nash and John.

"And...what if I didn't find it?"

"I hope for your sake you did. Otherwise you might find you don't have as many limbs tomorrow as you did yesterday. Stop wasting my time," Agent 15 growled sternly, squeezing the life out of the steering wheel with his clenched hands, wishing they were unleashed on a nice, firm neck.

"Look, I don't know what help it'll be, it made no sense to me. All it said was, J.A.W.S. HQ, 1593-22."

"Thank you, Faith. Now get in the car. I'm not finished with you yet."

CHAPTER EIGHTEEN

THE PIGEON AND THE PROTESTOR

A widely accepted opinion on modern-day Earth is that you make your own luck. Yet the word 'luck' is still used frequently when something unplanned or improbable happens. Often combined with a friendly expletive, the word might be used when a golfer hits a ball straight into the hole from a hundred yards. That would be seen to be lucky, yet paradoxically if that same shot had landed an inch from the hole it might be greeted with consolation and cries of 'bad luck'. Can luck really be measured in distance? If the best golfer in the world had successfully hit that same shot, that would be viewed as skill or even genius.

Some might say that the shot was nothing to do with luck and was instead the result of basic physics. A combination of the right speed, distance, direction and power placed upon the object whilst taking other external factors into account. That would suggest that luck can be controlled, that one has the ability to enhance the probability of being lucky. This view would be contrary to the 'luck' of winning the lottery where there is no skill or control involved. So some luck might be skill, and some luck might be chance. So, where does fate fit in? Fate appears to involve neither chance nor skill. It suggests that someone or something is in control of your destiny. With fate, there is nowhere to run and nowhere to hide. The outcome is totally inevitable.

Ian had often wondered whether he was unlucky or just incompetent. It was true to say he was often the perpetrator of his own misfortune. This was not called being unlucky, it was called being stupid. There was no denying, though, that he'd miss out on his fair share of chance along the way. Right now he was hoping and praying that fate might put in an appearance. He didn't feel confident in his skill or chance, so if he was going to succeed, someone else had to come to his rescue. It was to Ian's good fortune that fate was about to put in a guest appearance.

Ian had flown for about half an hour before he had found Number 12, Blackhorse Way, and surprisingly at the first attempt. This had been somewhat as the result of fate. He knew that the number fifty-seven bus went right up to the junction of Blackhorse Way, and he'd just happened to see that very bus pulling away from Trafalgar Square. He'd followed it until he caught sight of the distinctive, four-storey Georgian terraces that lined both sides of this short and narrow cul-de-sac.

Number 12, stood out like a sore thumb and had been the bane of fellow residents for over a decade. Every window from basement to roof was broken and had been shoddily boarded up with plywood. As out of place as a bacon sandwich at a bar mitzvah, Number 12 loitered awkwardly amongst its pristinely decorated cousins with their blossoming hanging baskets and colourfully painted façades. Each property, with the exception of Number 12, painted a different brand of bright hue with no two houses the same; pink, blue, cream and yellow, a seaside colour scheme in the heart of a metropolis.

Having visited it on numerous occasions over the last decade, Ian knew Number 12 well. Mostly he'd been there with Sandy, although occasionally, when it was deemed unsafe for Sandy to appear personally, he'd gone there alone on his instruction. It had been, and still was, the heart of the group known as Justice for Animals, Whatever Species, or J.A.W.S. The key to this place was that it blended in with the increasing number of empty properties that destroyed the fantasy of London's affluence. The illusion to the outside world was that the property only housed the occasional squatter, vermin or stray dog.

To the dismay of the neighbourhood, the police had never investigated any of the current occupants. There were several good reasons for that. These people weren't squatters. Therefore they did not involve themselves in some of the activities that such people are stereotyped for, careful to be extremely quiet and law-abiding. There was another fundamentally more important reason, though. The real owner of the property had allowed the occupants to live there and had struck a deal with the police to distance themselves from the property. Which is all very well really, as the security on the place was like Fort Knox.

All this was possible because the house was owned by one Sandy Logan. He'd used his connections to equip it with some of the most technologically advanced security devices power could buy. Even if the police did want to get in they'd need to be James Bond himself to gain entry. There was only one drawback to this security. When Sandy had arranged to have the keypads, cameras, infrared and voice recognition built in, he hadn't foreseen that Ian might need to gain entry without the use of his hands. It's an easy oversight in fairness!

Ian perched on the fence, scanning the familiar equipment used to keep the place a secret and allow members like him access. He guessed that the voice recognition would be okay and he remembered the PIN needed for the security pad. What he couldn't con were the cameras. If they caught a pigeon tapping the code in with its beak it might draw the attention of some of the people less sympathetic to a talking pigeon. Not everyone connected to J.A.W.S. was quite as tolerant as Violet when it came to animal protection. It was clear that some of the membership were less interested in the animal welfare issue and more interested in a damn good brawl. It suited Violet to have some of these characters around. Being a pacifist was one thing but she had no qualms if others felt the need to use violence.

There was one advantage of being a pigeon, even an unusually big one. You could fit into the small places of the world. Violet's quarters were, as Ian remembered it, at the very back of the building near the rear entrance. Violet believed that even with the security if anyone did manage to enter the site they would first and foremost be after her. That's why she had an emergency exit built near the back of the house that would allow her a swift retreat if ever it were needed. This getaway was via a cellar that led from Violet's bedroom, out under the garden and up through a public toilet into a small park area.

If he remembered how to get in, it would take him directly to Violet, and if she wasn't there now she soon would be. It was late evening by Ian's guess and she always came back here when she was in hiding, the only truly safe place for her to be. Over the top of Blackhorse Way he flew, opening up the panorama in the distance of a small park with its dense trees and untended lawns. It wasn't one of those fancy gated gardens found all over London, only accessible by rich local homeowners. This one was a public space and the types of people that visited at this time of night were best described as shady.

Ian landed gracefully at the front of the public toilets, carefully analysing the scene for any signs of the usual oddballs. The door to the woman's toilet no longer stood in its frame, allowing easy entrance for its unusual visitor. Ian searched his memory to remember how the tunnel worked. To get from the house to this side was easy. There was a button hidden in a bookshelf that opened a hatch in the floor. The tunnel had always been designed to be used to get out of the house, not into it. It was possible, but it had been made difficult to ensure that no one came across it by mistake. Access was neither easy nor pleasant. Ian hopped into one of the cubicles and onto the seat of the toilet. The trigger to open a hatch in the cubicle wall was located on the U-bend inside the toilet bowl.

"Oh shit," Ian muttered as he stared down into the murky waters of the pan. He wasn't just being figurative.

Up and down onto the cistern handle he jumped in a vain attempt to flush away the toilet's toxic contents. After several attempts only a tiny trickle of water ran down the inside of the porcelain bowl. If Ian was still wondering whether there was such a thing as luck, then he'd just found the answer.

"It's no good, I have to do it for Sandy."

He held his breath, hoping he knew how pigeons did it, and jumped head first into the bowl. On his first attempt the smell of the grimy water was so repulsive it made his insides turn outwards, rebounding him straight back out again. On the second attempt his beak touched the lever but he was unable to pull it forward sufficiently before running out of breath. He jumped out again, soaking wet and panting for fresh, clean air. Undeterred, for the third time he jumped back in. Gulps of sewage water ran down his throat at every attempt to bite at the handle. Time ticked by, ever closer to his need for air, as he thrashed around in the world's most disgusting bird bath. Eventually, either by skill, chance or fate, the lever came loose.

Clambering up the side of the bowl he used the last of his energy to heave himself up onto the edge. Whilst he was thanking the Lord that the ordeal was over, he become aware that he was no longer alone. A bedraggled and severely underdressed middle-aged woman stood limply at the cubicle door. Her lipstick and mascara had run to join each other on the sides of her face, creating a female version of the Joker. She attempted to brush the matted iron-wool hair from her eyes, revealing the true extent of her miserable expression. Clearly not having the best of nights, she'd popped into her usual place to shoot up the necessary dose of heroin to numb the rest of her evening.

What she hadn't counted on seeing was a pigeon, drenched from head to toe in shit, pop its head over the top of the toilet seat. Deciding wisely that another dose of heroin wasn't necessary, she left the cubicle in slow reverse. Chance might have finally shifted in his favour. Not only had she left without commotion, but also for the first time in the history of ever the hand dryer in the toilets was *actually* working.

A quick blow-dry did nothing to reduce the stench of his newly acquired aroma. But he was dry, if not a little permed. The gap in the wall had opened and he hopped down into the floor, following the sewer system that the tunnel had been crafted from. A few hundred yards from the entrance it took a familiar climb upwards to a spring-loaded trapdoor. Mercifully, it was far easier and more pleasant to open this entrance than the one in the toilet. There was a simple catch that released the spring, dropping the floor section in Violet's bedroom down into the tunnel. Remembering that the spring-loaded floor rapidly returned into position, designed to avoid any pursuers following after you, he flew without hesitation into the room.

The only light inside came from a small table lamp next to the bed. With limited sight, Ian made out the figure of a woman lying fully clothed on the bed, rumbling like a hippo in a sleep that was neither restful nor complete. The woman had the complexion of a person in their late-fifties, although Ian knew she was considerably younger. Without the use of products to improve herself, whether tested on animals or not, added to the conditions in which she lived had added years to her complexion. Unlike most women she was as natural as the day she was born. In her outlook if it was natural, it was good. If it wasn't, it was bad, there was only black and white with Violet. Would she change that paradigm, given that Sandy was most definitely grey?

Unsure of the reaction that he might get, Ian carefully made his way over to the side of the bed to check for certain that it was Violet Stokes. He'd been so focused on finding her, he'd given no thought to what he would do when he succeeded, never really believing that he would. How was he going to get her onside? Subtlety, he felt, was the order of the day. Unfortunately both subtlety and skill chose that moment to spontaneously abandon him. Attempting to land silently on the bedside table, he overdid the flight and careered into the lamp, which sent it and Ian down the side of the bed.

Half in and half out of sleep, Violet sat upright to locate the source of the noise. Violet's deep sense of anxiety meant that everything was bad news until it was proved otherwise. Struggling to search around the room, as the only light source was now rolling around the bedroom floor, her heart rate slowed in conclusion that her flailing arm must have dislodged the lamp whilst she slept.

She got out of bed to put the light back in its rightful place and to her great surprise found an unconscious pigeon spreadeagled on the floor. She picked it up, immediately more concerned for its well-being than its unusual appearance in her bedroom. With the careful touch of a vet, she placed it on the bed, assessing it for any breaks or bruises. Dazed, confused and unsure of his whereabouts, Ian opened his eyes.

"Hello. How did you get in here?" said Violet, like a caring pet owner exchanging unanswered small talk with a beloved animal.

"Violet, am I glad to see you," replied the disorientated pigeon, believing the question was his to answer.

In Violet's world of black and white, this fitted squarely into the black section. This was bad news for

Ian as her immediate reaction was to fight. Picking up the nearest object she started beating uncontrollably in the direction of the pigeon. The hardback book thumped at the bed hysterically as if someone afraid of spiders had just awoken to find that a group of arachnids were performing a Morris dance on their faces. Amidst the screams and thwack of book on furniture, Ian managed to retreat before his face was a permanent feature of Al Gore's autobiography.

"What witchcraft or sinister plot is this?" shouted Violet, throwing the book at the door frame where Ian had briefly settled to catch his breath.

Thinking quickly was not on the shortlist of Ian's attributes and it wasn't going to suddenly appear from nowhere. Fortunately for Ian, this was the point where fate put in a very welcomed appearance. Unannounced, a man burst through the door, narrowly avoiding another book that had been flung through the air.

"Violet, there's someone at the front door," said the man hesitantly.

"Who? Everyone we know is here for the meeting?" replied Violet, only half-taking her gaze away from the pigeon.

"We're not certain who he is, but he has the right codes and his voice recognition is in our records."

"Well, whose voice is it?"

"I don't quite believe it, Violet, but its John Hewson's."

CHAPTER NINETEEN

AN UNEXPECTED VOICE

As they stood in the doorway of Number 12, Blackhorse Way, the lack of activity in this unnaturally quiet road did nothing to quash John's anxiety. The only noise was the faint rumble of cars and buses trundling along the main road in the distance. John knew this was going to be one of the most difficult jobs that he'd faced so far. Not only did he have to get inside, he also had to explain how he'd done it. In front of him on the right-hand side of the door was a screen, keypad and speaker.

"Nash, I need to take a front seat on this if we're going to get in."

"Okay, John, I think that might be safer for both of us," replied Nash, who relaxed his mind and felt John seep across his body.

John opened the piece of paper from Nash's wallet to remind himself of the numbers, knowing that he'd only have one chance before the code randomly reset itself. He pressed each number until 1593-22 shone in LED brilliance. Then he waited. The intercom buzzed and the screen illuminated to show Nash's grainy outline against the moonlight. John tentatively pressed the button to answer the ringing and a male voice answered from inside the building.

"Declare yourself."

"It's John Hewson," he replied, concentrating all of his efforts on Nash's vocal cords. John was aware that when he took control of Nash's body he sounded different. But he didn't know if he sounded enough like himself to trick the system.

"Stand by for confirmation," the man's voice replied.

John stood on the doorstep waiting for approval like a new boyfriend meeting his girlfriend's parents for the first time, blood pressure slowly rising in anticipation of the outcome and his potential need to flee. The people inside these walls didn't take kindly to imposters and they wouldn't allow them to walk away unscathed. That was before he thought about being seen on this side of the doorway by the authorities who were already following him. This door wasn't just a barrier between two spaces, it was a portal from one dangerous situation to another. Inside the security room, Violet had just sprinted in to see what she suspected to be a hoax or some bizarre technical error.

"Let me see him," she croaked.

It had been some years since she had last seen John Hewson, so undoubtedly his features would have changed. Although he was barely an adult back then, even in the limited light and the poor-quality black and white CCTV image, she was fairly sure that this wasn't him.

"Show me the voice pattern."

The man responsible for security pointed to another screen where two wavelengths, one blue and one red, danced across it. They were almost identically matched on top of each other.

"There's no doubt, Violet, that it's John's voice. These things are accurate to one person in one hundred thousand."

"Don't underestimate the power of one."

"Do you want me to let him in?"

"What I want to know is why you're telling me that there's a dead man standing on my doorstep? It must be some trick?"

"Maybe he's not dead," replied the man. "People fake their own deaths all the time."

"Some do, although I don't think this person had the talent for it. Whoever he is, what's important now is how he got the code to come here tonight," replied Violet.

John was contemplating legging it. They must have caught him out and were now planning exactly what nastiness they were going to inflict on him.

"OK, let him in. Let's find out who he is. I want you to take him into the main meeting. I'll listen in for a while and then join you for my speech once I have managed to sort out my strange little intruder," she announced as she left the room in a blur.

The unexpected appearance of John's voice at the front door seemed to have calmed Violet down to the fact that she had discovered a talking pigeon in her bedroom. The distraction had also given Ian some valuable thinking time.

"John, sorry for the delay. Your voice record is rather old. I'll open the door."

John helped Nash exhale his relief.

Other than having a dimly lit quality, the hallway of this typically Georgian building had been beautifully kept throughout. In front of them a staircase engorged the centre of the room, turning to the left and the right as it reached the first floor and on into unseen places. In the centre of the ceiling a magnificent chandelier, decorated around its base with rings of red and blue crystal glass cascaded down to a great orb that hung like a silver moon in silent orbit. The security man didn't direct them up in the direction of the staircase, but rather down to the right where a less impressive staircase led down into the basement. John approached them nervously.

"The meeting will start in about twenty minutes," said the man, as he pointed them towards the stairs. "You'll find a number of people already down there so grab a cup of tea and make yourself comfortable."

John edged carefully down the narrow steps into an area that was even gloomier than the one they had come from. At the bottom there was none of the elegance that they had witnessed upstairs. This was what first-time homeowners referred to as basic. The bowels of the house had been completely stripped out to create a huge, sprawling open-plan cellar. Pillars at regular intervals were the last remnants of the walls that would have previously separated this vast chamber into small basement rooms.

The cellar itself was about forty metres long by about twenty metres wide, and housed a crudely built stage across the width of one end. The venue wouldn't have been out of place in the low-quality end of the Edinburgh Fringe. In rows facing the stage dozens of chairs dominated the floor space and at least half were already occupied.

Considering that there were about fifty people in the room, it lacked the volume level that John would have expected. Most of the people were sitting quietly, deep in their own thoughts. A few had huddled in small groups of three or four, whispering between swigs of tea from beaten-up china mugs. They were an interesting mix of people. If most people were asked to describe a bunch of animal welfare protestors, then they'd have pictured the same type of person. They'd be wrong. Here sat men in suits, well-dressed old-age pensioners, students, muscly builders, and some that you might describe as traditional 'crusties'.

John made his way to one of the back row seats where a man sat with his feet up against the row of chairs in front of him. Almost completely covered by a long, dark trench coat, his trilby hat was tipped forward to cover his eyes from view. John thought for a moment that he was asleep so, not wanting to disturb him, sat in the row behind a few seats to the right.

"Excited about the speech?" came a stony voice from the row in front, where the man quite unnaturally made no attempt to turn to speak with him.

"Yes," replied John, unmotivated to offer more than the very minimum of responses.

"I've not seen you at this meeting before. New to this, are you?"

"First one for a long time. What's your name, maybe I know you from then?" asked John, suspicious of this dark stranger's inquisition.

"I doubt that. I understand that Violet might have some rather interesting news for us tonight. Apparently we might find out what happened to Sandy."

"Really," replied John impassively.

"What's your guess, then? What do you think happened to him?"

This was a strange question to someone who had just indicated that they had not been involved for a long time.

"No idea," John lied, in a tone that would tell anyone the conversation was over.

"Oh, so you do know who he is, then?"

"Well, um, I didn't say that, did I?"

"But you implied it," said the stranger.

"No I didn't," huffed John.

"What does he look like?"

"What's that got to do with the price of fish?"

"It just seems odd that few of these people here," he waved his hand in the general direction of the others, "ever saw him in the flesh, that's all. I find it quite interesting that there was a man so influential in this organisation that almost no one ever saw him. It's funny, he could walk in the room and no one would know it was him."

*****

Gently, Violet pushed open the door of her bedroom, peeking around the side in search of her guest. In her absence, Ian had spent the time wisely. After catching his breath he'd taken up position at the highest point he found, the ceiling light. Fortunately, like all the others in the house, it had been turned off for some time, avoiding any potential singeing of tail feathers. Violet stared around the room clutching a metal fire poker she'd picked up en route.

"Violet, you must listen to me. I know it's hard to believe but I am Ian Noble. What's more, Sandy is also a pigeon," said Ian, not sure where to start and sure that it wouldn't matter, given the absurdity of the message.

"Where are you, creature of Satan?" said Violet, spinning around to locate its voice, brandishing the poker in front of her.

"Look, I know it's hard to take in, believe me, I'm still doing that myself. Let me prove it to you."

"I don't want to hear it."

"Just before Sandy died he left you a message warning you about a weapon that the government was making at Tavistock. Think, how else could I know this?"

"You couldn't know that. I'm going mad, tell me I am?" She finally looked up at the white bird sitting on the edge of a lampshade.

"You're not going mad. We need your help, Violet. We don't know how to get out of this. We think it has something to do with Emorfed."

"That's the name of the compound that Sandy talked about in his message," said Violet. "I've only given that information to one other person. It really is you. But it can't be."

"You must believe me. There's much more that you need to know. Sandy has told me all that he remembers."

"So why isn't *he* here?"

"Too risky, you know what they'd give to get their hands on him," cooed Ian from his perch. "You need to warn the others, mobilise them against it or this country might never be the same again."

AN UNEXPECTED VOICE

*****

The basement room was almost full. Only a couple of empty seats were dotted amongst the crowd. Over the last five minutes the volume had gradually faded in anticipation that the meeting was about to start. Out of a side door next to the platform, Violet Stokes burst in with a renewed sense of determination. She didn't look much different from what John remembered of her, even though many years had passed since their last meeting. Her dark hair was still matted and in desperate need of a wash. The worn and tatty recycled clothing was still a central feature of her appearance. The biggest difference was not how she appeared but how she acted.

John's outstanding memory was how her behaviour was always calm, at least amongst her own people. Just like making a successful complaint to a business, the best emotion is calm and that's how she approached her colleagues. Out on a protest march it was quite different. There she would outshout a town crier. Right now, as she shuffled her notes ready to address the crowd, her face was drawn and her body visibly twitched with anger.

"Friends, welcome to the quarterly meeting of Justice for Animals, Whatever Species, and as always thank you for being here. Never before has the name of our organisation been more appropriate than it is today. In the years that I have been a part of it there was one species that I never thought would need justice, one species that would never need our help. Today I have a very important campaign that I need all of you to commit to with the utmost sense of energy and urgency. This season we will be saving mankind, for it is our own species that is most at risk."

A surprised gasp went up around the room. People bickered and gossiped amongst themselves. Violet wasn't one for jokes. Behind her back it was once commented that she had the sense of humour of an organic chemist whose hobby was the history of motorways. This couldn't possibly be a joke. If it was, then her body language certainly wasn't letting on. There was only one person that didn't react in the way the congregation had. The man with the black hat in the row in front of John remained motionless. Even John was taken aback by the announcement. After all, he'd only come here to find Sandy and Ian, he didn't really have any interest in J.A.W.S., its campaigns or its objectives anymore.

"Quieten down, people," shouted Violet, uncharacteristically.

The group regained their composure.

"As some of you may know, Sandy Logan, one of our biggest contributors, has not been seen or heard from for some months. Until tonight, I had believed him to be dead. I believed this because he called me on the night of the Tavistock bombing to warn me about something that was hidden there. At the time the information he gave me was limited and I repeatedly attempted to contact him through the usual means. I gave the details to a reporter who investigated his accusations. It was through this journalist that I learnt that Sandy and Ian Noble had been killed in the Tavistock blast. This information was only partly true. Indeed they were in the blast, but they were not completely killed."

Violet had carefully chosen that last sentence to create the most ambiguity but the smallest amount of comment. The congregation started to mutter again but were cut off before they got into their stride.

"In fact, Ian Noble is here with me tonight and has given me the full and terrible picture that threatens our very way of life. The government has created a drug called Emorfed, which has a number of effects when taken. Primarily it permanently removes all human addiction, but in doing so has the side effect of quashing the human spirit. It redirects our desires, cravings, instincts and behaviours to a utopian model designed by the government itself. It's been designed to suppress mankind to act as model citizens. You've heard of genetic engineering, well, welcome to a world of spiritual engineering."

John was dumbfounded. How could any government go to such lengths to keep control of its people? This was misuse of power on an unprecedented scale, dictatorship by prescription. John considered what this drug would do to a human's soul. It appeared to John that with Emorfed, every single soul would turn out to be neutral. No one would be doing anything wrong, but likewise no one would have the inclination to help one another. They'd be like robots.

Having been to Limbo as a neutral soul, he didn't wish that on anyone, particularly as the decisions made there were by anyone's standards a little dubious. What was the point in him saving humanity, if humanity didn't end up being human at all? This news had even distracted him away from the news that should have made him dance in the aisles. Ian was here. All he had to do was to seek him out and half of the job would be done.

"Okay, I don't need to tell you the severity of this situation. I want you all to stop your current activities and follow a new strategy. This will be like nothing we have ever been involved with before. We can't merely campaign as we have done in the past, we will need to act in total secrecy. If this is to be stopped we need to infiltrate the very heart of government. Ian and I have talked through a plan and each of you will play your part. Jenkins, give me the attendees list."

She snapped her fingers at a spotty kid, standing unnoticed to her left, quickly passed her a clipboard, and hurried back out of sight. Violet's fingers tiptoed down the list, both counting the numbers and observing the names. Sporadically she would pick someone out and shout an action.

"Fletcher Conrad, I need you to talk to your contacts at Defra. Find out what they know about this…Sally Palmer, I need you to take a couple of your group down to the Tavistock site and stake it out. I want to know what goods come out and where they go…"

After six people had been given their duties she called out a name without appreciating its significance.

"Sandy Logan…" She paused. "Jenkins, come here, you snivelling little git. All I asked you to do was the bloody register."

Jenkins cowered over to Violet.

"It's not a mistake, Mrs. Stokes. He came through the front door with all the checks, I remember it."

"So, where is he, then?" whispered Violet sceptically, pretending to look around the faces in the crowd.

Jenkins pointed a finger over to the mysterious man sitting in the row in front of John. The fascinated congregation followed the finger.

For the first time the man turned to the row behind him. "Hello, Nash. Sit still. Once I have dealt with this lot, you and I need to have a little chat."

Lifting the hat from his eyes he let out a droll, sarcastic laugh, still bearing its monotonal quality. Poking his fingers into his eyes, he removed two fake contact lenses before peeling off a fake plastic chin and nose. Finally he removed a small metal object from the inside of his mouth that transformed his voice into something more friendly and welcoming than it had been. He started a one-man, slow hand clap.

"I must congratulate you on your extremely sophisticated, but highly ineffective security. It's a shame that the real Sandy is no longer able to keep you safe in this place, isn't it?"

"Who are you?" shouted Violet.

"Oh…ha ha ha…how sad that I know everything about you, Violet, yet you know absolutely nothing about me. Who am I? I'm your worst nightmare. I'm the man that's about to burn down your organisation and piss on its smouldering remains."

A number of the crowd had started a silent panic. They'd been sought out and were about to be identified. Some crept quietly towards the doors.

"STAY WHERE YOU ARE," Agent 15 bellowed. "There is nowhere you can go. The whole place is surrounded by my people. There's no escape."

"You're assuming that you'll get out of this room with your life," said Violet quite calmly.

"Oh, I'm scared," taunted Agent 15.

He'd anticipated the fact that he might be outnumbered by about one to a hundred and that they might attack him. He hadn't prepared for this possibility, though, because in truth he loved a good scrap, especially if the odds were almost impossibly against him. Maybe Violet had spoken too soon about the power of one.

"What are you going to do, you oversensitive bunch of hippies? You going to throw joss sticks at me, or chant me to death? That's your problem, you don't know how to fight properly. You've convinced yourself that you can win with words, when everyone else fights with fists. How very pathetic."

"GET HIM!" Violet shouted to the crowd.

"Oh shitty bollocks," gasped Agent 15, as a dozen or so of the gathering flung themselves at him from all angles.

Some saw this as an opportunity to retreat to the exits. John saw it as a fantastic opportunity to slip out unseen and look for Ian.

"BACK-UP!" shouted Agent 15 into a concealed radio, as he aimed punches in as many directions as possible.

As John found his way through the melee to the door at the back of the stage, dark-suited agents burst into the meeting hall.

CHAPTER TWENTY

THE UNFORTUNATE
STUPIDITY OF IAN NOBLE

The clamour of the fight escalating behind John grew faint as he searched everywhere to find Violet's bedroom. John hoped that the noise of trouble downstairs hadn't found its way through the corridors and scared off Ian. Only once, a decade or more ago, had John been inside this building and not as far into the property as this. He'd been a somewhat outer member of J.A.W.S. in his youth, his only real connection being his friendship with Sandy Logan. Therefore he had no local knowledge to aid his search. He systematically turned every door handle he found. Each wrong choice hastened the chance that someone followed him.

As he opened doors, scanned rooms and discarded them as dead ends, he thought about what he'd heard in the meeting. The news that a government could effectively change people's very way of being without them even knowing it sent a deep shiver through his soul. All the while that he had been in his present semi-deceased state he'd had at least some control over his direction. He'd decided to take Brimstone's deal, chosen who to possess on Earth, and co-ordinated the search for Sandy and Ian. The fact that some of these decisions had gone wrong was merely the consequence of being human.

That was the silent truth of Emorfed. It would stop people making mistakes or taking responsibility for themselves, all basic human conditions. It would affect everyone he knew and cared for. How could he do anything about it? A semi-dead person with a borrowed body was no match for the Prime Minister? It would have to wait. There were other priorities right now.

Success came after he opened the eighth in a long row of doors. Sitting on a double bed with his head stuck in a crisp packet was a bright, pure white and larger than normal pigeon. John had known for some time that Ian and Sandy had become pigeons but he still wasn't prepared for the reality of it. There was no doubt it was Ian. Who else was able to incapacitate themselves with a snack product?

"Is that you, Violet?" said the pigeon with the crisp packet head, trying ferociously to shake it off. "Can I get some help here?"

"Hello, Ian, I see you're still getting yourself into the wrong place at the wrong time," said John, gently lifting the foil bag off his head.

Ian panicked from the instant realisation that not only was this not Violet, it also was another person who knew who he was underneath his feathery disguise. After flying around the room like a hyperventilating balloon for a few seconds, he tried to decide whether this revelation was incredibly good news or unbelievably bad.

"Ian, you won't recognise me, but it's John Hewson. I, too, have had things done to me that I don't fully understand. We are both souls that have become squatters in other bodies. I know how you got like this," said John, trying as he might to keep track of the randomly spiralling bird.

"How do you know all this?" Ian replied, having finally repositioned himself in the only safe place he knew, on top of the ceiling lamp.

"I have been to the…other side."

"What, Australia?"

"No...the afterlife," John answered, remembering Ian's handicap and trying desperately to remain patient with him. "You have been affected by a phenomenon called the Limpet Syndrome. A human condition driven by a desire for your soul to remain on Earth when the physical body has no life left in it. I don't fully understand it if I'm honest. The consequence, however, is that the longer you remain on this planet, in this Universe, the more of a threat you are to it."

"I don't understand."

"You never really do, Ian," replied John sympathetically. "I'll try to make it simple. In essence, if you stay here the Universe will end. You don't belong here. You should be dead and the fact that you're not is making the Universe irritable."

"I don't care. I have to stay here. It's you that doesn't understand," said Ian, still not fully accepting of the whole pigeon thing, let alone this new exposé.

"Do you know why your soul remained here?" asked John.

"I think it has something to do with protecting Sandy, but it's very hazy, just emotions rather than memories."

John felt a great deal of empathy with Ian. Here was one of only three people in the entire Universe who had been through an ordeal similar to his. Ian, too, had felt the loneliness, wallowed in the confusion, and been consumed by the irrepressible thirst for answers. Experiencing death, whilst retaining certain emotions of a life not quite past but neither ultimately present wasn't an easy existence. The ultimate pity that he felt for Ian was that he had come to extinguish the flame that still burned brightly inside his soul, still very much alive. Would that make John a murderer? Did he have the courage to take that away from someone? He doubted it. Nothing had changed, he wouldn't have killed someone in life and that same attitude burnt within his soul, body or no body.

"Ian, the truth is I've been sent to bring you and Sandy back to the afterlife. If I don't then there will be no life at all, for anyone. Your existence is jeopardising every living thing."

To be told that you could be responsible for the biggest genocide in the history of creation can't be an easy thing to hear at the best of times, let alone when you're stuck in an oversized pigeon suit.

"How do you know all this?" asked Ian.

"I've been to Hell, Ian, and have it from a pretty high authority. I'm sorry but I have to take you back there."

"You realise if you do that, John, there may be no humankind to save?" Although this was uncharacteristically quick thinking, it was also a spontaneous acknowledgement of the truth.

"Do you think Emorfed is the reason why you're here in the first place, Ian? Maybe you triggered the Limpet Syndrome to stop it destroying humanity?"

"I think between me and Sandy, you're right," he replied, still clinging to the lampshade for dear life.

"The irony is by doing that you threatened it in an entirely different way."

"You may be right, but I must help Sandy."

Suddenly the bedroom door crashed open against the bookshelf and Ian and John were presented with an entirely different stand-off. Holding the expression of a man who wasn't going to take any more shit stood a bruised and bloodied Agent 15. Several new experiences had happened to him today that he wasn't entirely comfortable with, one of which was bleeding. Sure, he saw bleeding a lot. It was what other people did when they stood up to him. But when your own blood was spilt on the actions of a dozen unexpectedly aggressive hippies, you weren't going to put up with any trouble from a girlie musician and a big pigeon.

"Who's this joker?" said Ian.

THE UNFORTUNATE STUPIDITY OF IAN NOBLE

"Joker! Is this a joke?" said Agent 15, pulling a gun from his inside pocket and screwing the silencer in place ready for the shot.

As both of them had reason to believe that the aim would be at them, neither needed much further motivation to scatter. Ian's escape route from the lampshade started with a perfectly placed nosedive into the bookshelf. He careered into the copy of 'War and Peace', that he knew would trigger the opening of the trapdoor. Before John or Agent 15 reacted, Ian had flown through the trapdoor and into the tunnel.

John had to acknowledge that the man in front of him had a gun and was probably prepared to use it. Yet his only chance of finding Sandy was leaving down a secret passage. Agent 15 had to acknowledge that he couldn't interrogate Nash Stevens if he was dead, and shooting him would create a bag load of paperwork. Having weighed up the options, John made the brave decision to throw himself at the closing trapdoor, just before the door slammed shut behind him.

Before Agent 15 followed in pursuit he had some issues to deal with. One of the only living witnesses to the Emorfed project was getting further away from him, yet his attention was struggling not to be diverted to a much less important wooden object that he'd flung open minutes earlier. If someone else had opened, it then there would be no problem. But when it was his responsibility it was also his destiny on the line. Torn between two priorities, an argument broke out.

"You're being stupid, nothing's going to happen if you don't do it. You'll be fine," he muttered schizophrenically to himself. "It'll only take a few seconds. Isn't it better to be safe than sorry. No, I'm not going to do it, for once in my life I'm going to leave the fucking door open. Sod the consequences, I'm going after them."

THE UNFORTUNATE STUPIDITY OF IAN NOBLE

Unsure which book had been the trigger for the exit, he pulled them from their shelves at random like a burrowing mole. Through tearing paper and buckled spines eventually the trapdoor collapsed into the ground to signal the discovery of the correct one. Clambering down into the darkness his pursuit continued. The chase lasted ten seconds before he'd jumped out of the hole again. Running over to the bedroom door he hastily swung it back and forth three times before emptying a round of bullets into it.

"I need help," he said to himself, jumping through the trapdoor for a second time, moments before it closed shut again.

*****

As Ian flew down the tunnel towards the park toilets, he, too, had a dilemma to solve. There was so much that he needed to tell Sandy from tonight's events. But doing so risked bringing a fox into the chicken coop. Which would be worse? It wasn't Emorfed that had triggered the Limpet Syndrome in him, as he'd confessed to John. It was his stupidity at Tavistock that had triggered it. In all the years that he'd known Sandy, all he wanted to do was prove his worth. To be appreciated for a unique and valued talent. In whatever life he had left it was still achievable. Leading John further from Sandy might be his unique talent, even if that meant sacrificing himself.

As he reached the exit at the far end, he heard the echo of sloshing footsteps from the hollow behind drawing ever closer. There was no trace of the door's release mechanism as he searched in the darkness. The footsteps were almost upon him. If he couldn't find the exit, then maybe John would. If he stayed quiet enough he could wait patiently and escape unnoticed.

Unfamiliar with his surroundings and in his haste to catch up, John did not anticipate the end of the tunnel until he ran straight into it. The force of the impact catapulted him off his feet and with a thud he hit the filthy sewage that lined the stone floor.

"Awwwhhh! I can't see a thing. Ian, are you there? Do you know the way out?" yelped John pathetically.

Ian remained like a statue.

Feeling the walls like a blind man, John crawled to his feet, assuming that Ian had already found his way out and the door had closed behind him. John thumped every brick with his fists, searching for many minutes without success.

"Where's the bloody exit?"

Befitting of a man who had spent his entire career preparing for such situations, Agent 15's descent had been much more stealthy. In fact, the first news John received that his adversary was there was the searing pain of a gun handle striking the back of his head, forcing him to be reintroduced to the wet floor. The adrenaline that flowed through John came to an intersection labelled: fright, flight or fight. The slip road labelled 'fright' appeared to be already in use, 'flight' had roadworks blocking any access, and the only lane free of congestion for his adrenaline to run down was 'fight'. As it engaged throttle and hit full speed his arms thrashed forward as clenched fists firstly caught brick, then Agent 15's leg, before finally a left hook landed on something feathery.

Agent 15 switched on his mobile phone. In the glow of the light a man squelched around on all fours punching at invisible foes, whilst next to him a white pigeon lay unconscious with its feet in the air. The illumination made light work of discovering the resting place of the lost exit lever. As he pulled on it, the wall unveiled a filthy toilet cubicle and what smelt like several rotting corpses. As Ian's brain settled back in place and he regained consciousness, the fuzzy sight of the exit opened up the lane marked 'flight'. Still disorientated from the punch that had hit him in the dark, he flew straight into the stomach of John Hewson who had just risen to his feet.

John's adrenaline was still set on fight mode as he grabbed hold of Ian's scrawny feet. Driven by self-will and a power many multiples more than the lactose available in his muscles, Ian flew towards the exit, pulling John along with him. Agent 15 had a much more annoying instinct flowing through him than fright, flight or fight. Again he'd been responsible for opening the door and the only instinct he heard was the one telling him to 'quickly open and close the door three times'. Only this time the door had already swung closed and he was on the toilet side of the tunnel.

"Where's the bloody handle?" he shouted whilst searching the cubicles for a clue. All he found was a semi-conscious, half-dressed woman slouched on the floor next to the sinks.

"Hey, darling, you looking for some fun?" she stammered.

Agent 15 aimed his gun in the woman's direction. "No. I'm looking for a way to open this door and having gone over the point of frustration, fuck the paperwork, I'd be quite happy to shoot someone. Unless you can tell me how to open this door, then fuck off."

"I don't know how to open it, love," she said, quite unfazed by the possibility of a bullet in the head, "but you'll never guess what I saw coming out of that toilet earlier tonight."

"Then enlighten me, you scabby spac granny."

"A white pigeon covered in shit."

Without hesitation, Agent 15 launched his hand into the pan.

*****

THE UNFORTUNATE STUPIDITY OF IAN NOBLE

Ian pulled John with the strength of a Saint Bernard sniffing out a cat. Sadly for Nash, being dragged through the park by a pigeon hadn't gone unnoticed. Several late-night drunkards rubbed their eyes in astonishment at a grown man being pulled at speed, legs running furiously to keep up, across the park by an overgrown bird. One even used his phone to take a picture of it to endorse his drunken memories during tomorrow morning's inquisition.

"Ian, stop, let's talk about this. We're getting nowhere here. I'll rephrase that, we are in fact fast approaching the main road. Ian, you need to slow down now."

"If you want me to slow down, John, then you'll just have to let go, won't you?" mumbled Ian, quite out of breath.

They burst through the hedgerow and out onto the main road. There wasn't much traffic on the road at 2.30 in the morning with one exception. A red double-decker night bus was rounding the corner and heading straight towards them. John had seen it all right, but he wasn't quite sure if Ian had.

"Ian. Bus. STOP."

John instinctively let go and stumbled to a halt, wobbling precariously on the kerbside. The sudden reduction in weight had the predictable effect of speeding up Ian's progress at exactly the same moment as the bus passed by. The bus didn't stop. When it had driven by there was no sign of Ian's flattened outline on the road. It wasn't there because it took up a position that made driving a bus much more challenging. John sprinted down the street after it.

When the bus reached the next stop, to pick up and drop off the night's stragglers, John was still jogging down the road some fifty metres behind. Poor Ian had evidently been catapulted by the hard braking of the bus and was now spread out on the bus shelter's concrete floor. John quickened his pace. Maybe Ian was already dead and his soul had disappeared into the ether? When he picked Ian up he rejoiced that the bird was still breathing. On further inspection he diagnosed a broken wing and a beak that was definitely flatter than it had been earlier.

Ian opened his eyes to see that he was in the hands of his pursuer. Before realising the full extent of his injuries, his 'flight' instinct kicked in again. The attempt to take off with a broken left wing created a suicidal circular flight path that sent him careering into a dust wagon that was sweeping the opposite side of the street. The brushes sucked him under the vehicle with a crunch. John ran to the back of the wagon expecting the worst. No pale white bird floated out of the back with the black exhaust smoke. Instead, a small, electric-blue storm lit up the street as its crackling charge drew the attention of people nearby like a tractor beam. John remembered what he had to do, he just hoped he pronounced it correctly.

"Erior wit solsta trak. Erior wit solsta trak. Erior wit solsta trak."

Ian's soul froze and stopped emitting any kind of charge. It froze in the shape of a person for a fleeting second before it shot up into the air at an almost invisible speed. Moments later it was gone.

*****

Agent 15 stood at the door of Number 12, Blackhorse Way, one arm dripping with excrement and drenched up to the shoulder. He contemplated opening it, but decided to ring the bell. Another agent opened it for him.

"Why didn't you just come in, sir?"

Agent 15 shot him a 'do you really want to die?'-type of stare.

"Where is she?"

CHAPTER TWENTY-ONE

THE LIMPET SYNDROME

As morning broke over the rooftops of Gloucester Road, John knew they were in trouble a long time before Nash did. As Nash slept peacefully in his adopted bed on the second floor of Herb's town house, dreaming about some sordid tryst with a group of scantily clad groupies, John was watching it all unfold. Unable to wake Nash from his slumbers, the best defence he offered was the occasional unconnected swing of a fist or shake of the head.

Yesterday had been a good day. In fact, John had to admit it had been the best day he'd experienced since before his own death. Half of the job was complete and he was finally starting to believe that this ludicrously impossible task was somehow possible. Ian had been accounted for without John having to do anything unpleasant other than watch Ian effectively commit suicide. With the determination of a kamikaze pilot, Ian had helped return his soul and in turn keep everyone else's safe. All he had to do was find the last piece in the jigsaw, a job that was more than slightly hampered by the circumstances of a new sunrise.

It had been late when they'd returned to Herb's place. The sort of time only known to milkmen and early morning delivery drivers. When they'd finally got in, the house had been empty and there were no signs that Herb was back from his first-class strop of two days earlier. John could safely say that he was back now, and he'd brought a friend. Through a slightly raised eyelid he saw Herb sitting uncomfortably on the chair at the bottom of the bed, drinking tea from an antique blue and white china cup. A musty smell of dense smoke filled John's nostrils as another figure stood puffing on a pipe that he repeatedly relit with long, brown-tipped matches.

Now, when you've been to the places that John had, the one thing you couldn't deny was the existence of a higher power in the Universe. Something out there shaping and guiding the fate of millions. Refuting it would be like trying to argue that Oliver Reed was teetotal. The sight of a priest prior to his death would have gone unnoticed. But now that John was uniquely informed, the sight of a man wearing a white dog collar around his neck scared him to his very core. Just such a man was currently looming above him, making tutting noises.

Nash attempted to rub his face but the nearest his hand got was the air halfway between the two. It must have been amusing to watch a semi-conscious man trying to work out why his arms wouldn't go as far as normal. John knew why. All four of Nash's limbs were now firmly tied to bedposts, a sight that would have sent Nash over the edge with excitement.

"Nash, wake up. WAKE UP. I think I'm in big trouble," said John, placing as much of his concentration in Nash's ear as possible.

"Go away, it's too early," mumbled Nash as he opened his eyes a fraction and tried unsuccessfully to turn over.

Herb rolled up the newspaper he was reading and moved to the bed on the opposite side to the priest. If John hadn't been panicking so much he might have paid more attention to the way Herb had pulled off the manoeuvre with sobriety and grace. The Herb of a few days ago would have winced at the word 'sober'. But there was no doubt from his clean-shaven face, suitably dressed appearance, and lack of the hallmarks that usually accompanied his life of excess, that he looked respectable.

"Nash, wake up," urged Herb, shaking him by the arm more and more energetically.

"What?...Hey, it's dark in here...where's my friend gone?...the feathery one...you know the one."

"WAKE UP!" shouted Herb, so close to the ear where John had taken up residence that it forced him out like a bullet. He found himself down in Nash's abdomen, tingling like sherbet.

"I'm sorry, Nash, but this is for your own good. This man is Dr. Donovan King. He's a friend of mine, who has come to help you," said Herb, in a way that a parent might talk to a critically sick child.

"Nash, you don't need a doctor," thought John, crawling back into position. "Tell him to sod off."

"I don't need a doctor. I'm fine. Nice cup of coffee and a cigarette and I'll be awake," he said, trying to sit up, but being forced back by the ligatures around his wrists. "Hey, Herb, what's going on here?"

"It would appear that you have either gone mad or been possessed."

"Thanks for getting on-board, Herb. Tell me something I don't know."

"OK, I will. You're in a bottomless pit of trouble, free-falling towards jail, or possibly the lunatic asylum and almost certainly musical obscurity."

Herb opened up the newspaper to the front page. On the cover of one of the leading national newspapers was a half-page colour photo with the headline, 'Off His Rocker'. The grainy picture showed Nash in the middle of a public park holding a pigeon in full flight.

"That's not so bad, that could be anyone really, the picture's all blurry," replied Nash after a pause for thought.

As he continued to blather his defence, Herb flicked the paper over to page seven. This picture of Nash was much clearer. Hands raised in the air, Nash appeared bathed in an electric-blue cloud that swirled around the air above a cleaning wagon.

"Hey, that's not fair, I could be doing anything. That blue stuff has been Photoshopped on, it's a…" Nash stopped as Herb pointed to the bottom of the page where it read, 'see the entire video on our website.'

"How many hits?" whispered Nash.

"Since it was uploaded last night at four o'clock in the morning?"

"Yeah."

"So, you're asking me how many hits there have been in just over six hours?"

Nash nodded sheepishly.

"One hundred and twelve," answered Herb.

"That's not too…"

"Thousand," added Herb, "approximately of course."

"Oh. I suppose there's no such thing as bad…" Nash stopped when he saw Herb's face turn from contempt to bewilderment.

"Dr. King is here to help understand what's going on…" Herb pointed vaguely in the direction of Nash's head, "…in there."

"Tell him I'm not in 'there' anymore," replied John, as he squeezed himself up through Nash's throat. "Ask him what sort of doctor he is, Nash."

"What sort of doctor are you?"

"I'm really two doctors, Nash. As well as being a doctor in theology and a practising priest in…um… ah…you know?" he looked at Herb for clarification.

"The Catholic Church," Herb prompted slowly.

"The Republic of Ireland," Dr. King corrected him after seeming to remember. "I'm also a doctor of psychiatry. I believe that our behaviour is partly defined by Our Father in Heaven and by ourselves. The demons outside and the demons within, as it were."

"So, what are you going to do?" said Nash.

"Well, we have to exorcise the demons within," answered Herb, before Dr. King had a chance to stutter a reply.

Dr. King lifted a silver tray and placed it on the bedside table next to Nash who craned his neck to see that it contained a jug, several strings of beads, a book, a cross, a knife, a towel, a pair of plastic gloves and a pair of glasses. He was a little surprised and concerned by the knife. Dr. King placed his hands in the jug and removed fingers that dripped with blood. He wiped them on the towel and placed them inside the plastic gloves.

"Don't look so worried, Nash, this shouldn't be that...that...oh what's the word?"

"That what?" screamed Nash.

"Long," comforted Herb.

"Painful," clarified King, remembering what he wanted to say.

"His memory's not what it was, I'm afraid, but he's in his late-seventies so no surprise really," whispered Herb.

It was supposed to relax Nash. It failed miserably.

"Herb, tell this decrepit, dementia-riddled, Irish lunatic that if he puts so much as a finger on me, I'll rip it from its socket," shouted Nash, thrashing his body in a vain hope of loosening the ropes.

"You're really not in a position to threaten that, are you? Anyway, I don't have to... to...what's it called?" Donovan waited unsuccessfully for divine intervention to rescue him.

"Touch you?" offered Herb.

"Yes, that's right. Thank you, friend. Now I need you to let me talk to this John character. That is his name, isn't it?"

"Yes, but I won't let you talk to him. I need him. He's made me a better person. I feel secure now that he's with me, I won't let you get to him."

"We'll see about that, son."

"Nash, listen to me," said Herb. "No one likes change, but this situation is not doing you any good at all."

"I can't change, Herb. I don't have that choice," replied Nash.

"We all have a choice, Nash, even me."

"When have you ever bloody changed? You've been the same for as long as I can remember. You're a bloody hypocrite, Herb."

"Am I? Well, I've given up the booze for a start."

"You've given up booze, I don't believe it. What happened?"

"The night that I stormed out of here, when you were about to ruin your life again, I went out to the pub and got smashed. I didn't want to come back because I knew that she would still be here, so I ended up sleeping in a skip. I woke up covered in other people's junk. Filthy and broken, I sat there and I cried, I'm not ashamed to say that I wept uncontrollably. I realised in that moment that I was out of control. I wasn't acting like me anymore, I was acting on behalf of the alcohol."

"That's how you live, Herb. I thought that was how you liked it?"

"It was, but there's more to life than just what I want. Do you know what made me cry most when I was sitting there in other people's garbage?"

Nash shook his head.

"That I had failed you. Part of the reason for your behaviour is that I have acted as an appalling role model. I decided the only person who could change me, was me. You're the same, Nash. The only person who can decide how you want to be is you. Not John, not the government, not the press, no one but you."

Doctor King picked up the cross and held it directly above Nash's head, swinging it back and forward, whilst mumbling some claptrap of an unrecognisable language in his broad Irish accent. Nash wasn't sure if it was hypnotherapy, something more religious, or a combination of the two. But as he tried to block out the noise it crept back into his body like an infection. Somehow the words weren't being spoken to Nash's conscious self. They were being aimed somewhere deep within his subconscious, somewhere that Nash wasn't even aware existed. It was penetrating deep into his cells, absorbed into him like a breath taken into his lungs.

It might have been indecipherable to Nash but John sure knew what it meant. He translated it as easily as he understood the Polish cleaners in the hotel back in Camden. As the noises formed meaning, suddenly Nash's eyelids collapsed and his body fell limp.

"Nash, I need you to let me speak to him," asked Dr. King in a softly spoken tone.

"No," came a distant voice that was unmistakably Nash's, even though his eyes and mouth seemed to be tightly closed.

"Nash, where is he inside you at the moment?"

"Throat."

"Now, Nash, do you remember I had a knife on my tray?"

"Yes."

"If you don't let me talk to him, I'm going to…to… oh you know?" said King, gazing at Herb for help.

"Cut the cords and let you go," said Herb, not sure of the ending and offering a wild guess.

"Cut your throat open and release him anyway," King contradicted.

This seemed to have an instant reaction on Nash. Somewhere deep down, bubbling away, his natural instincts were telling his soul that it didn't really fancy that one little bit. Either Nash willingly offered access to John, or his body was going to find a way of doing it for him. Like a body rejecting an organ donation, the answer came quickly.

"OK!" shouted Nash in uncontrolled reflex.

"Come forward, evil spirit and speak," said Dr. King, affecting a tone that was more dark and menacing than the softly spoken Irish inflection that he'd used before.

"I'm here," replied John calmly, as Nash's mouth and eyes opened without concerted effort. There were no pupils evident in his eyes, which had been replaced by light red capillaries that chased each other across his white marbled eyeballs.

"Welcome, evil spirit."

"You seem very sure of yourself, don't you?" John answered.

"What do you mean?"

"It's evil. Something that you don't fully understand. It must be evil, mustn't it? You have no idea how wrong you are."

"You do not belong here, demon!"

"Demon, I take that as an insult. If you were facing one, as I have, you wouldn't have got as far as an introduction. A demon is driven by a need to destroy. It's only purpose is to feed on human spirit. Whilst I have been working hard to save them. Including yours, as it happens."

"I demand that you leave this body and this world. Go back to the place whence you came." Dr. King held his cross high above Nash's head.

"Who uses the word 'whence' anymore? What are you, a Knight of the Round Table? No. I'm not going to do that, I'm afraid. I have a job to do and if you won't accept that it affects you, then at least give the rest of mankind a chance to."

"Are you...are you...oh damn it!" stuttered King, again looking at Herb for support.

"Um...kidding?" he offered with a hunch of his shoulders.

"Threatening me?" came King's eventual response.

"No. But the truth is that if you go through with this you will be responsible for the consequences and you will be judged for it," said John.

"If you do not leave willingly, then I will draw you from this body and eject you into the burning fires of damnation," croaked King.

"You don't know the half of it," replied John, who had been nearer to damnation than any Pope, bishop or vicar was ever likely to.

John was starting to believe that the priest didn't have the power to remove him, even if he'd wanted to. King's religious beliefs appeared to be based on a naive collection of traditional views that John knew to be nowhere near reality. A combination of strong insults and cross waving wouldn't be enough. As John waited for the next level of encouragement, 'polite invitation', it was clear that he had underestimated this peculiar preacher.

Dr. King delicately placed the beads in the sign of the cross over Nash's body. Dipping the point of the knife in and out of the jug with the finesse of an artist coating a paintbrush, he flicked blood over his patient. Eyes magnified through thick glasses, he thumbed the book open to the appropriate page and once again started his incoherent chanting. With each crescendo of the incantation his arms stretched forward in a pulling motion, beckoning to John with his hands. To John's surprise he felt himself moving. When all you are is a very small ball of electric gas floating around in someone else's body, there aren't any easy ways of stopping yourself. He needed to think quickly.

Gathering speed at an alarming pace, it wouldn't be long before he shot out of one of Nash's orifices, and then what would happen to him? Could he die twice? Would he return to the Soul Catcher or maybe something worse? Whatever the consequences, he knew unequivocally he had to stay with Nash. In the whole of the Universe there was nothing more important than his utter desire to survive. As the light rushed through Nash's jaws, inviting him out to play, an uncontrollable energy exploded all around him.

Although gradual at first, an intense blue fire burnt in Nash's eyes before it eventually consumed the room with the intensity of a magnesium flame.

"I'm not sure if this is...this is...oh damn it?"

"Normal?" said Herb, his face etched with a sense of worry.

"Yeah," agreed King, bewildered by this unexpected side effect.

John burst through Nash's eyes like a comet, convinced that the next emotional memory would be the Earth rushing away from him, until it was merely a speck of dust in the distance. After a few seconds of unfamiliar calm, when nothing at all seemed to be flying past him, he glanced about. The bedroom, that John had so often seen through Nash's eyes, was lacking in the level of commotion that he expected. Both Herb and Donovan stood frozen in position like town-centre statues keeping guard over bustling shopaholics. No tick nor tock pattered from the timepiece on Nash's bedside table, all three of its hands having ceased movement. None of these revelations were nearly as exceptional as the discovery that John found closest of all.

The cloud of particles that embodied his spirit existence were projected into the room in the shape of a human. Not just any human, one he barely recognised from the distant past. It was John's. Although there was nothing normal about his actual structure. Every feature from head to hip to heel was a crackling malevolence of blue light, powerful and intimidating. Although his limbs moved freely, his mobility from the spot where he had landed was restricted. The light that tapered away from the back of his head shook like a rattlesnake, eager to extricate itself from Nash's eye sockets. The enjoyable nostalgia of being himself one last time was soon shattered by a voice.

"This is a turn-up for the books. That makes you number twelve," said a voice, no more than a whisper. None of the people in the room were talking. Whether it came from outside or inside him, John couldn't be sure.

"Who said that?" John whispered back.

"I said it," came the voice again, "and, although you think it's a whisper, believe me, I'm shouting from where I am."

"Where are you?"

"Very close and very far away at the same time?"

"I don't get it?"

"You're not meant to. I can't believe you're number twelve and I didn't know anything about you. They have been keeping you from me?"

"What are you talking about?"

"I'm talking about you and your ability."

"What ability?"

"The ability of a non-human to enact the Limpet Syndrome."

"This is the Limpet Syndrome?"

"Oh yes indeed. Welcome to the ultimate human survival mechanism. A unique trait that has evolved over countless millennia to protect mankind, and they don't even know about it. The most amazing of all man-made creations. Except, of course, you are not human."

"Yes, I am, don't oppress me," replied John indignantly.

"I'm not. You were human once. But now you are only part-human. A human in soul alone. Only eleven human souls have ever succeeded to do what you have just done. That also means you're not reincarnated, which is the normal consequence of the Limpet Syndrome in a human. So, I'd guess that you've been sent back. Am I right?"

"Who are you?"

"I'm part you and part me," said the voice ambiguously.

"I'm sorry, I think I'm aware of the 'me' part, but not the 'you' part?" replied John.

"Maybe you'll find out, one day. The more important question is what do you want to do now?"

"What do you mean?"

"Do you want to stay here, or do you want to let go?"

So much had been asked of him since his death but until now no one had asked him what he wanted. All of his energy had been focused on saving humanity and nothing had been reserved for saving him. What he wanted most of all was to put the world, and his place in it, back to normal.

"It seems, then, that your choice is made," said the voice.

"What? I didn't say anything," replied John.

"You didn't have to, John. If you want all of those things you cannot stay where you are. You must find another way to fight, and only you have the answer to that."

"What answer?" shouted John, "I don't have the answer."

"You're smart, John, you must know who holds the key to what you want?"

"Who? I don't know who you mean."

"You will, soon enough."

"When?"

"I don't know why they have sent you back. But I will find out. Whatever they've offered you in return, ask yourself, John, do you really believe that they will keep their side of the deal? They will not. They will do everything they can to cover up your very existence."

"Why should I believe some random invisible voice that might just be my own insanity?"

"Well, if you don't believe me, ask them yourself. There is only one person who can help you get back what was taken from you. But you must start fighting clever. It will become clear, but you must let go now."

John had no reason to trust this voice. It was hard to trust anything that you couldn't see. It wasn't the voice that was telling him to let go, though. He had already made that decision himself. It wasn't just for his benefit either. One of the side effects of his occupation of Nash was the dependency that it had created. If he didn't want to destroy that link he was no better than Emorfed.

"I'm ready to let go," he said.

"Good decision. Now before you go there are two pieces of information that will be useful. Next time you set up residence inside someone's body I highly recommend you spend some time in the frontal lobe. That's the bit of the brain that manages emotion and memory. You'll find it a lot safer there and they won't even know you're at home."

"Frontal lobe, got it."

"Secondly, when you are at your very lowest point, a place where even desperation or despair would be welcomed alternatives, when any glimmer of hope has been utterly extinguished, then you will have one, and only one, more chance to enact the Limpet Syndrome again. You'll know when that time comes. I won't even dare to explain the aftermath of using that talent a third time. Let's just say the power of it would be so intense we'd be finding bits of you from the Milky Way to Orion's belt. Just don't do it. Well, this has been an extremely enjoyable nanosecond of your life, but if you're ready, John, time to hold on tight again."

The light snapped from Nash's eyes like the breaking of an elastic band, and in an instant John was sucked out of the window, fired at regurgitating velocity through sky and space. Nash opened his eyes, his pupils having returned to their correct positions. The faintest sparks of electricity flickered off the lights and appliances before being absorbed into whatever stood in their way. Herb and Dr. King were aware that something had happened but had no clear recollection of what it was.

"I'm not sure what happened, but it would appear we've...we've...oh whatever."

CHAPTER TWENTY-TWO

TO HELL...AND BACK

"Brimstone, we've got a problem. I think you better get down here," came a voice wafting over the intercom system as Brimstone was taking a break in the Library.

"What seems to be the issue, Mr. Silica?" he said, calmly putting down a cup of frothing red liquid that overflowed with smoke and craning what neck he had towards the microphone.

"We have an unidentified foreign body inside the machine," replied Mr. Silica, in the tone of an apprentice who'd been left in charge on his first day and had accidentally been pressing the wrong buttons.

"That's impossible," Brimstone huffed. "The Soul Catcher can predict every soul in, and every soul out. I'm afraid you must be mistaken."

"If you saw the fireworks that I'm seeing, I don't think you would agree. Shall I just tell the team to ignore it and if they happen to be disintegrated in a ball of fire and time static, not to worry as they'll probably get compensation for their families?" came the sarcastic and jittery response.

"Alright, you don't have to throw a wobbly. It's still impossible, even if there is a little bit of a...situation," replied Brimstone, struggling to remove himself from his seat.

"I know that but what if something that should be impossible had been made possible? What if the Soul Catcher can't predict a soul that's not meant to be out there in the first place?"

"John Hewson," gasped Brimstone, finding an invisible power to leap to his feet, an action that took much longer for a three-foot-piece of rock than it would have done for anyone else.

*****

Inside the Soul Catcher, John's soul ricocheted off the insides like a pinball. The journey to Hell had taken just a few minutes travelling at a velocity close to the speed of light, but having previously experienced it was still no preparation for the complete and utter disorientation. The electrical charges of his soul were bumping around the walls like beans in a coffee grinder, emotions and memories in constant collision that created a weird and bizarre dreamlike state. These twisted recollections flashed in front of him in incredible life like detail.

At one moment he visualised the end of his first day at school. But not as he originally remembered it. At the old, rusty school gate, tearful and distressed by the realisation that twelve years of educational selection and humiliation had just begun, he was being collected. Not by his mother, as was the reality, but by his faithful dog Jelly whom he'd only bought when he was twenty-eight. To add insult to insanity, the Red Setter was dressed in a tatty corduroy suit and talked in the posh English accent of one of his ex-girlfriends, Trudy Sackville-Brown.

These twisted memories flashed intermittently through him one after the next, every example more absurd than the last, each no more than a second apart. As the walls of the Soul Catcher absorbed his speed, his own hallucinations began to wane. Although this was not the end of his discomfort. Around him, hundreds of other souls pressed against his own, whilst more and more were flooding into the round holding bay at the bottom of the chamber by the second. As the hundreds poured into the free space, the build-up of pressure was forcing the Soul Catcher to expand and grow. As souls collided with John's, so did the electricity and emotions that they emitted, overwhelming his memories with theirs.

*****

Brimstone and Silica stood gazing agog at the rapidly expanding bulb of the Soul Catcher. It was fair to say that neither of them had ever seen anything like it before. Brimstone placed a craggy hand onto Silica's waist, the highest point he could reach, in the same way a normal-sized person would place a hand on someone else's shoulder. It wasn't there long. He watched it slide effortlessly through the sand-constructed body and thump back against his own. The sand reassigned itself from other parts of his anatomy, refilling the area that Brimstone's hand had just displaced.

The usual hub of activity outside the Soul Catcher, the conveyor belt of vessols that carried new inmates away, the demons busily moving around like drones, had all ceased. Everyone had stopped to watch the event unfold. There was an eerie silence in the cavern, occasionally broken by the harsh sound of metal grinding on metal as the bulb tried to expand and break loose from its standings.

"Well, I think you were right, my friend. Definitely not normal," sighed Brimstone. "How many souls do we have inside?"

Silica reviewed the list that showed the number already inside and the number that were due. The one on the left ticked along, adding about a hundred or so every second, whilst the list on the right was also gaining numbers at pace.

"We've got eight thousand inside at the moment, and a torrent on its way. If we don't do something soon then I fear the whole thing will explode and we'll be picking up pieces of fractured souls for eternity."

"I'm guessing that John has blocked the exit. If we had nothing to put him in, then the machine would have stopped letting people out. It's an override to stop any leakage. I never thought when it was being built we'd ever use it. What we need is something to put him in, and quick," concluded Brimstone, waving over three of the demons who were still gawping, mouths open at the scene like bewildered infants watching a fireworks display.

"Right, go and find something to put a soul in. I don't care what it is, just go!" shouted Brimstone.

Five minutes later the three of them returned with an assortment of plastic bodies, dropping them on the floor in front of Brimstone and Silica. They retreated backwards as if their hunter-gathering would be met with disapproval. After examination only two of the vessols on the ground were undamaged, one of a young girl and the other of a shrew.

"A girl and a shrew," muttered Brimstone, scowling in the direction of his now departed minions. "So, Silica, if you'd just spent several months cramped inside another human, before having the discomfort of being shot like a cannon halfway across the galaxy, which would you rather be?"

"Well, it's not much of a choice, but I don't think I'd want to be a shoe," answered Silica.

"I think you've got sand in your ears."

Brimstone lifted the flaccid and empty body of the young female, attached the nozzle in its mouth to the end of the Soul Catcher, and fiddled with the control panel. The machine lurched around on its foundations for a moment before rattling furiously. The mass of the bulb sucked inwards, paused for a few tantalising seconds before explosively firing something forward like a huge reconstruction of the Heimlich manoeuvre. The young girl expanded rapidly as the pressure blew out the connection and the figure shot across the massive room. Silica dropped down to a stream of sand and scurried over to the place where it had landed in a crumpled heap against the craggy wall. He slid under the body and like a flying carpet carried the girl back to the machine.

John opened his eyes. Mentally and physically bruised from his experiences, he was still focused on what he'd witnessed and unsure as to whether the feelings were his or those that had pressed down on him. Above him, a familiar, square face loomed over him.

"You gave us quite a scare then, John."

"I didn't know you cared?" puffed John meekly, still gasping for air and clutching his head, which was pounding like a supersonic jet engine.

"I don't. I thought you were about to break one of the most amazing pieces of engineering ever constructed."

"That may be, but I never want to go through that ever again."

"Why, what was it like?" enquired Brimstone curiously.

"It was horrendous. On Earth you think that being squashed on a train with merely inches to move is horrible. It's not. That's just uncomfortable, inconvenient, even mildly disappointing. All you have to put up with is the sweltering heat, someone's breath on the back of your neck and the fear of being crushed. A fear that never develops. In there you're not just feeling other people around you, they are *in* you. Their fears become your fears. Their emotions become your emotions. I have felt the most impossible, incredible fear, the most desolate panic and the most uncomfortable, searing pain," John replied, still shaking from head to foot, his voice shallow and compressed by the weight of what he had learnt.

"This is Hell," said Silica in disdain. "What did you expect, a holiday camp?"

"You're right. I expected pain, fear, pity, shame, guilt, anger and evil. I found all of them. But not exclusively. I felt some things I didn't expect and certainly can't explain."

Silica and Brimstone looked at each other with concern.

"What exactly did you feel?" asked Silica.

"I experienced hope."

"Impossible," scoffed Brimstone, a word that was coming out of him today with increasing regularity.

"Not just hope, I'm sure I felt joy, too. Someone in there showed me sympathy as our two souls collided. How could I have felt that? What were those emotions doing in there?" asked the female version of John.

Brimstone held out a stumpy hand to help John to his feet. He now stood only a little higher than Brimstone, prompting him to look down at his new existence. Nothing really surprised him anymore. Although he was less than amused by his new physique, there were far more pressing issues to solve.

"Not everyone who comes here is *pure* evil, John. The world isn't black and white. It's not split up into evil and good people. You should know that having been through the back door as a neutral soul," replied Brimstone, having taken a few moments to contemplate how to respond to John's revelations.

"Maybe, but it felt more than that. If people still had some good in them, even though they were still destined to be here, surely the prospect of coming here would move all of those feelings away. When I touched those people's souls I didn't have to go searching for the emotions that I felt. They were right there on the surface."

"Look, this is a very interesting philosophical debate and it's not that I am not thoroughly enjoying it, but... why are you here, John?"

"Ian," shouted John, suddenly remembering the mission at hand.

"He's here, don't worry. I understand he's already causing havoc for Primordial down on level zero.

Again, why are you here? You have one more to go if you remember."

"Exorcism," replied John.

"No, I don't believe you," Brimstone huffed.

"Given that I was there and as far as I remember you were not, it certainly felt like exorcism. Let me see: man of the Church, lots of incantations, feeling my soul being drawn out through the eyes – yep, pretty sure it was exorcism," replied John, miming out each part of the process.

"You don't have to be sarcastic. If it had been exorcism we would have known. The Soul Catcher would have lit up like a red dwarf."

"Maybe it's broken?"

"Look, if you'd like to be a shrew and spend a few days in the company of Primordial then carry on, John. What we have to do is work out how to get you back down there again."

John was reminded of his experience of the Limpet Syndrome. The voice he'd heard had posed some pertinent questions that at the time he'd struggled to answer. It had suggested that there was one person who would be instrumental in helping him find a way out. A way of saving himself, not just everyone else. He'd not had much time to work it out whilst he was inside the Soul Catcher. There had been far too much going on. Soon he'd need to come up with a plan, before Brimstone escorted him up to the library to pick out another poor, unsuspecting victim. There was one particular aspect of what he'd been told that he was most interested in answering first, though.

"How will you get me to Heaven, when I complete my side of the deal?"

"What do you mean?"

"Well, I've been around most of this place. I've seen the Soul Catcher and how to go back and forward to Earth. I've seen the different levels and know what they contain. What I haven't seen is what instrument takes me there."

"Look, I wouldn't worry about it. We'll get to that if you succeed and if you don't, none of it really matters," replied Brimstone cautiously.

"But just how many people have gone from here to there before?" asked John, still stalling for time but equally interested in the answer.

"I'll level with you, John, not very many."

"Hold on. I've been to level zero. I've seen hundreds, if not thousands, of animals. Surely all of them must have been brought back by someone like me. What happened to all of them?" demanded John.

"If you succeed, I assure you the big man upstairs will make sure you get what you deserve. So let's stop wasting time and go find you another candidate?" he said, setting off for the library.

"No need. I already know who to choose. You've helped me to make up my mind. Thank you," replied John. "Let's fire up the machine."

The three of them made their way over to the still steaming machine. John stood at the now familiar controls, as Brimstone fiddled with the myriad of buttons and switches. His decision had now been made and whether he was right or wrong to choose would soon become evident.

"Who's it going to be?"

John leaned over to Brimstone and whispered a name into his ear.

"Can it be done?" he said, after pausing to see Brimstone's reaction.

"When you're here, John, almost anything can be done. Although I'm intrigued by your choice."

"I think I will keep my own counsel on that."

"So be it. It matters not who you decide to burden."

"There's something else, too. I need to break one of your own rules. I need you to send me back before the time that I last left Earth."

"John, you know why I can't do that: it could be worse than the current situation with Sandy. Two of your souls running around the place, it's not

267

recommended," said Brimstone. "You can't imagine the shit that I'll be in if it went wrong."

"What happened to, 'almost anything can be done here?' If you want my help, Brimstone, it's about time you gave me some of yours. I don't want to go very far back. A day or so will do it."

"OK, if it means getting it done, then we'll try. The compromise is that you must go nowhere near Nash, understood?"

"It is. I think he deserves a break anyway," replied John, unclear whether it was a promise he could keep.

Brimstone led the female infant John up to the nozzle of the Soul Catcher and attached the mouth of his vessol to the white, cone-shaped receptacle. He stomped back to the controls, set the co-ordinates and pulled a lever. Immediately the vessol dropped to the floor and once more John was in flight.

CHAPTER TWENTY-THREE

BEAKS, JAWS AND CLAWS

Truth doesn't live where it used to. In fact it recently packed its bags and relocated to a new town with no known forwarding address. Incognito, it has settled into its secret new surroundings like the member of a witness protection scheme. Occasionally someone will claim to have discovered its location. They'll back up these claims by repeatedly shouting in a loud and convincing voice until no one has the strength to argue anymore.

It used to be much easier to locate the twinned towns of truth and untruth. Truth was occupied by experts who wore uniforms and carried their qualifications proudly about their person in their deeds and the logic of their arguments. They were doctors, lawyers, scientists, policemen, even journalists. They were believable because they carried with them this really interesting stuff called evidence. Sadly, though, they weren't very confident at shouting erratically and waving their hands in the air. Politicians don't wear uniforms, haven't done for ages.

There will always be secrets in life. Our earliest childhood memories are crammed with parental directions that defined what we should and shouldn't do. Rarely was there any proper explanation as to why. The lack of explanation is often rooted in the perception that adults believe children lack the experience or mental capacity to understand it. Often the lack of explanation is nothing more than…there isn't one. Even the person handing down the advice can't justify it because they were never told the truth either. Yet inexplicably it remains part of their belief system forever unchallenged. Even in adult life this trait of truth being hidden or ignored continues. We're told what we need to hear, which isn't quite the same as the truth.

Byron's government was no different from any that had gone before it. Arguably this government was only like it *because* of what had gone before it. A culture had been bred into the fabric of the establishment mentality, both unexplained and unintentional, like a type of conspiratorial Tourette's. Some of this government's secrets had simply been policies continued on from past administrations, preserved like an immovable bad habit. There were many examples, and Agent 15 was about to walk down the corridors of one of them.

Fifty feet underneath the streets of the city, where Londoners navigated their robotic lives oblivious to its existence, lived one of these secrets. A place that had once been the epicentre of the country's struggle for freedom was now being used to keep people from it. Through a series of dried-out sewers, disused bunker offices held the types of people that the government didn't want us to know about. In a stretch of underground from Parliament Square to Whitehall, each desolate metre had been transformed into a network of dank prison cells. Each hidden behind Victorian brick arches, and most occupied.

There was no legislation that gave the government the right to keep these people locked up. After all, laws can't be broken if they don't exist. The general public couldn't protest against the decisions either because there was almost no knowledge that these people existed. Other members of the secretive organisations who knew these inmates didn't offer aid in case they ended up joining them. In their eyes these were the unfortunate fallen comrades, silently remembered for their sacrifice. Legal representation had been revoked to avoid a human rights scandal making it into the press and there was very little objection. Every part of their existence had been erased from memory.

Of the several hundred inmates imprisoned here, Agent 15 knew most of them. After all, he'd been responsible for inviting them. The dimly lit tunnels echoed with his footsteps as he strode on, nodding occasionally to the heavily armed military personnel who stood guard at regular intervals. Lichen-covered brickwork ordered iron bars to stand to attention in each murky entrance. Cell eighty-one was no different.

Agent 15's presence was the only prompt needed for the sentry guard to unlock the firm steel gate that separated the cell from the corridor. Before the guard opened the door, Agent 15 beat him to it. He opened it with a creak and closed it behind him. Only once.

Sitting composed and upright against the far wall was a familiar female outline, clearly unfazed by her seemingly difficult predicament. Although she displayed the emotions of someone in good spirits, the cuts and bruises that covered her face told a very different story. A smile crept through the foundation of grime that coated her skin, exuding a warmth normally reserved for the greeting of close personal friends.

"I was expecting you a little earlier," she announced.

"Bad things happen to those that wait. This place has a great way of helping people think clearer," he replied.

"Were you expecting my resolve to be broken by spending a few days here on holiday? I've been to far worse places in the world than this."

"That's not a surprise given the plague-infested holes that you're used to. Perhaps I should have sent you to a farm. You'd have been much happier there amongst the animals and their filth. But they count more than us, don't they, Violet?"

"I'd take one of them over you any day. At least they have some manners. I'd try to convince you, but I can see your crown of arrogance hasn't slipped yet," replied Violet, her voice remaining calm and neutral.

Agent 15 would have happily traded insults for hours if there wasn't a deadline to meet. It had appeared to Agent 15 that the PM's urgency to resolve the whole problem of Sandy had increased in recent days. Perhaps with the election only a week away he was getting anxious as to the potential disruption of loose ends.

"Interesting place this," said Agent 15 conversationally, rubbing his fingers over the bricks as if they might give up a story or two. "It's steeped in history. A dark and macabre one at that."

"Shall I ask the guard for a torch? You can shine it under your chin and try to be really scary," mocked Violet, for the first time pushing herself up from the rickety camp bed.

"Well there are many ghost stories in these tunnels. This was the very spot where Winston Churchill made the decision to condemn Coventry to the impending Nazi bombs, sacrificing thousands of civilians for the greater good. Personally, though, I like the earlier stories. In the 19th century this place housed a truly sinister brand of criminals," he said, closing his eyes and breathing in deeply. "Can you feel it, Violet?"

"Feel what?"

"The anger running through these walls. I can smell the wonderful aroma of horror and death filling my nostrils. It's like the atmosphere has been suspended untouched for two centuries ready to poison the next occupant. Breathe it in, Violet, take a really big mouthful until you're dizzy with the ecstasy of it."

"All I can smell is something foul that wasn't in here five minutes ago."

"Do you know they used to drag the most notorious mass murderers by horse and cart through the streets and then publicly hang them outside Newgate Prison? They don't allow that anymore, apparently people object. I do miss the stupidity of old-fashioned mob violence."

"Times have changed, maybe you need to keep up?"

"Things aren't that different. This is still where successive governments over the last century have brought people they wanted to forget about. I should introduce you to a few of them. We've got Lucan here somewhere, one of our oldest guests."

"Lord Lucan?" said Violet in surprise.

"Oh yes. He was far too close to the royal family to go on trial for his alleged crimes. The scandal would have been fatal for the establishment. In any case, the man is a turd of the highest order and deserves nothing less."

"What about justice? Does that word no longer have meaning in this country?" muttered Violet, demonstrating the first signs of irritation.

"Justice is subjective. A collective viewpoint of twelve humans not intelligent enough to understand the arguments," replied Agent 15 scornfully. "In any case, if the government can set the law, then it can circumvent it. Law or no law, it's our job to protect society from itself. Which includes keeping you away from them."

"Are you trying to provoke me?"

"I don't need to, Violet. That reaction, in fact all of your emotions, are instincts that you won't even know how to feel before long."

"I don't get you?"

"I need a second volunteer," said Agent 15, reaching inside his jacket pocket and removing a syringe that contained a light blue liquid that sparkled and danced. "You see, Violet, our first trial of Emorfed was inconclusive and I need to test it again. If you don't tell me what I want to know I will inject this into your neck and you will tell me anyway. On top of that you'll lose any motivation to fight me, or anyone else for that matter. Another victory for national security."

"I think you misunderstand my motives," replied Violet, "I think you and I want the same thing."

"I doubt that."

"I suspect that we are both trying to find Sandy Logan. Now if you do inject me with Emorfed I may be able to tell you, but I won't be able to help you."

"I don't need your help."

"I know Sandy. What's more, he sent Ian Noble to find me, which means he was seeking my help. If you let me approach him, he will not be suspicious of our meeting. It will give you valuable time to bring him in."

"Why should I trust you?"

"You shouldn't. I take no pleasure in aiding you or betraying a friend. But if it is my route out then I will take the selfish choice. In return for helping you, I must be released."

"What, so you can go on terrorising the scientific community?"

"I can't promise you I won't. Your choice. Who do you need more, Sandy or me?"

Agent 15 didn't have an opinion on this ultimatum, but he knew Byron did. What if a few laboratories were under threat because of his actions? If he brought Sandy in he'd remove the only eyewitness to the government's involvement in Tavistock. Who cared if he had to pick Violet up again later on? It might not take that long if he double-crossed her after she delivered Sandy to him.

"They tell me that your nickname is Violent Strokes. It's interesting that your friendships are so easily broken. You bark on about wanting justice, yet you're willing to rob Sandy of it. Perhaps you are not as strong as your nickname suggests," exclaimed Agent 15.

"We'll see, won't we?"

"If you are to be used as bait then you'll be electronically tagged until the operation is a success."

"Agreed."

"Where is our friend now?" asked 15 impatiently, already moving towards the cell door.

"Where would you expect to find a pigeon in London?"

"Trafalgar Square?" he replied. "How can you be so sure?"

"Ian told me. Now you're going to need help. I understand there are quite a few pigeons in that area."

*****

Four days had passed since Ian had left and the valley pigeons were making themselves right at home. Initially, Trafalgar Square had been as alien to them as a shark living in a fourth floor council house with a couple of water bottles strapped to its back. Like most things in nature they had come to accept the strange, symbiotic relationship between the humans and themselves. They came to believe that the threat level here was less than in their traditional surroundings. What's more, big, fat tourists wanted to feed them, for free!

They mixed with the locals without much fuss, too. Their city cousins were foolhardy and simple but survived this urban environment through a combination of confidence and luck. There they were flying aimlessly from one hand of food to the next, oblivious to the possibilities of capture or death. They sat on perches of man-made stone like they were branches of a tree, and flew without fear between bus and tramline. Convinced that they were some horrible mutation and not a related species at all, the valley pigeons observed their strange habits like a bunch of mystery shoppers.

It wasn't long before the braver, or possibly more stupid, of their number started to copy and learn this foreign behaviour. Once the line of least resistance was broken, once one or two did it, the rest followed like lemmings. Whether through natural selection or acquired behavioural conditioning, they were learning to accept this new way of life. As the days passed they had become hooked on free food and danger, as much as a junkie is to his next heroin fix.

Sandy's attention to them was minimal, even though their groups' number seemed to be growing daily. The initial fifty or so that had made the long and erratic journey here across various parts of the country, seemed to have grown into the hundreds. The ratio of country pigeons versus city ones was almost level, although it was becoming increasingly difficult to separate them.

Only some of Sandy's attention was being reserved for Big Bobby. Clearly not satisfied with the small amount of blurry video footage of two pigeons in conversation taken a few days ago, he'd used his uniquely American mentality to set up his very own London tourist attraction selling tickets to see the talking doves. Sandy had been careful to avoid any contact with Bobby, who was forced to coax the tame London pigeons to talk. He would have had more success getting a stone lion to roar. The pigeons were more than happy to support Bobby's endeavour if all they had to do was look gormless and eat sunflower seeds.

Sandy's attention had been largely focused on Ian's absence. This was partly borne out of a concern for Ian and mostly out of a concern for himself. Without Ian's total dedication and Violet's help, he had nowhere to turn. Too long had gone now to convince Sandy that all was well. Yes, it was possible that Ian had got lost or had simply forgotten where he was going in the first place. Yet with Ian's reputation it was just as plausible that the worst had happened.

Sandy had lost none of his intellect or intuition in his current incarnation. It was clear to him that if Ian had failed, he may well have disclosed more than Sandy would have wished. That's why he'd been on his guard these last two days, keeping as close to the pack as possible in order to disappear into the background.

When Violet arrived in Trafalgar Square that sunny June morning, Sandy had seen her well before she'd made it past the fountains. It was with mixed emotions that he watched her approach, unsure if it was a potential exit or his inevitable end. Before he was willing to reveal himself, he needed to know if she was alone. She strolled down the steps of the National Gallery towards the bulk of the valley pigeons who were collecting lunch at the feet of a school group. Other than paying a little too much attention to the pigeons themselves, Sandy noticed that she was acting normally, and there appeared to be no one with her as she approached the flock.

"Sandy," she whispered faintly to each of them.

"Cooo," came a response, as a speckled pigeon jogged and hopped away.

"Sandy."

"Cooo," replied another.

"Sandy."

"Cagoo," said two or three pigeons at once, eagerly advancing in search of food.

"This will take all week at this rate," she muttered under her breath. "Sandy."

"I prefer Minister," came a whispered response from the feathery crowd. Violet drew closer to pinpoint the exact pigeon that had answered.

"I thought friends called you Sandy?" replied Violet, moving deeper into the crowd, crouching down to increase her chance of hearing.

"It depends on whether I'm still talking to one, doesn't it?"

"Look, Sandy, come out of the crowd. I'm worried about my sanity and I think so is that group over there," she implored, pointing over to the group of school children who were pointing and laughing at this dishevelled woman on her hands and knees.

They weren't the only people to notice. Big Bobby was paying close attention to a woman bending down and whispering to a group of pigeons just across the Square. Anxious that someone else might muscle in on his unique and bizarre business empire, he crept slowly over to take a look.

"I'd prefer to stay in the crowd for the time being, Violet."

"OK, I understand. You've no idea how long I've been looking for you, Sandy. You need to come with me, it's not safe for any of us."

"Where's Ian?"

"He didn't make it."

Bobby, with all the stealth of a piano falling from a skyscraper, was now within earshot of the two of them. There was no doubt in his mind that they *were* talking to each other. Avoiding any tact or subtlety, he stood up and shouted to his group of punters, who had followed some way behind.

"I found them! She's talking to one of them now."

"Sorry, Violet," said Sandy.

"Sandy, don't go!" she shouted as he launched into flight with a number of others.

"Right, you'll all get a chance, one at a…" were the last audible words that escaped Bobby's mouth.

The small dart that was now lodged in Bobby's more than substantial arse had stopped him in mid-sentence. His outstretched body was now falling in slow motion towards the ground, hitting the deck with a thunderous noise that drew the attention of most of the tourists in the area. More darts flew out around them. Another of Bob's party hit the floor unconscious as one just missed Violet's ear. As she ducked out of the way, the Square around her was becoming a military zone.

Armed and uniformed personnel were aggressively sweeping the general public away from the area.

Violet had not discussed with Agent 15 how he was going to pick up Sandy, but she had no doubt this was it. A painful surge of guilt spread through her body at the realisation that she was responsible for bringing this upon him.

Lorries of men were pulling up in all directions. A dozen harpoons flew out from the top of Nelson's Column, smashing through the masonry walls of the gallery and other nearby buildings. The thick canvas ropes that they carried unravelled to construct a web of nets in all four corners of the Square, until the whole area above their heads was covered. Escape by air or foot was now impossible.

An inherent sense of panic struck the valley pigeons like the cranial lights had suddenly been switched on. Those instincts that had been subdued sprang back into action as they launched into the air in a vain attempt to escape the massive aviary that had been hastily constructed above their heads. The local pigeons stood around and watched. Many were themselves struck by darts and compliantly fell to the floor in a deep sleep.

Along every rooftop, hidden snipers rained a shower of darts into the Square, where pigeon and person alike scattered to avoid them. Men, women and bird fell where they were struck and before long the whole Square was a mass of bodies. Amongst them was Violet Stokes, struck by a dart in the back of the head. Through glazed, empty eyes she wasn't able to pick out the lifeless body of a pigeon that was far bigger than the rest.

CHAPTER TWENTY-FOUR

VOTE CASEY

"I'll ask you again, Prime Minister. How do you respond?"

The Prime Minister had barely registered the question. There were far more important things to consider than the stupid questions of some holier-than-thou, private-educated political journalist.

"He can't answer the question, Tristan, because he knows only too well that his policies on social mobility have been an utter failure. There is more poverty in this country than ever before and his turgid administration owes a four-year debt to each and every one of those poor souls that his party have conspired to hinder," said another voice.

The lights beamed down on the sharp suit opposite, his greasy hair glistening like a mirrorball. The grin on his face was a permanent blemish that attempted to deceive the viewers from the façade of his self-righteousness. There was an unusual lack of fight inside Byron tonight and the enemy smelt it. Uncharacteristically, he found this debate an inconvenience. A discussion rebellious in its desire to focus on anything of genuine importance. At least on the subjects that mattered he was acting, all Geoffrey Hitchins would do was dither. Surely the public would understand that this pompous, overprivileged moron would do a much poorer job than he had?

The cameras had zoomed in on Byron in hushed expectation of the response. The lights burned down on his slightly thinning hair and a line of sweat trickled down his brow.

"As usual, Tristan, you have asked the wrong question. The point shouldn't be about our perceived shortcomings, but about our substantial achievements," uttered Byron, finally revving up his verbal retaliation.

Geoffrey scoffed loudly.

"My party inherited a society utterly shattered by the very man who promises to fix it," added Byron, fixing his gaze at the alternative in front of him. "The opposition are interested in government, but not governing. The only chance for the British people is to embrace my manifesto and when they vote next Thursday they must remember the years of hardship and despair they faced under my honourable friend here. If they prefer not to relive it, then their only choice is to vote Casey."

The answer tripped instinctively out of his mouth, a pledge repeated habitually down his career, conscious that the game being played was, 'who do you trust most?'

"If the choice is so obvious to the people of Britain," jumped in Geoffrey, before the twittering Tristan was able to ask another question. "Then let him explain to them tonight, in honesty and with integrity, why he enforced a policy of taxation that inflicted terrible suffering on those in the most deprived parts of our country."

Byron struggled to remember the policy to which his accuser referred. He wasn't in the right frame of mind for soul-searching and he certainly wasn't prepared to justify his actions to an individual whose outlook on life made his skin crawl. A month he'd spent in manifesto launches, TV campaigns, speed canvassing, policy announcements and constituency coffee mornings. He was completely bored with the whole circus. Now it was all in the past all he really cared about was the future and making it a brighter one.

"I don't recall such a policy."

"I'm sorry, Prime Minister, did you say you don't recall?" pounced Tristan like a predatory lion who'd just spotted a gazelle with a gammy leg.

"See, he doesn't even remember his own policies. This man isn't just unfit for government, he's unfit for anything. I thought your manifesto was called 'Freedom for Britain'? Well, I suggest that the British people set this Prime Minister free from his undoubted suffering," goaded Geoffrey, auditioning to the studio audience who clapped enthusiastically in agreement.

"This country and its people will get freedom, I can promise them that. I will not stop until every man, woman and child in this country can wake in the morning with a stout heart and a clear head. I will work tirelessly to create opportunities for all, irrespective of what they look like, where they were born, or how they decide to live their lives. They will know what freedom from their pain really feels like and they won't even need to work hard or long for it," he answered with words devoid of spin or preparation. This was deep from the heart and no one watching doubted Byron's conviction.

"With respect, Prime Minister, these sound like the words of a despot, not a democratically elected leader," offered Geoffrey, taken aback by the delusion in Byron's response.

"With slightly less respect, at least the people know where they stand with me, and the polls still suggest that the overwhelming majority would rather vote for me than a man who stands for elitism and the fortunate minority," rebuked Byron.

"Thank you, gentlemen, that's all we have time for. A heated debate as ever," Tristan interceded, before the two politicians ended the programme in blows. "Whether you are convinced by the arguments that you have heard tonight or not, one thing is for sure, you will have the chance to demonstrate it at the ballot box next Thursday. From everyone at 'Election – You Choose', goodnight."

The lights dimmed for a moment as the candidates and their host sat in the gloom watching the credits usher across the monitor. Angry exchanges had been substituted for whispered tones away from the public jousting of the live televised debate.

"Well, that was jolly. I thought I just about won that one, Byron," joked Geoffrey. "Shall I meet you later in the ministerial bar for a couple of whiskies?"

"What?" replied Byron indignantly.

"Oh come on, Byron, no hard feelings. You know as much as anyone how this works. These events are all for show, we've been sparring like this for years. Are we going to fall out over rhetoric?"

"No, of course not," he said, snapping out of his trance. "But I can't tonight, there's a meeting I need to attend."

Byron's mobile phone displayed a number of missed calls, all from the same recognisable number, all demanding silently and impatiently for a reply. He got to his feet and strolled briskly away from the alien environment of the television studio and made his way out of the building. It was about ten o'clock in the evening but the bright full moon tricked the night sky into believing it was much earlier. Quickly he was ushered into his ministerial Jaguar, which was inelegantly mounted on the kerbside awaiting his speedy retreat. In the back of the car he slumped on the leather next to his Private Secretary who was clutching a clipboard that bulged with notepaper.

"Andrew, you look like you're organising a wedding. Why don't you get yourself some technology?" said Byron, commenting on the black folder bursting at its seams.

The man clung onto his clipboard somewhat offended that his boss felt his methods were lacking, even though he knew the PM couldn't wipe his arse without help. He drew out a piece of paper and passed it to Byron.

"You're a fine one to talk. You thought a laptop was a naughty dance," replied Andrew. "As you know, sir, I find working with bits of paper means I don't need to be constantly talking to the IT department about how to fix them. Unlike some of my colleagues."

Byron shot him a dirty look.

"Here are the details of your meeting," he said, handing Byron a compliments slip. "You're late, but then again why break the habit of a lifetime?"

"I won't need you for the rest of the night, Andrew. I'll see you in my office first thing in the morning," replied Byron, taking no notice of the piece of paper in his lap.

"OK," replied his assistant, hesitating before leaving the car. "Prime Minister, I'm not really sure why you are going to meet this guy. It doesn't appear to have anything to do with the campaign and we are fast running out of time. Is he a donor?"

"Of sorts, but it's of no concern to you," barked Byron, unhappy with his aide's interrogational tone. "You need not worry about the campaign, it's all in hand."

"But…we have less than a week left. How can you feel so confident when there is so much that could still go wrong?"

"You just run along and do what you do. Let me worry about winning the election, I have done it before, if you remember."

Andrew dragged his gangly frame out of the car. Bewildered and concerned by Byron's total arrogance, he watched as the Jaguar sped off into the night before raising his hand to hail a taxi. Byron picked up his phone, pressed seven on the speed-dial and waited for the response.

"Prime Minister," came Agent 15's familiar voice on the other end. "It is done."

"So, you have him, then?"

"We believe so, sir."

"I'm sorry, you believe so? Agent 15, you either do have the reincarnated form of Sandy Logan, or you don't. It's not hard to work out, there aren't many talking pigeons in this world."

"It's not that simple…we hit some complications. We had to bring in as many pigeons as we found at the location we were given. We couldn't run the risk of him escaping," replied 15.

"How many?" asked Byron, a tone of inevitable disappointment rearing up in his voice.

"Four hundred and fifty-two."

"Oh, not many, then. I'm slightly disappointed."

"On top of that we got Violet back, too," he added, hoping this news would act as a silver lining. "On the bright side there are millions of pigeons out there in the world, at least we've whittled it down."

"What are you going to do with them now?"

"We'll do what we always do with prisoners."

Byron knew what Agent 15 meant by this. The Secret Service were an unsubtle bunch and had removed the word 'diplomacy' from their induction binder. They just went about their methods in the quickest possible way, which usually meant more brawn than brain, usually with a great degree of success. Byron knew that the unfamiliarity of the species would not stop them using their barbaric techniques to extract what they needed.

"I'll be there as quick as I can. Remember, I want no harm to come to Sandy," demanded Byron.

*****

The moon that had shimmered so brightly on car windscreens and the glass buildings that surrounded the television centre now skipped mesmerically over the surface of the reservoir where, from the edge, Byron watched the gentle ripples of the water. Accompanied only by the calmness of the lake and the chattering of his thoughts, he stood alone. At his request his team of advisors and security guards had withdrawn, allowing him to meet his guest alone, unshackled from prying eyes and inquisitive ears. For some time he waited, completely still apart from the flapping of the winter coat that protected him from the cool midnight breeze.

The reservoir was small in comparison to the ones that take up vast canyons and valleys around the country. This was not one of those encircled by picturesque postcard mountain ranges or sweeping forests. This one was in the heart of London, enveloped by high brick walls that kept out claustrophobic apartment blocks. Even at midnight, with only the light of the moon for illumination, all sides of the reservoir were visible.

Byron raised his expensive wristwatch to his ear, confirming that time hadn't ceased completely, only to catch the glimpse of a figure moving slowly towards him. The man approaching wore a similarly suspicious long coat, his head hunched into his shoulders, seeking an escape route from the icy breeze. When he reached Byron there was no warmth in his reception, unimpressed to have been dragged away from whatever activity normal people do at this time of night.

If it wasn't for the strangeness of the location, there would be no clues that these men were expecting the other, a chance meeting of two lonely travellers. They stood in silence, each waiting for the other to break it.

"I thought we'd agreed there was no need for us to meet again," sighed the newcomer.

"I need to change some of our arrangements and be satisfied that you fully understand what is expected of you," replied Byron.

"We have been through it often enough," replied the man, "I risk as much, if not more than you, remember."

The two men avoided eye contact, as if the chance meeting of their gaze might bring the same result of meeting Medusa. It was a good job that no other human was in sight of these two dodgy individuals. They couldn't look any more dubious if they'd been wearing signs and winking insanely at each other.

The second man was considerably shorter and older: the top of his greying hair only just came up to the shoulders of Byron's six-foot frame. Dressed like he'd just left an expensive gentlemen's club, a gold pocket watch and chain swung from his double-breasted suit jacket that peeked out from his long coat, as his gleaming shoes were in competition with the moon itself.

"Dominic, we need to move the date. Next Monday is too soon, I want you to do it on Tuesday. That will give us less chance of something being discovered before the election on Thursday," stated Byron, his warm breath condensing in the air like dragon's smoke.

"What difference does it make, Byron? I have gone to great length and personal danger to ensure that both of us are kept 'uninvolved'. If we change the plan now we risk losing that anonymity."

"Nevertheless, that is what you must do."

"If you want to change the date then I'm changing the price. Another one million on top," demanded Dominic.

"I find your greed ironic."

"I'm not with you?" he replied quizzically, his eyes finally drawn towards Byron.

"The irony is that your deceit will remove from the human race the very motivation that has caused you to act."

"Well, you haven't changed the world yet, Byron. There's still time for some of us to profit."

"I wonder what the water company would say if they discovered what you had done? How would you be viewed, Dom? What would the members at your pompous gentlemen's club say?"

"I suspect they would raise a glass of whatever expensive wine I had just bought them with my ill-gotten gains and toast my endeavour."

"I find it abhorrent that I have to deal with an immoral mercenary. My only consolation is that slugs like you will never be able to act in this way again. You are helping to destroy the greed that you epitomise."

"Nevertheless, if you wish for me to aid you, then that is my price. You can keep your utopian ideology and do what you wish with it, you and the rest of them. I'm not interested in the outcome of your experiment."

"You will get your money. I hope you can find a hole big enough to escape to. It will haunt you and if you reappear, so will I."

"I'm sure I will manage."

"I need you to go through the plan with me one more time," announced Byron.

"We've been through it a hundred times before," appealed Dominic, tired of being pulled around on strings like the Prime Minister's very own puppet.

"Then we will go through it for the hundred and first time."

"OK, if we must. On Tuesday morning we will receive at our main waterworks depot a large container on the back of a lorry" Dominic regurgitated the plan in a slow repetitive fashion.

"And where is that depot?"

"Oh come on, do we have to go into that much detail? You know where it is."

"Humour me."

"Hemel Hempstead," sighed Dominic, continuing in the manner of an actor reeling off a well-rehearsed script. "The delivery will be marked for my attention and no other person will meet it. The goods-in department has been given the information about the vehicle and I will falsify the goods-in data, creating an entry for twenty-four barrels of folic acid."

"And what will be marked on the barrels?"

"Oddly, it will say folic acid," huffed Dominic. "Shall I go on? I'd like to finish before breakfast."

Byron nodded.

"The barrels will be taken into the processing plant and the team there will be told about the government's decision to add folic acid to the water supply to reduce infant deformities. The sample will be tested onsite, as everything else is, to verify its contents and to ensure its purity. Of course the real contents will not be tested, so we have created fake reports and certificates for the batch. Once presented with the forged documents, the production department will not query the strange colour of the contents."

"Why not?" asked Byron, believing to have found a flaw in the plan.

"Because they are underpaid morons who are not employed for their speed of thought or moral fibre. They will add it to the water system without a flinch."

"How long until it gets into people's taps?"

"Somewhere within twenty-four hours at the earliest. But by the Saturday the whole of the South-East of England will be having it in their cups of tea and bathtubs. Once your party has been re-elected and you have nationalised all the water companies under my leadership, then we will do the same for the rest of the country. You will have your utopia and I will have a newly discovered preference for bottled water."

"It all sounds too easy to me," muttered Byron.

"That's the beautiful thing, Prime Minister: it is. Now let's talk payment. When will my money be paid?"

"On Tuesday I will send someone with your money to Hemel Hempstead."

"Is that wise, sir?"

"I thought you'd be eager for it, Dominic?"

"Well, yes of course, but on the same day. Isn't that risky?"

"Everything in life is a risk."

"Who should I expect?"

"I will be sending two people to ensure that no mistakes are made. Don't worry, one of them is the best in the world at what he does. I have asked him to oversee the operation."

"This is totally irregular. I protest," argued Dominic. "We agreed that I would only use people that I trust."

"Yes, but I also need to use someone that I trust."

"What is his name?" asked Dominic.

"Victor Serpo," replied Byron.

"What about the other person that you speak of?"

"Oh, you don't need to worry about him. I doubt you will even see him," replied Byron.

CHAPTER TWENTY-FIVE

TRUTH AND LIES

When Byron finally reached the underground network of the war offices, deep beneath the streets of Whitehall, it was the early hours of Sunday morning. He'd caught a few hours of restless sleep in the back of his government car, before freshening up at his private apartment. The meeting with Dominic Lightower had gone exactly as planned and, although he felt on top of things, he had desperately wanted to get to Sandy earlier. There were four days until the election and only two before Emorfed would be let loose on the unsuspecting British public. That only gave him two days to take Sandy out of the equation.

Agent 15 was waiting for the Prime Minister at the entrance to the underground rooms in his now familiar black outfit. He, too, had slept restlessly for much of the night, but showed none of the typical signs of fatigue. All part of the training, it would seem.

"Prime Minister, welcome to our hostel for undesirables," he said, shaking Byron warmly by the hand and leading him through the inconspicuous door that led from the Home Office buildings and down underground via stone steps.

"Have you identified him yet?" Byron asked when they were far from the outside world.

"We believe so, sir. Although we've had no luck in making him talk."

"How did you work out which of them was Sandy, then?"

"We asked Violet really nicely," replied Agent 15, winking when he hadn't needed to. "We encouraged her to remember what might have been different about Ian compared to a regular pigeon. On top of that we have some of the best scientific minds working on tests to identify the DNA make-up, to see if we can identify him that way. The one that Violet picked out is being tested now, so we should have the results soon enough. Do you want to see him?"

"Very much."

As they walked along the row of worn-down brick cells, Byron glanced at each inmate that occupied them. Where once a human would have sat, now most contained pigeons. It gave it the feeling of an aviary rather than a prison. Some of the pigeons sat on the floor seemingly unfazed and even possibly enjoying the experience. Some flew around in a vain search for the exit, petrified by the men that stood guard over them. Occasionally a cell was inhabited by a human, some poor misfortunate soul still groggy from the effects of being shot by a military strength tranquilliser. One loud American voice was shouting insults and promising severe legal retributions.

"What were the characteristics that Violet mentioned?" asked Byron.

"She mentioned that he had very similar characteristics to his human form. Particularly that Ian was an extremely pale person and his pigeon had been pure white. So we had a look at Sandy's profile and got one of our boffins to do a match," replied Agent 15, reaching into his pocket to produce the world's most ludicrous photo e-fit of a purple-coloured pigeon with a bald patch and bristly chin.

Agent 15 stopped at cell one hundred and fifteen and pointed into the cell. His expression beamed with the same satisfaction a cat shows when it brings a dead mouse to the feet of its slightly disgusted owner. The pigeon in this cell had been tethered to the bars of its cage by its feet, wings and head, a process that had caused its feathers to be displaced all over the floor. Bloodied and blackened, its body displayed the results of undisclosed implements ripping at feather and skin. A woman in a white coat and spectacles was still probing it maliciously with a mini-cattle prod. As a gloved hand shot in and out of the cage, the other took samples with a needle. On another table a second scientist was running blood samples through a three-foot analyser as the constant droning sound of a printer reeled off the results.

"Agent 15, your work here is complete. You have exceeded your brief and I must ask you to do so once more," said Byron, turning away from the pigeon's despicable torture.

"The job isn't complete," replied Agent 15. "We've not positively identified Sandy yet."

"He's safe. As long as he's unable to bring attention to Emorfed in the next few days, I'm happy. I have a few things that I must attend to here, specifically with Violet Stokes."

"What would you have me do instead?"

"You must get personally involved in bringing Emorfed to the people. On Tuesday morning a batch of twenty-four barrels will be delivered to the main waterworks of Southern Water in Hemel Hempstead. The lorry is parked up in what remains of the Tavistock Institute. I want you to drive it. When you arrive you will be met by their Chief Executive Officer, Dominic Lightower. He'll know what to do. I want you to assist him and make sure he follows my exact instructions."

"You want me to be a courier?" grunted 15, clearly of the opinion that this was well beneath his station.

"No, I want you to take responsibility, Victor."

"How did you get that name?" he growled viciously, pulling Byron into one of the empty archways and leaving his normal composure behind him.

"Did you forget? I'm the Prime Minister. You seem to be under the impression that you run this country.

You don't," whispered Byron close to Agent 15, but out of earshot of anyone else.

"How naive," replied Agent 15, smiling and loosening his grip on Byron's collar.

"I'm sorry, I'm naive, am I?"

"You really don't know who I am? You think I'm some sort of lapdog that runs to return the sticks that you throw. Be careful, bad owners tend to get bitten," replied Agent 15, before marching off down the corridor.

Byron glanced back at the pigeon being subjected to its sickening treatment by the hands of the two scientists. He shook his head and continued up the corridor. As before, he scanned each of the cells, quickly verifying each occupant. Most of them were subdued either chemically, physically, or from the despair of their utter solitude. One occupant was less subdued. A female voice echoed down the tunnel, screaming at anyone who had the misfortune to pass by. To confirm his suspicion, Byron wandered down to the cell in question as two guards were trying to calm the occupant with all means available, legal or otherwise.

"Hello, Violet. Finally our paths cross," said Byron.

"Prime Minister, you must listen to me. You must stop this. Search your conscience, stop this madness," she implored.

"No, no I don't think I will if it's all the same to you."

"But you can't possibly understand the plague that you are about to unleash on humanity."

"I appreciate your concern, Violet."

"NO YOU DON'T."

"Did you ever consider your conscience over the years? Ever stop to consider the innocent people that died by your actions? When your crude incendiary devices ripped their bodies apart, did you consider the pain and anguish that they suffered? Did you consider the families that you destroyed, or the children destined to grow up with less parents than God intended? I don't think you are qualified to lecture me on morality."

"You have to fight for what you believe in."

"I quite agree. I guess that makes it alright, then?"

"I'm very aware of the guilt that I have to carry. Are you? Recent events have made me understand that I have done wrong. I am determined to make amends. I have changed: if you give me the opportunity I will show you what is possible," begged Violet through the bars of her cell.

"Changed? Perhaps. But I can't risk the likelihood of a relapse to bad habits, so Emorfed will insure your change is permanent."

"If you can't see the side effects then you are truly lost. You're going to destroy spirits with the ease and normality of flicking a light switch."

"I'm not lost, Violet. I know exactly what I'm doing."

"You must let me out. I must be allowed to finish what I started," shouted Violet, shaking the bars of the cell with both hands.

"You will get your freedom, Violet, along with everyone else. I promise you that. Goodbye."

Byron continued on a well-rehearsed path as Violet's screams gradually faded with every further step taken. As each cell was observed with a glance, almost immediately he moved to the next. Just at the point when he believed that he would never find what he was searching for, he stopped in his tracks and stared again into cell number three hundred and eight. A shadowy feathered outline was hunched in the murkiest corner hiding from view.

"Guard, open the door please," asked Byron.

"Yes, sir."

"I'd ask that you disable any surveillance equipment and move away from this place as quickly as you can," added Byron.

"Sir, I cannot leave my post. We have our orders."

"Then you have new ones."

What was so exciting about the pigeon in *this* cell, compared to the other hundred or so in this part of the network? He placed the key in the lock and pushed it open. Byron waited patiently on the other side until everything he'd asked for had been completed and the sound of the guard's feet faded into the distance.

"Hello, Sandy," he said as he entered the cell.

There was no reaction from the pigeon who'd immediately recognised his visitor.

"Strange that you have so little to say. You had such a reputation for being outspoken," stated Byron as he sat down on an ancient wooden office chair that had been waiting idly for the room's previous purpose to be called back into action again.

"Where shall we start, then?" said Byron.

Sandy remained motionless in the shadows.

"It's strange, I'm not usually very good at recognising old colleagues. You know what it's like in politics, all those wannabes and old-timers. They rise and fall like a pair of cheap tights. Oddly, though, I recognised you straight away. Clearly, it wasn't because of how you look. Do you know what it was?"

There was still no acknowledgement from the bird.

"It was the smell that gave you away. Power has an odd sort of smell. It bites the nostrils. It's a pungent, aggressive sort of smell, hard to explain really. I'm good at recognising it, though, I smell it on me."

The pigeon strolled out from its corner with a very human swagger. There was no little hop forward, bob or characteristic turn of the head. Its mannerisms gave the impression of a bird that had been hypnotised in some strange experiment.

"That's better. I can see you properly now. You do have some of Sandy's features I see," offered Byron, leaning down to come into eyeline with the purple-feathered creature that was trying to stretch itself to its most upright position.

"Well, I've lost some weight," said Sandy. "What do you want?"

"The really important question, Sandy, is do you repent?"

"Intriguing question. You are not normally a man who cares for others. You only care about yourself. Why would that interest you?"

"You don't know the real me, Sandy. Time is tight so I'll ask again. Are you repentant?"

"That depends on what you are asking me to repent?"

"Everything. Every underhand, illegal or immoral act that you have conspired to, or personally carried out in the last twenty years," replied Byron. "To all intents and purposes you're dead, that must have made you reflect? Are you willing to change in character?"

"Perhaps you didn't fully understand my real character."

"I knew enough to make a judgement. You showed enough of your ambition and selfishness for me to feel confident in my own instincts."

"Or maybe I'm just a good actor?" countered Sandy.

"Either way, its not important now. I need to know what you were really doing at Tavistock on the night of the bombing," asked Byron, trying to avoid any further verbal jousting.

"I was trying to save lives."

"Yet you killed many more than you saved that night. What did you know about Emorfed before you went there?"

"Nothing. I still only know what I discovered in the brief time that I had there. It's obvious that you are going to use it to subdue the human mind, which is enough information to know you should and will be stopped."

"Your current position would suggest an improbable boldness, my friend. How do you intend to stop me? Are you going to peck me to death?" Byron chuckled alone to his own joke.

"I'm tangible proof that life always finds a way."

"Well, let me enlighten you. What I can tell you, Sandy, is that Byron intends to create a race that is impervious to temptation and weakness. He intends to suppress the very soul inside us. What you must know now is that the soul is very real. It has depth, feeling and potential well after death. The flesh's function is to carry it around this Earth, but what's inside is all that we are."

"Why do you talk about Byron in the third person like that?" enquired a confused Sandy.

"Because, like the human body's function, he is here to serve the same purpose. Byron, too, has changed and if I am going to help you – no, us – then I need to know that you are willing to take at face value what I am about to tell you."

"What do you mean?"

"Byron's only purpose is to carry me around. I am John Hewson. I've been sent here with the single purpose of taking you back to the afterlife. If I fail then your presence in this form will create a crack in the Universe," announced John.

Sandy circled the words around his head. Once he was certain they were correct, he burst into laughter. He rolled around the floor, banging his wings on the stone tiles and chuckling with a sound that resembled a bird being strangled.

"That's the most preposterous thing I've ever heard in my whole life, or death, come to think of it," spluttered Sandy.

"What, more preposterous than a senior political figure being reincarnated as a pigeon, you mean?" scoffed John.

Sandy stopped laughing as he considered the parallel.

"If you are, John, as you say you are, how did you get inside the Prime Minister?" goaded Sandy, hopping onto the desk in order to analyse him further in case there were some obvious external signs that he'd missed.

"To simplify it, the same way that you found yourself inside a bird. It's called the Limpet Syndrome and the only difference is that Byron is still alive in here. I'm just suppressing his soul, borrowing his body. Once I've gone he will be back to normal, well almost normal anyway."

John explained to Sandy the situation that they had both found themselves in. He described his journey to Limbo deep inside the Swiss mountains, the process of the Limpet Syndrome, the Soul Catcher, the library in Hell, level zero and the fact that they had until the solstice to get Sandy's soul back. He also explained how he had managed to capture and send back Ian, before he, too, had been returned through his exorcism. After about an hour of explanation, Sandy jumped onto the steel bed to contemplate what he had heard.

"I've seen some pretty weird goings-on over the last couple of months, so I can't totally dismiss what you say out of hand, however unlikely it might sound. How can I be sure that John really is in there somewhere?" He flapped a wing around, pointing at different areas of Byron's body.

"When we first met each other in Blackpool all of those years ago, when you convinced me to join your group, we used to go to a pub called Mallards. You used to order a pint of mild and smoke Gauloises cigarettes. You nicknamed me 'high horse' because of my tendency to check the legality of all of our actions, something you felt held us back. Does that convince you?"

"There are a few people who might know that, but tell me, you once bought me a pin badge that went on the left side of my black jacket. What did it say?"

"I never bought you a pin badge because the ones you had were totally stupid and completely unfunny. Plus I'm tight," replied John without thought.

"My God, it is you. I didn't even know that you were dead," said Sandy. "What happened?"

John once again returned to the manner of his own death. The memories of that moment were still just uncoordinated fragments seeking some thread to bind them together. There again was the car bonnet crumpled into the postbox, followed by the figure of an old man peering through the broken car window. The mysterious young girl, hair as white and fair as a unicorn's, that he'd swerved to avoid. He considered whether at the speed he had been travelling it was likely that the crash would have been fatal. He surely hadn't been driving fast enough to have done that much damage? The smell of the fuel still swirled around an inextricable part of his memory. But how could the fuel tank have ruptured if he'd hit the postbox straight on? On reflection, he'd been so busy with the bigger questions of why, that most of these details had never occurred to him, let alone been answered.

"I think I died in a car crash, but I'm not quite sure how it came about," John answered. "It can wait, we have no time for that now. We must act quickly."

"Look, you told me what happened to Ian and what must happen to me, but why have you taken all this time telling me about it? Why haven't you just killed me and uttered the same incantation you used on him?" asked Sandy, bravely facing the elephant in the room.

"There's little point in saving the world, if what remains is not worth saving. I need to stop Emorfed. If you help me, I also believe I have found a way to get both of us out of our fate. I have been to Hell, Sandy. It's an unimaginable place that doesn't befit the descriptions given to it. I do not wish it on you. Will you help me, help us?"

"I will. What do you want me to do?"

"You need to do as Byron says," replied John, smoothly returning to his host's persona.

Byron explained his plan before they both left the cell, Sandy flying out as quietly as possible. Attached to one of his feet was a tiny camera that Byron had placed there before departing. Sandy flew deeper into the heart of the complex, following the tunnel to where Byron had described an exit by way of a disused air duct. Byron set off to find a guard.

"Who's in charge here?"

"Sergeant Wallace, sir."

"Okay, I want you to take these release papers to him as quickly as you can," demanded Byron.

"Yes, sir." The guard took the papers that Byron had just removed from his pocket and scanned them for the correct official signatures and seals.

"What would you have me do with Foster and Stokes when they are released?" asked the guard. "Should they be followed?"

"No. I promised Violet her freedom. You might suggest they go far away and find somewhere they can't be detected. I hear Cornwall is nice this time of year."

"It will be done. Forgive me, but I expected to see a different name on the papers."

"Whose?" asked Byron.

"Your daughter's."

CHAPTER TWENTY-SIX

INTO THE SHADOWS

"Where is she?" John shouted, his rage bubbling through every limb of Byron's body.

"She's where we were told to put her, sir. She's in cell number four hundred. In the hospital wing," replied the guard.

"What's wrong with her?" John demanded. "Speak quickly if you want to keep your job."

"She's recovering from some side effects, I believe," replied the guard, "but Doctor Trent is responsible for that department. She'll be able to give you an update."

The guard moved out of striking distance, wary that the Prime Minister appeared to be holding him solely responsible for her condition.

"Side effects from what?" John bellowed, rising in stature.

"I wasn't told, sir. It's classified."

John swivelled Byron's not inconsiderable frame around and set off at a jogging pace. Off he went down the tunnel in the direction where he'd seen Sandy in cell three hundred and eight. How could this have happened? He'd been inhabiting Byron's body for weeks, since *before* he had met Faith at Herb's apartment. When did Byron give the order to have Faith interned here? Had it been premeditated? A compulsion driven by doubts over his daughter's loyalty? Nothing to do with what had happened that night? How could he do this to his own flesh and blood?

By the time he'd reached the bottom of the long, dusty tunnel, drops of sweat dripping down Byron's chubby face, his mind was no clearer on the situation. The end of the tunnel was blocked off with a strong, thick, wooden door with three large iron bars running from one side to the other. A small shutter had been positioned in the middle and a red cross on a white background had been shoddily papered onto one side. The sound of John's fist bashing furiously on the door echoed around him. The shutter opened and a pair of brown eyes glared back at him.

"We're not expecting anyone?" came a gruff, ugly female voice from inside. "Who is it?"

"It's the Prime Minister."

The eyes peered even more intensely up and down his body, piercing the gloom of the underground lights.

"No it isn't," came the response. "Where's your visitor's pass?"

"I don't have one," replied John cautiously, before adding more sternly, "I don't need one."

"Everyone needs a pass. These people might be extremely contagious and if you don't have a pass then it means you haven't signed the health and safety disclaimer," croaked the jobsworth's pair of eyes.

"Here's my visitor's pass," he replied, holding up his Houses of Parliament security pass, "and if you don't open this door right now, I will personally ensure that you will soon become an inmate here rather than an employee."

John had never been a person particularly concerned with power. But he had to concede that sometimes it was quite useful. The choice to possess Byron had been a risky one. It was never going to be an inconspicuous role to play, but so far it was paying off. The only side effect was his sudden change in character, day by day he felt himself becoming more like Byron. Even though it was still John's soul in control he'd never experienced anger like this in his whole life. In general he hated conflict but over the last few weeks it felt like his soul was trying to make up for lost time. Whether this had been Byron's influence or a change in his own outlook, the verdict was still out.

The sound of three bolts opening and the slow creak of the door proved that John had got his point across adequately. The cells on the other side were no different from the ones that John had spent the day searching. The only significant differences, on this side of the wooden barrier, were the white coats worn by the guards and the sporadically placed medical instruments that cluttered the corridors, impatiently waiting a more permanent home.

"Where is Dr. Trent?" demanded John.

"I'll go and get her," replied the pair of eyes, who had mushroomed into a short, plump woman who nervously cowered somewhere below John's knees.

As John waited restlessly for Trent to make an appearance he glanced amongst the cells, possessively seeking another glimpse of Faith's addictive energy, the spark that had set his soul alight at their last meeting. His borrowed heart was running wild, torn between the urgency of his own desires and concern for her condition. Maybe subconsciously this opportunity had influenced his choice in picking Byron as his next host? Was the selfishness of his own soul leading him against his will, taking away any sense of control he had left?

"Can I help you?" came a softly spoken voice that glided through the air behind him, shaking him from his internal debate.

John was surprised to find that Dr. Trent was a woman, cementing the stereotypes that even dead people are capable of. Descending from a short, white lab coat, tanned legs wrapped in black, knee-high boots, she stood in an elegant, relaxed fashion more akin to a catwalk model than a scientist. When you spent your working life cooped up in a dark tunnel with infectious and dangerous individuals you'd be forgiven for being just a little bit edgy. Yet Dr. Trent appeared to revel in it, unfazed and unaffected by the claustrophobic unpleasantness.

"Sir, I can't tell you what an honour it is to have you here. I never imagined that I would meet the man responsible for giving me the best job in the world," she said, eyes as wide as saucers and swooning like a teenager meeting a film star. She played with her long, auburn hair and fidgeted awkwardly on the spot. "We don't get to meet many dignitaries down here. To what do we owe this great pleasure?"

"I need to see Faith…my daughter," John added, with a slight sense of the peculiar about it.

"Of course, Prime Minister…and can I add how brave it was of you to choose your own daughter to be the first person to enter this bold new world of ours. She's still adjusting to the effects of Emorfed, but in general it has all gone as we expected. The limited testing that we managed to do at Tavistock made all the difference, I must say."

"You've given her Emorfed. That's not brave," replied John cursing under his breath, "it's callous and cruel. The whole programme is nothing short of a crime against humanity."

"You may be having second thoughts now, but don't forget this is science. It's all about progress and you can't stop progress."

"Don't count on it."

"Prime Minister, it's scientists' job to break boundaries."

"Dr. Trent, there are many things in science that were developed because it was *possible* rather than desirable. Humanity's curiosity will almost certainly be its downfall. The atom bomb, chemical weapons, genetic engineering, cloning, all examples of science that can no longer be undone. I will not allow this monstrosity to be added to that list. Morality can't be mixed in a test tube," cursed John, almost as angry at science as he had previously been at religion.

Morality had never played a big part in Dr. Trent's thought-processes. A follower rather than a leader, she used her superior intelligence and skill to push the boundaries of scientific know-how simply because someone had asked her. It never entered her head that it was possible to add the prefix 'con' in front of science in order to challenge the ethics of her experiments. That was the arena of politicians and lawyers. There was no reaction to John's moral rant. She just continued along her rational viewpoint to which she had been manacled for as long as she'd owned a white coat.

"What you have done, Prime Minister, is remove the very worst of human nature with a single treatment that's safe and quick. My only concern is that we have yet to perfect its replication. We have produced a few examples that are very close in chemical structure to Emorfed. But none of them seem to have the same effect on the frontal lobe," she exclaimed. "We understand that you were given the substance. But we have no records as to by whom or which organisation. Do you have the original formulation?"

Given it? Well, this was new. Who had given it to Byron? When time was a less important commodity than it was now, he'd need to find out. What he knew for sure was this was a piece of good news. A finite supply with no process for duplication meant destroying the current batch would give the human race a fighting chance when he'd 'moved on'.

"Are you saying there is a limited quantity of this stuff?"

"Yes, until we can replicate it. There appears to be a constituent part that, as far as we can make out, doesn't really exist. It's preposterous, of course, we just haven't worked it out yet."

Nothing was preposterous in her world, just unexplained. There was a computerised error message etched on the scientist's face, unable to process the realisation that in a world governed by fact and certainty, this was a mystery. How would she react if he'd told her everything that he now knew? She'd probably combust like a silicon chip being provided with too much electrical charge.

"How much of the stuff is there?"

"The batch that has been sent out to Hemel Hempstead is almost the lot. The rest is just a small quantity of test samples that we are using for live experiments," she replied.

John's anger subsided for a moment. Hopefully if all went to plan with Sandy, that would be the end of it. Forever removed from the fingers of such reckless and morally suspect chemists.

"Let me take you to see Faith, and then you can see the success for yourself," said Dr Trent, leading John towards her cell.

There was no security at the entrance of cell four hundred. The door was unlocked and had been left open against the outer bars. The interior was also much different from what John had seen before, more attune to the inside of a mid-priced hotel than a prison cell. Soft furnishings blended in against tasteless floral wallpaper. A TV in the corner of the room sat talking to itself, whilst the lights, of which there were many, were beating out brilliant tungsten-white light. There was a deep sense of warmth and hospitality awarded to this place. But it felt false as if a shroud had been placed around it to distract attention from reality.

In the middle of the cell, seemingly unaware of the concocted external stimulus, stood Faith. Immovable, her eyes were transfixed on a point in the distance, invisible to anyone else but her. The warmth and energy that had so stimulated John at their first meeting had been siphoned away. The scientists had decanted her spirit and replaced it with a grim and inanimate persona. Hair lay limply against a grey and lifeless face drained of colour, her once radiant smile grafted from her face and replaced by a vacant expression.

"What reaction have you had from her?" John asked, quietly.

"You don't have to whisper, Dad, I can hear you," replied Faith, lips barely moving but with a voice as strong as a megaphone. She clicked out the words like a ticker tape of computerised binary code, monotonal in delivery and as grey as her complexion. There was no other movement. Her eyes still pierced the wall and, if he didn't know better, her sound could have come from any of the machines out in the hallway.

"See, she still recognises you. Your medicine has not damaged her. You have improved her," commented Dr. Trent, disturbing his fixation on her patient. "She has memories that stretch back to childhood, just like anyone else. Unlike you and me, though, there is no emotion connected to those memories."

"How can that be possible?" asked John.

"The memories she has described are very clear. Memories are stored in the grey matter of the brain but the emotions that bring those memories alive are connected to something much deeper. So deep, in fact, that modern medicine doesn't understand it."

"I think I might be able to shed some light on that," said John under his breath.

"Other people can describe their feelings, yet Faith can voice no opinions about her memories. If you or I were to think of something from our past we might express the memory, or even show physical signs of that emotion. With Faith, there is nothing other than fact. She does not feel anger, she does not feel fear, and she does not feel desire."

"As well as those frailties, you have also robbed her of happiness," John responded disparagingly.

"Strictly speaking, you did that," she replied. "I only administer drugs, people like you write the prescription."

"I recall a similar defence was made by Nazi prison guards. It didn't work for them and it won't for you."

"I do not fear progress, sir," replied Dr. Trent as if she herself had been included in the Emorfed trials. Even though John knew he had not given the orders, he was responsible for not doing enough to stop them. Byron's failures were his also.

"What have I done?"

"You have created a perfectly balanced human being," replied Dr. Trent, sympathetically placing her hand on his shoulder.

"No. She *was* perfect, and you have removed the elements that made her unique. You have extracted her vibrancy...her colour...her character," said John, tears welling in his eyes.

John moved closer to Faith, taking in every part of her appearance. It was hard to observe her without feeling like an art critic assiduously appraising a controversial still life painting. As he came closer he noticed her eyes were clouded with a dense mist.

"There is darkness here," she droned.

"But it's so light, is there something wrong with your eyes?"

"There is a shadow. A shadow of darkness around me. It creeps within me," she replied, with no semblance of fear or worry in her voice. This was no more than a factual observation that required no opinion or explanation. Faith wiped a tear from Byron's face. Her hand was clammy and cold as if all the heat that shone down on the room from the burning lights was being reflected from her back onto the walls.

"How do you feel?"

"Normal," replied Faith through chattering teeth.

"She's perfectly well," added Dr. Trent, deflecting the hidden criticism.

John's outstretched finger pointed at the chemist, as malice flamed in his eyes and his body shook with fury. "You have done enough damage here. Although you may not be responsible for this crime, you are accountable for your part in it. You must seek forgiveness from your soul. Be grateful that you still can. In future think about answering your own conscience, rather than your orders. Leave."

She had no intention of going very far. She had been warned that an unnamed person might come to disrupt her work and she had been told what to do if it occurred. These orders had come from a high authority, although she never guessed that she would have to use them against an even higher one.

"What can you tell me, Faith?" asked John.

"It's cold and dark. I feel the shadow upon me."

"Are you frightened?"

"I'm not sure what that is."

"Do you feel anger?"

"What is anger?"

"It's what I feel now," replied John. "It's the burning in your blood, rising in your veins. It makes you want to lash out and fight when the very worst has been done to you."

"No, I do not feel that. My body feels heavy, like I am carrying a great weight. The shadow fills me from my toes to my head, influencing my thoughts. I don't have the will to fight it," Faith replied.

"What about Nash? Do you remember Nash?" asked John trying to find any reaction that might be described as an emotion.

"Yes, I remember Nash."

"How do you feel about him?"

"I feel nothing. He is a man I know," came the dry and soulless response.

John fell to his knees, tears now flowing freely from his eyes, bouncing like raindrops onto the flagstone tiles. John had felt some excruciatingly painful things in the time since his death. His father's screams, the desolation that awaited him, newborn babies ripped from life in front of his very eyes because of where they were born in the world, were all amongst the worst. But this, this was the most desperate thing he'd witnessed yet. What made it worse was that he did not know how to fix it. Throughout his journey he'd believed he still had some element of control. That destiny was still something he was able to define and direct. The reality was quite different.

"I'm sorry, Faith," he cried as he hugged her legs, rocking back and forward like a scorned child seeking forgiveness.

Faith stood unmoved and unresponsive. After several minutes of self-indulgence, John got back on his feet. Faith was gone, but he'd stop this happening to anyone else. That was what mattered now.

"Father, there is something different in your eyes."

"Those are tears, I doubt whether they are something that you will ever experience again. At least you won't feel the sadness that I feel now," he sobbed in response.

"I didn't mean the tears. There is something inside you that I do not remember. You are not the man that I knew. The shadow can see something bright that fills your mind, not something ...someone. The shadow can see you."

John had no idea how she appeared to be talking about John's soul buried deep inside Byron's body.

"I think it is time that we removed you from this place, Faith."

He led Faith away from the hospital wing and back up through the tunnel. As their surroundings grew darker, Faith placed her hands out in front of her to feel her way through the darkness, describing as she went in a controlled and unemotional manner the thickness of the shadow that surrounded her. When they reached the end of the tunnel uninhibited, John found two people he recognised. There, waiting for their release, were Fiona Foster and Violet Stokes. Both had to be immediately restrained by their guards.

"If I ever find you," blurted out Violet, "I will put you in the same condition that you so willingly subject on others."

"I did what you asked of me," replied John. "I released you when I had the power to throw away the key."

"It will not be forgotten," barked Violet. "That debt will be repaid in full."

"Very well, do what you will to me. In return for pursuing me I ask something of you, Miss Stokes. I am putting my daughter into your protection, so that I can no longer be a danger to her. I trust you, Violet, to do the right thing. Take her far away from this place. Keep her safe and keep her hidden. Then if you feel the need to wreak your revenge on me, you will know that you have in your possession the one thing that will cause me most pain, and that will be revenge enough."

"Why would you do that?"

"If you can keep yourself hidden from me for so long, then you can also keep Faith hidden from me. I know your compassion and I know no harm will come to her."

"What if I won't do it?"

"Then I will send Agent 15 to hunt you down, and this time I won't give him any restrictions. He will use his own instincts and you really don't want that. I'm prepared to do anything to keep Faith away from me."

"Then I have little choice."

"Thank you. One final thing. If you see me again, use everything in your power to protect yourselves. She must not be allowed to see me, and I must not be allowed to see her. Is that understood?"

"It is," replied Violet.

Holding Faith's hands in his, he relaxed his control of Byron's frontal lobe to allow Byron one last glimpse of the daughter whom he underappreciated.

"I want you to see what you have done to your own flesh and blood. One of the most beautiful souls that I had the pleasure to meet," thought John.

Byron's eyes, that for so long had been occupied by John's, saw the outside world for the first time in weeks. There in front of him was the shadowy and dour shape of his daughter, grey and bland.

"See what Emorfed has done to her, Byron. I hope it is the last thing you ever see. I hope you will repent it every second of whatever life you have left."

Then as quickly as Byron had seen it, it was gone.

CHAPTER TWENTY-SEVEN

DOWN THE DRAINS

Agent 15's heightened sense of suspicion had been burning with the ferocity of an industrial blast furnace even before he'd received the phone call. Something didn't feel right and, in his insatiable desire for control, that was unacceptable. Why was he being asked to do a job that anyone with half an ounce of wit would be capable of? As he drove the wagon around the more than necessary number of roundabouts that was Hemel Hempstead, the fragmented pieces of intelligence he'd pieced together did cartwheels around his mind.

This meaningless job had been assigned to him on the pretence that the Prime Minister needed someone to 'take responsibility.' That single word bothered him because it had two possible connotations. One demonstrated the unwavering faith that the Prime Minister showed in him. The alternative suggested Byron needed a fall guy if the plot didn't go to plan. But which one was it? Byron's long-standing loyalty to him could not be overlooked, yet neither could Agent 15's belief in his own judgement. The recent changes in the Prime Minister's behaviour had fertilised a suspicion that permeated through Agent 15's nervous system to the very tip of his trigger finger.

One piece of intelligence that stoked the fires of his distrust radiated from the election. Why had Byron called it so soon? Governments went to the electorate when they were popular. They had at least another year to improve on their dismal approval ratings before going to the polls. Agent 15 had assumed that the effects of implementing Emorfed would reduce the nation's inclination to vote for change anyway.

Another piece of information was of even greater concern than the election. Only an approved handful of people knew Agent 15's real name. What was Byron trying to achieve by using it openly in front of others? It was totally against protocol and potentially dangerous to both of them. Yet, Byron had revealed it to someone outside of the government. Someone, by all accounts, who was seriously lacking in scruples. If Dominic Lightower was willing to betray his nation, surely he'd have no problem betraying him? If Byron hadn't used one of his fake names then there must have been a motive for using the real one?

The phone call from Dr Trent had sealed it. When she'd described the Prime Minister's attitude to the effects and use of Emorfed, Agent 15 was convinced he knew what 'responsibility' really meant. Now time was his primary enemy. Every mission had to be flawlessly planned, every eventuality simulated to ensure success. It was his job to leave no stone unturned. If stones were found they were generally interrogated, analysed and subjected to waterboarding before being turned over, usually three times. Minutes from his rendezvous, none of the normal preparations were possible. He'd have to use his training, wits and intuition. Screw it, he always had his gun. As the main gates approached, devoid of security checks, he made one final phone call.

"Agent 12, I have a small job for you," he bellowed into the speaker.

"Where are you, 15? We've lost your position, your tracking device has been deactivated."

"That figures. Look, I want you to put a trace on someone for me."

"No problem. Who do you want us to follow?"

"The Prime Minister."

"You must know that only one person can authorise that?"

"Yes, I know, it's the Prime Minister. I recognise the absurdity. What Prime Minister is likely to authorise someone to spy on himself. It doesn't matter, I have a higher level of permission," replied Agent 15.

"Oh yes, what's that?"

"I'll shoot you if you don't do it," replied Agent 15 calmly. It was the kind of response that would be very hard to ignore. Everyone knew that if Agent 15 wanted to shoot someone, he shot them.

"Okay, consider it done," came the response after a brief pause.

Agent 15 pinned a named security badge to his navy blue overalls as he alighted from the truck's cabin. Stripped naked in black, bold font his real name announced itself to the world. In an instant this single act destroyed years of misinformation designed to keep him in the shadows. Now only the gloom of night-time hid him. As he accustomed himself to a new environment his attention was drawn to the top of the water company's service vehicle.

As statuesque as a lion prowling its prey, his eyes pierced the gloom, convinced that his ultra-sensitive ears had picked up an unusual rustling noise on the roof. When you've been trained to the level of Agent 15, you weren't like ordinary people. In this situation most people would jump at every patch of dark or imaginary noise. If Agent 15 thought he'd heard something, then it was fact. There were no coincidences in his world.

"Victor Serpo?" came a quiet voice from the shadows, as a fully suited Dominic Lightower shuffled forward tentatively to greet him.

"I'd prefer if you referred to me as Agent 15," he replied gruffly.

"Yes, the Prime Minister said you might. Although given the gravity of what we are doing here tonight, I think it might be folly if I introduce you to the other workers using your Secret Service moniker," replied Dominic. "Don't you think?"

"He seems to have thought of everything," replied Agent 15 sarcastically, confident that Byron had not considered what Victor was capable of.

"My money?" hinted Dominic, straddling the pathway in an awkward mix of defiance and false bravery. The two eyeballed each other for a split second, analysing their relative strengths.

"In the van. All cash, all unmarked."

"Good," said Dominic, rubbing his hands. "Shall we get on, then? I have no desire for this to go on any longer than necessary."

"Sure you don't want to check the money for yourself, Dominic? I'm told that I have not always been…reliable with the truth, particularly when I have ulterior motives," offered Agent 15 with a weak smirk.

"I'd like to say I trust you, but I don't. Yet neither do I have the luxury of the time needed to quench my curiosity or challenge your authenticity," he responded, waving at a group of burly shadows in the distance. "These gentleman will unload for you, Victor. Let's make our way to the laboratory and delay no longer."

When they reached the rear entrance to the facility, Dominic swiped his security card to enable a large, open aired gate, positioned within eight-foot-high barbed wire fences, to swing forward and reveal a dozen sewage tanks. As they walked along the gantry the rotating steel arms of each tank slowly swirled its contents, each exposing a uniquely different odour. To the untrained eye the tanks transformed gradually from ones that appeared totally pure to those that would make the average man immediately retch on the introduction of the aromas to their nostrils. Due to familiarity and sheer bloody-mindedness, neither of them reacted.

In the middle of the facility a side walkway led them towards a sizeable yet out of place Portakabin. The dwindling lights from the building were involved in a desperate struggle to escape from its grubby windows. One of these windows rattled shut suddenly as the metal catch was released from its hook.

"Just the wind from the turbine," offered Dominic, noticing Agent 15's immediate interest. "Happens all the time, I wouldn't let it worry you."

Stepping inside the cabin, Agent 15 was grateful to be away from the stench, not that he would have let on. In the cluttered disorganisation of the lab, three employees busied themselves amongst the test tubes, Petri dishes and condensers. They operated with the tenacity of worker bees, none of them in the slightest bit interested in acknowledging their visitors.

"Welcome to the lab, Victor. Not a particularly impressive part of the tour, I'll admit. Over there are our three lab rats. No one knows what they really do, but I'm told someone would revoke our licences without them." Dominic chuckled, failing to suppress a vacuum of empathy for their total insignificance. The scientists continued to ignore them.

"Okay, listen up, you lot. This is Victor Serpo from the Environment Agency. As you know, he's come to audit our processes and from now until he leaves this is his domain. To put it more bluntly, on your way please," barked Dominic at his lab rats.

They rose on cue and two of the three marched out of the cabin, stooping as they went to avoid eye contact. The third approached Dominic subserviently, as if he was not really allowed to converse with someone of a higher rank in case it resulted in instant dismissal.

"Excuse me. Is it possible…you know if it's not too much trouble…if we're allowed…I wanted to ask if we could get pest control in here again." The man trembled his request, visibly shrinking on every word.

"This isn't the time," replied Dominic, pointing suggestively towards the door.

"It's just…I think I saw a rat in one of the corners over there." He saw Dominic's unsympathetic expression. "Well, it'll probably be all right. I mean, who doesn't like rats? I love them."

His voice disappeared with him as he left through the door backwards, expelled by Dominic's disdainful stare.

Agent 15 was already down on his knees, searching around in the corner highlighted by the man's pointed finger, convinced that he had seen a pair of eyes glaring back at him from under the dusty bench. His attention was diverted from this quest as the door of the cabin opened again and a scruffy man stuck his head inside.

"The barrels are out on the gantry. We'll wait for you to verify them and then lob them into tank number nine," said the man. The door closed again, leaving Dominic and Victor alone inside.

"Let's get these certified and be done with it. I need you to sign these," stated Dominic. "If they see my name they'll immediately be able to trace the contents. If they trace you, well they'll never find you, will they?"

"I'll make sure of it."

He wasn't entirely comfortable signing these documents. Not because his name was traceable: it had been removed from all existence by his employers many years ago. The real issue was he didn't have a signature. It wasn't something he needed. Checking to see if there were any CCTV cameras that might place the name of Victor Serpo and him in the same place, he proceeded to invent a signature for himself and repeated it on twenty-four separate pieces of paper. A newly invented inky squiggle was all that was needed to incorrectly certify that the contents in the barrels were folic acid.

"Good. I've backed up the certificates by adding a real sample of folic acid to the sample racks over there. That will verify the contents if anyone does try to trace them. It's quite incredible how simple it is to poison a nation," remarked Dominic.

"Are we done here?" replied Victor, clear that he had no intention of drinking anything out of the tap in the next month.

"Not quite. I thought we should watch it going in, just in case," replied Dominic. "We wouldn't want to disappoint our employer, would we?"

They left the Portakabin to discover that twenty-four large barrels, accompanied by four burly men, now occupied the narrow gantry. As Dominic closed the Portakabin behind them it seemed to act as a signal for the four men to start working. They simultaneously put out their cigarettes, one or two of the butts ending up in the nearest tank below.

"Oh well, if Emorfed doesn't do it, at least some of them will choke on a fag end," replied Dominic scathingly.

Victor Serpo wasn't listening. His attention was yet again intensely focused on the side window of the cabin.

"What is it?" asked Dominic.

"The window that slammed as we came in."

"What about it?"

"It's open, and on the catch. We didn't do it and neither did the scientists," added Victor, who was now over by the window examining it.

"You're quite jittery for a secret agent, aren't you?" whispered Dominic. "It's a window, get over it."

"What your underutilised, peanut-sized brain can't fathom is that observations like that don't happen by chance. I have survived fifteen years in this job because I notice things. I'd be dead if I didn't. You may find out how that feels before sunrise if you continue to ridicule me."

"Look, you can worry about an open window if you like, but I'm going to make sure those idiots put this stuff in the right place," replied Dominic, wandering off in the direction of the tanks.

Tank nine was one of three purified containers in the complex. The water from tanks nine, ten and eleven all went straight into the mains water network, and from there into every tap, cistern and boiler in the South-East of England. As each barrel was lifted, opened and emptied, even in the murk of night-time the electric-blue liquid lit up the water. Blue whirlpools shone out like little beacons before mixing in the water and fading out of sight. As the last few barrels flowed over the edge of the gantry, Victor joined the mesmerised audience.

"Happy?" asked Dominic.

"Rarely," replied Victor.

"So this is it. A great new dawn. The liquid will mix for six hours and in the morning we will open the sluice gate, allowing the water to drain off into the networks. It will meet the water flowing through the mains system and by Thursday morning every man, woman and child will be drinking, cooking and washing with it. Odourless, tasteless and invisible, no one will notice the difference. There will be no resistance, just change," said Dominic giving a running commentary that had not been asked for. "What do you think, Victor?"

Victor Serpo had not been listening one bit to Dominic's rambling. All of his senses had been drawn to something in the distance. Something perched on one of the central arms that swung through the sewage of one of the adjacent tanks. Finally, without moving, he answered Dominic's question.

"Don't you have big pigeons around here?"

His hand had already reached for his gun and in a flash a bullet exploded out of the barrel.

*****

The cameras settled on Byron T. Casey, sitting erect in his leather chair surrounded by his plush office within the Palace of Westminster. The normal frills that accompanied party political broadcasts were conspicuous by their absence. No overproduced video introduction of the Prime Minister out in the community. No transitions from one strapline to the next. No rallying music. Just the Prime Minister looking serious. Unlike the dozens that had gone before it over the weeks of campaigning, this broadcast was live. The cameraman counted the Prime Minister in with his fingers. Three, two, one.

"Tomorrow you will have the opportunity to vote for an administration that you believe will work for you to create a better future. A better future for yourselves, your families and your communities. Tomorrow morning you have the responsibility to vote for the party that has your best interests at heart. A party that is selfless and determined. A party that will be in power, but not under its spell. A party that has a track record of making the right decisions on the big questions." John cleared Byron's throat. "The party that can deliver on all that I have spoken of, is *not* this one."

There was an audible gasp from the small television crew assigned to capture the Prime Minister's words. They checked through scripts and cue cards in case one of them had made some heinous error that would come back to bite them.

"Even though, I'm sure you'll find such advice unusual. I'd like to take a few minutes of your time to explain. There are good reasons why I ask, if not implore, you to vote for anyone but my party. This institution has consistently used power for the wrong reasons. Always thinking of its own interests before those of its citizens. Its moral insolvency can no longer be bailed out by mis-sold sentiments. You deserve better."

Senior party members appeared at the back of the room wearing shocked expressions across their pallid faces like clowns with hurriedly applied make-up. They acted out exuberant charades in their leader's direction, but it was no good. Byron wasn't going to be swayed. This suicide was being broadcast live and they were going to be forced to watch it unfold in front of them.

"This evening I was notified of an example of this government's deceit. For the sake of the election and the safety of the British people, I need to tell you what I have learnt. On Tuesday night, without my knowledge, a member of the British Secret Service instigated an attempt to poison a large section of the general public."

The party faithful joined the gasps within the room. John reached inside Byron's jacket pocket and pulled out a corked vial of liquid. Glowing with its own internal energy, the liquid moved furiously to escape the glass. It clawed its way up the sides of the tube, occasionally emitting a low groan that caused the crew to cover their ears.

"This is Emorfed. It's a powerful and odourless liquid that was discovered by a secret scientific department housed within the now defunct Tavistock Institute. If just one drop of this substance is consumed, it would steal from the recipient all emotion and desire. It was designed for one purpose and one purpose only. The complete control of the human race. Those affected would no longer show malice and anger to others. There would be no weakness or lack of willpower. Although this would create a society of compliance, it would also remove something much more crucial. It would remove what makes us unique and brilliant, our soul."

He placed the vial back into his jacket and the room dimmed. Drawn in by some powerful subconscious desire for its contents, several of the people in the room showed visible disappointment as it was removed from view.

"On Tuesday night," John continued, "the agent that I spoke of, acting on the orders of his department and aided by the Chief Executive Officer of Southern

Water, poured twenty-four barrels of this liquid into the water supply. Now I would like to show you the proof of this by playing you a short video clip."

John nodded to the television producer, the pre-agreed signal to play the DVD he'd given him earlier that evening. The producer looked down at his hands with a new nervousness, as if what he'd been innocently holding was Emorfed itself.

Filmed by someone seemingly suffering from delirious tremors, the grainy footage shook from one gloomy shot to the next. As the film lolloped through the scenes, in need of a much longer stopover at the editing suite, John gave a commentary for the viewers. The first scene revealed a man jumping out of a truck and placing a badge on his blue boiler suit.

"The man you can see now, viewers, is Victor Serpo. He is known normally by his Secret Service code name, Agent 15. This man's motive appears to be driven by a thirst for power. We have discovered from colleagues that he believes MI5 and MI6 hold the real power in this country."

Shakily the picture pulled away from Victor as his glance came to rest on the unidentified cameraman. Now all that was visible was the white roof of the van and the accompanying soundtrack of a strange heavy breathing.

"Although you cannot see the other person in this shot, you are listening to the voice of Dominic Lightower, the formerly well-respected Chief Executive of the water company and non-executive of a number of other well-known British institutions. He is also a member of one of the most prestigious gentlemen's clubs in London, where I'm certain he is being blackballed at this very moment." John afforded himself a wry smile as he visualised the event. "Dominic demonstrates how greed can affect even those that already have more than they need."

The next section showed an interior environment. The legs of a table obstructed a full view of the room, but on the other side was a bench cluttered with chemical apparatus. Two figures were busying themselves amongst the bubbling and smoking conical flasks, whilst a third was cautiously edging away from the camera. The picture jerked across towards the door as two additional pairs of legs hastened into the room. It was impossible to visually confirm who these two individuals were. But when they talked, the voices matched those from pictures taken near the truck.

"What you are hearing now is Victor Serpo and Dominic Lightower falsifying the certification, which is a necessary step for any substances that are added to our water system or sewage plants. Stop the video for a moment please. This document shows that the barrels have been signed off as folic acid. You can see here the signature of Victor Serpo, who I guarantee does not work for the Environment Agency." He indicated for the film to continue.

The last shot of the tape was being taken from a distance where it was impossible to distinguish any dialogue. What the video showed clearly, though, was the many barrels of blue liquid being poured from a gantry into one of the large, circular water tanks. The scene focused back over to Victor, pistol drawn. There was a flash and the film ended.

"Clearly some of you will be concerned for your welfare. This video was filmed last night and none of the contamination will have reached your taps. The water system is being flushed to dilute the presence of Emorfed, but this will take up to two weeks. In the meantime, do not drink or bathe in the water if you live in London or any of the other Home Counties. A full list of affected areas is available on the Environment Agency website. Free bottled water will be available at all supermarkets, and large bowsers will be placed on every street corner until it is again safe to use the normal water system."

It was an impressively polished speech from what was, after all a dead weatherman. Ironically it was just the kind of address that would make the public even more confident in the person delivering it. John knew this, so there was one killer blow yet to be dealt.

"I personally had no prior knowledge of this event until I was tipped off yesterday. However, it occurred on my watch. So before the Opposition parties call for my resignation, I shall give it to you directly. As of today, I am stepping down as leader of my party and your Prime Minister. It is not my concern who runs in my place, although I'm in no doubt they will be up all night arguing and fighting about it. Remember tomorrow, use your vote responsibly. Thank you."

The red light on top of the camera flicked off to simultaneously indicate the transmission was over and set in motion a violent free-for-all. Having spent the preceding ten minutes boiling through shades of red, the senior party members now took their opportunity to pounce. Highly valuable film equipment was knocked from its stands as cameramen and producers stood idly by or ducked for cover. One of Byron's ministerial colleagues leapt forward, wrestling him to the ground. Punches, delivered by characters unaccustomed to the manoeuvre, flew from all angles, mostly missing their intended target.

"Security," wailed John from within the melee.

"You're not going to get prime ministerial benefits anymore, Byron. You've ruined us," screamed one of the more elderly and once gentile of the gathering who was in the process of removing his shoe to use as a missile. They knew that this was the end of their empire and possibly their personal reputations.

Within minutes a number of aides came to the Prime Minister's side, dragging him from the scrum that was now his office. It was only good fortune that most of these rescuers had *not* been watching the broadcast. As a few of the ministers attempted to remonstrate with them, John managed to pull himself out of view and into the next room, locking the door behind him.

Sandy flew ungracefully down to meet him from his lofty perch in the high ceiling of the magnificent chamber. A large part of his left wing had been pulverised by the bullet that Agent 15 had dispatched at the end of the video. There would be time for such stories. Now the more pressing question was the means of their escape.

"It's time to come clean, John. We've solved the Emorfed problem, it's time you told me about the plan for us," chirped Sandy.

"What, now?" murmured John, as he watched the door he'd locked take a pounding.

"As good as any. Were you expecting to walk out of here without getting lynched? You're an enemy of the state now."

"Okay, I'll tell you," John answered. "It's extremely risky, but the way I see it, what have we got to lose? We need to get to a place in Switzerland that I have only been to once before. I have no real understanding of how to get there. But if I've guessed correctly, getting in won't be a problem."

"What's in Switzerland, other than chocolate and clocks?"

"Limbo."

"What?" asked Sandy quizzically.

"It's where they process neutral souls. Where they can change them from neutral to allow them to journey onwards," he answered.

"I'm still not with you."

"You will be, when we get there. The problem is I'm not sure how we're going to get there. I hadn't anticipated just how much of a stir I was about to create. I also hadn't anticipated that I might not be able to slip away from here unseen. I think public transport is out of the question," he joked.

"I'd say so."

"The solstice is in three days' time. We really need speed on our side," added John.

"It would appear to me that you need a private jet."

John considered this for a moment. Surely Byron must have known hundreds of important and influential people who would have access to a plane? Many of them would have been thankful for what Byron had done for them over the years. No doubt there would be some that would aid him. But could he trust any of them? They might be the same as Dominic. This was much too important a decision to take chances on people he didn't know. John would have to seek help from people he trusted and only one of those had access to a plane.

CHAPTER TWENTY-EIGHT

CURIOUS FRIENDS

Herb clung to his comfy sofa for moral and physical support as forty years of excess drained from his shaking body. No one ever said giving up an addiction was going to be easy. It took a high degree of self-control, buckets of positive attitude, and a dramatic change to one's behaviour. These radical changes often meant you needed to distance yourself from the places, people and times where you are most at risk of a relapse. When everywhere you went, and everyone you associated with, had a link to booze, that made the challenge even greater. Herb wasn't just giving up drink, he was giving up his way of life.

The only person that Herb felt confident enough to help him was Nash. Not because Nash didn't like a drink: he did. But because Nash knew him like no other did. Other than alcohol, Nash was Herb's life and he was beginning to realise that he had a duty to demonstrate to his protégé that drink and drugs weren't the answer. Granted, he hadn't been the best role model on that front over the last twenty years. It was never too late to make amends. If only he wasn't having the sort of withdrawal-influenced hallucinations that would have sent Keith Richards over the edge.

Whilst Herb's attempt to dry out was a mountain with no sign of a base camp, Nash was having no such trouble with his own inner demons. For the first time in years he felt in charge of his life. He'd finally buried his drug dependency in a deep recess of his brain labelled 'ill-judged decisions'. In the week since parting company with John, he'd managed to pen a whole new album of work, inspired and enabled by what had happened over the last month. What's more, he was finally at ease in his own skin.

"Nash, cup of tea?" whimpered a crumpled Herb, half-sitting and half-lying on the sofa. Nash arrived moments later clutching a mug of tea, a pot of which must have been on permanent brew in case of an emergency.

"How are you feeling today, Herb?"

"They were back again."

"Who were back again?" asked Nash, glancing around the room for evidence.

"The talking flowers in their plant pots," replied Herb, pointing at the mantelpiece, whose only contents were a paperweight and a carriage clock.

"There's nothing up there, Herb. It's your imagination. The doctor said it might last for a couple of weeks," explained Nash, examining the mantelpiece just in case.

"I don't understand. Nothing has changed. When I was hammered out of my mind I used to see weirdness like that all the time. The only difference is I used to think it was normal and find it rather amusing," said Herb, sitting up fractionally to drink his tea. "Now it scares the life out of me. I wish they gave me something stronger for it."

"You're already on three different pills. If you take any more we'll get you off booze and you'll be addicted to prescription drugs instead."

"Maybe I've just got an addictive personality. I wouldn't mind some of that stuff the Prime Minister was talking about last night," said Herb, searching as all addicts do for the mythical magic bullet.

Herb merrily slurped his cup of tea and as Nash watched he spontaneously put his hand to his mouth to stop himself from yelping. Some habits were just so difficult to change. He hoped that by boiling the water some of the contamination might have been removed. To avoid thinking about it further, Nash went to collect the post that he'd seen on the doormat on his way to serve Herb his drink. Collecting the few letters that lay there, he returned to the living room to see if there had been any change in Herb's outlook.

"Anything good?" Herb pointed at the letters Nash was holding.

"One bill, couple of bits of junk and…" Nash stopped in his tracks as his eyes fixed on a brown envelope.

"What is it?" asked Herb cautiously, struggling to show the physical posture that might demonstrate concern.

"It has a stamp that says, 'Office of the Prime Minister'," he murmured, as his newly found self-confidence was effortlessly chased off by anxiety.

"It's probably just a warrant for your immediate extradition to Switzerland, or possibly a death threat for porking his daughter," replied Herb, feeling laughter run through him and welcoming its return.

Nash didn't laugh. He opened the letter and scanned it for a few moments.

"I don't believe it," said Nash, reading the details again.

"What is it?"

"Pardon," stammered Nash.

"I said, what is it?" replied Herb, slightly louder than the first time.

"I said it's a pardon," replied Nash slowly, as if Herb had gone deaf. "I've been given a full pardon by the British and Swiss governments for any involvement in the Geneva massacre. It's signed by the Prime Minister. Apparently they have found some evidence that totally exonerates us."

"Us?"

"Yes, me and John."

"John's gone…hasn't he?" Herb inquired cautiously, in case he'd come back without his knowledge.

"Yes, of course, totally."

"So why do you look so miserable? You should be happy. This means you can go back to normality, or at least your version of it. On top of that we..." He stopped himself. "I mean *you*, can make a shedload of money by selling the story."

"There's more in the letter. It says in recognition of the Prime Minister's generosity, and as a condition of the agreement, I must stop seeing Faith. In fact, it's a bit stronger than that. There's something about an unusual technique for the removal of a vital reproductive organ if I even attempt to see her again."

"She's just a girl, Nash, give it up," said Herb, attempting to offer consolation whilst at the same time being quite pleased with this second clause.

"Well, I guess he's not the Prime Minister anymore, what can he do to me now? As long as we don't get caught."

Before Herb had the chance to argue there was a deep and loud knock at the front door. Nash waited to see if there was any likelihood that Herb might get up to answer it. There wasn't. Nash got to his feet, wondering how long he might remain as his friend's permanent servant. For the first time in a week he opened the door unconcerned as to what or who might wait on the other side. At least until he saw who it was. The doorway and its occupant fell away from Nash as his body went limp, his mind went blank and his head hit the tiled hallway.

*****

Ten minutes had passed before Nash came around. A deep, throbbing pain stabbed at the back of his head as the living room and its contents span like a kaleidoscope. Propped up by the leather sofa, that had until recently housed the incapacitated Herb, he tried to focus his muddled vision on the two characters above him.

"Are you all right, Nash?" came a voice that even in his current state he knew immediately was not Herb's recognisable Scottish accent. Rubbing his head in a vain attempt to restore his vision, he noticed that the figure gazing down at him was doing likewise to his *own* head. Eventually the man came into focus.

"Oh shit!"

Nash jumped out of his seat and, like a spider retreating from a rolled-up newspaper, scurried to the other side of the room. With the composure and skill of an astronaut who had just had his first experience of the Vomit Comet, he picked up a fire poker and brandished it in no particular direction.

"I haven't seen her. She's not been here, I promise. Herb, hide the cheese grater, quick!" he shouted in reference to the distinctive threat outlined in the letter.

"I see you got my message," replied Byron calmly, quite unsurprised by Nash's reaction to seeing him. "I'm not here to hurt you, Nash. I need your help."

"What do you want from me, Prime Minister?" uttered Nash feebly, keeping the fire poker outstretched, still wobbling it about inoffensively in mid-air.

"I'm not the Prime Minister anymore."

"What do you want, Byron?" rephrased Nash.

"No, I'm not Byron either."

"What?" said Nash, examining the bump on his head again in order to check whether the extent of the damage was escalating.

"I understand twins often have such a close bond that they often feel pain or emotion when the other experiences it," said Byron, removing his hand from his skull to expose a trickle of blood. "It's interesting but I never believed it before today. Do you see what I'm getting at, Nash?"

"You're my twin?" bemused Nash, with a shrug.

"No," Byron sighed. "I was making a comparison, that's all. Having occupied your body for so long, when you fainted to the floor I mirrored your pain quite psychosomatically. They did say there were some side effects, I just assumed that they would only affect you."

"John?" Nash lowered his weapon and cautiously approached Byron to check his instincts. "How? Why?"

"How? Almost the same way that I encountered you. But this time I chose Byron and found a way to control him completely. Why? Well, it was the only way to stop him winning."

"So was it you that sent me the letter?"

"Yes, I wanted to put things right."

"But why did you threaten me?"

John had no way of knowing at the time of writing Nash's pardon that he would ever see him again. His decision to ward off Nash from seeing Faith was John's first selfish act. After all, his soul was still human, he was still capable of it. Maybe that's what was meant by being dead jealous. The truth was he didn't want anyone to have Faith, although he knew all too well that it was impossible for him to have her either, whether due to his condition or hers.

"She's not the same anymore. Byron used her to test Emorfed. It must have been after she left here and before I got to Byron," John replied apologetically. "She will be protected and concealed, in case her disorder is discovered and she is exploited by less virtuous people."

"I could protect her," answered Nash.

"She's away from both of us now."

"Why should she fear me?"

"The truth is that she is now incapable of showing you the same love that you do to her. I asked her about you, Nash. She doesn't feel anything for you. I'm sorry, but I'm protecting you as much as I am her."

Nash dropped the poker to the floor and slumped against the sofa, sobbing uncontrollably. Even though he was a renowned womaniser who had accumulated a collection of beautiful groupies in every town from

Bangor to Bognor, in truth it was all part of an image that he himself had helped to create. Of course, he never complained. But secretly deep down he knew it was a false persona. Faith wasn't just another sycophantic fan, sculpted from a stockpile of silicon and cosmetics. Nor was it the taboo and triumph of bedding the Prime Minister's daughter that made her different. There was real affection between them. So much so it had been one of the motivations for him cleaning up his act.

Nash wiped his tears and appealed to the room for comfort. Herb was sitting completely still and upright in a Georgian antique chair in the corner of the room. The colour had drained from his body and he was no longer sweating profusely.

"Another cup of tea, Herb?" Nash offered, believing this to be no more than one of his 'odd' moments.

"Where did the shadow come from?"

Herb replied with a tone of voice characteristically familiar to John. He'd heard it only two days before. He knelt down at Herb's feet, knowing that the darkness that Herb was experiencing would disable him from seeing more than a few feet.

"I see you, John. You're back," stated Herb, groping forward to allow his hands to confirm what he believed his eyes were seeing.

"How can you see me?"

"The shadow is drawing in on me. I can feel it in my bones. It surrounds you also. Your soul has been ripped in two. The energy is burning you up. Right there," came Herb's one-dimensional reply as he placed a finger on John's forehead.

"What do you mean it's been ripped in two?"

"John...your soul is burning out," added Herb.

"What's wrong with him?" asked Nash.

"Has he drunk the water?" inquired John.

"He's drinking thirty cups of tea a day. I just forgot about the warning," replied Nash. "I thought it would be fine if I was boiling the water."

"No. I'm afraid not. The Herb that you know has just left us. This is what Faith has become also. This is why you will find no happiness with her."

"What have I done to him?" sobbed Nash once more, placing a hand on Herb's shoulder but producing no reaction.

"You have removed his pain," replied John, "but at a price. You can't help him now."

"I'm sorry, Herb, I love you like a father. I wanted so much to help you. I wanted so much for you to be proud of me."

Herb remained vacant as Nash hugged his waist, desperately trying to defibrillate a positive reaction. Nash hated himself. Why was it that only now he told him how he felt? Now, when it was too late.

"Nash, there is more suffering on its way. You can't help Herb, but you can help me," demanded John.

"What help can I be? I can't even look after my friends."

"I need you to call Syd. Get him to ready his plane for one last flight."

"Where are we going?" asked Nash, rubbing his eyes with his sleeve.

"Switzerland."

The eyes rolled in Nash's head, his body crumpled like a concertina and once again he hit the floor.

*****

It was late evening on Thursday the nineteenth of June when Nash pulled up at Fairfax airfield, parking Herb's pride and joy at an angle that monopolised three parking spaces. The gash on the front of his head throbbed in perfect harmony with the one on the other side of it. Anyone not familiar with the activities of the last few hours would quite reasonably believe he'd recently been through a poorly performed lobotomy. The rotor blades of Syd's now familiar Cessna plane were already whizzing around impatiently, confirming the request for a swift and immediate departure. As John and Nash navigated their way across the runway, a third passenger was standing impatiently on the tarmac.

"Took your time, didn't you?" Sandy cooed.

"Well, we had a little trouble with a patient," replied John.

"This will be the other one, then," muttered Nash trivially. Once you'd seen one talking pigeon, the novelty wore off somewhat.

"Yes, this is the other pigeon," John replied. "Any trouble getting here, Sandy?"

"No, I took the train. The wing wasn't up to flying yet," replied Sandy, meekly trying to raise his damaged limb.

"Wasn't that a little risky?" asked John, who had a vision of Sandy sitting in first-class alongside the pristine-suited businesspeople, reading *The Times* and commenting on the 'bloody railways'.

"I didn't travel *in* the train, I travelled on it. Quite a rush, I can tell you," replied Sandy, noticeably more fluffed up than usual.

"Come on let's get on-board," said John.

"Nash, you've done enough. I see no reason for you to come with us. Thank you. You helped save humanity."

"I like that," said Nash. "You've just given me a name for my new album. Don't take offence, John, but I do hope we don't meet again, it's just getting too painful."

"None taken. Good luck with everything."

"You, too," answered Nash, as Sandy and John made their way up the short mobile staircase and onto the plane. Not content with the assumption that this time John would leave him for good, he waited to see the plane take off and be fully reassured.

"I think it might be best if you make yourself scarce, Sandy. I find it tiresome having to explain why you can talk," suggested John, as they entered the plane and saw no obvious sign of Syd.

"I'll find somewhere quiet," agreed Sandy.

"Syd, we're ready to go," shouted John as he approached the door of the cockpit. It swung open to meet him, but it wasn't Syd. Wearing a blue boiler suit that no longer sported a security badge, Victor Serpo was brandishing a pistol complete with silencer.

"Going somewhere?"

"Short holiday," replied John timidly, reminding himself that as far as Victor was concerned he was still Byron, at least visually.

"Where is your companion?" demanded Victor, eyes unwavering from his target.

"What companion?"

"I think, 'We're ready to go,' was the shout, was it not? Where is your feathered friend?"

"Look, this is between me and you, not him," replied John.

"Probably, but that depends on who you really are. This is certainly not between me and Byron. It is clear to me that the real Byron would not have relinquished power quite so readily." Victor took a bottle of pills from his trouser pocket and swallowed a few of the orange tablets as he continued to keep the gun and his eyes transfixed on his prey.

"Stressed?" asked John.

"Never," replied Victor. "They suppress my little *problem*. There will be no distractions. I will not allow you to escape from me this time."

John was not in a position of strength. In front of him was one of most lethal individuals on the planet, who, to make matters worse, was carrying an extremely quiet gun. That person had just been framed for a major government deception live on national television by Byron. It was understandable why Victor might be miffed. John had clearly discovered a newfound ability to annoy people. The facts were simple. Victor had a weapon and in response he had a first-class degree in bullshit and a talking bird. First things first.

"Look, you're right. I'm not Byron, at least not totally. You and I have met before, although you would not recognise me even then. At 12, Blackhorse Way, the day we caught Ian, I was possessing Nash Stevens. What I learnt that night convinced me that I had to stop Byron going through with Emorfed. I was right to do that. Have you seen what it does, Victor? I have and it's not fun," explained John, waiting to see if any of this information was going to make sense to his opponent.

"You must be John Hewson?" remarked Victor. "I don't know who John Hewson is, or what he's doing here. But I'm going to put a stop to it."

"Ha! You have no idea how stupid that sounds," laughed John, partly amused and partly stalling. "This goes way above your head, a power at work that even I don't properly understand. How do you intend on stopping me?"

"Well, you may have noticed that I am holding a gun," replied Victor sarcastically, "and you are not."

"Right, and what good will that do exactly?"

"I'll kill you, you moron," Agent 15 snarled angrily. He'd never been mocked in this way before, at least not by someone standing in his cross hairs.

"No, you won't. You would kill Byron. Now that may be no great loss for either of us, but in effect you might as well turn the gun on yourself. If I don't get Sandy back to where he belongs by Saturday we're all dead. If you were stupid enough to pull that trigger the first thing you would see was a dead body and moments later you would see a blue cloud of electricity hovering above it. Then that cloud, me, would be gone. What's more, there's nothing stopping me coming back as you. That's the power you are up against."

"Maybe I'm willing to prove you right. All I want is the bird, then I can clear my name and regain my place."

"Is power all you care about, Victor? Is it that important to you?"

"Yes," he replied without flinching. "I had everything and everyone that I wanted. I changed lives with the flip of a coin, brought down governments and destroyed institutions. That's real power."

"As I have recently found out, there's nothing that humanity really controls. It's a fantasy, an illusion," replied John, running out of ways to break down Victor's granite-thick dogma.

"The bird," Victor commanded again, clicking the safety catch on his gun in a threatening manner.

"And if I hand him over, what would you do then? Try to convince whoever has been re-elected that in some way a pigeon was responsible for the Emorfed fiasco? I think I might stick around, it might be quite entertaining. You'll be in the loony bin quicker than you can say 'split personality'," added John, growing in confidence and urgency.

There are definitely things that you shouldn't do when someone with limited tolerance and a total disregard for life points a gun at you. One of them is to suggest defeat. It tends to result in the last mistake that you ever make. John had pushed Victor too far. But whether by luck, chance or fate, several events happened at once.

The daylight that had been seeping in through the aircraft's windows was suddenly muted as a dark swarm flapped against the glass. A ferocious army of winged soldiers pecked desperately against the windows in a concerted attempt to break the glass. Through the cacophony of noise, Victor made his way to the side door to see what the commotion was. As he opened it a stream of pigeons finally broke through, joined at that very moment by Sandy from an overhead locker. He'd been listening intently to the

340

conversation, waiting for the right moment to make an entrance. This audible sign seemed as good as any.

The sudden appearance of so many birds presented Victor with a difficult dilemma. What did he aim his gun at? One pigeon, or the mass that were now trying to squeeze in through the opened door? He didn't get the chance to decide. A lump of wood came flying through the door. It clobbered him on the back of the head and knocked him to the ground. In a last-gasp act of retaliation an instinctive shot discharged from Victor's gun, smashing through one of the windows.

Sandy swooped down and plucked the gun from Victor's hand whilst John launched Byron's huge frame onto the beleaguered and damaged secret agent. As more birds swarmed into the aircraft, John tried to establish what had just happened. There in the doorway was Nash. In one hand, hanging from a piece of rope, were the airplane chocks. The other hand was flapping wildly to stop the mob of pigeons from messing up his hair. Sandy recognised the pigeons instantly as his valley relatives. Forever they'd been following him, trying to protect him as one of their own.

"Get off me, fatty," Victor shouted, wriggling about to escape the one-man pile-on.

"Don't just stand there, Nash. Get some rope," John shouted. Victor was tied and gagged securely before what had happened was properly dissected.

"Where did you come from? Not that I am not eternally grateful, you understand," said John.

"I think you might be right about that bond between us, John," replied Nash. "I was standing there waiting for you to take off and I felt this inexplicable sense of danger. Not mine, but yours. Something was telling me to go to the plane."

"Something?"

"Well, someone, I think," replied Nash. "Somewhere deep down inside me, I heard a voice."

John guessed that whoever had been guiding him was now guiding Nash. If he guessed correctly he'd soon find out who it was. For now, they had a flight to catch.

"Where did all the birds come from?" said Nash. "I was waiting at the door, trying to decide how to get in and what to do, when this huge cloud of wings descended on me."

"That'll be my family," replied Sandy.

"What?" replied John and Nash together.

"They think that I'm one of them. I suppose you can't blame them. I was born, as it were, into their flock. They've followed me everywhere and put their lives on the line to protect me."

"Maybe some things in life are more important than…well life," said Nash poignantly.

John knew exactly what he meant. He knew that Nash would have swapped places with Herb in a heartbeat, just as he would sacrifice himself in the end if he needed to.

"Nash, help me get Victor off the plane?" asked John. "Sandy, go and find Syd."

They dragged Victor down the stairs, purposely bumping his head on every step. John had already removed the gun from Sandy and decided to keep hold of it just in case it came in useful.

"When we're clear of the runway I want you to let Victor go," John instructed Nash. "He's done all the damage he can do."

Syd had been found tied up in one of the sheds that surrounded the airfield. Although unhurt by his experience he was eager, as they all were, to get as far away from Victor as possible. All three of them made their way back onto the aircraft, leaving Nash and Victor to watch them take off into the beautifully clear sky. The throng of pigeons took off in unison with no chance of keeping pace.

CHAPTER TWENTY-NINE

THE LONGEST DAY

The aircraft flew all night. Not because it had to, but because it was at John's request not to land at night. His instructions to Syd had been to continue to circle over the Swiss Alps as long as the fuel load would allow. The sun rose from behind the mountains, framing a magnificent scene worthy of any postcard. As John watched it from the cockpit he knew that this was the penultimate time the sun would rise before the solstice. The start of the longest day. Tomorrow, when that sun reached its full height, the world would find out whether there would be another.

"I'm getting low on fuel," Syd indicated the dial on the dashboard. "Which airport do you want me to land at? I'll need to radio clearance."

"We won't need an airport, Syd."

"Come again," replied Syd and Sandy in unison.

"We'll be taking a slightly more direct route. I can't run the risk of being recognised at an airport, however remote. I also can't afford the time needed to get from the airport to where we are now."

"What exactly do you mean by a more direct route?" chirped Sandy.

"I mean this," said John, reaching behind his seat and removing a parachute pack that he had quietly placed there earlier in the journey. He offered it up to the air like a trophy.

"You're crazy!" shouted Syd.

"It's very possible."

"Have you ever plummeted at one hundred and twenty miles an hour and felt the power of the wind force your body in opposite directions?"

John considered the two journeys he'd taken at the speed of light, through and out of the Earth's atmosphere, into the odd black hole or two and right to the very limits of human knowledge. "It's really no problem, I've gone faster."

"Who knows where you'll land?" added Syd. "Around us is some of the most inhospitable terrain in the world. That's if you survive the landing, which could be on a glacier the size of a small country or on a precipice where blizzards will catapult you into a deep abyss."

Syd was not the only one against this course of action.

"What about me?" added Sandy.

"Sandy, I thought you'd have noticed by now that you can fly."

"That won't be flying, John, it'll be falling uncontrollably. I can tell that you've never flown before. It takes more than just gravity. Believe me when I tell you it takes a while to perfect it."

"You'll be fine and honestly it's the easiest way," comforted John. "Syd, how close above Jungfrau can you get?"

"In this weather, about ten thousand feet. If you want to land in a specific place then you'll need to skydive for as long as possible, otherwise you'll be dragged off course by the wind. If your chute is going to open in time you'll need to pull the cord at least a thousand feet from the ground. But by then you'll need to pull the cord straight away or they'll be searching for a John-shaped fissure."

Syd changed direction sharply, bringing the plane down and to the left. Where the skies had been perfectly clear, out of contact from any major weather issues, they were soon blinded by dense cloud and fog.

John put on the backpack and placed goggles over his eyes.

"OK, as far as I can tell from the equipment, we're within the area of Jungfrau," Syd shouted down the plane at them. "The chances of you landing in the right place are tiny, but hopefully you'll be within a three-mile radius."

John forced open the side door and was knocked over by the power of the oncoming elements that searched for shelter inside the relative cosiness of the plane. There was no change in pressure on account of the bullet from Victor's gun that had destroyed one of the windows and made for a rather noisy and cold journey. Sandy was backing away from the door.

"Look, I'll hold onto you until after I pull the chute, that way you should be protected until we're closer to the ground," said John, beckoning Sandy over.

"I suppose you've gotta go somehow."

"If it's any consolation, if you do die again, you'll survive. God knows in what form, though. Ready?"

"As I'll ever be."

John tucked Sandy under his arm and looked down into the cold, bitter sky, offering a nod to the gods. As he leapt out he immediately felt the force of the elements batter him upwards. It was a breathtaking experience where any sense of human control became an utterly distant notion. It was only the sight of the plane disappearing in the distance that qualified in which direction he was moving. His outstretched arms, drawn to their furthest possible position by the forces of nature were the first indication that neither of them contained a pigeon. With the mountainous white earth expanding rapidly beneath him, he pulled the ripcord, silently thanking the Almighty as he watched his parachute unravel correctly. His pace immediately slowed, allowing him to search the sky for his lost companion.

What had he done? Sandy was nowhere to be seen. Had he beaten impossible odds to find Sandy, only to lose him at the final hour because of his own stupidity? The approaching ground revealed specific features rather than the nondescript, craggy white mass he'd first witnessed. He didn't really know what he was looking for, other than a soft landing. Through the swirling snowfall he spotted a distant building perched on the peak of a mountain, its man-made metal and glass frame at odds with the surrounding desolation that Mother Nature had moulded for thousands of years.

If he landed somewhere near it he could escape the elements and just possibly ask a few people for help. Discovering an anonymous talent for controlling a parachute he was going to land quite close to it. Right next to it. ON IT! He pulled furiously on both of the cords to slow himself down. But it was too late. A heart-stopping ripping noise followed as he came to rest suspended in mid-air.

The chute was wedged precariously on the corner of the metallic roof, forcing him to dangle helplessly in front of a huge glass window built to show off a vast, glacial valley that stretched almost as far as the eye could see. There were no lights on inside the building, but as John peered through he thought he made out a shop and a cafe. Where *had* he landed? He struggled to free himself, spinning in circles and twisting the ropes of his parachute every time he reached for safety. The building had been constructed on the very edge of a precipice and his ripped chute was the only thing stopping him falling hundreds of feet to his demise. He immediately stopped struggling and started shouting.

*****

At the moment John jumped from the plane, Sandy had been torn from his grip and catapulted downwards like a stone. No parachute was going to slow his descent. The competition between the battering winds and the uncontrollable force of gravity had conspired to drag him some distance away from where John was falling. Eventually his friend disappeared from sight. The speed and disorientation of his plummet muddled his senses to the point of unconsciousness and hurried him into a decision.

He forced his head into a nosedive and painfully pushed open his wingspan, the air whistling through the wound in his left wing. The speed of his fall initially increased, but slowly the aerodynamics of his body shape finally came to his rescue. It pushed him into a horizontal position like a world war pilot pulling a burning aircraft up from a seemingly disastrous dive. Moments before he careered into the mountainside he regained full control, gliding tantalisingly close to death several metres above the snow. Lifting his feet to land, they hit the icy surface at speed. Slipping and sliding like a comedy duck, he punctured a snowdrift with a thump.

The creature that eventually crawled out, caked in layers of snow and gasping for air, had a passing resemblance to another, recently deceased, pigeon. Although he shook off most of the snow it was impossible to dislodge the cold absorbed into his feathers. If he was going to survive in this inhospitable environment he'd have to find somewhere warm and safe. Around him was a low, wide ravine that was cornered by three jagged peaks in a triangular formulation. In the cliff face, at the base of one of the mountains, nestled a weather-worn hut raised on stilts. A wisp of grey smoke billowed from the chimney.

*****

It was eight-thirty in the morning and the three staff members of the Jungfrau visitor centre were standing in the viewing gallery staring agog at the *thing* that hung limply in front of their huge, panoramic window. They were used to seeing the magnificent view that made a less than exciting job far more bearable. Today, that magnificent view was being ruined by a hysterical idiot hanging upside down, pointing at a tangled parachute and drawing his finger across his throat. He appeared to be talking to them, but the three-inch glass was rebounding his message back down at the vast valley.

On the other side of the glass John saw three woman with confusion etched upon their faces. They had barely moved since one of them had flicked all the lights on, illuminating him against the backdrop. Their lack of urgency suggested to him that being courteous to customers was probably a struggle, whilst rescuing one from certain death was totally outside of their job descriptions. They also appeared to take no regard to his desperate pleas for assistance.

"I'M GOING TO DIE!" he shouted to the valley again.

*****

It had taken Sandy about an hour to drag his battered body up the steep slope to where he'd seen the smoke rising into the sky. When he reached the cabin he was relieved to find that it was real and not a consequence of his scrambled brain playing tricks on him. The building appeared, at least on the outside, to be designed from discarded planks of wood, worn and tired. Its weathered walls held back the elements by pure good fortune. It had tricked itself into believing that the uniquely chaotic way that it had been built banned it from collapsing in the face of all laws of physics. The few windows that it had were small and firmly closed and the entrance door was misshapen and small, as if the elements had eroded it over time.

Sandy struggled through the piles of snow to greet the door, tapping it twice with his beak. After several minutes the door opened. A scraggy beard, whose last shave was in nineteen-seventy nine, emerged from the sanctuary of the cabin attached to a scrawny face. The only other aspect of the person that Sandy saw, through the fraction of door that he'd opened, was a layer of dark green Gor-Tex. The man, bewildered as to who might be walking the mountains at this time of the morning, opened the door enough for Sandy to hop through unnoticed. For a final time the bearded waterproof scanned the barren wasteland, tutted to himself, and closed the door from the onrushing elements. Without removing his thick layers of warm insulation, he made his way back into the cabin and up a flight of stairs.

At the top of the stairs a scantily furnished kitchen, where beaten pots and pans adorned cluttered work surfaces, encircled a long, Viking-style wooden table that stretched across the width of the room. Unlike most kitchens, this room was a place of refuge for all manner of paraphernalia. A menagerie of once colourful ropes lay piled in a corner like a poorly managed reptile house, whilst a dented tool kit sat prominently next to a kettle that whistled warmly from the stove. Another equally bearded man with blackened fingers gazed through the condensation-soaked window.

"Qu'est-ce que c'est?" he said, as his colleague entered from the stairway.

"Rien," came the muffled reply from lips unseen but most certainly there somewhere under his bushy mane.

In truth, Sandy and John were less than a mile away from each other, not that they knew of course. They had to find each other, and quick. Which explained his rather rash next move. He jumped up onto the table, sending both men into prophylactic shock.

"D'où viens tu!?" screamed one of the men after gaining his composure. Sandy had no time to explain what these two mountaineers were about to witness, or any grasp of the French language to help him.

"Look, by any chance has either of you seen a parachute landing near here?"

The haggard men tried to verify with each other that they weren't the only ones hearing a talking bird. The pigeon had broken into an elaborate game of charades.

"Fièvre de cabine?" one questioned the other.

"Pa-ra-chute," Sandy repeated slowly and loudly as he attempted to mime the shape of a parachute with his frozen wingspan.

*****

John had been hanging around, quite literally, for about four hours. Finally they had discovered the inclination, if not the exact means of rescuing him. The former, John suspected, being a much more difficult a job than the latter. Although the latter wasn't going to be easy. They couldn't reach him by land because land was some considerable feet below them, a fact that John was now more than familiar with.

To make matters worse the viewing gallery had begun to fill up with interested and bemused tourists. Most of them had made the journey by train and on foot to see one of the most magnificent glaciers in the world. A spectator of several ice ages, this awesome spectacle of ice sheets, that had moulded the valley over countless millennia, was a mere distraction compared to the sight of an inappropriately dressed man floating upside down in front of it. After all, the glacier had been there forever, and this might not last that much longer. John's suffering was compounded by the endless photographs and video footage being taken. He couldn't wait until they made their way into the public domain. If he hadn't already destroyed Byron's reputation, this ought to do it.

He watched as the red-fleeced staff members gathered around, hopefully to discuss his removal. One of them was analysing the pages of a large binder that John guessed might be the staff manual, although he doubted whether this situation had ever been simulated and planned for. The staff members dispersed, either having agreed on a plan or conceded to John's permanent residency as a regular feature of the Jungfrau tour. After a long period of inactivity a face appeared next to the metal guttering above John's head.

"Comment ça va, monsieur?" came a sarcastic voice, partly dissipated by the wind. John had been a relatively competent French speaker in life, but he hadn't used it for years.

"Tu te fous de ma gueule," he replied, remembering some of the more colourful phrases that a foreign exchange student had once taught him at college.

A rope was slowly reeled down to him, until it bobbed in front of his eyes. He wrapped the length around his waist and tied four or five unofficial knots, tucking them tight.

"Allez."

As the weight transferred from the cords of the parachute to the rope it triggered a switch in his focus. Taking in his surroundings he reminded himself of the reason he was in this predicament in the first place.

Along the line of mountains that fought through the clouds, occasional shards of sunlight escaped through the gaps that it found between the two. Stalked by one of these mountains, a small cabin on stilts hid in its shadow. A few hundred metres above its peak a shot of thin, blue light pierced a hole in the cloud allowing more of the sunlight through. John's heart leapt. This was the sign he'd prayed for. A message from Limbo beckoning him home. All he needed was to find Sandy again.

The new local celebrity composed himself in the warmth of the visitor centre. He posed for a photo or two and signed some autographs, each time remembering to sign 'Byron', not 'John'. With his heart rate back to a semi-acceptable level and the blood fully balanced to all parts of his body rather than just his skull, he readied himself to set off again. He thanked his rescuers, even though they had been less than competent and were still somewhat perplexed by proceedings. John conjured up some French in his head and managed to secure a fleece, waterproof jacket, thermos flask of coffee and walking boots for the next, and hopefully last, part of his journey.

Jacque, the man who had rescued him from the roof, led him through the crowd to an exit that would lead him on the hour-long journey to the position that John had indicated on the horizon. The sun had passed the midday point, which left less than twenty-four hours before it cycled around again to its highest point of the year. Then what? With renewed vigour he left the building to a huge cheer, although no one was quite sure what they were cheering for.

The snow crunched under foot as he set off up the slight incline. Although the distance was short, the air was thin, and pulling Byron's obese body across it would be a challenge. John was about halfway to his destination when he caught sight of two dark green figures hurrying away from the cabin in his direction. Pulling heavily laden sledges and travelling at twice the speed, they were clearly fitter and better prepared than John was. With fear as well as snow in their eyes, they did not stop when they reached him.

"Arrêtez-vous, Monsieur. Un oiseau démoniaque dans la cabine. Repart tout suite," they muttered, gliding across the snow as quickly as the water ran off their waxy waterproofs.

John attempted to translate the words that he heard. He understood the words 'cabine' and 'démoniaque'. He knew the word 'arrête' meant stop. Stop, the cabin's possessed? Deciding that made no sense, he racked his memory in search of the missing words in the sentence.

"I remember 'oiseau'," he said to himself, "but what was it? Peach stone? No, what would 'The cabin has been possessed by a peach stone' mean?"

He kept plodding slowly through the two-foot snow.

"It sounded a bit like wagon. What the hell is a demonic wagon? It can't be that. Oiseau," he repeated several times over, before it finally hit him. "It's bird, of course it is. A demonic bird. Sandy!"

Undeterred by the build-up of lactic acid that drowned Byron's body, his legs worked at an unfeasibly quick pace. Ten minutes of frenetic walking later he'd reached the cabin, almost braking its fragile hinges as he burst through the door.

"Sandy!" he shouted. "Are you in here?"

On the first floor of the cabin the answer to his question was thawing off in front of the dwindling embers of the fire. Sandy sat snivelling and spluttering in the relative warmth, having almost returned to his distinctive original colours.

"John, next time you have a good idea," Sandy chattered, "keep it to yourself."

"At least you haven't spent the morning swinging by a thread," John replied. Empty packets of biscuits were strewn around the floor. "Looks like you've had it pretty good."

"If you want to keep your eyeballs, I'd stop if I were you. You didn't have to deal with the hairy twins and their total hysteria. Now that you've put us here, I hope you know what to do next?"

"Yes. It's around here somewhere, we just have to find it."

"Find what?"

"The entrance to Limbo. I saw a blue light coming out of the mountain. I'm convinced it was a soul cast from Limbo. Let's spread out and look for it. I'll look around the slopes, I need you to fly up to the summit and see what you can find. I'll meet you back here at the end of the day."

Over the next few hours they explored every possible nook and cranny on the mountainside. From high peak to shallow contour they searched for the entrance, neither knowing whether an entrance existed or not. The mountain bullied and harassed their efforts, shedding massive rocks from its giant shoulders, unwilling to allow any clues to its secrets. The weather was as equally uncooperative, unleashing a fierce horde of sharpened ice crystals in their path. When the sun had moved out of sight and the conditions became impossible, they retreated to the sanctuary of the cabin. Exhausted, they collapsed in front of the fire to defrost frozen limbs and exchange scant information.

"Nothing," said John both as a question and a summary of his day.

"I watched the peak for hours and nothing came from it, blue or otherwise," replied Sandy, his chest panting frantically for air.

*****

Daylight broke for the twenty-first time of the sixth month and both Sandy and John hid from it under borrowed sleeping bags. John's stomach woke with an enormous sense of foreboding that soon spread to the rest of his body like a cancer. This day had been engraved on his conscience. He'd always believed, always hoped, to avoid its consequences when the day eventually arrived. How wrong he'd been. The human race had been saved from the emptiness of Emorfed. But his own emptiness, his own impending solitude, was more and more certain. In order to save humanity for the second time in a week, and sacrifice himself in the process, it was time to initiate plan B.

He nudged the lump in the adjacent sleeping bag where Sandy had presumably been lost during the night. After much flapping and cursing, Sandy's head appeared at the end of his sluglike chamber.

"Ten more minutes," he croaked, head retracting back under like a gopher.

"No time," replied John. "We're all out of it."

Sandy reappeared to see that John was pointing Victor's gun at him, "What are you doing?"

"We can't find the entrance, Sandy. I can't help you as I promised. But I can't risk the consequences of the solstice. I'm sorry."

Sandy's face flooded with the fear of his own reckoning as the shiny barrel of the gun shook uncontrollably in John's hand. Accustomed to a more confident master, the metal felt alien in his palm. As Victor had done before it, the weapon cast doubt on his courage to fire. Two parts of John's will wrestled with each other, stricken by stalemate. There was an anger desperate to pull the trigger and a logic stopping him doing so. How could he weigh up the importance of one life above another? Would he save billions or take one life needlessly?

"You can't do it, can you?" said Sandy, after several minutes. "You're no killer, John, you just haven't got it in you."

"I thought, given the gravity of the situation and the choice that I had to make, it might become easier. At the end of the day you're only here because you wanted to do good. It's not your fault things ended like this. I won't be an accomplice for someone else's mistake."

John lowered the gun and sank to the floor. Weakness was overcome by anger as he repeatedly punched the floor until his knuckles cracked and bled. A shriek of pain leapt from his mouth and in that moment the mountain roared back its disapproval. The cabin shock uncontrollably as if John's roar had finally found the one weakness in its chaotically mangled structure.

Anything that had been stationary was now mobile. Objects were flying from shelves as the furniture shifted around them unaided. The magnitude of the juddering increased as a full-scale, seismic event threw them from one rickety wall to another. As timbers ripped like sails in a hurricane, the unbearable noise of rock colliding with rock echoed down the valley. Dust filled the air around them and the darkness engulfed the cabin. Holding anything that resembled a solid object, the occupants and the remains of the building sank into the ground. They fell uncontrollably into a deep crevice that had opened up in the Earth beneath them.

Unlike the fall from the airplane, which had been uncomfortable yet planned, this experience was terrifyingly brutal. Fingers became numb from the pressure of clinging on, as they dodged the rocks that had pulverised what remained of the roof and joined the cabin on its descent. Then as quickly as it had started, everything stopped. Sandy and John jerked upwards on impact with the ground. But the remains of the cabin didn't stay at rest for long. After several hesitant seconds it slide across a smooth, convex surface, before coming to rest in a heap of fractured planks and battered tiles. A slither of distant sunlight crept in from the outside world thousands of feet above them into the newly carved-out crevasse.

John opened his eyes, half-expecting to see Brimstone's craggy face or the excruciating pain that came from being sucked through the Soul Catcher. He got neither. In fact he saw nothing at all. If he hadn't known better he would have sworn that this was what death really felt like. How many times had he *died* so far? There was no way of predicting what it actually felt like, maybe one day he'd find out.

Slabs of timber, rock and ice lay over his body, yet as he attempted to move he found to his surprise that none of his limbs had been shorn off or shattered. Unable to predict the obstacles, he crawled out of the rubble and walked into a soft metal wall, wet and cold. The part of his arm that he'd placed forward to stop his fall was being sucked in by the liquid metal. He wisely pulled it back before he lost it forever.

As he analysed the barrier like an architect studying a new structure, he found the metal was soft and malleable and deduced that its properties must have cushioned the falling cabin. The cold metal sloped away from his body above and below him. When he pushed forward it sprang back into its original position. It acted like a plastic but had a metallic feel in all other respects. He had only seen it once before and it filled his heart with hope.

"Sandy!" shouted John.

"I'm over here. Follow the light."

"What light?" replied John, following the sound of Sandy's distant voice and finding to his surprise a gleam of light creeping from the metal sphere a few hundred feet away.

Using his hands to gently follow the curvature of the wall, he followed the sound. When he reached the light it came from a small, circular opening that allowed entry into the sphere. Sandy stood inside taking in the interior. The illumination came from a long, white cone that hung from the ceiling.

"Is this what you were looking for?" asked Sandy, his head fixed on the view.

"It's the place that I sought, but hoped that I would never have to."

"I've never seen anything like it. What is it?"

"This is Limbo. It's where they process the souls that have no charge. The neutrals of the world, neither good nor bad."

"Isn't it about time you explained to me what your plan is?" demanded Sandy. "I've gone on faith so far."

"Soon," said John. "Let's get down there and I'll show you."

John scanned the gloom, expecting to see figures going about their business. The lack of any people in the vicinity gave him a sense of unease. The cabin had come to rest at the top half of the massive sphere, so John and Sandy had to carefully and quietly stroll down the smooth metal steps to reach the bottom. When they arrived the things that John had seen on his last visit were still in place.

The dock, where he had stood utterly confused as his counsel had unsuccessfully fought his case, and the raised, throne-like seat that Laslow had occupied, were all unchanged. All these items brought back painful yet insignificant memories. There in the centre of the room was the thing he was most interested in. The long, thin white cone that stretched hundreds of feet from the roof to about six feet from the shiny, polished floor.

"OK, this is it. Sandy, this device ionises souls. It can be used to charge a neutral soul to either positive or negative," he said, grabbing the lever on the floor and dragging it from its central position to where it was marked on the floor 'positive'.

"I don't get it," replied Sandy.

"You are a negative soul, Sandy. But I can't send you where those souls go. You and I deserve better. So *we* are going to determine our destiny, rather than wait for judgement to be given. Stand here please," John indicated a spot directly underneath the ioniser.

Instinctively he found the switch. A jet of white light illuminated the feathery figure below it. Sandy wasn't altogether happy with the plan unfolding in front of him, but the alternative wasn't worth thinking about. John raised the gun and once more aimed it at Sandy, hoping this time he would have the bottle to pull the trigger.

"I *can* do this," John said to himself. "I'm sending him to a better place, I'm not killing him."

"I don't think you want to do that, John," echoed a cold, callous voice high above him in the void of the sphere.

CHAPTER THIRTY

THE VIVISECTION OF
MANKIND

"Who made you God, John?" demanded an ancient figure moving down the levels of the sphere with the agility and speed of a man a tenth of his age.

John peered up at the approaching figure, his gun still fixed on Sandy. The voice alone was enough for John to know who he was up against. He'd never expected this to be easy, he expected someone might try to stop him. Now he knew who.

"You did, Laslow."

"Really, I must have missed that," said Laslow.

"You remember. It was the moment you took control and made my choices for me. After that, I had to take things into my own hands."

"And you think shooting this poor creature will help?"

"It's a start."

"You won't go through with it. You proved that up in the cabin, you just haven't got it in you," taunted Laslow. The black hood and cloak that Laslow had worn at their last meeting in Geneva were replaced by a pinstripe suit four sizes too big for him that did nothing to hide his weathered skin.

"We'll see," replied John defiantly.

"The trouble with people like you, John, is that they lack foresight. You're more concerned with the mundane than the significant. You have become consumed by the trivial over these past months. What will happen to others? How people will feel? The impact on the ordinary individual? But most of all you lack the courage to pull that trigger. That's why you'll fail to do it."

"What do you want from me, Laslow? I have done everything asked of me," replied John, refusing to be drawn into his meandering accusations.

"LIAR," Laslow boomed angrily. "You've done what *you* thought was important. Since your very first step, every one of them has been in the pursuit of your own selfish outcome. In doing so you have flaunted every gram of your human weakness. Every time it was predictable and, as it happens, necessary. No one told you to come here. No one told you to stop Emorfed. No one told you to hide Faith. These are not my commands, are they?"

"How do you know all this?" said John, scratching his head with his free hand in order to massage his head into understanding. In response, a single laugh bounced around the metal sphere. The laugh had no way of escaping and simply resonated on like a never-ending echo.

"I find it amusing that your tiny, human soul believes you have reached this far on your own. It's frankly laughable. I have been with you at every step of the journey. It was me that made sure those steps reached this point, at this time. Like the plastic bodies that you've seen in this place, you are my vessol, John."

"Who *are* you?"

"Why are humans so interested in questions, when they have no faculty for accepting the answers? You do as we tell you. Now put down the gun."

If this wasn't a character assignation then the bruising insults certainly amounted to a damn good hiding. It wasn't just accusations about him. They were about the whole of the human race. Fury bubbled through him. He'd done so much for others and yet he was being accused of selfishness. Of all the results he wanted, his own future was the one thing that still appeared at the bottom of his priority list.

"Why shouldn't Sandy go to a place where he can be at peace? He has done more to save humanity in the last few days than the world's politicians pooled together. No one will write plaudits for him. What do you care anyway?"

John pulled the safety catch off his weapon and found, not for the first time, someone pointing a gun back at him. Sandy was suddenly feeling a little exposed as the only individual in the room without a gun. But now he and John were both staring down the barrel of one.

"I don't care John," came the ill-tempered response.

"Then let us do what we please," shouted John. "Let us be."

"Why should I do that? There are rules, you know. It's not for you to decide the polarity of someone's soul," answered Laslow, his footsteps finally reaching the same level of the sphere as John.

"Why not? I have suffered injustice. Isn't it about time I inflicted some."

"Then do it, if you feel that way. This has never been about him, John," replied Laslow with a grin to shock the most dedicated of dentists.

"What?" John stuttered.

"It's not about him," Laslow repeated, nodding towards Sandy.

"What do you mean it's not about *him*? I've spent months tracking *him* down. I've been through the most unbelievable and hideous of journeys to bring *him* here."

"It's about you, John. It always has been," croaked Laslow, revelling in John's expression. A gaze of such utter confusion it resembled someone struggling with an unfathomable mathematics calculation or the age-old riddle of why women needed so many shoes?

"What do you mean, me?"

Laslow looked at John with an air of disappointment. He pitied John's lack of foresight. It was incomprehensible to Laslow that someone could pursue a course of action for so long without any indication that it was a hoax.

"You actually thought the Universe was going to collapse, didn't you?" said Laslow.

"Um," replied John, with an expression that said, 'yes', 'what?' and 'of course not' all at the same time.

"If the Universe was fragile enough to be split in half every time a soul went walkabout, it would have destroyed itself in the Neanderthal period. Look around you, John."

John took in the magnificent yet horrifying surroundings of Limbo. A place of chilling beauty created by the magnitude of some great unseen power. The metal in the walls oozed around him, a living, breathing structure made of a substance alien to planet Earth. In the middle of it all was this tiny speck of life, dwarfed by the sprawling behemoth that towered high above his head. Just one stitch in the infinite tapestry of existence.

"*They* created structures like this and the places you have seen at the end of time. They don't need you to save it. But they do need you to save them."

"You're not making any sense," said John, mouth still swung open so wide it was dramatically changing the external pressure in the room. Laslow went back to square one.

"How did you get here, John?"

"I went to Hell, twice. Spent three months possessing two notable personalities, fell through a massive crater in the very mantle of the Earth..."

A raised finger stopped John in his tracks.

"How did you get past the security guard at the airport?" enquired Laslow.

"I don't know."

"Who told you what to do in the hotel corridor?"

"I'm not sure."

"When you ran out of fortune, who has been guiding you through your journey?" goaded Laslow, spinning a riddle that John would need help to find the answer to.

"I don't know."

"When we last met I said that there were powers at work beyond your wildest comprehension. The power I referred to was partly my own. It has been by my will that you are here. I have controlled your every move," said Laslow, "even your own death."

John's memory cast itself back to the moment of the car crash. The moment he drew his last breath. The incident that in all probability could not, or should not, have caused his death. He closed Byron's eyes and pictured the scene in his mind. The broken postbox, the smell of leaking fuel, and the warm trickles of blood running down his face. Harder than he had done before he attempted to focus on the old man peering over the windshield of his car. A man of impossible age. A man whose skin clung tightly to his skull, whose eyes burnt with an anger unparalleled to anything he'd witnessed before. The face that had for so long been blurred, developed in his mind like a roll of old photographic film.

"YOU!" he turned the gun away from Sandy and pointed it directly at Laslow.

"Finally you show some real emotion. It's anger, not compassion, that drives at the truth. Do you want the truth, John?"

"I WANT MY LIFE BACK," screamed John, pulsating with so much fury his soul wanted to leap out of its body. "I WANT THE LIFE THAT YOU HAVE STOLEN."

"Interesting how you attack me for dabbling in the fate of others. What about your own acts of manipulation? Yes, I have influenced you to aid my agenda. What of poor Byron? Have you not also done the same to him? It's Byron that stands before me in mortal peril, a puppet to meet *your* ends. Have you spared a thought for his destiny?"

The irony was not lost on John. Laslow was right. Byron might have been an abhorrent individual capable of stealing the souls from the very people he should have been protecting, but what right did John have to judge him? What right did John have to lead him to his death?

"It's different. Byron had his chance, he deserves everything that he gets. He was also responsible for dominating people against their will," replied John with an argument that just seemed to play into Laslow's hands.

"Playing God again, John? I see that two wrongs do make a right. Very well, in that case I accept your absolution."

"No, it's different. I'm doing what is right."

"Who's to say what is right?" replied Laslow. "One man's view of right is alien to someone with opposing opinions. A terrorist fights for a cause he believes in, just like your friend Violet. Does it make her right? Whose perspective is acceptable? We've all been doing it, John. You, Byron, Violet, even Sandy here. We have all used our will to define the outcome that would best suit us. The difference is that I have no conscience to regret my actions, so sue me."

"It's different, I AM RIGHT," raged John.

"You're a pawn, John. An insignificant piece easily sacrificed but totally unable to influence the outcome of the game. We oversee a billion human experiments here on Earth. Each one moved around the board and changed for our own amusement. The only difference between you and me is the scale of the power available," replied Laslow, instinctively knowing which buttons he needed to press to stoke John's aggression. After many years of scientific observation he knew how humans behaved.

John in an instant did the only thing that would give him back a semblance of control. His anger helped turn his gun back at Sandy and without hesitation or mental debate he fired a single, silent shot. The bullet pierced Sandy's chest and the corpse of a blue-grey pigeon hit the floor. It was followed swiftly by a blue, gaseous form that floated underneath the ioniser for a moment, and a fraction of a second later it was gone.

"That's how insignificant I am. Your words might cut at my soul, but they can't change the past," John said calmly.

"Proud of your power, are you?"

"I feel sorry for you, Laslow," replied John.

"I really wouldn't."

"You may have started out as a human, but you have lost all human qualities. Your power is worthless. Real power isn't the ability to harm or meddle. Real power is overcoming your frailty when every sinew of your mind tells you it's impossible. Real power is facing up to your problems when you want to hide from them. Real power is picking yourself up from a fall and redoubling your efforts. Real power is the strength to choose what is right. I just did what was right, not what was easy."

"We'll see. These things have a habit of correcting themselves. You can't fight what you don't understand," replied Laslow still appearing calm and controlled. "Now that you have dispatched your friend, perhaps we can start with the real business?"

"Not until you give me some answers, even if I can't live with them," demanded John, fearing the same fate as Sandy and developing a sudden thirst for understanding. He knew in his heart he was only stalling the inevitable.

"We have time?" Laslow replied, glancing up at the ioniser for a moment.

"When you spoke to me during Nash's exorcism, I was under the impression that you were on my side. Whose side are you on?"

Laslow's demeanour changed. The corners of his chiselled jaw straightened, removing the psychotic grin that had been permanently etched on his face. His nostrils flared like an agitated dragon and it was clear that John had said something that Laslow had not expected. Something had momentarily broken Laslow's control and John's emotions and memories whirred around Byron's head in order to find it and use it to his advantage.

"Mine," Laslow grunted. "I'm only on my side."

"It wasn't you. So, if it wasn't you, who was it?"

"Baltazaar," whispered Laslow under his breath.

"Who's Baltazaar?" asked an intrigued John.

"You should choose your friends more wisely, John. If you really care about humanity in the way you suggest, then you'd be best to stay well clear of him. Baltazaar is no friend of humans."

"Given the choice between him and you at this moment, I'm not swinging in your favour. In fairness he's not pointing a gun at me," John replied sarcastically.

"You think you're so clever revealing him to me. In truth, it's your biggest mistake to date. If you have spoken to him it means you have experienced the Limpet Syndrome for yourself. Which means that you have suddenly become extremely dangerous. Only eleven others in your position have done that and I've killed six of them," explained Laslow, taking another glimpse at the ioniser, waiting for an invisible signal that would bring the toying of his prey to an end. "It's almost time. Do you have any other questions while we wait?" Laslow added flippantly.

"Yes, as it happens. I'm intrigued as to why a man who has the ability to melt things with the power of his own finger needs to carry a gun?"

"Very good, John. Now we get to the real points of interest. What do you know about the solstice?" asked Laslow back on message and impressed that John had noticed the irregularity.

"Longest day of the year, middle-aged men dancing around with bells on their flares, and until recently the destruction of time and space," John scoffed.

"There are some other important qualities about the solstice you may not know. When the sun is in its highest position in the Northern Hemisphere it literally stops. Its name comes from the Latin 'sol' and 'sistere.' 'Sistere' means 'stand still' and 'sol' means…"

"The sun, or possibly a refreshing Spanish lager?" John was tiring of Laslow's games of intellect. He knew he was about to die again, and all this did was delay the inevitable.

"Neither. It can mean sun, yes, but it actually refers to the soul. The soul stands still. In medieval times people would light huge bonfires to ward off evil spirits. Although the stuff of pagan propaganda, it wasn't so far from the truth. If you know where to look for it, anyone's soul can be seen at the point of the solstice, particularly if there is more than one of them."

The timing couldn't have been more fitting. John couldn't say how long he had been underground since the earthquake, as time had become an unfamiliar concept in this foreign place. When they had fallen through the Earth, the Sun had only just risen. Outside in the world it was now creeping into its final position. As it did so a shaft of light burst down and out of the ioniser, brighter than a thousand lasers. The metallic gloom disintegrated as the whole of the sphere burnt with the reflections emitted from every slope and curve. John blinked uncomfortably trying to adjust to the dramatic change of conditions.

"See. There you are, John." Laslow was pointing his finger directly at John. He was pointing at the exact position in the frontal lobe where John had been situated for several weeks. "I see the light is dim. Can you feel the shadow yet?"

To John's surprise a spot of bright blue electricity throbbed through the translucent skin of Laslow's head, and it wasn't alone. There was a faint blue colour across the whole of Laslow's body. This light was paler and stretched. It did not emit the same energy and brightness as the one that sat in his forehead.

"There is another interesting fact that I know to be true," Laslow offered. "At the zenith of the solstice there are certain midsummer plants that have incredible healing powers. Even the power to bring back the dead. Plants just like this one here."

He held out a plant with delicate white flowers that he'd plucked from his pocket. As the light bathed his hand the flowers seemed to grow by some form of accelerated photosynthesis. John had no idea what the significance of this was, other than proving that Laslow had finally lost the plot.

"To answer your question about the gun, I find the healing power of this plant doesn't work on bodies that I have turned to ash."

A gunshot echoed abruptly through the sphere. The sound danced around forever like the laugh had done before it. John felt a force from Byron's chest that jolted him upwards and out of his position, pushing him through the mouth and into the brightness. Although he felt Laslow's presence he no longer visualised it. Outside of Byron's body a shock of electricity struck out at him as if it was trying to find protection. There was a brief battle between his soul and this other entity before he felt the inevitable familiarity of being flung skywards with an incredible force and the density of a burnt-out star.

Laslow edged forward to the crumpled, bleeding and broken body of Byron T. Casey. There on the glossy, cold surface lay a hollow body once home to a great, proud yet wayward politician. Death had come to him in a flash. A pain-free experience many in life would have appreciated. Clutching the white flowers in his hand, Laslow knelt down and whispered in Byron's ear.

"What are we going to do with you, then?"

CHAPTER THIRTY-ONE

TIME IMMEMORIAL

There were no special arrangements for John's final visit to Hell. No unique greeting or welcome party. No entrance by the back door or extended occupation of the Soul Catcher. There was no need for it. If he hadn't suspected it before, then the meeting with Laslow had confirmed it. There were no deals with the Devil. Now he was a soul like all the others on the final journey that would lead to damnation. He had been part of a game in which his participation was still unclear.

He left the Soul Catcher as quickly as he had entered it, and for that he was extremely grateful. The idea of having to spend more time being bombarded by the panic of the wretched mass within filled him with uncontrollable anxiety. Before he knew what had happened he was standing inside his vessol manacled by the hands and feet and lined up on the conveyor belt with all the rest.

Expecting to be housed in something ghastly or inappropriate, he looked down at his plastic body to see how he would spend eternity. What final humiliation was the Devil going to deal him as a constant warning to others? It wasn't a surprise that he did not immediately recognise the figure that he occupied. After wearing so many different disguises in the last three months he'd forgotten what the real John Hewson looked like. It felt uneasy to be inside his own skin, even a plastic version of it. The truth was that John didn't know who or what he was anymore. Perhaps being John Hewson *was* the ultimate humiliation? Why did it matter anyway? His soul was broken, whatever vessol he was inside.

John recognised many of figures that were busy making this endless process run smoothly. Brimstone stood by the Soul Catcher busy with his daily, never-ending workload. The steaming molten figure refrained from curiously looking over to where John was about to disappear from sight. John had become an invisible acquaintance, someone that he'd endured because he had to. Just waiting for the moment when he'd show his real feelings.

Around John stood hundreds of vessels of every possible demographic; females, males, young, old, short, and tall. All equally damned, all dressed in their white plastic and all undoubtedly consumed by fear and doubt. These were their plastic graves, whether they were held in them for the rest of eternity, or they were consumed by their despair and recycled into space. He pitied them for their fear. At least he knew what he was about to suffer and in some way was prepared for it. The only consolation was that Sandy would not face the same punishment.

As the conveyor belt crawled slowly along, occasionally stalling to welcome another inmate, John was aware that he was entering a part of Hell that he had not seen before. The conveyor belt led into a cave that was relatively small compared to the endless caverns of the inner levels. Inside, the main conveyor burrowed through an eight-foot-high steel arch that resembled a metal detector from an airport security checkpoint. On the other side of the arch the belt split into ten separate conveyors that sped off at different gradients into the holes in the wall.

The conveyor stopped as each vessol reached the arch. There a lamp beamed down from the top, bathing the figure in brilliant light and highlighting the blue soul within. As the light scanned the soul for a few seconds a glass panel to the left presented a solitary number. As the never-ending line of vessels passed by,

John observed the numbers that flashed on-screen. A three, then an eight, a one, and very occasionally a ten. The majority of the numbers were between one and three.

Those in front of John would have been desperate to know what these numbers meant. Not only did he know, but he also predicted what number would flash when he reached the scanner. They'd place him where he would receive the most punishment. The vessol in front of him went through the apparatus and the number flashed with a big, bright ten. 'Lucky sod,' John thought. Knowing that the character in front of him must be a seriously nasty piece of work didn't stop a bout of jealously within him. What he would do to swap places. The survival instinct of a doomed soul, desperate to avoid the fate that it knew would come.

John's turn arrived and the mechanism's light shone through his prosthetic body. It analysed his every emotion, like a computer scanning for viruses. Maybe it was his imagination but it appeared to be taking a lot longer for him than it had for some of the others. Some of the vessols had only been under for fractions of a second before a verdict had been revealed, as if there was little for the device to discover. Finally a number flashed on the screen. It was a twelve.

The machine seemed just as perplexed as he was. So far, on his previous visits, he'd been from level zero to level eleven, and to his knowledge there was no level twelve. The machine stopped with a grinding shudder, unsure of its next command. There were only ten conveyors and it was being asked to use number twelve. It searched for a piece of programming script that had been lost in the depths of its design.

John racked his memory to locate any reference that he had to a twelfth level. He knew that there were ten for inmates, Brimstone had shown him that when he'd first arrived. He recalled the lift that they had taken to the library on level eleven. Then it struck him like a punch to the face. There were twelve numbers on the lift. It was the only level whose contents had not been discussed. Was that a good thing? If level ten had been the closest level to the Devil himself, where souls were treated like royalty, was this place better or worse? Perhaps he *was* being rewarded for his efforts after all?

"Take him down," called a voice a little way below to John's right. He was lifted down by a demon that appeared to be a cross between a bolt of lightning and a ball of fire. The charged electricity from the demon's hands pierced the vessol and the whole of John's soul was left numb. The figure dumped him roughly onto the stone floor.

"Thank you, Mr. Volts, I'll deal with him now," said Brimstone, walking casually towards one of the exits. John shuffled after him, which even in death is hard to do when your legs are manacled.

"What's happening, Brimstone?" he called to the small, bubbling figure now some way in front of him.

There was no response.

John's question fell on deaf ears, although it was unclear if Brimstone had anything that even resembled ears. When they reached the lift that they had taken so many months before, at least by John's calendar, they both got in. Brimstone pulled out a small stepladder from a corner of the lift to enable him to reach the button marked 'level twelve', which was normally unused and out of reach.

"What's on level twelve?" asked John, now able to get some form of eye contact with Brimstone.

"You'll find out when you get there, won't you?"

"You promised me, Brimstone," beseeched John. "You said that I would have my freedom."

"That'll teach you to make deals with demons, then, won't it? Besides, you got two or three more months of fun out of your life, didn't you?"

"Fun. You call that fun?" John exclaimed. "I think I would have had more fun if I'd stayed here!"

"I wouldn't bet on it," said Brimstone. "Anyway, the deal we agreed was not something that was in my power to offer. Maybe he will be more sympathetic?"

"Who's he?" asked John as they reached the top of the lift shaft. Again there was no answer.

The rusty door swung open to reveal level twelve. The first thing that struck John was the lack of edges around him, atypical of all the other areas that he had seen. From one to ten the levels sat on a cliffside that ran in a huge oval teetering over a central chasm that revealed each of the levels above and below. There were no cliffs towering around the edges of the highest level. On level twelve only the great desolation of space stretched out infinitely above them. The stars and constellations lighting up the sky like an immense Christmas tree, the very last window on John's Universe.

Amongst the stars, suspended in zero gravity, were hundreds of metal boxes fixed to the ground by thick, wrought-iron chains. Each box appeared to be the size of a small car but was the shape of a cube. They floated hundreds of feet up in the air, yet the screams from the inhabitants were as clear as if they were parked on the ground. Below these strange prisons was a vast, round table built of smooth, black rock. Positioned around it stood dozens of beautifully constructed jewelled thrones. Each of these massive chairs would make John look like a toddler if he'd sat in one. Each throne had a different gemstone motif, branding the owner that would sit there. Of those waiting for their masters, only one was occupied.

As John was ushered towards the table the figure of a man sitting perfectly still watched them approach. This was not the type of demon that John had come to expect. There was no predominant element that made up his anatomy. The man's blond hair nestled neatly just above his shoulders, and there was an uneasy but friendly feel to the electric-blue irises that peered towards them. He projected the essence of purity, a white gown accentuating his tanned, smooth skin and the very sight of this exceptional man lifted John's mood, pacified by the pull of his gaze.

"You have been very busy, John." The figure got to his feet and moved around the table towards him.

"Who are you?" asked John politely, expecting the same level of non-responsiveness that he'd been getting from Brimstone.

"I am Asmodeus, keeper of Hell and the Devil's will," he replied in a soft, captivating voice.

"Oh," replied John, still unclear quite who he was, but certain that he was someone serious.

"And you are John Hewson. The seemingly ordinary man with an extraordinary desire to meddle in the affairs of others. I have sent for you because I sense that you want something from me, John?"

"I only ever wanted what was promised."

"Do you deserve it?"

"I did what was asked of me."

"You cannot lie to me, John." Asmodeus's voice hardened and again fear reappeared in John's mind. "You were told to send Sandy's soul back to us. But instead you attempted to send it somewhere else. Somewhere it did not belong. We cannot have a mortal playing with immortality, can we? Maybe there are a few others that you wish to save while you're at it?"

Asmodeus strutted over to an elegant silver platform where two clear-glass decanters stood filled with faint blue gas clumped together in a cloud-like form. The gases were less lively and duller in colour than the other souls that John had witnessed.

"Do you know what these are, John?"

"Souls."

"Almost," replied Asmodeus. "They are pieces of souls. They have been splintered from their host before their time. They wait for the remnants to join them. They wait impatiently for their shadow."

"The shadow? I've heard that phrase all too often," replied John, considering his conversations with Herb and Faith.

"These represent the other side of Emorfed," replied Asmodeus. "These part-souls must wait for their Judgement Day, idle and untouched. They will attempt to rip apart anything that they come into contact with. They know no rational thought and will consume themselves and their surroundings unless they are reunited. They are no good to us. I hate their very presence in my kingdom. They're a plague with no known cure."

Spontaneously he opened one of the jars and poured the contents into his mouth, which prompted his features to distort. The hair on his head descended down his back and curves appeared on his chest. As his body shrank by a good foot, his face now displayed a feminine quality. In a smooth, fluid motion the man who had stood before him was now a much more familiar figure.

"Faith," John shouted in hope.

"No, not quite. Still Asmodeus, but you clearly recognise the soul within," he replied in Faith's hypnotic tone. "I will let you see her in a minute, if you can deal with it."

"What is this? Is this just part of your cruel game?"

"We will never again receive these hideous creatures, these half-souls, and for that I have you to thank. Emorfed would have made a human race devoid of spirit, and if that had happened, what would become of us? We would diminish, no part to play in the laundering of sin. There would be no souls for us to feed upon, no pain to mete out. The purification of the damned would be unnecessary."

John never considered that his actions had actually kept Hell in business. It was an unfortunate side effect. Mankind had kept its humanity and with it kept the vile cruelty of their end after death.

"I've helped you after all, then," replied John, growing in confidence. "Surely I deserve some recognition."

"I'm scared," came the voice from Asmodeus. "Help me, I can't deal with it anymore. They are tearing at my mind. I can't get away from them."

Influencing the reaction of the physical form where the soul lay, the female figure was sobbing uncontrollably. Although John knew that this was some sick joke, he was unable to separate his fear of Asmodeus and his love for Faith.

"I'm here, Faith. It's John."

"Who are you? You're one of them, aren't you? You're just here to hurt me!" she screamed, retracting as he got closer.

"No. I'm here to help you. I will comfort you. I must save your soul, or I cannot live with mine!" he shouted.

"Your soul is not worth saving!" she screamed. "The heat from your shadow burns me. Go away, foul and hollow beast."

"You cruel bastard," John shouted. "You're just playing games with my mind. This is just part of my punishment. I don't care what you do to my soul anymore, I've already won. I beat you. Sandy escaped this foul place. Do what you want with me, but you've lost." His anger burst at the seams of his vessol, and sparks of electricity whipped forward from the valve in his throat, trying to physically attack Asmodeus.

Asmodeus vomited Faith's soul back into the glass bottle and replaced the stopper. As he did so his body convulsed violently, morphing from the slender Faith into an altogether different creature. The demon's body rapidly expanded into the air as both legs welded together as one. Where his kneecaps had once been something was desperately trying to escape the confines of his flesh. With a ferocious roar the head of a lion surged out. As it gnashed the air in front of it, more of the lion was revealed. Wings forced their way out of the body and legs that followed. Whilst the legs were developing their own safari exhibit, Asmodeus's body was also changing. Thick, black, matted hair, that ripped through his white gown, was sprouting from his torso.

Then as a final act of terror the centre of his face split open like a snake shedding its skin. The head of a bull was first to hatch out of his severed face. The heads of a goat and a man quickly followed it. John cowered on the floor from the three-headed demon that sat regally upon a winged lion, belching out fire that blackened all that it touched. The twenty-foot-high monster loomed above its victim, wielding a blazing staff sharply pronged at one end. The three heads were covered in bleeding wounds that dripped down into a disgusting pool on the floor.

"You have shown your true colours, John, so I will show you mine," boomed Asmodeus, prowling ominously in a circle around him. "Why do you lie to yourself? You haven't won. You worked out the truth long ago. It's time you faced up to it. You can't avoid it forever. How many lives do you need to live before you accept it?"

"What do you mean, lives?"

"This cycle will just continue until you accept what you already know," taunted Asmodeus.

"What am I supposed to know? I don't know what you mean?"

"Yes you do. It's called truth, John. Why do you think you felt such hope from the other souls that you encountered inside the Soul Catcher?"

John suspected he knew why he had felt souls around him that appeared to hold emotions out of step with that dark place. The problem was accepting the only explanation that seemed likely to him. Perhaps the Soul Catcher didn't just attract negative souls? It would explain why there were souls with positive emotions congruous to their surroundings. The real question in John's mind was why?

"Let me give you the truth that you are so keen to avoid," growled Asmodeus, reading John's mind.

Asmodeus raised each muscly arm in the air and brandished the razor-sharp claws that extended from each finger. The claws sliced away at his hairy chest, ripping through the flesh of his abdomen. John recoiled in disgust as blood and guts splattered to the floor and a vile odour of death and disease seeped from the open cavity. When he finally turned back to look at the disturbing sight he wished he hadn't. Inside Asmodeus's chest where most veterinary scientists would have hoped to find vital organs, hung the blackened bones of his ribcage. Holding the ribs like the bars of a prison stood the blue and grey plastic figure of a pigeon.

"You see, John, there is no sanctuary for man!" bellowed Asmodeus. "No escape from fate."

"You said you would save me, John," echoed Sandy's voice from his hideous cage, before the body resealed itself, silencing him forever.

"It's not possible. It's another one of your tricks. I sent him back as a positive soul. He should never have come here."

"That all depends on where you think positive souls go, doesn't it?"

John didn't reply. Everything that he knew about the afterlife was based on what others had told him, not on what he knew to be true. Just like every seemingly convincing politician, scientist or preacher, Brimstone had made a passionate and compelling case and, as he had done countless times in his life, he'd believed it. When you're scared or tired maybe you lack the motivation to challenge or test the evidence for yourself? It appears truth is what you believe it to be.

"You knew the truth the first time you arrived here, you just decided to reject your own instincts," declared Asmodeus. "You could not believe that your precious father was evil. You were right. So, why is he here, John?"

"How can you detain him if he does not belong here?"

"Every soul belongs here," laughed Asmodeus, a noise as terrifying as anything that John had heard before.

"How is that possible?" John stuttered in response.

Asmodeus ignored the question, grabbing John by the head with a powerful arm and lifting him off the ground. The lion padded off in the direction of one of the metal cubes that stood on the floor, its door swung open in anticipation. There was nothing inside it. The only contents would be what you brought in with you.

"You destroyed everyone you tried to help? Let me show you your reward for doing what you thought was right." All three of Asmodeus's heads spoke in unison. "Byron is dead. Faith and Herb broken. Sandy damned for eternity. That's your legacy and you will have to die with the consequences. Guilt that will last until the end of time itself. That's the only punishment that you will need."

John landed in the empty metal cask like a discarded piece of meat. A thick, black windowless metal grave, empty other than for his own torment. The door slammed shut and the light in John's world went out. As the sound of heavy chains dragged across the stone floor to winch him into place, he made one final desperate plea.

"Where is Satan?" screamed John as loud as possible.

There was no reply.

"Is he too cowardly to deal out justice for himself? I demand to see him!" John continued, hoping for one final answer. A reply echoed through the box, as if Asmodeus's mouth was pressed up against the outer wall.

"You've already seen him," boomed Asmodeus.

"What?" shouted John.

"More than that, John, you've made him stronger."

"When?"

CHAPTER THIRTY-TWO

THE THIRD LAW

The only thing in the darkness was fear. It didn't come from the darkness. It bled from John. There is nothing to fear from darkness, it's one's own psychology that produces panic. After all, there is nowhere to run from yourself. There's always a way of overcoming solitude, if you can find something within yourself for comfort. Most people can find a reason to ease their loneliness. John found nothing of comfort anymore, his hope had been completely drained from him.

Even his positive memories were turning against him. They were lies built on false beliefs to trick him into a pseudo-happiness. Even the ultimate escape route of giving up had been removed. He would stew with his guilt and despair until the end of time, a moment that might never even exist. He envied those that had been in such agony on level one. They relied on stimulus, however awful it might be.

The ghosts of his memories screamed at him in the darkness. Although he was unaware of it, the screams echoed from his own mouth. An uncontrolled psychosomatic reaction to a blood-curdling nightmare from which he would never wake. The ghosts called to John in the nothingness, screaming their accusations and judgements. Occasionally it would feel so real he'd reach out to feel who was behind him.

"John, you have cursed your family, they are all destined to suffer in life and beyond."

"John, there is no sanctuary for man. No sanctuary for man."

"All hope is lost, only pain remains."

"Faith will suffer the most. She will never wake from the shadow."

"How does it feel to suffer like me, John?"

"All of your lives have been a failure."

"Humanity is lost, you have cursed them all."

Then one voice wrestled his attention from all the others. A voice that he'd only heard once before.

"John, there is always a way out. Remember, when you are at your very lowest point, a place where even desperation or despair would be welcomed alternatives, when any glimmer of hope has been utterly extinguished, then you will have one, and only one, more chance to enact the Limpet Syndrome again. You'll know when that time comes."

*****

Brimstone was tinkering with the Soul Catcher when the call came from level twelve. Something wasn't right with the massive machine that towered above him. It wasn't the first time that the machine had been quiet, but this was ridiculous. When time was no barrier, waiting just wasn't something that happened. It wasn't as if there was a day when less people died and Brimstone got a well-earned break. That was what it was like now, though. There just weren't any souls that wanted to be caught.

The space on the other side of the wormhole, that separated Hell from the Universe, teemed with blue specks of energy. The souls were out there, they just weren't coming in. Brimstone looked again at the two lists on the screen. The one on the right was jam-packed with names, all related to one of the bright spots that glistened up above him. The one on the left showed only one entry. Brimstone stared at the list in absolute confusion.

One entry sat there, incommunicado. Existing but in the same way not. Something living namelessly inside the bulb. How was that possible? There was always a name. This entry simply read, 'unknown'. Age and sex showed as blanks, too. There was none of the information that normally told Brimstone how they were to be suited. It wasn't even a reincarnated soul, that would still have given some information. This was something new.

He tried several times to coax it from the Soul Catcher, but it just wasn't going to budge. In the end he was forced to turn the machine off hoping, although unconvincingly so, that the machine might reset itself when he turned it back on. He sent the other demons to different parts of the complex to carry on some other pressing tasks and turned to answer the call that had summoned him up to level twelve. When you were called there, you went, no questions asked. As soon as Brimstone had moved out of sight, a thin, blue, silvery leak of gas seeped from the end of the exit valve of the dormant Soul Catcher.

*****

"What's going on?" asked Brimstone as he joined a small group of demons who were standing staring up at one of the metal boxes that levitated in the air.

"The screaming has stopped," replied one, without moving his eyes from the box.

"So?" huffed Brimstone. "It's not my domain, what do I know about it?"

"It's John Hewson's box," came the reply from another.

"SO," hissed Brimstone, annoyed that he'd been summoned away from a rather more important matter down below.

"It means he has...passed on," came a growling voice, that joined the group from the shadows. Brimstone didn't need to look around to see who it was that had spoken. Only one creature growled like that.

"It didn't take long for him to diminish," added Asmodeus. "It's extremely disappointing."

The demons seemed to instinctively know what was now required of them. They grabbed the thick metal chain like a tug-of-war team and slowly pulled the metal box from its position in situ in space.

"Why do you need *me* here?" Brimstone asked Asmodeus.

"I thought you would be interested to know," he replied. "Having spent the most time with him, I thought you might be able to offer some explanation, why it was all so quick."

"Weak," croaked Brimstone. "Simple as that. Now if you don't mind, I have a little trouble of my own."

*****

Brimstone was hot, even for him. He'd marched as quickly as his short, stumpy legs carried him, back down to the broken machinery. He switched the Soul Catcher back on and it rocked into life. The screens flashed on, and he breathed a sulphurous sigh of relief. The left-hand screen was blank and whatever had appeared there was nowhere to be seen. The list on the right was slowly and surely traversing over. Everything in Brimstone's world appeared to be back to normal, except for one tiny, and seemingly unimportant thing. A small, red light flickered on the dashboard of the console.

He knew what it was. He knew when it came on. It was the light that indicated that the Soul Catcher had become a soul thrower. If *he* hadn't reversed the Soul Catcher, then someone else had. Had it been on before he left and he just hadn't noticed it? Maybe it was just another malfunction, nothing to be worried about.

"Brimstone, level twelve. NOW," came the call again on the tannoy. He stared up in the air and wondered if his legs were capable of another twelve-floor dash.

*****

John's solid metal box lay at rest on the floor. An even bigger crowd than before surrounded the front. They pushed for position to peer in, fascinated by the interior. Brimstone's view was blocked and he couldn't quite see what all the fuss was about. Asmodeus wasn't amongst the crowd, but he was definitely within earshot. He was single-handedly ripping down all the other metal cubes from their positions and smashing their contents onto the ground. The floor shook so viciously they felt it all the way down on level zero. All around them, smashed boxes presented the remains of ghostly, plastic figures sprawled where they had landed.

Brimstone pushed his way through the legs of the crowd until he got to the front of the queue. The door of John's cask was open on one side, revealing its almost empty cavity. On the metal floor of the cube lay the flaccid and empty vessol of John Hewson's last resting place. It was in exactly the same condition as when Brimstone had attached it to the Soul Catcher in anticipation of John's arrival.

"John's gone!" Brimstone gasped out loud.

The demons around him seemed unwilling to nod in agreement in case it stood against them in any future promotion.

"He must be around here somewhere?" Brimstone appealed to the other demons.

"We've done a complete scan. The majority of him is gone," replied a purple demon constructed completely out of iodine.

"What do you mean, the majority of him?" questioned Brimstone.

"Well, his energy appears to be here, but his soul has gone."

"Maybe he has diminished, then," Brimstone replied, pointing a craggy finger into space. The other demons shook their heads.

"It's not possible. He must have been recycled. If not, Asmodeus will rip this place apart if we don't find him. Including us," replied Brimstone.

"Look inside the cask," added another of the demons from the throng.

Brimstone's molten skin produced a red glow all over the shiny metal walls as he walked easily into the cube and found and what the demon must have been referring to. On one of the walls an inscription had burnt through the metal. The marks had been melted into the side but were quite clear and easy to read. In letters, six inches in height, running around the walls read, 'Remember Newton's Third'.

"What does it mean, Brimstone?" asked one of the demons from the crowd as he re-emerged from the cell.

"John's gone," replied Brimstone, "but not for good."

OUT NOW

SOUL CATCHERS
How to Survive the Afterlife Book 2

33378983R00225

Printed in Great Britain
by Amazon